Cooking
the Books

Books by Kerry Greenwood

The Phryne Fisher Series
Cocaine Blues
Flying Too High
Murder on the Ballarat Train
Death at Victoria Dock
The Green Mill Murder
Blood and Circuses
Ruddy Gore
Urn Burial
Raisins and Almonds
Death Before Wicket
Away With the Fairies
Murder in Montparnasse
The Castlemaine Murders
Queen of the Flowers
Death by Water
Murder in the Dark
Murder on a Midsummer Night

The Corinna Chapman Series
Earthly Delights
Heavenly Pleasures
Devil's Food
Trick or Treat
Forbidden Fruit
Cooking the Books

Short Story Anthology
*A Question of Death:
An Illustrated Phryne Fisher Anthology*

Cooking the Books

A Corinna Chapman Mystery

Kerry Greenwood

Poisoned Pen Press

Poisoned Pen Press
6962 E. First Ave., Ste. 103
Scottsdale, AZ 85251
www.poisonedpenpress.com
info@poisonedpenpress.com

Printed in the United States of America

For David Greagg, an angel in wombat form…

With many thanks to Jenny Pausacker, Ika Willis, Chip Granger, Jean Greenwood and the people who send me intriguing emails in the middle of the night. And to Belladonna, my constant companion while writing.

Please note that although there is a film studio at Docklands, it is not called Harbour Studios and bears no resemblance to my studio. This whole book is a work of fiction. As is the city of Melbourne itself.

Satan finds some mischief still for busy hands to do.

—Charles Dickens, *David Copperfield*

Chapter One

I was supposed to be on holiday. So what, you may ask—in fact, Daniel was actually asking—was I doing in the bakery? Apart from, self-evidently, baking?

'Bosworth Jumbles,' I explained.

He smiled at me. My heart did a complete flip-flop with pike. Beautiful Daniel, my Sabra turned private detective, who out of all women in the city picked me, an ample size 20 who worked too hard making bread at my bakery, Earthly Delights. Since the advent of Daniel I have become susceptible to the idea that miracles might really happen. He is tall, dark and gorgeous with a faint whiff of mystery. I am short and mousy and smell mostly of flour and honest labour. Not seductive.

'Why jumbles and why Bosworth?' he asked.

My apprentice, Jason, a recovering heroin addict, had taken his holiday pay and gone surfing. My shop was closed until the end of January, and my two assistants had gone to an audition for a soap of some sort. I should have been relaxing, but I didn't seem to have the knack.

'The cook died rather than disclose the recipe,' I said. 'Mrs. Dawson is giving an afternoon tea and she wanted some traditional English munchies. And as she is a famous retired society hostess, I like to think that the fact that she chose me as her baker is a great compliment.'

'How do you mean, died?' Daniel sounded intrigued.

'Was executed. He deserves to be remembered. He was Richard the Third's confectioner, a highly paid position,' I told him, forming the jumbles into little heaps on my baking sheet. 'He went with Richard to the battle of Bosworth Field, where the King was defeated and the cook was captured. Henry VII offered him his life if he would give him the recipe for these sugary little treats. He refused, and after a week Henry VII had him executed. But the cook gave the recipe to one of his jailers and the local bakers made them for centuries, all through the Tudor period. Just to remind the rulers that there had been a good king who was usurped and murdered.'

'Sedition by cookery. Impressive,' he murmured. 'What else do we have here? Isn't that fruit mince?'

'For Eccles cakes,' I agreed. 'When the parliamentarians banned Christmas, the bakers of Eccles made these little mince tarts instead of Christmas pudding. I don't know if it was just because they had a stockpile of the main ingredient, or because they wanted to bring a little joy into people's hearts in those joyless times.'

'Possibly both. And these?'

'You can have one. Or two,' I conceded. 'They're singing hinnies. Like the song.'

'*She can cook an Irish stew, aye, and singing hinnies, too,*' he sang, a pleasant tenor somewhat obscured by crumbs.

'And otherwise there are some Bath buns and a sand cake.'

'Sand cake,' he said flatly. 'Even for a superlative baker, sand is not a good ingredient. I recall those childhood beach picnics. It grits the teeth. Love the singing hinnies, though.'

'Sand cake is not made of sand,' I informed him, opening the oven to insert the jumbles and remove the cake. 'It's made with cornflour so it's sandy in texture, but no real sand is used in the construction, I promise. Otherwise she has potted shrimps, which I made yesterday, to eat with brown bread, and cucumber sandwiches, which also contain—'

'No sand. I understand now,' he assured me. 'How much longer will these historical sweeties detain you?'

'Just have to get the jumbles out of the oven—ten minutes or so. Can't ice the cake until it's cold.'

'I notice that none of the feline contingent have descended from the sun porch to supervise your labour,' he observed.

'Lazy creatures have been taking nonstop naps,' I said, wiping flour off my forearms onto my strong green apron. 'Though the Mouse Police are still catching rats down here at night. But they probably think that is sport, not work.'

'Cats don't do the "w" word,' he agreed solemnly. 'Even the maître d'hôtel Horatio only supervises.'

Horatio is my tabby and white gentleman and he does, indeed, oversee the moral and aesthetic standards of Earthly Delights. I sometimes feel that I cannot live up to him. He is an aristocat.

'Have you heard from Jason?' he asked, leaning a hip against a mixing tub.

'Postcard,' I said. I ducked my head at the missive on the counter, which boasted the single line: *luv the beech but its hotte.*

Daniel read it. 'His spelling is very Middle English, isn't it?'

'The picture is of Lorne. Surely he can't get into too much trouble in Lorne.'

'I don't know—can he swim?' asked Daniel.

'No idea,' I replied.

'And where are the girls?'

'At an audition for a pilot episode of a soap called *Kiss the Bride*,' I said. 'This is their second call back, so they might even get parts. I do hope so. Might even make them put on a little weight.' The girls are fervent devotees of the Goddess Anorexia. I live to see a little more flesh on their bones.

The jumbles announced by scent that they were cooked. I took them out of the oven and tumbled them gently onto a cake cooler. Then I mixed and drizzled the lemon icing over my sand cake.

'All finished. You want to help me carry them up?'

'What about scones? Afternoon tea ought to have scones,' he objected, taking up the large tin tray loaded with food.

'She's making her own, of course,' I told him. 'Up to the roof, Madame is entertaining in the garden.'

I can't imagine how the roof garden at Insula escaped unscathed when the building was allowed to run down in the sixties. A lot of Melbourne was trashed at the time. The elevator goes right there so they can't have missed it. Intervention of fate, I expect. Fate likes a good garden as much as anyone else. There is a statue of Ceres with her arms full of corn, copy of a Roman original, in the glassed-in temple, but there is also a rose bower, a lot of wisteria, and even Trudi's linden tree. Mrs. Dawson's table was laid out under the wisteria. There were no blossoms on it, of course, it being January, but delightful pale green leaves and a lot of diffused light. She had lovely china, gold and blue, and a massive samovar which Trudi was even now wheeling up to the right of the hostess.

Trudi is Dutch and sixty and wears blue and is the only person whom the freight elevator obeys. Her appearance is only unusual in that she wears a ginger kitten of fiendish aspect on her shoulder. Meroe, our witch, says he is not really diabolical; only humans have the spiritual software to be devilish. He just has a small kink in his feline soul which renders him mischievous. That's why he is called Lucifer. He's getting bigger, which is a sobering prospect...

He made a wild dive for the cake—Lucifer will try to eat anything—and was hauled back by his harness. That harness has been the thwarting of a lot of potential adventures, especially those involving Lucifer and the fish pond in the atrium. For Insula is a Roman building, and what is a Roman building without its impluvium?

We don't know much about the lunatic who built Insula like a Roman tenement. There was a fashion then for exotic buildings—Moorish, Arabic, old English Gothick. It has some deco features but when Professor Dion ordered his apartment decorated after designs from Pompeii, they fitted beautifully. He is, for instance, the owner of the only ancient Roman TV/DVD cabinet in the world. We are a jolly collection, except for Mrs.

Pemberthy, who is there to curdle the milk of human kindness and make one desire state-sponsored seclusion of everyone over eighty-five with a small rotten doggie called Traddles.

Mrs. Dawson, urbane and elegant, was wearing what my grandmother would call a hostess gown in swirly shades of rust and apricot. She is an example to us all. She surveyed the provender as Daniel and I laid it out next to her cucumber sandwiches, the potted shrimps and their thin-sliced brown bread, and a mound of scones with concomitant jam and cream. Her scones looked very good. I would have guessed as much.

'A feast,' she told me. 'Thank you so much, Corinna dear. The ladies ought to be arriving. I've stationed Dion in the atrium to welcome the early birds. I shall now descend and join him.'

She flung a cobweb-fine muslin cloth over the feast and departed in a flourish of skirts.

'What a woman,' sighed Daniel.

'She is indeed. How about a tiny snack of our own?' I asked, with deep political cunning. I hoped to decoy him into my apartment for a little afternoon delight. I don't think I fooled him for a moment, but he fell in beside me willingly. In the interests of truth, I did intend to offer him tea. And cakes. As well.

All was going according to plan. He drank my Earl Grey, he ate a jumble and a slice of sand cake (I had made double, for my kitchen as well as Mrs. D's tea) and was about to kiss me with the kisses of his mouth in proper biblical fashion when the doorbell rang shrilly.

Damn.

The door was answered—however grudgingly—and Kylie and Goss danced into the room, waving bits of paper and laughing. I was not in the mood for laughing and dancing, but I tried. The whole building is sort of *in loco parentis* (as the professor calls it) to the girls. They are so young and on their own.

'What?' asked Daniel, also uncomfortably halted in mid-kiss.

'Contracts!' they cried.

'You got the job?' he asked.

'We got the job! We both got the job! Speaking parts! I'm the kooky girl, Goss is the loser one,' cried Kylie. 'It's an office. Ooh, tea. Can we have some? We missed lunch.'

'Certainly,' I agreed, surprised. 'Get yourselves a cup and a plate each—would you like one of my jumbles?'

'Looks good,' said Kylie, and they both tucked into jumbles in a way which would have made Richard III's martyred cook glad. I was just wishing I had made some more when I was given a typescript to read. It was a mass of convoluted phrases but seemed to be a hiring agreement for the pilot episode of *Kiss the Bride*, binding them to what seemed like frightful hours—six am to nine pm with extensions if necessary—and a condition that they didn't lose or gain weight. Or so much as breathe a word about the show to anyone at all, even their mothers, unless required to do so in supervised interviews. They could be sacked for a list of crimes, including persistent lateness, using drugs or alcohol, something which I had to read as moral turpitude, like getting in trouble with the law, and whenever the director felt like sacking them, he or she could. I would have protested but they had clearly already signed them—and the money was quite good. I nodded and handed the papers back to Kylie, or possibly Goss. They change their appearance so often that I get confused.

'I've got an appointment for my hair tomorrow,' breathed Goss, or possibly Kylie.

'Hair?' I asked, at a loss.

'Well, duh, Corinna, the kooky girl always has red hair and the loser's always a brunette. It's sort of the way things are,' explained the girl. 'I'm kooky so I'm going to be fire-engine red, and Goss is going to be brown for the future.'

The speaker was thus revealed to be Kylie and I realised that I would be able to tell them apart for the duration of the pilot. Goss, brown; Kylie, red. That would be a change.

Daniel was trying to catch my eye, making drinking motions. I briefly mourned my lost orgy. But yes, their triumph ought to have champagne. I got out the glasses. Daniel got out the emergency bottle of unexpected-good-news champagne from the fridge.

We all drank. After a glass each, the girls giggled and fled, saying that they had to get online to tell Facebook the good news—so much for their contracts, I almost said, but if the employers of modern young women don't know that every spare thought goes onto Facebook, they should not be employing them—and looked at Daniel.

'Where were we?' he purred, and filled my glass again.

Oh yes. That's where we were...

◇◇◇

I woke alone. Since the advent of Daniel, I had been finding my old bed a trifle constrained what with Daniel and Horatio and, of course, me, so I had bought a new bed roughly the size of a field, which easily fitted me and Horatio and Daniel with room left over for several haymakers and possibly a picnic. Horatio had tapped my cheek with an imperious paw, conveying that it was Cat Food Time and to look sharp about it. It further suggested that taking an impromptu nap was the province of the ruling species (i.e., cats) not the subservient (i.e., humans).

I can relate to that. I sat up, draped in my new blue sheets, and looked around for my lover. Gone, but there were noises suggestive of activity in the kitchen. I dragged on a silky robe and pottered out to investigate.

Thumping noises indicated that Daniel was making chicken schnitzel, so I found the peeler and began on the potatoes. We had become so used to working together that I didn't need to be told that mashed spuds were the accompaniment to Daniel's excellent schnitzel, and the salad was already chilling in its iced water. Yum. Making love makes me hungry.

Horatio was also hungry and discussed his gourmet cat food eagerly. Potatoes on, I wandered down to the bakery to feed the Mouse Police, a rough and ready pair who secured the night hours against rodents with tooth and claw. I was just laying out the cat meat which they get as a treat once a week—they seem disinclined to eat their prey, which is fine with me—when someone rapped, quite hard, on the bakery door. Since there was a large polite sign which indicated to the enquirer that we were closed until after Australia Day, I ignored it. Then they knocked again.

I was in a drowsy, pleasant mood. I opened the door to say, 'Sorry, no bread,' when a frantic hand seized me and dragged me into the street. I was about to deck my attacker—I do not allow myself to be dragged—when I recognised her. Almost. I had seen her before, somewhere...wearing a uniform...yes, of course, it was Thomasina, head girl and hockey fiend, from my very tough girls school. She had never been at all friendly toward me. But she hadn't actually mistreated me. I freed my arm from her anxious clutch.

'Corinna!' she cried. 'I thought it must be you! You've got to help me!'

This was a bit much for the hungry end of a delightful afternoon.

'Why?' I asked simply.

'Because we're old school mates,' she said. 'Because you're the best baker in town—everyone says so. Please!'

'Suppose you come inside and tell me about it,' I said, not wanting to conduct this interview in the street. 'But I haven't got long—I have a dinner date.'

'You?' she asked with that touch of incredulity which flicks a fat woman on the raw. I resolved that I would try to do the Christian thing and forgive my enemies, but that did not require me to present the other cheek. Especially since the Thomasina I remembered had a formidable right hook.

I sat her down in the assistant's chair. She had aged badly, looked haggard and lined. One advantage of being fat is that one does not wrinkle like the slim and gorgeous. Her hair had been a strong blonde. Now it was almost as mousy as mine. And she now wore glasses. I admit that I gloated, just a little bit. Corinna, your karma!

'What's this all about?' I asked.

'I started a company, catering for big events,' she told me. 'Gourmet food, you know, best of everything, hire my company and we do the works: decor, cutlery and crockery if required, flowers, staff, food, wine. The best people recommend us. You must have heard of us. Maîtresse.'

'I've heard of you,' I agreed. One saw announcements in the fashionable press about weddings, for instance; dresses by someone or other, event by Maîtresse. So Thomasina had done well. Good for her. 'What has that got to do with me?' I asked.

'My baker has gone to Malta for his father's funeral,' she said, making a raking grab for my arm again. 'I've got a big commission for a TV pilot. Not much going on this early in the year, most people are on holidays, this could make a big difference to us.'

'Who's us?'

'Me and Julia. You remember Julia.'

'I do. I had a crush on her in year eight.'

'I've had a crush on her ever since school,' grinned Thomasina. 'And luckily she likes me too—we're an item, so remember that if you recall your crush while you're working for us.'

'I don't know what you want me to do…and time is ticking on.' I hinted. I almost hoped that Daniel might wander down to find out what was keeping me. Even a stone butch like Tommy would have to admit that he was gorgeous…But nothing would deflect her from her mission.

'Make bread!' she screamed. 'We've got this contract, food for the cast and crew, matter of twenty people, three meals a day, and snacks, mounds of salads, hundreds of sandwiches, canapés, afternoon tea—and no bread! It's a nightmare!'

'Plenty of bakers around,' I murmured.

'But not the best! I need the best. Maîtresse needs the best, that's what we do.'

'And I'm the best?'

'Everyone says so. The stock exchange party made a lot of talk. Even Mrs. Dawson employed you for her afternoon tea.'

'Word gets around!' I said, amazed.

'It's a very small world and it never stops gossiping. Expensive, they say, but excellent.'

'I'm on holiday,' I temporised. 'My apprentice is away.'

'I can hire you as many helpers as you need. Please, Corinna!'

'All right,' I said. I had been bored. I don't have a talent for relaxing. Daniel had just told me that he had a new case which would occupy a week, so we couldn't go away. 'What do you want, and for how long do you want it?'

We started to plan. When Daniel finally did come down to see what was holding me up, she heard his footsteps and looked up from an order sheet. And her expression was all that I could have desired.

I introduced her. Her mouth was still open in an O of astonishment. I had the orders and Daniel had made his effect and in any case I was starving.

'What's the name of this TV show, anyway?' I asked as Tommy prepared to go.

'Oh, didn't I say? It's a soap called *Kiss the Bride*,' she answered, and took her leave.

Chapter Two

We had the argument—well, discussion—over the excellent chicken schnitzel and veggies.

'But you are supposed to be on holiday,' he protested.

'I know, but you're working, so we can't go anywhere, and I might as well be building up a holiday fund. And I don't have to get up so early. Six o'clock. Not four. Only bread for twenty, not the whole city and all those restaurants. I can do it alone, use only one mixer, clean up by myself. Tommy offered me a helper—I shall see if I need one. I wouldn't trust her helper not to nick my mother of bread and my best recipes and start up her own bakery. Apparently it is well known that I am the best,' I said, fluffing out my feathers and preening a little.

'Well, I suppose so,' he conceded. 'And you can keep an eye on the girls.'

'I won't be on site,' I pointed out. 'Just down in the bakery as usual.'

'I wouldn't rely on it,' he said. 'I know about old school friends. You can have first go at my car—and Timbo if you need a driver. I'm going to be on foot most of the time. This is a city mystery.'

'Not another missing son or daughter?'

'No, a missing bundle of bonds.'

'How did that happen?'

'Ah, there you have me. An intern had them, having just been to the Prothonotary's Office. Her mobile was out of credit so she went into one of the few remaining phone boxes, with the papers, and rang her office. There was some panic there and she was told to return right away. She was so upset by what was said that she flew out of the phone booth and…'

'Left the documents behind,' I concluded. 'And when she returned?'

'They were gone,' Daniel told me. 'She saw a homeless man walking away, but only remembered him later. Poor girl. So I'm searching the lost and strayed for a million dollars in bearer bonds.'

'They could have just ended up in the bin, or in the derros' campfire down by the river,' I commented.

'One has been presented at a Lonsdale Street bank,' said Daniel.

'Oh. Were they successful?'

'Yes, they cashed it. A man, they said, unshaven, much tattooed, dressed in an overall. So someone who knows what they are has his hands on them. And if they aren't found that poor intern is going to be sacked.'

'Tough call. Wide search. What's for dessert?' I felt I needed a change of subject. It would be a terrible thing to ruin a promising career so early…

'Peaches,' said Daniel, and fetched them. They were splendid, exuding a rich cold liquor such as is served in Paradise.

Then there was no reason why we shouldn't relax, watching *Doctor Who* and eating the rest of the Christmas chocolates, which even Horatio did not wish to share.

Tomorrow I was going back to the bakery, and I felt very pleased about it. Not only was my old school fellow Tommy paying above the odds, but she had stared at Daniel, gobsmacked, and something inside of me, some old school-aged injury, started to heal. And who would have guessed at Julia? Julia was a butterfly, a delicate little gauzy thing with an overprotective mother and a penchant for pink. Of course, she was sixteen when I had last seen her. She might have had a buzz-cut, adopted Gothism, or become buxom.

I went to bed early, as Daniel was going out on the Soup Run in pursuit of his papers. What could a collection of the homeless and desperate want with a packet of bearer bonds? But the sale meant that one of them must have known. Fallen stockbroker, perhaps, derelict banker…

◇◇◇

I must have dozed off at this point. When next the world declared itself it was six am and time to get cooking.

I rose, I washed and dressed, I donned my overall and my solid shoes. Bakers who wear sandals find out exactly how hot spilled toffee topping is. I still had the scar from that burn. There are other ways to acquire empathy with victims of lava spills. Better ones.

Horatio was waiting, politely, for a dab of my butter as I reached the stage called toast and contemplation. He is a royal beast and only asks for a token tribute. I read through Tommy's list again. Lots of bread, certainly, low-sugar, low-salt, no-cal health bread—erk—and real pasta dura, made with yeast. Rolls. Brioche. Muffins.

Ah, muffins. Mine were perfectly all right, but those made by Jason were superb. He, however, was learning to surf somewhere on the coast, and the cast of *Kiss the Bride* were going to have to ruin their diets for the high-cal and high-sugar with the standard Corinna muffin. Blueberry for today, as I had a lot of blueberries in stock. Those frozen ones were perfect for muffins, thawing neatly in the mix and thus not overcooking.

Down to the bakery to stagger slightly as Heckle and Jekyll collided with my ankles, one from each side. They are rough but affable mousers and ratters (and occasionally, strangely enough, spiderers and pigeoners) who decimate the rodent population and thus earn their kitty dins. During the day they snooze on a heap of flour sacks, their preferred couch. During the night they hunt, and last night they had done well. Three rats and five mice were laid out on the doormat.

I disposed of the slaughtered and fed the Mouse Police. They dived on the food in a blur of black and white fur as as I put the first mix on to rise. The bakery was loud with appreciative whuffling, always a charming sound. I mixed and measured. When I sat down for my cup of coffee everything was in train.

I opened the street door so the Mouse Police could scoot out and extort endangered species scraps from Kiko or Ian of the Japanese restaurant. The weather was temperate, which is a signal that it is about to change. In Melbourne, a city whose climate can only be called 'unstable.' If by unstable you mean that it is blowing a hot gale before lunch and raining like the Flood after lunch. This makes Melburnians flexible and agile. You have to be, to dodge the hailstones. Some of them are as big as tennis balls, I swear.

The paperboy slung the plastic-wrapped paper, hitting the half-open door with a thud. While Heckle seemed to have forgone his usual amusement—bringing down runners by threading between their feet—the paperboy remained fair game, if only the battle-scarred old veteran could work out a way of bringing down the bicycle safely. Heckle growled the sort of growl which a baffled tiger might have emitted when robbed by fate of his destined antelope. Then he slouched off to join his partner in demanding fish with menaces.

He went around Mrs. Sylvia Dawson, retired society hostess and vision of style, even at this hour. Mrs. Dawson has great authority. The Prof calls it *auctoritas* and says, a little sadly, that he never had it. Mrs. Dawson has it. It even works on cats, a difficult audience to daunt. She gives Insula tone. Today she was wearing a light leisure suit in dark brown, the colour of bittersweet chocolate, and an apricot silk shirt. She goes for a walk every morning to assuage her puritan conscience, which then allows her to spend the rest of the day in sybaritic pursuits. I have always wondered what sybaritic pursuits are. Did they have a connection with the nymph pursued by a satyr over Professor Dion Monk's door?

'Corinna! You're back at work?'

'Special order. I was getting bored with nothing to do. Can I give you a loaf of pasta dura?' I had made a few extra loaves for local consumption.

'You certainly can. How very pleasant! I need some breakfast. I've just seen your Daniel wandering among the homeless. He told me he was getting nowhere, so expect him back soon.'

This was good news. I am always pleased to see Daniel. I wrapped a loaf and handed it over. She gave me the exact change and walked off. I watched her straight back. She had probably learnt deportment by walking with a book on her head. Mrs. Dawson could carry the collected works of William Wordsworth on that trim silver hairdo.

But this wasn't getting bread baked. I returned to my ovens. The Mouse Police returned from their fishing expedition and flopped down on their flour sacks. All was peace and tranquillity in Earthly Delights. For a change.

When the loaves and muffins were out of the oven—and smelling ambrosial—the carrier arrived from Tommy and took them all away, and I was left to clean up. End of morning's work, and I was conscious of a glow of achievement as I locked up and climbed the stairs to my own apartment.

'Corinna's a baker again,' I sang to myself. Now I, too, could find something sybaritic to do. Having earnt my repose.

This took the form of a bath in violet bath foam. I dressed in a light cotton gown adorned with blue batik butterflies which Jon, our global food-relief guru, had bought in Laos. It is made to a pattern which at one stage requires the sewer to turn the fabric through four dimensions and which always baffles me every time I make it. But it is loose and gorgeous and flatters my size-20 body. It was probably going to be a hot day. But see previous comments about Melbourne.

I was reading the paper—always a dangerous proceeding, with the world in the sad shape that it is—when Horatio (who finds fresh newspapers an excellent spot on which to sprawl, sparing me the international news) raised his head and pricked up his admirable ears, which meant a visitor was impending. He always hears them before I do. And sure enough the bell rang and Meroe was there.

Meroe is our professional witch, seer and supplier of all manner of occult paraphernalia to the gentry, proprietor of the Sibyl's Cave and devoted slave to her familiar, the black cat Belladonna. She had a basket of her magically derived salad leaves. She offered it to me.

'For lunch or dinner,' she said. But there was something on her mind. In a strong light, she might be seventy or forty: I have never been able to decide. Gypsies are like that.

'Come in and I'll make tea,' I offered.

'Chamomile,' she selected, which meant that she was really worried. And it had seemed like such a peaceful morning up until now. But that was Insula for you. The price of living in a small upright village was that everyone's worries were yours.

I conducted her and the leaves (yum) to the kitchen, that ancient female refuge. She shed today's wrap, which was a length of blue silk figured with masks of comedy and tragedy, and I made tea. I allowed her time to sip it and gather her thoughts.

'The girls came to me last night for a tarot reading,' she said slowly. 'And it showed that they would be undertaking a new enterprise in which they have every chance of success.'

'Good,' I encouraged.

'But I have seldom seen a reading so hedged about with danger,' she told me. 'Peril. I did not know what to advise, except to tell them to be very careful.'

'What sort of peril?' I asked. I supposed that a studio could be dangerous—trip hazards, falling booms. I really had no idea what a film set was like. But every human endeavour these days is beset with electrical wiring.

Meroe sipped more tea. 'Secrets,' she said reluctantly. 'The reading was surrounded by secrets. I don't like it, Corinna, I don't like it at all.'

'But this is what they have always wanted to do,' I said. 'It would be too cruel to forbid them to embark on their life's ambition.'

'That is why I did not do so,' she snapped. 'I just warned them. It would be better if you could accompany them. Earthly

Delights is closed. I would feel happier if there was a reliable person looking after them.'

'Meroe, I'm on holiday!' I protested again. 'The girls don't need a chaperone. They're nineteen years old. They think they're grown-ups. This is their great adventure.'

'It may prove more adventurous than they can handle,' she warned. It was too much. I had been seduced into making bread for the wretched program. I wasn't going to waste my life hanging around the set annoying the girls. But it is never wise to say an outright 'no' to a witch.

'I'll think about it,' I said reluctantly.

Her beautiful smile illuminated her face.

'Thank you, Corinna, I knew I could rely on you.'

She finished her tea and took her leave. I grumpily washed the breakfast dishes and was attempting to recover my equanimity when the key sounded in the door and Daniel arrived. He kissed me hello. He smelt gamy and his cheek was scratchy. It had clearly been a long night.

'I need a shower and some food,' he announced, and went into the bathroom forthwith. I exchanged a glance with Horatio. Both of us were feeling a tad put-upon.

However, we got out the eggs and sliced some bacon and soon the scent of a proper cooked breakfast tempted a clean, damp, famished spectre out of the bathroom and into the kitchen.

'Food!' he exclaimed. 'Corinna, I don't deserve you.'

I refrained from murmuring agreement. I supplied him with eggs, bacon, grilled tomatoes and fresh sourdough. He ate it all. He must not have pinched a sandwich from the Soup Run or eaten at all for the whole night. I made myself coffee and tried one of my muffins. All right, though not a patch on Jason's. I wondered how my wandering apprentice was getting on and hoped he wasn't sunburnt. Before he had dragged himself off heroin, he didn't go out much in the daytime.

Daniel sipped his coffee, looked at the muffins and shook his head, and spoke at last.

'That was a long night,' he said. 'I must have covered miles and miles. All for nothing.'

'Didn't find a thing?' I asked sympathetically.

'Nothing but rumours,' he told me. 'Everyone is talking about a great treasure being in the possession of a group of drunks. I heard it at several places. But it happened on the other side of the city, wherever I was. That is the hallmark of an urban legend.'

'The German shepherd choking on the burglar's fingers?' I offered.

'The car thief with Granny on the roof rack,' he agreed. 'Always happened to a friend's aunt. In another city. I'm chasing phantoms,' he said sadly.

'Never mind. Perhaps we can do some psychical research and nail them down to a place and time.'

'And a reason for haunting. I'm almost at the stage when I'm ready to try it. I might ask Meroe. She's probably on first-name terms with every spook in the city.'

'She's been here already, with premonitions of doom,' I told him. I related the gist of Meroe's tarot reading.

'And what did you reply?' he asked, smiling at last. Ah, the healing influence of food.

'That I'd think about it.'

'And?'

'I've thought about it and I'm not going to do it. I can't see a way of smuggling myself onto the set and, in any case, what could I do about the danger? She was very unspecific about the threat. It could be anything.'

'Threats are usually people,' he pointed out.

'Even so,' I said firmly. I wasn't going to burden the girls with my presence. They didn't need a bodyguard. And on the off-chance that they did, I wasn't one. The only thing I am good at subduing is yeast. That takes all my energies. Having made my stand, I kissed a freshly shaven cheek. Mmm. Salty goodness, as Xander would say. 'I can think of a way to take our minds off our problems,' I hinted.

'Oh, I do so need distraction,' he said, and kissed me in turn.

It was an afternoon full of kisses. If we are talking about deserts, I do not deserve Daniel.

◇◇◇

Answering the phone. Never a good idea. It is sure to be 1) a Mumbai call centre selling free mobile phones; 2) some lunatic doing a survey; or 3) someone who wants something. Usually money.

I unwisely picked up the phone while I was preparing dinner. This had the effect of ruining my temper and getting onion juice on the handset, both bad things. On the line was my school acquaintance Tommy. She was in a state. The voice was as tense as a cat trespassing in the yard of a big fierce Rottweiler.

'Corinna? Is that you?'

I suppressed the retort that I was the only one likely to be answering my phone at this number and told her that I was, indeed, Corinna.

'I need a favour,' she quavered.

'I thought you might,' I agreed.

'I need you to come in with the bread tomorrow. Just for a few days. My pastry chef has broken a leg. Why the silly bitch wanted to go rollerblading at her age I'll never know.'

'No,' I said.

'You owe me!' The cat had now sighted the Rottweiler and it was off its chain.

'How?' I asked, reasonably.

'At school. I never told who tripped Susie into that mud puddle when she was wearing her new white pleated skirt. Not even under torture! I knew it was you! I saw you!'

'Oh,' I said. One of the few warming memories I had of my school days was the memory of watching Susie, in her new skirt, tumble into the puddle. And I had, actually, tripped her. I hadn't thought anyone had been a witness to my crime and I felt a pang of not-unpleasurable guilt. Susie had been one of my chief tormentors. She had had that mud puddle coming. 'Right.'

'So you'll come?' The cat was within a pace of the fence.

I felt what Meroe calls the tides of fate turning. I succumbed gracefully. As gracefully as possible.

'You'll have to pay me,' I said.

'Full wages,' she said. The cat was on top of the fence, out of range of the teeth. 'As well as the fee for the bread. Just hop a lift with the carrier. It's only Docklands. Not far.'

I put down the phone. Damn, damn, damn. I went back to chopping onions, grumbling.

'It might be interesting,' Daniel offered, tasting my tomato sauce with capers and anchovies and approving.

'It's only for a few days,' I conceded. 'And I might be able to keep an eye on the girls. As Meroe asked. It is always wise to accede to the requests of a powerful witch. Do you think this needs more salt?'

'A touch more,' said Daniel, and there we left the matter.

It was a very good sauce, anyway.

After its consumption Daniel went out to pursue his lost papers and I watched *Dollhouse* series 2, about which I am still ambivalent, before putting myself and Horatio to bed for an early start. I had prepared my bag: good apron, spare socks in case the freezer failed and I got soaked (this had happened before), one good knife and my favourite Venetian-glass rolling pin. If I was going to make pastry, it would be good pastry.

I fell asleep full of forebodings. I didn't like being manipulated, even by fate. Manipulated to what end?

Presumably fate knew…

Chapter Three

But there was bread to bake the next morning, so I baked it. The Mouse Police performed their morning rituals—display hunting trophies, eat breakfast, scamper off for tuna scraps—and curled up to snooze the day away on their flour sacks. I took in an order of flour, made muffins, drank coffee, sifted sugar over my not-as-good-as-Jason's muffins (strawberry) and awaited the carrier. I hadn't worked in a kitchen for years, not since I started Earthly Delights and abandoned paid employment.

Commercial kitchens are fraught places. Ordinary kitchens can get intense, especially when two people are trying to do things and they get in each other's way. Domestic murders happen in kitchens, where there are a suitable array of objects both sharp and blunt with which to commit them. I had worked in places which were more like war zones than places of culinary refinement. I was, therefore, a little anxious when I hopped, as instructed, into the anonymous white van for the short trip to Docklands.

All drivers of anonymous white vans have a hidden flaw. In some it is that they channel Ayrton Senna and one arrives at a destination—if one arrives—feeling like one has fallen from space without a parachute. Some smoke like chimneys. Some avoid washing and laundry, presumably for the mortification of the flesh. It is as though they know they are multifold, and need to stand out from the pack.

This one whistled. Quite tunefully, I admit, though it was getting on my nerves by the time we arrived. 'Heartbreak Hotel' has never been my favourite song. Strange selection for a young man, who must have got his driver's licence a scant six months ago. By mail.

Docklands is huge. We trolled along the avenue of palm trees to a large building, painted in a cheerful grey colour. It looked like a wartime Nissen hut. There were probably reasons for this. Over the front door was emblazoned HARBOUR STUDIOS with a logo which vaguely resembled a boat with sails, or possibly a seagull after collision with a helicopter. We zoomed around to the back entrance, where the kitchen was, and found ourselves in a grimy paved car park spotted with a few discouraged trees (palms) and a huge stain where someone had spilled something like red wine. Or blood, of course. My driver chuckled.

'Beef burgundy, and didn't she go mad!' he explained.

I expect she did. Beef burgundy takes ages to make and the ingredients are expensive. That must have been enough beef stew to feed a whole crew—utterly wasted. I felt sad.

The driver waved me toward a kitchen door—you can tell by the smell, the rubbish bins, and the butts of those slipping out for a smoke between courses. Because smoking is disapproved of, no one provides receptacles for the butts. I suppose there is logic in there somewhere. But it makes all places of tobacco resort unsanitary.

The kitchen was large, full of people, steamy from various pots and noisy. As expected. Tommy sighted me and dived through the ruck.

'There you are!' she exclaimed, as though I had kept her waiting. 'Pies today, pies, fillings are over there, staff toilets and lockers over there, coffee over there.' As she was brandishing a large knife, I did not protest at my welcome. I stashed my basket, washed my hands, put on my apron and took possession of my pastry corner.

You need a light hand—and a light heart, so the saying goes—to make pastry. Mine was all right. The secret is to keep all the ingredients cold. Pastry was invented in cold countries where you could only get things warm by sticking them in an oven. You could keep things cold by merely leaving them on the bench, or, as in the old days in Wales, making your Welshcakes with snow. This may have led to excellent scones but it also led to incurable chilblains. I preferred the Australian climate and reliable refrigeration. I checked my list, which was posted next to the working surface. Ingredients. I found flour, salt and butter, granulated and powdered sugar, milk and a row of large plastic containers marked *Chicken pie*, *Apple purée*, *Beef pie* and *Berry pie*. There was also a goodly array of tins and a commodious oven.

So I made pastry. The list demanded ten of each pie. I made Grandma's shortcrust for the sweet pies and my own buttery puff for the savoury and soon I had a collection of lumps of dough chilling down for rolling. Then I had time to draw breath.

The kitchen smelt gorgeous. There seemed to be a table laid out against the far wall and I wandered over to it, hoping for a cup of coffee at least. I found that it was the Salon des Refusés of any kitchen: stuff which hadn't quite worked which the staff were enjoined, sometimes at gunpoint, to eat. Instead of food which might be profitably sold to the starving public, of course. There were wrapped rolls and sandwiches and muffins—mine—a pot of something which smelt like minestrone and a tray of hors d'ouevres. I wasn't really hungry, but I could certainly pick a bit after all that kneading.

Two people were already standing at the table; a young man and a young woman. By the tattoos and piercings I guessed they weren't actors. They both smiled at me and moved aside.

'Go ahead,' one invited. 'It'll only go to the poor if we don't eat it. I haven't seen you before. You the new pastry Nazi?'

'That's me,' I agreed. 'Corinna Chapman. I'm actually a baker, but don't tell anyone.'

'Promise,' said the young woman. Her hair, I couldn't help noticing, was tortured into a thousand dreadlocks. I wondered if they hurt. I wondered how she slept in them. 'I'm Gordon and this is Kendall. We're the writers. Try the little pastry boats.

Poor old Em made them just before she went off on those roll-erblades and fell.'

I bit into a *petit bateau*. Flaky pastry, creamy asparagus fill-ing. Poor old Em was a good pastry chef. I hoped she would be back very soon.

'Writers? Isn't the program already written?' I asked, trying a little pie which proved to be filled with chicken and sweet corn.

'TV doesn't work like that,' Kendall said. Tattoos, dread-locks, piercings, to match his co-writer. He had a strange, rasp-ing voice. Had he been yelling a lot lately? 'TV gets written then rewritten. Especially with Madame Superbitch Molly Atkins dictating terms,' he added, gloomily crunching up a piece of cucumber as though he personally disliked it.

'And then rewritten,' agreed Gordon. 'Oops, here she comes. Remember, smile, and tell her it's all low-fat.'

They decamped. A tall woman, clad in a fluffy pink velour gown and a turban, had stalked in through the other door and now stood next to me. She loomed.

'Isn't breakfast ready yet?' she demanded. Lovely voice. Beautiful face. Eyes like chips of sapphire, lips like rose petals. Pity about the manner. It would have been considered impolite in one of the Old Regime in Russia who was dealing with a serf.

'Just coming,' sang Tommy, appearing at my elbow. 'Go through and we will be serving directly. And you, Corinna, aren't those egg and bacon pies ready?'

'You didn't ask me for any,' I responded.

'Special order, little egg and bacon pies for our star, Ms. Atkins.'

'Low-fat,' snarled the star, departing as requested in a flurry of baby pink. I waited until the door slammed.

'Look, Tommy, you didn't order them, and I haven't made them,' I said firmly.

'I know, I know.' Her face crumpled. 'But make me some? Say six? She didn't demand them until five and I didn't have time. Besides, I can't make pastry. Please? She'll be bearable if she isn't hungry.'

'You're pushing this friendship further than it will go,' I warned, but went off, securing myself a cup of coffee, to find the eggs and make more pastry. After all, I was there to make pastry.

As I rolled and crimped I was conscious of curious glances from the room. The sandwich hands had completed their mound of wrapped comestibles and were starting their clean-up, which for some reason always involves retrieving tomato slices from the floor.

Everyone in a kitchen looks superficially alike: white cap, white coat. I stashed the egg and bacon pies in the oven. They ought to be delicious: free-range eggs and the best prosciutto. But definitely not low-fat, not with all that Parma ham. As I started on the beef pies I considered my company.

Not a friendly kitchen. No one had greeted me or offered to show me where the coffee was. Efficient? There was no shouting, no clanging of dropped or thrown pots. Everyone seemed to know what they were supposed to be doing, and to be doing it. Sandwiches were made, eggs were being fried, bacon crisped, tomatoes grilled, mushrooms seethed. Apparently we offered a full English breakfast, which was ambitious. My bread was being sliced and yesterday's was being toasted. Someone was making a ratatouille; I could smell the eggplant cooking. The vegetarian option, no doubt. I missed one scent: garlic. Ratatouille needs garlic. Beef pies in the oven, I said as much to the chopper-and-slicer on the next bench, a tall thin pale cook who resembled a stick of celery. He giggled.

'Not in this kitchen,' he told me. 'Hi! I'm Lance. They call me Lance the Lettuce Guy. We're feeding actors. They spend all day breathing into each other's faces. No garlic and precious few onions.'

'I hadn't thought of that,' I confessed. 'Could certainly take the passion out of a love scene.'

'Especially if it's Ms. Atkins,' he whispered, using a piece of cucumber as cover. 'She threw a pink fit one day because that poor camera guy was eating mints. She hates the smell of mint. Or so she says.'

'She's powerful?'

'It's all a merry round of "Who's Queen?" What she wants, she gets. She's on a fearsome diet and demands low-fat everything, but if it's really low-fat she flings it away and says it has no taste. I'm glad I'm on salads. If she puts on a gram it'll all be your fault, you watch.'

I began to wonder what I had got myself into. I could be sitting on my balcony right now, caressing a cat and drinking a G and T. Of course, I could do that when I had all the pies done.

So I got on with the pies.

As the first lot came out of the oven I slotted in the next lot. A servitor came to collect the special order for Ms. Atkins. She was a thin nervous girl, rather pretty, with dark hair in a ponytail and no makeup. She reminded me of a trapped mouse I had once rescued from Horatio, who had no idea of what to do with it once he had cornered it. It had shivered under a crumpled bathmat, its little beady eyes bright with terror. It had not offered to bite when I picked it up and took it down to the street and let it go. I suddenly remembered its little trembling warmth in my palm as I gave the small pies to the girl with the warning that they were hot and it would not do for the star to burn her mouth. Her hands shook as she took the tray. Poor little mouse!

'Emily,' sympathised Lance the salad maker. 'What a life!'

'Ms. Atkins' assistant?'

'Personal slave to a superbitch,' said the salad maker's mate. 'Hi, I'm Kate.'

'Corinna,' I replied. 'Why does she stay?'

'She wants to be an actor,' said Kate. 'It's an addiction, like wanting to be published or revealing your secret identity as Superman in Federation Square on a Sunday afternoon. A mania. Everyone wants to be an actor!'

'Not me,' I disclaimed.

'Nor me.' She passed a bowl of salad to a server outside the door. 'Ms. A is powerful. You must have seen her on TV.'

I confessed ignorance. Kate raised an eyebrow.

'She's been in every soap,' she told me. 'Ever since she was a child star. It's what she does. Lately she's been in a bit of a hiatus—surgery, you know.' She grinned. 'They must have pinned her eyelids to her ears. Something I'd love to do, by the way.'

'So, you've given up your membership of her fan club?' I asked.

Kate laughed, sounding surprised.

'You're all right! We thought you were a best girlfriend of the boss.'

'Never,' I said. 'I'm here because of a nifty bit of blackmail and a lot of begging.'

'She's good at that,' responded Kate. She went back to her salad and I went back to my pies.

They were turning out well. You never know with pastry. Mostly it obeys the laws of physics but sometimes it doesn't. I glazed the apple pies—the last—and began to clean my pastry board. Several people smiled at me. The scents cleared now that all the food was out on the buffet, steaming in the bains-marie I had glimpsed outside the kitchen. There was a general sense of relief. Some people went past me to the outer door, presumably for a smoke. There was a step to sit on.

My feet were beginning to complain. Also my back. And my task was completed. I thought I had perhaps better say goodbye to Tommy before I stripped off my apron and removed the flour from my person, so I finished the cleaning and went walking.

I could not see her anywhere in the kitchen, so I shucked the apron and went out into the studio.

There was a crowd round the food, buzzing with conversation. Kylie and Goss spotted me immediately. Spines stiffened. Was I here to do the unforgivable adult thing and interfere? I waved a hand at them, trying to express 'This wasn't my idea.' Nice-looking people surrounded me. Beautiful people. One young man turned and gave me a smile which would have made a seraph envious.

'Hello, you're new!'

'I'm just your baker,' I said, dazzled. Such perfection! Hyacinthine curls in ebony, swarthy skin, white teeth. A dimple. Of course.

'I'm Harrison,' he announced. 'If you made this bread, you're as good a baker as I am an actor.'

'Thank you,' I said, not sure how to take this.

'Couldn't you just take him home and cuddle him all night?' asked another young man wearily. 'Stop harassing the help, Harry, or I'll film you exclusively left profile.'

'Ethan! You wouldn't!' exclaimed Harrison.

'You watch me,' threatened Ethan. 'Any more of that scrambled egg left? Grab it before the crew eats it all,' he advised.

Harrison uttered a famished squeak and dived back into the pack. Ethan grinned. He was large and mid-brown and looked calm, which would be an asset on a film set, I was beginning to realise. He rested his plate on a plastic-enshrouded table and fished a small bottle from his pocket.

'Spice it up a bit,' he explained, waving the bottle in my direction. My nose wrinkled.

'Chili oil?' I asked.

'Ms. Superstar hates hot food,' he explained. 'I like a bit of heat. So I bring my own. Nice to meet you.' He looked past me at Ms. Mouse, poor thing, bearing a cup of hot coffee toward one of the little cubicles marked DRESSING ROOMS. His face softened. Serious interest there, I thought, or maybe just sympathy. Ms. Mouse could do worse than repose on that manly bosom.

My curiosity was piqued. What an interesting collection of people! Kylie and Goss slid through the crowd and grabbed me, an arm each.

'What are you doing here?' demanded Kylie. 'You're not checking up on us, are you?'

'No, I'm baking pies,' I said. Their long fingernails were digging into my skin. They looked like small predatory birds. 'Really. Tommy's an old school friend and I owe her a favour and the pastry chef has broken her leg.'

'Oh yeah, I heard about that.' Kylie released me.

'So did I.' Goss released me. 'Well, all right then.'

'I'm just looking for her so that I can leave,' I added. They both relaxed. Then I made a tactical error. 'Did you get some breakfast? The food looks good.'

'We don't eat breakfast,' said Kylie.

'Not when we're working,' added Goss.

And they stalked haughtily away. Oh well. Suddenly, I missed Jason, a handy and reliable appetite. And it was time I left.

Then something occurred which was quite unacceptable to any civilised mind. Savage. Brutal. The door of one of the cubicles was open, and I heard a voice insisting, 'No, you eat one first.' Which was overlaid on a frantic protest of: 'No, I can't, you know I'm gluten intolerant! Please, Ms. Atkins, don't make me!'

Through the opening I saw Ms. Atkins standing over her assistant and forcing one of the little pies—my pies—into her mouth. I was reminded of me giving pills to a cat. Cats are not cooperative when it comes to medication. The struggle involves towels, bandaids, Betadine and pain. This one was unlikely to require iodine but otherwise was similar. I was shocked. Poor Emily was recoiling in fear and no baker can stand seeing someone reduced to revulsion by their works of art.

'I'll eat one,' I volunteered boldly. What if Tommy sacked me? I didn't want this job anyway. I heard an intake of breath behind me. But I walked in and took the pie out of the long-nailed hand and munched it up. 'Delicious,' I announced. It was, too.

There was a moment of perfect silence. Then Molly Atkins began to laugh. She had a lovely, rich laugh. The audience laughed as well, out of sheer relief. Emily made her escape. Then Ms. Atkins sat down in her chair and began to eat her breakfast, and I turned away and ran straight into the arms of a stocky woman, who shook me by the shoulders.

'You've got a nerve,' she said admiringly. 'Who are you?'

'Corinna Chapman, the baker—those were my pies. Who are you?'

'Tash,' she said. 'I'm the director. Thank you. I never like to start the day with a nice tantrum.'

She was taller than me, a stalwart figure in blue jeans and a saggy T shirt. Her hair was plaited in two long braids over her shoulders. She had frank blue eyes and really only needed a straw to chew to complete the picture of a wholesome country girl, dreaming of rustic pursuits and hayfields and able to carry a pig under each arm. I liked her immediately. She let me go and turned to the attendant crowd, who were still giggling.

'Ten minutes,' she announced.

They scattered. I found Tommy and bade her farewell, and walked home up the tram route, anxious to get back to Earthly Delights and my preordained date with a gin and tonic.

This, however, was not to be. As I rounded the corner into my own street I saw Daniel, comforting a young woman who was crying like a fountain. This must be his intern client. What to do? Should I invite her up to my apartment? I didn't want to do that. Start inviting Daniel's clients to my own house and there would be deserving cases sleeping on the floor. And Horatio would object.

I waved a hand toward the little umbrellas outside Heavenly Pleasures, which had just opened again. This is an expensive gourmet chocolate shop and a state of emotional collapse called for strong measures; i.e., a Heavenly Pleasures hot chocolate. Not to be even contemplated by those of a diabetic disposition, it is so thick as to be almost solid. In homage to the proprietor's Belgian ancestry, it is accompanied with a dollop of whipped cream, sprinkled with cinnamon. I ration myself to one a week. It soothes the soul.

And this poor girl had a soul evidently troubled enough for several vats of chocolate. Daniel introduced her as 'Lena' and she gave me a damp little paw to shake. I seemed to be surrounded by maidens in distress lately. As we waited for our chocolate I examined the client.

Fat girl. Unhappy about it. This was evidenced by the straining seams of her charcoal jacket and skirt. Women who know and have accepted their magnificent fleshliness buy or make clothes which are roomy, even loose. Those still convinced that a crash diet will reduce their waistline to a size 14 will stuff themselves into a size too small and be uncomfortable. And wear black because they think it makes them look thinner. Which it doesn't. She had olive skin and dark eyes and long black shiny hair in a bun. Indian, perhaps?

She stopped crying and dried her face and sipped at the drink when it came. I did too. It was wonderful. If I was concocting a last meal this chocolate would have to be part of it. After a few cups, one wouldn't mind being executed so much. Serenity in a cup.

'It's just that internships are so hard to get,' she mourned. 'I was so happy when Mr. Mason said I could come. I'd be good at accounting if they gave me a chance. But I know they'll sack me and then no one else will employ me. And I'd be better if they didn't yell at me all the time. The partner comes in every morning and kicks the filing cabinet and yells 'Hello, stupid!' at me and that sort of sets the tone for the day. I get nervous and I drop things and misread things. They tell me I'm useless and I *am* useless. And now…'

'Haven't you got any friend in that office?' I asked, looking for some silver in the cumulo-nimbus lining.

'No, well, there's the other intern, her name is Claire. She doesn't say nasty things to me. Sometimes we have lunch together. She's on a fierce diet so it's good for me.' Unconscious of irony, Lena drank more of the lethal Heavenly Pleasures brew. The chocolate was doing its healing work. Lena's face had dried and her eyes were clearing a little. But they were still as red as coals.

'I have to get back,' she said, glancing at her watch. 'I'm in enough trouble without being late. Thank you,' she said to me. 'That was an amazing treat. You'll let me know, Daniel?'

'I'll let you know,' he replied. And Lena bustled away.

'Poor girl,' I said.

'Indeed.'

'How have your enquiries progressed?'

'They haven't,' he confessed. 'Rumours and more rumours. I'll have another trawl tonight. What about you?'

I told him about the studio, the crew, and the remarkably bad behaviour of the star.

'More bullies,' he answered. We sipped chocolate in silence. It was, however, wonderful chocolate. I paid Julie and we went back to the apartment for some afternoon delight in preparation for an early dinner and then more wandering in the underworld for him and a lot of sleep for me. That studio had been a very stressful workplace. I wondered why anyone took up acting as a profession. Early hours, temperamental coworkers, and long periods of time when nothing was happening. There must be rewards. I just couldn't see them.

Chapter Four

Morning announced itself with the alarm, and I supplied myself with coffee and toast before I stepped down to the bakery to start my loaves. The mail yesterday had included another free postcard, this one advertising mineral water baths, on which Jason had scrawled: *Think I'm getting the hang of surfing. And camping. Luv.* I could not read the postmark. Was he still in Lorne? And staying out of trouble? I missed my apprentice as I hauled sacks of flour and measured and mixed. Jason had been strong and willing and quick to learn. I wondered if he would fall in love with surfing and follow the trail to the Queensland sun. I hoped not.

Bread was baking and I was drinking my third cup of coffee, which I never pour until all the heavy work is done, when there was a respectful tapping at the street door. When I opened it there was a neat young woman dressed in a white overall.

'Tommy sent me,' she said. 'She called me last night. In case you needed any help.'

'Well...' I hesitated. Did I need any help? I had run Earthly Delights on my own before Jason's advent and I seemed to be coping with doing it again. She read my expression.

'Please,' she said. 'I could be good if anyone gave me a chance. I've got my pastry cook's certificate but I've never done any bread.'

'All right,' I said grudgingly. I could not ignore an appeal like that. 'But if I find that you've pinched my mother of bread and started your own bakery, I warn you, I'll sue.'

'Not a chance,' she replied, coming in and bending down to stroke the Mouse Police. 'Who's a gorgeous kitty-cat then?'

Heckle looked offended. He had taken a great many pains to be accepted as a tough streetfighter. He did not appreciate being addressed as though he was a fluffy toy. The young woman realised her mistake.

'Oh no, you're a big tough bully, aren't you? I had a cat like you called Attila Mouse Ripper.'

That was more like it. Heckle let out a faint, rusty purr and angled his jaw into the caressing hand. I smiled.

'Sit down, have some coffee, don't talk a lot unless you need to ask a question and we shall manage. What's your name?'

'Bernadette. People call me Bernie. Just black, please. What's on the menu?'

'Muffins, brioche, rolls, bread. All the dough is on and rising. We just need to make the muffins. You any good at muffins?'

'No idea,' said Bernie. 'Give it a go.'

Well, she had the proper baker's taste in coffee and maybe she would be helpful, at that. I turned over the recipe, the tins of apple filling, allowed her to collect her ingredients and showed her which oven to use while I got on with cleaning the mixers. And I covertly watched her, of course.

She was neat. Her hair was short and neat, her overall was neat, her feet were neatly shod and she didn't waste a movement. Although she had evidently not made muffins before, she worked out that they should not be overmixed and dropped the batter (neatly) into the pans in the recommended time. Then she looked around for something else to do, and I directed her to take the rye bread out of the oven. This she managed without dropping the loaves or burning herself, which is not as easy as it sounds, that oven having been designed by someone who hated bakers or ran aBandaid franchise. She didn't ask a single unnecessary question that whole morning's work. I was impressed with Bernie.

When the carrier arrived, we packed ourselves into the van for the trip to Harbour Studios with the glowing consciousness of a good day's work already completed. The driver was still whistling 'Heartbreak Hotel.' I wished he wouldn't. I started a conversation to cover the sound.

'So you're not aiming to become a baker?' I asked Bernie.

'Pastry chef,' she replied. 'I admire what you do, of course,' she added hurriedly, in case I might be offended, 'but I just love pastry. There is something magical about it.'

'Yes. That's how I feel about bread,' I assured her. 'And if you don't feel like that, you have no business being a baker. The hours,' I added, 'are a killer.'

'So they are,' she said. 'This catering firm is my first real job. It's a bit stressful,' she said dubiously.

'Get used to it,' I advised, hanging on to the panic strap as we veered round a truck. 'All commercial kitchens are nervous places. Customers demanding food, only a certain number of bread rolls that they can usefully eat without spoiling their appetite, something always going wrong—overcooking, under-cooking, curdling sauces. No wonder chefs used to drink like fish in the old days.'

'Some still do,' said Bernie.

'Not this one, though?' I hadn't noticed any alcohol available except for use in sauces. No open bottles of brandy on the sink. No bodies on the floor, either.

'No, though everyone yells a lot.'

'Par for the course,' I said.

'And then there's the actors,' she went on, settling into her subject.

'Fraught?'

'Congenitally. They're a funny mixture of in-your-face arro-gance and terrible vulnerability. I get on better with the TV crew. They've just got a job to do, and they do it.'

'Anyone in particular?'

'Ethan,' confessed Bernie. 'But I don't think he's even noticed me.'

'Keep feeding him,' I said. 'And keep up the supply of chili oil.'

'Oh my God, he hasn't still got the chili oil?' She clasped her hands on her breast. The reaction seemed extreme.

'Yes, he was pouring it on his scrambled eggs yesterday. Why?'

'Tash said she'd kill him if she caught him with the stuff again. You see, someone—not Ethan, of course—mixed some in Ms. Atkins' chili con carne when we did Mexican and she burnt her mouth: couldn't do any more work that day. Cost Tash a day's shooting, because she's in almost every scene. They shot around her but now she makes that poor PA taste all her food. And Emily's got all sorts of dietary problems and allergies.'

'Yes, I saw her doing that yesterday. I think Emily needs a new job.'

'Oh, so do I, but she wants to be an actor and Ms. Atkins could call in some favours and do wonderful things for Emily. So she puts up with it.'

I was spared the necessity of a reply, because we had arrived at the Harbour Studios kitchen entrance and it was time to go and make pastry.

Today's lunch theme was Mediterranean, so I was making tarts and pizza. I set my dough to rise while I inspected the fillings for the pissaladière. Excellent. Someone must have stayed up late to make it. Onions and yes, here were the anchovies, but no garlic, of course. Pasta was being made and rolled. Sauces were being concocted. The usual breakfast—bacon and sausages and eggs, mushrooms and baked beans—were being fried and poached. The air was full of the most wonderful smell as the food was carried past to the bains-marie outside the kitchen door.

The sandwich hands were slicing rapidly; tomatoes, cucumber, beetroot in aspic, egg, lettuce, cheese, ham, my bread. Constant practice makes sous chefs very good at knife work. They seldom cut themselves. However, sometimes they do.

There was an exclamation and one of them dropped her knife. It clattered on the floor. The worker rushed to a sink and held her hand under the tap. The water ran red.

I was unoccupied, as my dough had yet to rise, so I went looking for the first-aid box and the fluoro Bandaids, which we use so that one cannot escape into the food unnoticed. I found the box and overheard a most peculiar conversation.

'This morning?' asked Ethan the director of photography.

'Tomorrow,' said Ms. Emily. There was a sly, gleeful undertone in her voice which I did not like.

'Tomorrow,' agreed Ethan, and they went back to the table and I carried on with my Florence Nightingale routine before Kate bled to death. She had managed not to bleed on the food, which is always a chef's first duty when injured. It was not a bad cut. I patched it easily with glow-in-the-dark green bandaids and went back to my pizza.

Tomorrow? What was going to happen tomorrow?

While I thought about it, there was food to construct. In the making of pizza there are two imperatives: 1) a very hot oven, and 2) a minimum of toppings. In origin they were, after all, a snack to be eaten while walking, leaving one hand free to pinch attractive bums and fondle appreciative waitresses. Or fend off irritated slaps. Bernie came to join me and we worked in silence. Gradually the trays vanished under dough which I rolled and then spun in the air.

This attracted quite an audience as catering tricks often do. I tried to ignore them in case I got distracted and dropped the dough or, even worse, lost control of it and draped some poor innocent bystander in a floury shroud. That had happened before. But I was aware of the two writers, making notes. I had no idea what they were doing in the kitchen and I hoped those dreadlocks were secure. Gordon nudged Kendall and Kendall nodded emphatically. They were plotting something.

'Teach me how to do that!' Bernie pleaded.

'It's centrifugal force,' I explained. 'Gravity or something. You want the dough to make a flat disc, and the easiest way to do it is to use spin. Not that much spin,' I added, as her first attempt slid toward the edge of the bench. 'Gently. It's yeasty. Yeast needs to be handled with care and respect or it will sulk and refuse to rise.'

'This isn't as easy as it looks,' muttered Bernie, trying again and achieving a lopsided ellipse.

'But secretly she's really his mother,' said Kendall to Gordon.

She laughed, a deep gurgle, and replied, 'Yes! That's the subplot. Of course!'

They both hurried off. I assumed this was the nature of soap operas and paid little attention.

The audience began to fade away. Bernie sweated over acquiring the skill. She was a very determined young woman, I gave her that. But the dough would be overworked soon. I was just about to interfere when she achieved the perfect disc and slapped it on an oven tray. She turned to me, her face bright with joy.

'You did it,' I said, patting her on the shoulder. 'Well done! Now you can do the rest while I get on with my onion tart.'

'Can I?' she said breathlessly. I felt like a benefactor, which was silly, because I was sure that she had the knack and her pizzas would be as good as mine, or better. After all, I had made the dough.

Tommy bustled over to the pastry corner as I was sliding the last of the pizzas into the oven.

'Wonderful,' she said. 'Bernie being useful?'

'She's excellent,' I told her. 'She could get a job in any pizzeria in the land.'

'Have you finished your list?' she asked.

'Yes, that's the last.'

'Good, then would you like to watch a rehearsal? They're just starting. Bernie can mind the oven.'

'Why not?' I was curious. I took off my apron and cap and rolled them for washing, told Bernie to watch her cooking times, then joined Tommy as she went into the large studio.

It was transformed. A set had been built. It was a strange construction. Open at the front like the diorama I had made from a shoe box as a child. It had desks and phones and a potted palm that was obviously pining for its tropical home. In front was a wilderness of wires and cameras and people. On the set were Kylie, dressed in a subdued skirt and twin set in which she would ordinarily not be seen dead, and Goss, wearing the same with a much shorter shirt and a tighter top. Ms. Atkins, off camera, sat on her plastic chair as if it were a throne. The gorgeous Harrison, in Lycras and carrying a bicycle helmet, waited off the set, as did a grey-haired man, a girl dressed like Tank Girl with platforms, I swear, at least ten centimetres high, another young man in a T shirt emblazoned with SAVE THE WHALES and Tash, the director, looking like she was longing for her rural retreat.

A young man snapped a clapper together and announced, 'Scene three-oh-one.'

I noticed that Ethan and his crew were watching, but I could not detect any cameras operating. I looked at Tommy.

'Just a rehearsal, no need for cameras yet,' she told me. 'We can talk. Grab a chair and let's sit over here, where we can see.'

I complied. Ethan was lounging beside me, staring very intently at the brightly lit set. Goss cleared her throat. The actors were all watching Tash.

'Action,' she said.

Goss asked, 'Where's Ms. Yronsyde?'

'She's not in,' said Kylie quietly. 'Not in a good mood, either.'

'Chloe, she's never in a good mood,' said Goss. 'I don't think she has "good mood" on her database. What are we arranging today?'

'Need a new venue,' replied 'Chloe.' 'I can't get a reply to my emails from that harbourside place. You'd think they didn't want our business.'

If this was a sample of the dialogue which was supposed to support a whole series I couldn't see it catching the popular imagination. Tommy nudged me.

'It's about the people who arrange weddings,' she whispered. 'That's Chloe, who's quiet, and Brittanii, who's kooky. The geek girl is Felicia. Actually, Abby can't even work a mobile phone, but she's supposed to understand all the computers and so on. The grey-haired man is the accountant, Darryl, and the blond Elton is Matt the office boy and personal assistant. Harrison plays Adam, the courier. He's the love interest. One of them, anyway. Pretty standard soap,' concluded Tommy, as Tash sent us a warning glare.

I had never been seduced by soaps. Not even *Desperate Housewives*. And it did not look as though I was going to be. After a few more lines of this clunky dialogue, however, the door swept open and Ms. Atkins as Ms. Yronsyde appeared.

And she lit up the set. Really. Her perfect face was enamelled to the point of mask-like immobility. Her scarlet claws slid up the sides of her tight red suit. She had presence. The tension in the room went up like a lift and the actors started to respond to each other. The pace picked up. I sat up straighter.

'Chloe' and 'Brittanii' snapped into their lines. The grey-haired accountant, entering, was unable to throw a wet blanket the whole length of the set, though he was obviously meant to be a dreary figure. When Ms. Yronsyde went into her office, pausing at the door to deliver a blistering snub to 'Chloe,' Harrison the beautiful sauntered onto the set and the air went electric with URST.

'You see why they put up with her,' said Tommy. I nodded. The woman was a bitch, but she was playing a bitch. She was utterly natural.

'There's nothing like it,' said Tommy dotingly.

'I expect not,' I responded weakly. I had never seen anything as sexy as Harrison. The Lycras moulded his thighs and buttocks, shaped like those of an Athenian bronze boy I had seen in the National Museum in Athens. He moved with the conscious grace of a ballet dancer. I was finding it difficult to breathe.

'Gorgeous, isn't he?' remarked Ethan. 'Pity he has a head full of feathers, like all actors. Tell him he's beautiful and he'll be happy all day.'

'You're not bad-looking yourself,' I told Ethan. He suppressed a smile and looked away from me. Point made, I turned my attention to the action again.

Everyone feels better when you tell them that they're beautiful. Admittedly, I did not have a lot of experience...until Daniel had arrived. He really thinks I am beautiful, God bless him. I still feel that he ought to get his eyes checked.

Reminded of what joys awaited in my bed, I stirred. Tommy grabbed my arm.

'They're getting to the good bit,' she whispered. She was fascinated. I wasn't, but it seemed rude to rush away. So I sat on the hard plastic chair and watched as Harrison—screen name Adam—cast his spell on the office of Kiss the Bride. He smiled seraphically. I heard Ethan mumble something about a close-up as he witnessed that smile. Then he sashayed out with a large box. I heard someone close to me sigh. Another one who appreciated beauty. When I looked around, the only person close to me was Emily.

The plot concerned finding a new venue for the wedding reception, the old one having burnt down most inconveniently. There were suggestions of arson. The accountant warned that they were running out of money and could not spend a lot more renting the new one. The geek girl rattled her computer keys and advised that they had three point seven hours to make a decision. Ms. Yronsyde reproved Matt for looking sad, and it became apparent that she was a bully because the reason for his sadness was the death of his mother the day before. The scene finished with Matt bursting into tears and being comforted by the geek girl and Brittanii. And Ms. Yronsyde stalking into her own office and slamming the door.

There was a general sense of relaxation until Tash went to the front with a notebook and began tapping keys.

'Notes,' she said firmly, and I made my escape.

Back in the kitchen, Bernie had successfully laid out all of the pizzas. They smelt divine. She was cutting them into neat slices with a pizza roundel. I really wanted to pinch one of them—margherita is my favourite—but I decided to refrain. Unless she offered. They were her works of art, after all.

Fortunately, she offered. Heavenly. The cheese was melted but not toughened, the tomato sauce was first rate and the basil agreeably abundant. Those actors were well served. I said so. Bernie beamed. I took the opportunity for some gossip. Actually, she started it.

'How did the rehearsal go? They looked pretty wooden to me yesterday.'

'They were until Ms. Atkins marched in,' I said, wiping crumbs off my lips. 'She's amazing.'

'Great presence. She started off as a model, you know. Even when she was seventeen she could stalk along with that model walk, and she found out that she loves an audience.'

'Is she married?'

'Was married, now divorced. Didn't fit in to rich society. They took a dim view of her temper. Not done for members of the tennis club to stamp their feet and scream,' said Bernie bitterly. I wondered at her tone. It sounded like she took this personally. Was Bernie the product of one of our excellent private schools who had abandoned 'hit-and-giggle' afternoons for terribly early mornings and pastry? Was she a disappointment to her wealthy parents, who had a daughter who was clean, neat and sober but not, as it happened, marriageable?

Now why I had I thought that? I shook my head and Bernie mistook the gesture.

'Sorry, you probably play tennis,' she said.

'Certainly don't. Silly game,' I assured her. 'Now, you need to serve lunch and I need to go home. See you tomorrow?' I asked, gathering up my bag.

They were carrying out lunch as I exited past the rubbish bins and went back to Earthly Delights, which could be considered a tennis-free zone. They had tried to teach me at school, but because of my fine natural clumsiness I had never made it past the hit and had certainly not arrived at the giggle. One advantage of being a grown-up was that no one could make me shuck my clothes, stuff myself into a pair of shorts, and run out onto a freezing paddock to play hockey with an opposition who regularly maimed public-school girls. Life was tough on the young.

◇◇◇

Insula, when I reached it, was free of hysterical young women. It was also free of Daniel, regrettably, who had his own apartment and crashed there when he felt like it. Horatio was waiting at the door, anxious for a stroll on the grass and a possible encounter with Mrs. Pemberthy's rotten little doggie, Traddles. Horatio could defeat Traddles with one Look. It was always worth watching. So I found the drinks container and took it and Horatio up in the lift to the roof garden, one of my favourite places, to sit down and contemplate the beauties of nature.

The temple of Ceres had been constructed by the same lunatic builder who had designed Insula to be entirely Roman. It had a life-sized statue of the goddess, her arms full of corn. Under her feet was a very comfy stone bench, on which I deposited myself and my cat, poured my drink (with a small libation to the Mother) and found a women's magazine. It had presumably been left by that same Mrs. Pemberthy, who was also in sight, urging Traddles to pee on a daphne bush. Horatio stalked off into the undergrowth on his own occasions and I leafed through the brightly coloured pages. Thin women in silly clothes. Celebrity gossip about celebrities unknown to me. I was getting bored—I didn't recognise any of the names—when I sighted a familiar face. Molly Atkins sneered out of the paper. Well, well.

I settled down to read the article. It said, in a breathless rush of superlatives, that Ms. Atkins had a part in a new, hush-hush project being made at Harbour Studios. That her clothes were more amazing than ever and her tragic past seemed not to be cramping her creative style. Tragic past? Molly Atkins struck me as someone who caused tragedies, not suffered them. The author did not explain, assuming that I knew all about it. Just then Mrs. Pemberthy arrived, accompanied by her small, smelly, scruffy terrier, to reclaim her magazine. I held it out.

'There's an article about Molly Atkins,' I explained. 'I saw her today and I was curious.'

Mrs. P's face lit up. 'You saw her? What's she like?' she exclaimed.

'Looks just like her picture,' I answered carefully.

'No, really, Corinna.' She sat down next to me. 'You're the lucky one!'

'I'm just in the kitchen,' I told her. Mrs. Pemberthy was a poisonous old bitch and was not to be crossed lightly. She made tenants' meetings hell and was always trying to get rid of my cats on the grounds that they were unhygienic. I did not want to needlessly offend her. Now she was settling in for a nice long gossip. Damn. I always knew women's magazines were a bad idea, just as Grandma Chapman had said. Though that did not affect her affection for the *Women's Weekly*.

'She's a bit temperamental,' I offered.

Mrs. P bridled with pleasure. 'They say she's an absolute monster,' she replied. 'I'm sure she's an immoral woman,' she added, sucking her false teeth.

'Well, she's playing a superbitch,' I said. 'Perhaps she feels she has to get into the part. Beautiful clothes, though.'

'Too short and too tight,' said Mrs. Pemberthy.

'Yes, well, they were rather short and tight,' I agreed. Disagreeing with Mrs. P always required preparation. And earplugs. 'I really didn't see much of her. I was baking.'

'I'm not surprised that she's got a temper, considering what she's been through,' opined Mrs. Pemberthy cosily. This was shaping to be the friendliest conversation I had ever had with her. A gust of lavender water and mothballs engulfed me and I tried not to sneeze. 'Does she look older and fatter in the flesh?'

'I suppose,' I said feebly. 'What tragedy?'

'Oh, her husband left her and then, just as she was preparing the party for her only son's eighth birthday, he was struck by one of those wicked cars and died. Poor little boy. You wouldn't think a mother could get over something like that.'

I couldn't imagine what use Molly Atkins would have for a small child, except maybe as an entree, but I did not say so. I haven't had children, what would I know? Come to think of it, Mrs. Pemberthy had borne no children, either. But she was wiping away a sentimental tear. Traddles, assuming that I had caused his mistress to weep, bit me on the ankle. Horatio, appearing from the bushes, scratched him. He yelped. Trudi emerged from the arbour and yelled.

Then it all got a bit mixed but eventually Mrs. P departed with Traddles and her magazine, mouthing curses. Leaving me to soothe Horatio, who was licking dog blood out of his claws with every sign of enjoyment, and Trudi to break out the first-aid box and hand me Betadine and Bandaids. Her kitten, Lucifer, observed from her shoulder. He did not object to blood but Betadine made him sneeze.

After all that excitement Trudi sat down on the bench with me to share a companionable gin while Lucifer played 'King of the mountain' on her shoulder and Horatio ignored him. Trudi prefers her gin unadulterated by such abominations as tonic water, despite the risk of malaria. I chatted about gardening, about which I know very little, and wondered how, indeed, a mother could get over the loss of a son at such a young age. Was this secret sorrow the reason why Molly Atkins was such a bitch?

No, I concluded, but it might have exacerbated her naturally acquired tendencies. Poor woman. However, she was not my concern and Trudi was talking about one of her favourite flowers, the *Rosa gallica*, and I listened and sipped and nearly snoozed for an hour, very comfortably.

Then Horatio rose to his paws and indicated politely that he would like to return to prepare for his afternoon nap, and I took myself back to the apartment. I was pooped. I joined Horatio on the couch for a little nap until something happened, a skill I have learnt from close observation of my companions.

He kindly allowed me a share of the mohair blanket and we snoozed. There were plenty of things I could be doing—consulting tomorrow's menu, preparing fillings and feeding the improver, cleaning the flat—but time spent recumbent on a couch with a charming feline is never wasted. Besides, my ankle hurt. Being self-employed has its worries and its pains, but it also has a lot of pleasures.

We woke about an hour later when Daniel came in. He was grimy and tired and in need of a shower and some lunch, so I got up to prepare it while he washed off the night's labours. Horatio grumbled, turned around, and resumed his slumber. I zapped some frozen pea soup in the microwave. With a dash of cider vinegar and my fresh rye bread, a feast fit for a king. A rather greedy king, perhaps; Henry VIII, say. I could see Henry hogging his way into pea soup. Daniel ate more neatly but he was just as hungry.

'Nothing?' I asked sympathetically.

'Perhaps something,' he said. 'I'll know more tonight. Now if you don't mind, beautiful lady, I might join Horatio on the couch.'

And he did so, leaving me with a frantic fit of industriousness. That nap must have refreshed me. I washed dishes. I changed and washed my sheets and a few other bits and pieces which needed cleaning. I had to go down to the bakery to the washer, so I read tomorrow's menu, groaned a little at the extent of the requested sweet cakes, and chopped a lot of nuts for the various Middle Eastern breads. I resolved to go and buy the baklava from Kyria Pandamus. She made the best baklava I had ever tasted. Therefore I went out into the street, leaving the bakery in the charge of the Mouse Police and the sleeping Daniel in the charge of the Stripy Gentleman. Any burglar would be glared into submission before the Mouse Police hunted him down and pinned him under paw.

◇◇◇

The shop was, as usual, crowded. Cafe Delicious caters for the workers of the world, bless it, and therefore does a full range of sandwiches and rolls, two made dishes, salads, and an array of cakes and dainties. Presiding over the Greek coffee was Del Pandamus, patriarch of the family and overruled by no one but his mother, the Kyria, who required deference. And got it. The power of little old Greek ladies who would weigh in at six stone in a drenched army overcoat is remarkable. But Del was a benevolent despot and everyone liked him. I, personally, doted on his Eleutherios Venizelos moustache. He whiffled it.

'Corinna!' he roared. 'Coffee?'

'Baklava,' I said. 'I need a whole tray. Can you manage?'

He looked at his mother, who was sitting in a corner crocheting lace. She nodded. Good, one less task, and my baklava had never been truly satisfactory. I think it's like scones—you need to make the dish for twenty years until you get it right. Then you can make it wearing a blindfold and with both hands tied behind your back. More or less.

'Ten minutes,' Del told me. '*Café hellenico?*'

'*Metriou,*' I agreed, ordering my Greek coffee half-sweet. Fully sweet removed teeth.

Another copy of a women's magazine lay on the table. I sat myself down in a cane-bottomed chair to wait and idly leafed through it. More faces I knew. Here was Ms. Atkins again, in a silver and black ballgown, flanked by poor Emily in a black dress which did her youthful slimness no favours. It was fussy and fluffy and had far too many frills. The story informed me that Emily was considered a 'rising young star,' which was nice, and that Ms. Atkins had been quoted as saying 'she loved Emily like a daughter.' How sweet. And here—well, well—was Ethan the cameraman, in a superb suit and white tie. He was very handsome and knew it; he had a self-satisfied half-smile which said 'I just know you admire me—and you are so right.' He was captioned as extremely successful, the hottest property around, staying in Australia to make this new hush-hush project instead of going to America where his talents had been appreciated and bulk money had been flung at his head. There was a hint that he was difficult to work with; the story said he had gone through ten assistants in a year, and that said assistants were suing him for all manner of abuses. Pity. I liked Ethan. On the other hand, I reflected as I sipped my coffee, gossip mags are not be relied upon.

My attention was attracted to two young women sitting near the door. One was poor Lena, still looking sodden. With her was a thin blonde creature in a very sharp suit. Both ordered undressed salads (this always annoyed Del, who made a ferocious brown vinegar dressing and loved to pour it lavishly over the leaves). This must be Claire, who sympathised with her co-worker. Claire was picking at her plate as Lena poured out her troubles. I could not hear what they were saying but I saw Claire put out a delicate hand and pat Lena's plump paw. Nice girl. My baklava arrived, my coffee cup contained only grains. I paid up and left.

I folded sheets, ironed a shirt, swept a floor, and still Daniel slept. Finally I sat down on the other couch with my novel and devoted a few hours to reading about Jade Forrester's complicated romances. That would keep me gainfully employed until dinner.

The whole flat was so quiet that a passing mouse would have made a sound like a trampling elephant. It was lovely. I was a very lucky woman.

Chapter Five

I had received an email from Jason and I was puzzling over it as I rose the next morning to wash, drink coffee and eat leftover muffins and a boiled egg with soldiers. Admittedly Jason has only a passing acquaintance with spelling and knows no grammar, which is why he can read Middle English cookery books without training. Chaucer was, so to speak, phonetic. Once you voice 'gyngylyng' aloud and realise that it is 'jingling' you're away. Even so, the email was a mystery.

He had written: *Yu miss me? I mss yu. Fud herer gud. Got jb sht orDr. cook. Fun. Jason.* I assumed it meant that he was working as a cook of some sort—*sht ordr*, was that order? Short order?—and being amused. It's texting that really ruins the vocabulary. Of course you have to have one in the beginning to ruin it. I replied that of course I missed him but all was well at Insula and left it at that. If I told him I was working he might cut short his holiday and rush back to help, and Jason had never had a holiday before. I wanted him to enjoy it.

Meanwhile Bernie was waiting below with the Mouse Police, each one of them anxious to show me something and be rewarded. In the case of the Mouse Police it was deceased rodentia and in the case of Bernie it was an ancient cookbook. I poured out the ration of cat munchies for Heckle and Jekyll and, to the sound of crunching, I examined the book. It was, I realised, a later compilation including *The Goodman of Paris* and was stuffed with recipes requiring things like elderberries or primroses, both hard to get in Australia. Some of those combinations were strange. Apple and fish? Fish? I suppose you would eat anything in the midst of a very cold winter, with snow on your chilblains and a diet of very old salt pork and strong ale your only prospect until the crocus bloomed.

'Nice,' I said, returning the book. 'What did you have in mind?'

'Some of the cakes would be interesting. We'd have to lay in some marzipan. They lean very heavily on almonds. Fantasies, they are called.'

'Yes, and they are really not very suitable for the lunch tables at present,' I said, hating to disappoint her. 'Let's put it to one side just for the moment and get on with the blueberry muffins, shall we? Have you shown that book to Tommy?'

'No,' said Bernie. 'I just found it.'

Of course. She did not want Tommy to steal her idea for medieval cakes. Silly of me. Bernie had her name to make as a pastry cook.

We began making muffins, bread, the usual tasks. I tried to cheer Bernie by telling her about my English tea for Mrs. Dawson but she remained crestfallen. I did not even think she was listening until she said abruptly, 'Can I have them?'

'Have what?' I looked up from caressing an onion loaf into its proper shape.

'Those recipes.'

'Certainly,' I said. 'They're very old and don't belong to anyone. Take them, and it's our secret, right?'

'Right!' Suddenly there was the enthusiastic Bernie again. I sighed inwardly. The young. So easily crushed, so lightly elevated.

This day the driver was whistling 'In the Mood.' I supposed that was an improvement.

Harbour Studios was much as expected, at least in the kitchen. Noisy today. Someone's mayonnaise had curdled. There was much screaming about who put the eggs in the fridge overnight instead of leaving them out to be room temperature to combine with the room temperature vinegar and the room temperature oil. I threw in some advice (put a cube of ice and a new egg yolk in it and keep beating) and withdrew to the pastry corner, where there was a list of stuff to be made and not a lot of time. Mayonnaise was not my problem, thank God.

Today was to be Greek in theme. This meant that I had already made most of the sweet treats (Greek shortbread is heavenly) and I had purchased a tray of Kyria Pandamus's incomparable baklava. Cheating has its rewards. There was, however, the filo challenge.

Bernie had not worked much with this very crispy pastry, so I instructed as I went.

'It's as thin as paper and shares some of its properties,' I explained, laying out the pastry and covering it with a wet tea towel. 'If it dries out it rips and the filling falls out. Now, remember all you learnt in primary school about origami and it goes…so.'

I brushed with melted butter, cut the pastry into strips, put on a dollop of mushroom filling, and folded it up into a triangle. Bernie was impressed.

'Neat!' she commented. 'Can I try now?'

'They're all yours,' I said, ceding her the filling and going on to make the cheese-and-spinach triangles of spanakopita.

The salad makers were slicing silverbeet and leeks. Vegetables were being roasted. Cauliflower was being steamed. This was going to be a feast and I almost wanted to stay for lunch.

I made a couple of chicken pies and a few chickeny triangles with the last of the filling. I loathe waste. Bernie was shoving trays into the oven, ranked with perfect triangles like a geometry example. The mayonnaise panic appeared to have died down. The kitchen smelt wonderful: chicken in red wine with figs, roasted beetroot. Poultry and fish with that divine Greek sauce made of lemon juice and honey. And underneath the stable familiar breakfast scents: frying bacon, grilling mushrooms. Mmm. You almost didn't have to eat, just breathe deeply.

Unoccupied until something cooked, I took out some of the trays of toast to the table and met the full force of actors, head on. Ethan the cameraman was there, looking sardonic over his heavily doctored scrambled eggs. He stretched out a long arm and snared a piece of toast. I brought him the tray and he selected and crunched another.

Close to his side was his assistant. She introduced herself as Samantha as she took some toast. She was a robust young woman with a healthy appetite. I am always delighted to see people eat happily. Her mound of scrambled eggs was almost as high as Ethan's and unadulterated with that fiery oil. Ethan clearly had not been introduced to the idea that chili oil was a condiment, not a food group. I wrinkled my nose at the smell. He grinned.

With both hands holding the tray, I could not scratch, and I did not want to sneeze on the toast so I set it down and turned to go back for more. I caught Ethan squeezing something in his pocket. I checked. Not anything indelicate. A box-shaped thing. He cocked his handsome head as though listening. I couldn't hear anything but the usual babble. Ms. Atkins, I assumed, was in her cubicle. With, I also assumed, Emily. The rising young star. Poor child. I could not see her rising any time soon. As soon as she stuck her head up she would be firmly suppressed by her mentor. Toast. I went back for more.

Bernie was surveying her crispy filo rolls with great pleasure. I enlisted her to carry more provender and we were busy for half an hour. Tommy was mediating the mayonnaise row. It seemed that a humble server had seen the eggs left out on the bench and had ignorantly put them away. He had thought he was being helpful. He was now being firmly disabused of this notion and was almost in tears.

Kitchens. They are a stringent arena. I sighted Kylie and Goss picking at some eggs. Good. They had to eat something in preparation for a long day's work. Tash the director was ploughing through a mound of bacon and poached eggs as though stoking a boiler.

'Filming today,' said Harrison, taking a mouthful of kedgeree. 'That's why everyone is on edge, Corinna. Pepper, please.'

'I've got a question,' I said, passing him the ground pepper.

'I am at Madam's service.' He bowed slightly.

'Why doesn't Tash replace Ethan, if he and Ms. Atkins are such bad friends?'

'Oh, the hard ones first,' he quoted *The Goons*. 'Well, dear, it's a matter of filthy lucre. Big money is backing Ethan because he's the flavour of the month. Without Ethan, no show. And Molly hasn't had all that many offers lately.' He lowered his voice. 'She's getting on a bit, even for a superbitch. Though she does seem to be channelling the ageless Joan Collins. Therefore, she stays even though she despises Ethan and he stays because this is his big chance. Do have some of this kedgeree, it's excellent,' he added in a louder tone as Ethan heaved into his orbit.

'Good idea,' I told him, and picked up a plate for myself. There were lots of leftovers and the actors and crew were beginning to drift away. I was eating pleasantly when Molly Atkins emerged from her dressing room. She was perfect, down to the unchipped scarlet claws and the perfection of her shoes. I could not imagine how she could walk in them. Stiletto heels. Bright red, of course. Ethan gulped down the last of his breakfast and grinned at her. It was not a charming grin. She noticed him, stiffened, was about to deliver a blistering rebuke and then— didn't. At her heels scuttled Emily, looking harassed.

Odd, but, like the mayonnaise, not my problem. Back to the kitchen, Corinna.

Tash called 'Ten minutes!' and the film day began.

Mine was ending. I was pleased. I tasted one of my spanakopita, and then, on Bernie's insistence, one of her mushroom ones. Perfect. Crispy and tasty. I said so. Bernie beamed. Time to leave on a high note. I left.

◇◇◇

Home again. The couch contained Horatio, drowsing, and the bed contained Daniel, sleeping. I know when I'm licked. I took off my baker's clothes, put on my gown, and joined them in a small refreshing nap.

Afternoon declared itself with a shaft of light through the curtains. I rose slowly. Daniel was cutting a baguette in preparation for lunch. I really wasn't hungry. I watched him make a salade Niçoise and ate a token mouthful or two. Then another, because I love anchovies. So does Horatio. Those furry fish are so tasty.

'How was your night?' I asked.

'Good. I've got three names. The trouble is that everyone in that drunks' camp down by the river is known by at least three names, some of them quite unprintable, and tracking them down is going to be difficult. Because even if they do know a Spazzo, it might not be the Spazzo I am seeking.'

'And they may not want to tell you where he is, assuming they know, and assuming he hasn't moved on.'

'That too,' he agreed gloomily. These nights among the lost, stolen and strayed were beginning to get Daniel down. There's only so much squalor that one man can handle. Horatio sat down for a really thorough wash and I watched him.

'What say I come with you?' I asked.

'You're working, so you need your sleep,' he replied.

'Not tomorrow. Tomorrow the whole lunch is being catered by a rather famous Thai restaurant. And how that touchy collection of diners are going to cope with the chili in Thai food is not my problem.'

'I would really like some company,' he admitted.

'Good. Then let's have a lazy afternoon. Egg and bacon pie for dinner—I made us one while I was constructing the others. Then we can go forth and find out what we can…er…find out.'

'Nice,' said Daniel, and kissed me, which is ample reward for a space of time mixing with the dispossessed. I picked at the olives in the salade Niçoise and stopped asking questions and the afternoon passed very pleasantly with me doing my own accounts and Daniel watching *Babylon 5*.

I love doing my accounts. It's probably a character flaw.

That fiendish north wind was still blowing when we set out, on foot, toward the river. I was sweating by the time we crossed the bridge and began to descend through the park into the underworld. The stone steps were designed for ladies in crinolines, so they are very broad and shallow (falling over in a crinoline was a deeply embarrassing experience, as I had found once during a school play). Leaves were being torn from the English trees and flung past us like dirty confetti. Even the Australian trees were bowing before the gale. Apart from anything else, it was very noisy. It was like trying to converse while a train is pulling into the station. There are many things I loathe about Melbourne, and one of them is this habit of the hot wind to just manifest itself like the Demon King in a pantomime and desiccate and destroy everything it touches. Kepler, Jon's lover, who is Chinese, calls it 'Dragon's Breath' and that is a good name. We don't have a name for it, just 'that bloody north wind.' Cops say that after it has been blowing for a while, tempers are frayed, nerves scraped raw, and homicides happen. It is at the height of a north wind episode that people decide that they really cannot stand their neighbour/spouse/children/drinking buddy/man who just looked at them funny and try to obliterate him/her/them with a handy axe. I can understand that. Other places call it *mistral* or *khamsin*. It's unbearable, whatever you call it.

But down under the trees the fury of the gale was foiled by the foliage and the solidity of the Victorian garden design. The old builders didn't take any lip from Nature. If she talked back, they felled her. They built walls to conduct the respectable feet of the gentry to points of botanical interest and they labelled every tree. It must have been nice to be that sure about everything. I'm not that sure about anything.

But under the canopy the natives were restless. We heard voices, now that it was quiet enough to hear anything. There was a party going on under the trees on the edge of the river, where the locked boathouse loomed and its security system provided light. There was a fire—even on such a night as this!—and men sat around it, toasting sausages on sticks, leaning back on stacks of boxed wine.

'Someone's come into money,' said Daniel.

They were ragged and pitiful, the rejects. Clothes which might originally have been good—I saw at least one handmade suit, fraying, the stitching coming adrift—trackies, polo shirts,

T shirts, they were all filthy and falling apart. The bodies underneath were malnourished, white and skeletal. Their hair was long and they reeked of cheap wine and dirt. But their eyes, oh, their eyes were glittering, and I felt that I had strayed into one of Dante's less pleasant Circles of Hell. I wanted to run away. But I had volunteered so I stayed.

Daniel walked easily into the encampment and leant on the boathouse door. The eyes examined him. Not a cop, not a social worker, not someone coming to do them either good or harm against their will. Not another drunk who might fight them for their bounty. Not, in point of fact, important, and they soon looked away from him. A man in a partly destroyed suit half stood and asked him, 'Want a drink, mate?'

'Looking for Spazzo,' he said clearly.

'Over there,' said the suit. 'Him and Pockets got lots of wine,' he added, and sank down to his seat again in the contaminated dust.

Daniel hoisted himself off the wall and sauntered slowly to the other gathering. The little fires dotted the river bank. I knew from recent museum research of middens that the local Aboriginal people had built little fires like this at about this time of year, to feast on mussels and dance away the Big Heat. How surprised they would be at their replacements. Disgusted, too, I expect. These camps knew no gods except Alcohol.

Daniel repeated his request for Spazzo at the next fire and found him. He was a thin, small, hairless man in old track pants, reclining on a pile of wine boxes like a pasha and very pleased with himself. He had a wide and toothless grin, surprisingly like that of a baby. Daniel accepted a plastic cup of wine from him and sat down on his heels to talk. Spazzo was happy. He was afloat on a sea of Yalumba Autumn Brown and sinking fast.

'You've got lots of wine,' observed Daniel.

'Lots!' gurgled Spazzo. 'Lots 'n' lots.'

'Where did it come from?' asked Daniel.

'Bought 'n' paid for,' said Spazzo with dignity. 'By my mate. My good mate,' he elaborated.

'It's good to have a mate like that,' said Daniel. 'What's his name?'

'He's got lots of wine,' said Spazzo. 'Lots 'n' lots of wine.'

'And his name? Tommo, was it? Big bloke, red hair?'

'Nah,' replied Spazzo scornfully. 'Tommo's got black hair. Pockets's got no hair. Pockets's me mate.'

'The mate who gave you lots and lots of wine?'

'Pockets did,' agreed Spazzo.

'Perhaps if I ask him he'll give me lots of wine, too,' suggested Daniel.

Spazzo was too happy not to feel regret in crushing this delightful dream.

'Nah, he's got no more,' he said sadly. 'Said we had to make this lot last. Said to keep some for tomorrow. But where can I keep some wine with all these bastards ferreting through the bushes? Better drink it all now,' said Spazzo, gulping down some more. The sweet scent of the fortified wine combined with the human stench was making me nauseous.

'Where can we find Pockets?' asked Daniel gently.

'Dunno. They might know,' said Spazzo, waving an uncoordinated arm in the direction of downriver. We went that way, past the little fires. I was sweating like a pig. Plump persons seldom tolerate heat well.

Then we found Pockets. He was reclining on a throne made of wine boxes. He was a bald, skinny man in a grey dustcoat which some amateur hand had sewn with extra pockets, hence the name. He had a bunch of papers in his hand and was perusing them by firelight through pickle-bottle glasses. Cryptic crossword puzzles, mostly filled in faultless calligraphy. And in biro. I was instantly reminded of an ex-boss of mine. Same glasses. Same squint. Pockets caught sight of me and began to rise, which was courteous of him. He managed to get to his feet and then sagged down. Daniel helped him to rebuild his seat and lowered him into it.

'Lady,' said Pockets in a cultured tone. 'Welcome to our humble camp.'

'Sir,' I replied. 'Thank you.'

Around him the revellers groaned and screamed and bickered. Pockets sat in an oasis of silence and was the most puzzling creature I had ever seen.

'My name is Daniel,' said my beloved. 'I am looking for some papers which were left in a phone booth. Would you know anything about that?'

'Oh yes, Daniel,' agreed Pockets, smoothing out his bundle and sliding them into a pocket. 'I am responsible for the medium of the printed word in this city.'

'I see.' Daniel sounded calm. 'And where are those papers now?'

'In their proper place. There is a proper place for all papers. They are written, see, that makes them sacred.'

'Of course,' Daniel assented. 'And their destination?'

'Filed, my dear sir, filed properly.' Pockets seemed to think that was the end of the conversation and took a deep draught of his wine. 'Of course, some careless person should never have left negotiable instruments in such a place. Corrupt. Careless. People are so often negligent with their certificates.'

'And you took care of them?' asked Daniel.

'That is my duty as an officer of the court,' said Pockets. He sounded so sane that I wondered what he was doing here in the drunks' camp. Then I found out.

'Which court?' asked Daniel.

'The Lemurians appointed me,' Pockets informed us. 'Prior to their takeover they want all the papers to be in order. The paperwork must be done, indeed it must. The takeover is imminent, my dear sir. Imminent. I expect them every day.'

'The Lemurians?' Daniel's voice was free of irony.

'Of course. You must have seen them. All of us have seen them. That's why we're down here. They will land on the river when they come in their great mothership and we will be here to greet them.'

'I see. Who provided the wine?' asked Daniel.

'Oh, that was Mr. Raban at the wine shop. He is a generous man.'

'I need to retrieve those certificates,' said Daniel. 'Can you tell me where you have filed them?'

'In their proper place, as I told you. Have they sent you to spy on me? I have been faithful. I take into my custody all the printed words and find them filing places. If I have missed one it was not my fault!'

The brow wrinkled, tears were forming behind the spectacles. Daniel patted Pockets on the shoulder and the man shied away like a frightened horse.

'No, no, they are pleased with you,' he said. 'You have done well. We'll be leaving now,' he added, and I followed him to the next camp, where we might find more information.

We didn't. Daniel dragged a fallen drunk away from the flames and looked at me in the hot firelight.

'We go home,' he said, and despite heat and exhaustion, I passed him on the stairs.

The big wind caught and battered us as we fought our way home, into Insula's air-conditioned silence. I dived into the shower, anxious to rid myself of wood smoke and filth. Daniel joined me. Gradually, as the hot water washed away the squalor, I started to relax. I unhitched my jaw, which had been clenched tight. That had been a truly hellish visit.

Dried and be-gowned I poured myself a drink. Good cognac, to abolish the scent of cheap sweet sherry. Daniel joined me on the couch.

'Phew,' he commented.

'I could not agree more,' I said. 'So, what do we know?'

'Pockets had the papers,' he said. 'He must have been a banker or a lawyer before the paranoid schizophrenia got him. Wasn't that a Gargantua and Pantagruel scene, the drunks reposing on boxes of wine?'

'I thought it was more Dante's inferno,' I said, sipping. Daniel nodded.

'Perhaps. However, Pockets has filed the papers "in their proper place."'

'So that the paperwork will be in order when the Lemurians arrive. But where is the proper place?'

'There you have me. I shall go back tomorrow and try him again. Perhaps I should tell him that the Lemurians have indeed sent me to spy upon him and check that he is carrying out their wishes.'

'Who are the Lemurians?'

'There was a mythical continent called Lemuria,' said Daniel. 'Or so I'm told. The Lemurians live in the middle of the hollow earth and rise periodically to see how civilisation is getting on.'

'If the only thing they saw when they rose was that camp, they'd give up on humans and sink down again,' I opined.

'Too true.'

We mused for a while. Outside the dragon's breath wind tore at the leaves and lashed the side of the building with its burden of filthy dust and valuable topsoil. It was a disgusting night, but here inside it was clean and cool.

We went to bed. It seemed a life-affirming thing to do, and might have even convinced the Lemurians, had they existed and been present, that humanity was worth another few thousand years.

I went back to sleep after suppressing my alarm clock. Lovely.

◇◇◇

Then it was really morning again. The big wind had gone. Melbourne was twinkling under a sharp sun which penetrated corners and revealed dust and spider webs. I forced down an urge to start cleaning and decided that I should deal with that backlog of emails while Daniel went out to meet with his client Lena and tell her that he had made a little progress. One of the bank bonds had been sold, we knew that, and it seemed likely that Pockets had sold it and paid for that deluge of wine. The rest must be somewhere. And who knew what a 'proper place' was to a man as unhinged as poor Pockets?

Emails. Hundreds of them. Well, not really, but they can build up into a disheartening number if ignored for any length of time. I kissed Daniel goodbye, took my cup of coffee to the desk and called up the messages.

Mostly spam. Pathetic pleas from Nigerian bankers. Appeals for more money from every charity available. Nothing to be done about them. Unsubscribing merely draws attention to the fact that this is a live account. I deleted merrily. People inviting me to buy plants, clothes, fabric, ties, annuities, penis enhancers, Viagra and hampers. I declined. And—aha!—another communication from my errant apprentice.

Fud gud, he began. *Got jb as cook. Good mny. Mss u.*

And what to reply? I was glad that he had a good job, though he was supposed to be on holiday. I was glad that he was eating well. I replied thus. I missed Jason. But nothing was going to make me text my messages. I didn't know the conventions. If you are going to insult someone, Grandma Chapman had said, insult them on purpose.

The sunlight continued to stream through the open curtains, revealing every spider web and the thin coating of dust on every surface. I gave in and found the broom. As I swept I wondered what strange turn of mental disorder had brought Pockets to his present situation in life. He had been, like me, a professional accountant. Mental illness owes no one any favours. It is an equal opportunity destroyer. Sane today, awaiting the Lemurians tomorrow. My meditation was making me gloomy. I decided to go up to the roof garden with Horatio and regain my perspective.

When I got there I found Therese Webb sitting under the statue of the goddess, stitching very small beads onto a length of red satin. I offered her a drink but she declined.

'I really need to get this done,' she explained, politely removing Horatio's exploring paw. 'No, not the satin, dear, it marks so easily. I came up here because daylight is so much better for beading.'

'Special commission?' I asked idly.

'Yes, for a TV show. Something to do with weddings.'

'*Kiss the Bride?*' I asked. 'I'm baking for them.'

'What a coincidence,' said Therese, setting a miniscule stitch, knotting it, and breaking off the cotton. 'There, all finished. What do you think?' She shook out the cloth. The red satin was studded with tiny red beads. They swirled up from what must be the hem in perfect, graceful curves.

'Lovely,' I said. 'A work of art.'

'It should be, considering what they are paying for it,' she answered, folding the satin and putting it into a plastic bag in case Horatio decided that satin was the ideal fabric for exercising the claws. 'I don't usually undertake such fine work since my eyes got so bad. But if it will help the girls in their careers, it's worth a little eye strain. Funny, when I heard the name of the show I thought it would be a wedding dress, and white on white is even harder on the eyes than red on red.'

'I wish you had made my wedding dress,' I found myself saying. I had been trying to avoid memories of my wedding to that snake, James. But they had been arising ever since I had started my work on *Kiss the Bride*.

'I would have been delighted,' she said. 'I could fancy a little drink now, Corinna. What was your dress like?' she asked, as I poured her a gin and tonic.

'Horrible,' I said, remembering it. 'Half a size too small, blinding white satin and very heavy. What with that and the veil I looked like a frosted cake. And I felt like an overstuffed sofa.'

'With your colouring I would have used ivory and a matte finish. Crêpe, perhaps. A belled skirt and a loose bodice, perhaps a sweetheart neckline. Pearl beading…Satin is a very unforgiving fabric.'

'Especially to the fleshy. I hated it. I gave it to the op shop the day it came back from the dry cleaners. Weddings! Impossible to believe that they are still so important. Your degree, your PhD, the publication of your first book, your Nobel Prize—minor events compared to your wedding day.'

'Princess for a day,' mused Therese.

'Happiest day of your life,' I said. 'A terrible expectation.'

'So it is, dear, but humans are like that. Have you seen the girls? How are they managing?'

'They seem fine. I even caught them eating a little.'

The conversation wandered into less depressing channels. I finished my drink and took Horatio home. My mood continued gloomy. I could not see how Daniel was going to bribe or persuade Pockets to tell him where he had filed the documents. And I really did not want to remember my wedding—a fiasco—but I seemed stuck with it. Nasty.

So I constructed a very elaborate roasted chicken with lemon, honey and brown rice stuffing for dinner. Cooking is a great comforter. Eating might make Daniel feel better, too. It always worked for me.

And it did, too. By the time we reached cheese-and-port we were merry together and contented. I raised the question which had been weighing on my mind.

'What do you think about marriage, Daniel?'

'Is this a proposal?' He raised his glass and quirked an eyebrow over it.

'No,' I said hurriedly. 'Not at this present time,' I temporised. Who knew? I might want to marry Daniel at some future time. In an ivory crepe dress with a belled skirt and pearl beading. 'No, it's this soap. *Kiss the Bride* is a wedding planner and it's a huge business. Flowers, venue hire, dresses, presents, invitations. I'm wondering how it is that getting married is suddenly the finest thing any woman can do.'

'I don't think it's sudden,' said Daniel. 'I think it's always been seen that way. The seventies was just a blip. Walking barefoot through the buttercups to the celebrant. Picnics on the grass. People have always made a big deal out of weddings. My cousin...'

'Your cousin?' Daniel seldom talks about his family.

'My cousin Sara,' he continued, 'decided to marry the man her parents had picked out for her. She liked him. Still does, as far as I know. She planned a nice quiet ceremony and a little gathering at a restaurant for a few close friends. But by the time her mother had finished with it, Sara was hosting the feeding of the five thousand and a spectacle which would have staggered Heliogabalus, and she didn't speak to her mother for six months. Her relatives, of course, were all fighting among themselves and several lifelong feuds were started. Her mother required medical treatment for shrieking-induced throat injuries and her father retreated to a kibbutz and picked melons. He said he liked the melons because they didn't scream at him. So,' said Daniel.

'So, indeed,' I agreed.

'Sometimes it is the only way that a girl can exert control over her life,' he commented. 'Not in Sara's case, of course. Some young women feel helpless to resist the zeitgeist. Once they have declared that they are getting married, they become "brides" and are swept away in a flurry of confetti.'

'Yes, I can see how that would happen. The same thing as happens to people who are elected politicians and become politicians overnight. More's the pity.' I picked at a little more King Island Cheddar.

'My own wedding,' he told me, 'would have been perfect in its way. We were both soldiers on active service so we would both wear uniform. Only parents could attend. It would have been charming,' he reminisced. He did not often mention his prospective marriage to a fellow soldier who had been killed shortly before the ceremony. I didn't know what Jewish marriages were like, anyway. I vaguely recalled something about a canopy, a smashed glass…I held his hand as he endured a wave of sadness. Poor Daniel. Almost a widower so young. He caught my line of thought and smiled at me. 'But now I have you,' he said, and kissed me. He tasted of cheese and port and was altogether delightful. I shelved the topic of marriage and sank into his arms. Horatio, who was sitting on my knee, was affronted, but you can't please everyone.

Chapter Six

Kiss the Bride's set was buzzing when Bernie and I arrived (the driver was whistling 'Moon River', which I quite liked). I could not put my finger on it but there was a heightened sense of anticipation. Tommy rushed over while we were still unloading bread, wiping her forehead with a red handkerchief. It was a hot day, but not that hot.

'Bernie working out?' she demanded.

'She's very good,' I assured her.

'Filming today so our timetable is altered. Lots of snacks for delays. People always get hungry when there are delays. Lots of little pies and tarts, the list's posted,' she said, and hurried away. I looked at Bernie, who was already looking at me.

'Pies,' she said.

'And tarts. Let's get started.' I led the way into the kitchen, which was loud with blasphemy because the white sauce had curdled and once that happens there is no resurrection. The disgusted cook was about to begin again and was screaming for the fine flour, the butter, and some peace and quiet. Well, she got the flour and the butter, at least. Everyone was on edge. Bernie and I aimed to create an oasis of calm in which to work and largely managed it, because no one was paying any attention to us. Also, the kitchen was full of actors and crew, requiring special breakfasts or accompanying someone who did, and getting in the way. It was like trying to cook in the middle of a herd of cross, uncooperative cows who were about to haul off and let the milkmaid have a hoof in the centre of her apron.

Tommy finally took charge and banished all but the actual workers. To massed complaints the extraneous removed themselves and we got on with constructing the required comestibles. Bernie had an inspired hand with pastry. Hers was better than mine. I was not jealous. I made better bread than anyone I knew.

Pies filled with chicken and leek, beef burgundy, cheese and spinach, and tarts made of everything except cement. They went into the oven pallid and came out of the oven golden and the sight of this growing array gladdened my heart. Savoury scents enfolded us. Bernie smelt spicy, due to rather specialising in apple pies. Breakfast was being set out as we came to the end of the fillings and decided that we deserved a cup of coffee and a little sit-down.

The coffee was easy. The rest was only available if we went outside and sat on the concrete step or grabbed an audience chair and watched the set. So we did that, and found ourselves next to the writers, Gordon and Kendall.

'This is always the most exciting bit,' Kendall informed me, shaking his dreads. 'When it goes from our heads onto the page and then onto the screen.'

'Scary, though,' remarked Gordon.

'So who's that?' I asked, observing an elderly man in shirt sleeves being fussed over by several assistants, who were bringing him tea, smoothing his cushions and turning away a big light so that it did not shine in his eyes—all with an air of veneration which might be considered proper in a cathedral.

'Oh, don't you read the gossip mags?' asked Kendall. 'No, I guess you don't. No sensible person does. Just us showbiz folk. That's Mr. Leonard, superstar where hair and makeup are worshipped. He's here to criticise the role of the hairdresser and offer suggestions. He still works,' she added. 'He came in at five-thirty to do Ms. Atkins.'

I could see Ms. Atkins, who was sitting very still so as not to smudge her maquillage.

'So, what's happening today?' I asked, thinking that I ought to get back to my ovens in case Tommy had something else for me to do.

'You've got the idea about the show? The Kiss the Bride office runs everything connected with a marriage. And each week we have a new wedding and a new set of problems. That can range from problems between the bride and groom, problems with the suppliers, problems with the family. After all, a wedding is the only theatrical experience where you cannot control all the cast.'

'And you have only one performance,' added Gordon.

I was looking at Mr. Leonard. He was small and dapper. That shirt was handmade. His hair was white and flowed back from the high unlined forehead in lustrous waves. He reminded me more of a conductor of an orchestra than a makeup person. He was magnificent. As I was staring, he turned his eyes on me and for a moment looked straight into my face. And he smiled. A small wintry smile, but a definite smile. This caused the fluttering assistants to redouble their efforts. They all looked in my direction and one came rushing up to ask me to attend on the presence.

Carrying my hard-won coffee, I complied. All around me the actors and crew were settling into their places. Mr. Leonard offered me a well-manicured hand and I took it.

'Hello,' he said in a deep, rich, London-club voice. 'You're new.'

'Corinna Chapman,' I introduced myself. 'I'm just a baker.'

'I thought so,' he told me. 'A very dear friend of mine was a baker. I have always henceforward loved the scent of flour and yeast. Would you care to sit beside me? It is refreshing to meet a woman with such good skin who does not use cosmetics,' he added.

An assistant fetched me a chair and I sat down. This was unexpected.

'I always forget,' I apologised for my naked face.

'You don't need it,' he said soothingly. This voice must have contributed to his success. It was like honey, rich and sweet. You just wanted to keep listening to it.

'But makeup and hair is your business,' I protested. He smiled his little smile again.

'These people—' he indicated the actors with a wave of his patrician hand '—are fragile. They don't seem so to an outsider but they are brittle. Frail. They need to apply a mask in order to know who they are. And it is my trade. I apply their masks. I make them real. I tell them that they are beautiful. Actors are massively self-involved. They have to be. Their bodies are their livelihood. A spot, a wrinkle, a white hair, the least increase in weight—disasters. Horrors. They need to be comforted. It is a very hard life. I'm glad I never felt drawn to it.'

'Me, too,' I agreed.

'Consider Molly,' he continued. I was a little intimidated by this rush of confidences. How could I repay it? I didn't feel like handing over a chunk of autobiography to this elegant puppet-master. 'She's terrified that she is getting old and fat. Usually she would have a tantrum. But she needs this job. So she is sitting very still, and the only sign of strain you will see is the way she is chewing off her lipstick. It will have to be done again. Ah, good, there is my Gervaise. He will repair it.'

Gervaise was an outrageously camp young man in skin-tight jeans and a Mr. Leonard T shirt that showed off a lot of very burnished muscles. He undulated over to Molly and produced a palette and a series of brushes. He also said something to her which made her laugh.

'He knows my methods,' purred Mr. Leonard. 'Trained him myself. He's done a very passable job with the ingénues. Young faces present difficulties,' he told me. 'They are not fully formed. But they are a nice blank page if made up by a master.'

Kylie and Goss were also sitting carefully in upright chairs, waiting for their cues. I almost didn't recognise them. Kylie was subdued. A mousy girl without any attractive features. Goss was vivid and cheeky, a little bit punk.

'Astounding,' I said. Mr. Leonard was gratified.

'It's all just masks, dear,' he said cosily. 'Emphasise an eyebrow, suppress a quirk, thin or thicken a lip. But they are very interesting masks.'

'Silence,' called Tash. And we fell silent.

The sequence today was about the Bellefleur wedding. Ms. Bellefleur was an oppressed girl who always did as Mother said. Mother was an overbearing old fusspot who questioned and quibbled and swore. Her husband was crushed. The groom was irritated. The girls were hyped up and the dialogue shot back and forth. Then the actor hair and makeup person fussed in and was instantly nailed by the bride's mother. Mr. Leonard leant forward, paying close attention. 'Oh, dear,' I heard him murmur in that woodwind voice.

I looked around. Everyone was watching. Except Kendall and Gordon, who were staring at Mr. Leonard. Finally Molly Atkins entered and demolished the whole cast: makeup person, mother, father, bride, groom and office staff. Then Tash called a halt and said to Mr. Leonard, 'Your opinion?'

He paused for a moment. Then he said, 'Not bad,' to a collective sigh of relief. Kendall and Gordon came to his side. 'Perhaps a few little suggestions,' he told them. I slipped away.

I had almost got to the kitchen door, carrying my empty cup, when Molly Atkins sighed and collapsed.

There was panic. Her assistant was the first to reach her, and then the entire cast milled around picking up arms and legs and imploring her to speak before Ethan the cameraman gathered her up and carried her to her dressing room. The unit nurse was summoned. Tash ordered everyone back on the set to get them out of the way and soon a harassed-looking young woman appeared, carrying a medical bag. She was shoved into the cubicle. The murmur of voices came to me as I stood at the kitchen door.

'What's wrong with her?'

'Heart attack?' suggested Harrison.

'We're doomed if she can't go on,' said Kylie.

'Not doomed yet,' said Goss. I applauded her optimism.

'We can shoot around her,' suggested Ethan. 'Put the under-study on.'

To my astonishment, Tash nodded, yelled a few orders, and Emily—that little mouse!—appeared in a red suit. Had they stripped Molly Atkins as she lay unconscious? What sort of world was this?

The play went on, but I went into the kitchen, my spiritual home. I caught sight of Emily straddling a chair, head back, mouth open to deliver a blistering line. She was so like arrogant, confident Molly Atkins that I shivered.

Bernie, beside me, was shivering too.

'Actors,' she commented.

'Indeed,' I agreed.

We took another cup of coffee out onto the back step, after all. We were joined by some of the catering staff, all worried.

'I really need this job,' said Lance the Lettuce Guy. 'The hours fit in with mine. I have to pick up the kids from school.'

'What do you think's wrong with her?' worried Tommy. 'What did she have for breakfast?'

Heads shook all round. Finally Bernie volunteered that she had been told that Ms. Atkins did not want any breakfast, just a cup of tea. Black without milk or sugar. Tommy cross-examined the step-sitters. No lunch, apparently, and no dinner, either. No one had seen Ms. Atkins eat anything the previous day.

Tommy heaved a sigh of relief and groped in her apron pocket for a cigarette. She lit it and said, 'Well, at least it isn't my food that's to blame,' and there was a general agreement. It struck me that no one was at all worried about Ms. Atkins herself. But it wasn't my business and I just drank my coffee. Come to think of it, I wasn't concerned about her, either. Tommy finished her smoke and said, 'We'd better get back and see what's happened,' in the tone of one inviting her friends to a judicial murder.

Tommy bustled off to find out what was happening and I fell in behind her as though I had every right to be there. The kitchen was loud with wailing about their future and I have never had any patience with wailing. Until you have reason to wail, of course.

The filming was going on. Emily in her red suit was providing the lines for which the others would react. I gaped at her for a few moments. There she was, cruel, arrogant, Ms. Atkins to the life: even her voice was a ruthless mockery of the honeyed tones of the star. The crew had converged, in a huddle of cameras and booms. I was confused by the way the action kept stopping and starting. It wasn't like this when Tommy and I were in the school play, when one had to keep going despite falling sets and forgotten lines. She had made a memorable Julius Caesar to my Calpurnia. Emily had to say over and over again, 'Of course, you've never been interested in appearances, have you?' and she was doing it perfectly. No droop, no loss of intensity, even through endless repetitions. Curious. This wasn't acting as I vaguely knew it.

We entered the little cubicle where Ms. Atkins lay and were greeted by the actress herself, eyes black with outrage, and the kneeling medic, who looked like she would prefer to crawl under the couch than continue to tend her patient.

'There's nothing wrong with me!' Ms. Atkins snarled. Well. At least she wasn't dead.

'You fainted,' the doctor pointed out. 'People don't faint for no reason. Your blood pressure's a bit low. How much have you eaten today?'

'Nothing,' snapped the actor. 'I had some tea.'

'You need some food,' said the attendant. 'Let's see you eat something light and then I might let you try to get up.'

'Soup, then,' conceded Ms. Atkins. She caught sight of Tommy at the door. 'Get me some chicken soup,' she ordered.

'Chicken soup, right away,' agreed Tommy. She ushered me back into the kitchen.

'She's all right,' Tommy announced to general sighs of relief. 'Needs food. Make Jewish chicken soup, Henry. Slice the celery very fine, remember what happened last time.' Then she said to me, 'Choux pastry, I think, Corinna—profiteroles and cream puffs? We seem to still have a job.'

'For the moment,' I said, and went to find Bernie. Choux pastry is a bugger to make and I was hoping a recent graduate would have a better hand with it than me. It ought to be like the Snark, 'meagre and hollow, but crisp', and mine had shown tendencies to be solid, indigestible and burnt.

When I informed Bernie that she could have the honour of making the choux pastry, she beamed at me and thanked me profoundly. I felt like a fraud.

As I was watching chocolate melt—always an engrossing occupation—I reflected on the look I had caught on Ethan's face as he carried Ms. Atkins to her room. He had looked guilty. I knew that expression. He had looked like a boy whose mother was making penetrating enquiries about the strange disappearance of the last slice of pizza and had not entirely accepted his explanation that aliens had taken it for testing. But what connection could the star's anorexia have to Ethan? Had he said something to her about her getting fat? This was quite probable. The two of them had an agonistic relationship. Snipe, snarl, snap.

Bernie's choux puffs came out of the oven looking gorgeous. My cream was whipped and my chocolate icing melted. We made a pyramid of them which would have made pharaohs fight for our acquaintance.

I noticed the chicken soup going out to Ms. Atkins. It smelt delicious. Daniel would have approved. A store of the very best stock is essential to the good governance of any kitchen, and this was clearly twice-cooked mother of stock, so concentrated it was almost demi-glace. That ought to build Ms. Atkins up to her fighting trim.

After which she would be going out to demolish poor Emily, who had had the nerve to wear her clothes and speak her lines as well as she could wear and speak her own. I did not want to watch this. I did watch, however. Inadvertently. Kylie and Goss, lurking by the door as they were not required on set, made frantic gestures to me to come and join them. As my work was done, I had no excuse. I sidled out into the main hall and was instantly grabbed, one to each arm.

'What happened?' hissed Kylie.

'To Ms. Atkins?' completed Goss. They sometimes did this, sounding like the Bobbsey Twins. Who were really before their time.

'She fainted from lack of nourishment,' I told them. 'Which is now being provided. She ought to be back with us very soon.'

'So that's…' said Goss.

'All right,' concluded Kylie. 'But why has she been fasting? We've been eating because Tash says she'll sack anyone who fasts during shooting. She watches, you know. Tash sees everything.'

I could believe it. I was just managing to remove my mistreated arms from their grips when Ms. Atkins, full of chicken soup, issued forth from her dressing room like an army with banners. Mr. Leonard hurried over to her but she brushed even that great artist aside. Holding his useless makeup brush, he watched her as she strode to the set, shoving aside the crew.

'I'm back now,' she announced in a steely tone. 'Thank you, Emily,' she added, as Emily, crestfallen, slunk off set to her side. 'Now, where were we?'

The cast readjusted themselves. Harrison, waiting for his entrance, sighed, 'Magnificent.' Emily fumbled for a hand-kerchief. Ms. Atkins was in entire possession of the room.

I was going home. I did not like the company in which I found myself. I shucked my apron and started walking.

Home was lovely; devoid of actors, pique, pain or humiliation. Also devoid, alas, of Daniel. Horatio and I had a quick drink on the roof and then I decided to deal with my emails. Amid the usual dross was one from Jason. I knew that he didn't have a laptop so I assumed that he was writing from an internet café.

Job hard. Fd gd. How things? Miss yu.

I wondered what to reply. I could say the same about my present life. Food was undoubtedly good. Work was hard. I missed him, too. We had adopted roles from Patrick O'Brian's *Master and Commander* and I missed not having my midshipman.

Daniel came in as I was pondering my reply. He read the email over my shoulder and chuckled.

'What should I reply?'

'Just as you feel,' he advised.

So I replied *Things good. Miss yu tu*, which was all true. Daniel kissed the back of my neck. 'You'll be a geek before long,' he told me.

'So, "How things?" as Jason would say,' I asked him.

'Terrible and sad,' he replied, quoting A. A. Milne. 'I have reached a dead end. Pockets seems to have had the documents, and he has, as he told us, "filed them in the proper place." The only way I can find the proper place is to follow Pockets. I have been doing that. But he has nothing he deems worth filing so he hasn't been near his stash. I have been leaving printed papers about with elaborate casualness all night and he hasn't even noticed them. A police patrol threatened to pick me up for littering.'

'What have you been using as bait?' I asked.

'Just newspapers and so on.'

'Why not give him these,' I offered, handing over a bundle of financial documents. 'They're copies of my shop accounts. Perhaps he will consider them worthy.'

'I'll try it tonight,' said Daniel, kissing me again. 'And how are things at the soap set?'

I told him about Ms. Atkins' collapse.

'The really unpleasant thing was the way they just re-formed and went on,' I said, putting on the kettle. 'And that Emily was a perfect copy of the star. No, not a copy—a pastiche. She just put on the red suit and the personality with it. It was very strange. Would you like to go out to dinner?'

'I would,' he said. 'You must be tired of cooking. Where shall we go?'

'Let's just walk around and see what's open,' I suggested. Melbourne is a good place for this. There are innumerable— well, I expect the Chamber of Commerce has counted them, but I haven't—cafés and bistros and little restaurants which only seat twenty people on old orange crates. They come and go and reopen with a new specialty daily, so there is always something surprising available. And you need to enjoy it while you can, because it might not be there when you thread the alleyways next week and find that it has reinvented itself as a Moroccan takeaway.

I finished my accounts and Daniel consulted with his Black-Berry and then we issued forth into the warm dusk, in search of a diverting culinary experience. Summer had relented for the moment and I was not sweating into my decorated kurta by the time we found a little Japanese restaurant in Bourke Street which had an encouraging population of Japanese students in search of tori teriyaki just like Mother makes. We were drinking our miso soup when I became aware that other persons had felt the need for some Tokyo cuisine.

Ensconced in a booth were Ethan, Emily, Tash and an unknown female with glasses. I thought she might be one of the crew. They were laughing and drinking sake. I pointed them out to Daniel and explained who they were. He was already rising from his seat. I joined him and we went over to the TV table.

'Eth!' exclaimed Daniel. 'I thought it might be you!'

'Daniel!' Ethan stood up, always an unwise thing to do in a Japanese restaurant if you are over two metres tall. He ducked his head under a hanging ornament and gripped Daniel's hand. 'You still haunting the city, then?'

'You still making pictures?' asked Daniel.

'Yep,' said Ethan.

'Yep,' said Daniel.

Some sort of ritual exchange, I assumed. Emily caught my eye and shifted uneasily in her seat. The woman with the spectacles introduced herself as Sasha, the producer of *Kiss the Bride*. I was vague as to the respective roles of producer and director. Sasha was small, thin, and fined down to the bone, with a nose I could use to cut cheese and very bright eyes behind the pickle-bottle lenses. They had almost finished their dinner, while I was aware of my stomach making grumbling noises. The table was covered with bits of script. Tash gave me a big grin chock-full of country goodness.

'Join us?' asked Ethan. 'Only we've got to go soon.'

'Just came to say hello,' Daniel said. 'Nice to meet you all.' And he ushered me back to our table, on which now reposed rice, tori teriyaki, that strange and fascinating Japanese coleslaw and potato salad and Daniel's sashimi, which he loves even more than the Mouse Police do. I poured myself another cup of green tea and picked up my chopsticks.

'So you know our Ethan?' I asked. 'How?'

'Met him when he was doing a documentary on the homeless. Showed him around the traps and introduced him to Sister Mary. He went on the Soup Run. Twice. Once with a camera and once on his own, just to help.'

'I have never seen him without a camera,' I told my beloved. 'Look, he's got one now. At dinner.'

'Film people are strange,' agreed Daniel, picking up another piece of tuna and slathering it with the ferocious pale-green wasabi. 'It's almost as if they can't be in the action; they are always observers. They see the world through the lens and it sets them apart. That's why he came back the next night without the camera, I think. And he was good with the kids.' He heaved a wasabi-scented breath. 'They don't have access to any good role models and they aren't used to strong men who don't hit people. One of our lost souls attacked him because he was new and instead of punching him Ethan just enfolded the kid in a big bear hug. By the time he let go the kid had stopped freaking out. I like him,' concluded Daniel. 'This wasabi is really strong,' he added admiringly, wiping his eyes on his paper napkin.

Pausing only to marvel that people would willingly inflict wasabi on their innocent mouths, I hopped into my chicken, which was excellent. But the crowd in the booth drew my attention. They were chuckling, snuggling close, popping bits from each other's plates into mouths as though they were mother birds. Daniel followed my gaze.

'All the earmarks of a conspiracy, eh, Corinna?' he managed through the scalding of the horseradish. I was intrigued. What was poor Emily doing, cuddled close to the bulk of Ethan, giggling at his jokes, in company with both the producer and the director?

It was none of my business. But still.

I shook myself, summoned up some civilised conversation, and paid attention to my dinner. Melbourne was striding past. Office workers were going home, all still glued by one ear against a mobile phone to their business and their boss. Bits of Japanese and scraps of English floated past us. Daniel and I are both eavesdroppers by avocation, and he was nearer to the *Kiss the Bride* table. I could tell from his expression that he had heard something interesting.

We paid and left and in the warm street I snuggled up to him and demanded, 'All right, what are they talking about?'

'Replacing someone called the Superbitch,' he replied.

Chapter Seven

We discussed it all the way home and reached no conclusion—mostly because we lacked enough data. In any case, I said firmly, it was not our problem. Daniel reluctantly agreed and we shelved the matter. We spent the evening watching *Doctor Who*—I was still undecided about the new Doctor—and then I went to bed with Horatio because Daniel was about to set forth on his Pockets-watch. He loaded his satchel with a thermos of iced lemonade and stowed away a packet of chicken sandwiches. He was obviously going to be out all night.

So I and my cat put ourselves virtuously to bed and slept the sleep of the healthily exhausted until it was six and time to let Bernie in to start the day's baking. While nibbling my toast with blackberry jam I noticed a piece of pale yellow paper on the kitchen table. It was grimy with fingerprints. When I turned it over, it read *Truth lies*. Cryptic. Something of Daniel's, I assumed, and went down the stairs to feed the Mouse Police, count the slain, and put the rye bread on. Today, from my list, was going to be Hungarian. You cannot have Hungarian food without rye bread.

I was thudding and kneading while Bernie—with, as usual, not a hair out of place—made Hungarian honey cake. I considered that grubby bit of paper. Where had Daniel found it? Was it the product of a strange mind, like that man who painstakingly lettered *Eternity* in beautiful copperplate all over Sydney? Or Jason's friend who had been arrested as a graffitist when he returned to finish his tag, which consisted of fluffy white clouds against a blue sky with the legend *Aspire?* Jason's friend had explained his tag as an exhortation to youth to rise above poverty and mischance to greater things, and apparently the magistrate had believed him to the extent of giving him a non-conviction community-based order. Why write *Truth lies?* An expression of existential despair? A philosophical statement? Or was it just the port-and-battery-acid speaking? These were deep matters but I ran out of patience with barren speculation quite quickly and got on with the bread. I sprinkled caraway seeds and got the whole baking into the oven before I poured my second cup of coffee, which Bernie took as an invitation to converse.

'What do you think was wrong with Ms. Atkins?' she asked.

'Famine,' I replied. 'Silly woman hadn't eaten for two days.'

'She must have gained weight,' Bernie told me. 'Emily says that Ms. Atkins weighs herself at the exact same time every morning. Nude.'

'Sick,' I commented.

'Apparently a lot of them do it,' she told me. 'They have a mass weigh-in for the players and anyone who gains weight will be told to go on a diet. It affects continuity, you see.'

I could not see that a kilo or so was going to make any difference to a camera. I said so. Bernie shook her head.

'It's not Ethan who insists on it,' she said dotingly. 'He likes to see people eat. He said so.'

'If he offers you any of his scrambled eggs with chili oil, refuse,' I advised. 'That stuff will slaughter every tastebud you own.'

'I like hot food,' she told me. Ah, that Ethan's attractiveness transcended cuisine. I smiled and went on with my coffee. The bakery was full of the scent of honey cake. Superb. I asked about the recipe.

'The secret is to mix the honey in really well,' she said, deflected from dreams of Ethan. 'If there's any left on the surface of the mix it will burn. It still tastes nice, but it's black.'

'Good for a Hallowe'en cake,' I observed.

'Oh, special occasion cakes are such fun.' She clasped her hands in rapture. 'Birthdays, Christmas, Easter cakes, Hallowe'en cakes. I am going to have such a fun career if I can get a job. I made a Simnel cake with the marzipan decorations for my masterclass. I formed and tinted them like primroses. I got an A.'

I determined that, if I had any influence, Bernie should get a pastry cook's position somewhere. Marzipan is notoriously difficult to deal with and Simnel cake is not an easy thing to construct. It has eleven adornments on the top, one for all the apostles except Judas. Servants used to be given one to take home to their parents on Mothering Sunday.

Unfortunately for those who do not like it, however you colour and flavour it, marzipan still tastes like marzipan…

Bread out of the oven, cakes packed in their plastic containers, we waited for the carrier. This time he was whistling 'Eve of Destruction.' I wondered at his musical elevation from Elvis.

To this accompaniment I asked Bernie for her interpretation of 'Truth lies.' She said immediately, 'It's one of those contradictions. Like "military intelligence." Why do you ask? Did you see it on a wall?'

I murmured something about you never knew what you'd find on walls these days, and we discussed the admirable Banksy all the way to the Harbour Studios.

There we found the usual cast and the usual tasks and set to work—as usual. I was becoming familiar with the rhythm of the studio. First thing, the whole cast and crew milled around, getting breakfast, chatting, texting and talking, drinking coffee and being summoned away to be dressed and made-up. Tash was always to be found sitting in front of a laptop, her assistants beside her, working out what was to be done today. She was usually forking in her scrambled eggs and ham with her non-typing hand. Everyone had a mobile phone. Some—the girls, for instance—had two. Though only the girls would try to talk on the two of them at the same time. Fortunately they only had two ears.

Harrison was always to be found gazing at his own reflection in the polished top of the bain-marie. At first I had wondered what he was doing. His face was doting, even gentle. Then I realised whose divine image had captured his regard. Actors.

Ethan and his chili eggs always had a cloud of admirers. He had a certain presence, I had to admit—big and calm, like a life-size teddy bear. His crew sat at his feet—literally, in some cases—and all females seemed to find him irresistible. He was lord of all he surveyed. No wonder he didn't get along with Ms. Atkins. She acknowledged no royalty but her own. And where was she today?

Ah, there she was, stalking through the throng, choosing a few tidbits from the breakfast table. Emily dogged her heels, as downtrodden and meek as yesterday she had been fulsome and dominant when channelling Ms. Atkins. The saggy T shirt hid her svelte body and her soft floppy hat, plonked on her head like a candle-snuffer, obliterated her handsome profile and her curly hair. Protective colouration, I have heard it called.

I grabbed a cup of coffee and went into the kitchen to make some more Hungarian cakes. Bernie was in full control of this process and I was no expert on cakes so I leant against the bench and watched the rest of the kitchen concoct borscht, cabbage rolls, goulash and what smelt like a rather good chicken stew. Strudel was being constructed, apricot cake, sour cherry cake, and Bernie was making a raspberry cream roulade. I held my breath as she laid out her sponge base and slathered on the filling then began to roll it, very carefully. Roulade is a bugger to make. If the sponge cake is too cold, it cracks. If it is too warm it cooks the filling and goes soggy. I had rarely attempted it because I got so cross when it would not cooperate. But Bernie was a heaven-born cake maker. The roulade rolled up enthusiastically and looked like an illustration in a cookbook.

'Excellent.' I applauded and she blushed.

That was the high point of the morning. As I had completed my tasks, I begged a chunk of the apricot cake for Daniel and took my leave. I left Bernie to her butter cream filling for her hundred-layer cake and I left Tommy to her argument with her assistant over who had failed to purchase sufficient sour cream

for the Hungarian menu—practically everything Hungarian
has sour cream in it. Tommy stuffed a note into my hand as I
went past the discussion. I assumed it was tomorrow's menu and
popped it into my bag. Filming was just beginning as I closed
the outer door and ran straight into Gordon and Kendall, the
writers, whispering almost mouth to mouth. They sprang apart
as though surprised in some deep conspiracy. I greeted them
politely and they goggled.

This TV world was as strange as an Animal Planet documentary about the depths of the sea, I thought, and walked on,
cradling my cake.

◇◇◇

At home I found Daniel. He looked rough. He was drinking
double-strength black coffee and scowling over the grimy piece
of paper. When he saw me he gave me a perplexed smile.

'Come and help, Corinna, I need a mind that does crossword puzzles.'

'At your service, Gov,' I said. 'Perhaps this small offering
might console you in your plight. It's Bernie's Hungarian apricot
cake. Try a spoonful or so and tell me of this mystery.'

'Yum,' he commented, tasting the cake. 'Pockets dropped this
yesterday. I think he knows that I am following him. I think he
left it for me. Therefore it is what we in the detective business
call "a clue." Except I haven't the faintest what it means.'

'You do think it means something?' I asked. 'Rather than
being the deranged product of a grog-destroyed mind?'

'Probably,' he confessed. I sneaked a tiny taste of the cake.
Delicious. 'But I haven't anything else to go on. What do you
deduce from "Truth lies"?'

'It's ringing a faint little bell,' I said. 'Biblical. A biblical bell.
But it wasn't "lies." It was "lieth." Pour me some of that coffee,
will you?'

Daniel supplied me with the restorative brew. I was just about
to give up when I remembered. It was so sudden that I looked
up to see if I had a light bulb over my head.

'Lieth. "Truth lieth at the bottom of a well." That was it.'

'Wonderful,' said Daniel. He leant over the table, seriously annoying Horatio (who was sleeping on the table in the time-honoured manner of all felines) and kissed me. He tasted of apricot and coffee. 'And I think I know where the next clue is.'

'We don't have a lot of wells in the city,' I protested. 'Not anymore, as far as I know. I mean, there must have been wells sunk by the original settlers, but we've got water mains now. Fountains, yes, before the drought we had a lot of fountains.'

'True, all true,' he said. 'Come on.'

We left Horatio in full possession of the table and Daniel swept me out of the apartment and into the street. Degraves Street was full of coffee drinkers and students discussing Street Art and the validity of tagging as we passed. I panted after my beloved as he clove his way through the latte-sippers. Then we were into Flinders Street and crossing the road past my favourite hatters and into the forecourt of the station.

Flinders Street was built in the spacious days when a station was the hub and centre of all activity in a city. I have always doted on its quirky design. Did it really need minarets? Why not? I can hear the architect say. And let's throw in a few battlements as well in case of attack by, as it might be, Fenians or Communists or Bankers. Make the facade really high and make sure that no one can miss the clocks—after all, this is the nineteenth century.

I scuttled after Daniel as he swept around the station to the St. Kilda Road side. There was a huge cathedral-sized space inside. It was always populated with coffee sellers, God bless their mission to mankind, a florist for those pre-emptive apologies, and several fast-food joints. Also charities hoping to sting a few tired travellers for a series of good causes. For such as was left over from the casino and betting shop. Daniel stopped beside a wishing well set up by People For Social Justice. It was attended by several young persons in T shirts which proclaimed their mission and a fine assortment of hair; from dreadlocks to a buzz-cut which a Marine might consider overly severe.

'Daniel,' said the partially bald one. 'You going to contribute?'

'I might,' said Daniel. Suddenly he was unhurried and casual. 'How's it going?'

'People just love to throw money into wishing wells,' said the young man. 'It's weird.'

'But I bet they throw other stuff as well,' commented Daniel.

'Oh yeah, hamburger wrappers, train tickets, that sort of thing. Yesterday we got out fifty-three dollars and eighty cents, a Malaysian coin, four buttons, two biros and a lot of paper.'

'Any of it interesting?'

'You are one weird dude,' said the buzz-cut admiringly. 'As it happens, yes. A note. I think I've still got it...'

He felt in pockets which were hard to open because his jeans were as tight as his skin. Finally there was a crinkle and he handed Daniel a grimy piece of parchment. Same paper. I looked over his shoulder as he opened it. Filthy fingerprints had marred the writing. I read with difficulty the legend *Mary Mary*.

'Thought it might be a message,' said Buzz-cut.

'It is,' said Daniel. 'It's a message to me. Can I keep it?'

Buzz-cut shrugged. 'What's it worth to the hungry and homeless?'

'Twenty,' said Daniel, holding out the bank note.

We departed to a chorus of thanks. Bless the young who care about the lost and strayed. Someone has to.

'Mary, Mary?' asked Daniel.

'It was a song,' I mused as we walked. 'On the radio when I was a child. The Beatles? No, not the Beatles, the Monkees.' I sang him the song. Daniel listened carefully.

'Not really helpful,' he commented.

'No, it isn't, is it? Songs with women's names in the title were popular. I was named after one. Dylan. "Corinna, Corinna." Still, I suppose it could be worse. I might have been called Sunshine or Moonshadow. Or Blossom,' I said, naming some possibilities.

'I think Corinna is a perfect name for you,' said Daniel. I took his arm. The day was yet young. I was getting peckish. I was about to suggest an adjournment for lunch when I thought of something.

'Nursery rhymes.' I stopped suddenly, causing an inattentive gentleman behind me to almost collide. He glared, brushed the front of his immaculate suit, and went round me.

'Nursery rhymes?'

'You are assuming that Pockets wrote these notes, aren't you?' I demanded.

'Yes, it's his handwriting; I could probably get fingerprints off the paper if we have to prove it. Why?'

'He's not likely to have heard of the Monkees, but he would have been sung Mother Goose in his childhood,' I stated.

'Who is Mother Goose?' asked Daniel. Just occasionally we came up against a massive cultural difference and this was clearly one of them.

'Little verses which are told to children,' I said. 'Usually had some remote political or religious point. Like "Georgie Porgie" which is about a king. Or "Ring a-Ring o' Roses" which is about the Black Death.'

'Very interesting,' said Daniel, puzzled. 'But what...'

'Listen,' I told him. '"Mary, Mary, quite contrary, how does your garden grow? With silver bells and cockle shells and pretty maids all in a row." It's about Mary, Queen of Scots. She liked gardening. In the French manner. Very formal. And she had four attendants all called Mary. There's a folk song about them.'

'That must have simplified summoning them. Just call "Mary!",' said Daniel. 'Gardens?'

'We just need to find a garden with silver bells or cockle shells,' I told him.

'And pretty maids all in a line?'

'Row,' I corrected.

'Nothing comes to mind,' said Daniel. 'May I invite Madame for a walk in the park?'

'Why not?' I assented.

It was a pleasant day, though the sun gave promise of searing the city later in the afternoon. Daniel and I strolled easily toward the nearest park, Flagstaff. We went along Little Lonsdale Street, which has always fascinated me. Odd trades abound in that steep, narrow thoroughfare. Umbrella repairers, outré little boutiques, people who copy CDs and supply the techie trade, map makers and costume jewellery shops loaded with enough glitter to stagger a countess. When we came up to the gardens I was a little breathless and longing to sit down, so we did, next to the trees wreathed in tin to repel possums (it seems singularly ineffective) and hung with fruit bats resting up after a long evening mugging someone's orchard.

The trouble with gum trees is that they do not provide good shade, turning their leaves to shed the load of the light. I rose and we began to walk through the park, across the dry grass. A sign proclaimed that Street Art was to be seen, and so it was. To me it always looks like someone has randomly glued a lot of industrial rubbish together but I know nothing about art. Junk, junk, more junk, then—Daniel let go of my hand and ran, and I followed after him. A series of almost life-size babushka dolls, largest to smallest.

'Pretty maids all in a row,' Daniel exclaimed.

'Look for a bit of paper!' I urged.

The base of each babushka was cemented into a block of concrete. This had been hastily assembled because some of the cement had cracks in it. I scouted round one way, Daniel the other, and I saw him stoop.

'Pockets?' I asked, meeting him at the end of the line.

'Pockets,' he said, grinning. He unfolded the spill of paper.

'*There was a crooked man*,' he read. 'You know, poor Pockets is really unhinged.'

'It's another nursery rhyme. "There was a crooked man, who walked a crooked mile, and found a crooked sixpence upon a crooked stile. He bought a crooked cat, who caught a crooked mouse, and they all lived together in a little crooked house."'

'Truly, our cultural differences are profound,' he remarked. 'Now at the same age, I was learning that my father had bought a kid for three farthings.'

'A kid?' I was startled.

'A baby goat. What do you think Pockets means by the crooked man?'

'No idea,' I replied promptly. 'It might be worth looking up what the original meant. All those rhymes had some point when they were made up. In that endeavour, Mr. Google is our friend.'

'So he is,' agreed Daniel. 'How about some lunch?'

'Let's go home,' I said. 'It's getting really hot.'

◇◇◇

The apartment was cool and tidy and I fired up the computer as Daniel assembled some salad sandwiches and Horatio, dislodged from his snooze on my chair, went to the kitchen for a few munchies to settle his newly awakened nerves.

I googled.

'I don't see that this will help,' I told Daniel as he sliced beetroot. 'It's about the Scots general who signed the covenant, Sir Alexander Leslie. The "crooked stile" is the border between England and Scotland and "they all lived together in a little crooked house" is about the Scots and the English coexisting in peace, sort of, after the covenant was signed.'

'What was the covenant?' asked Daniel, and the history lesson lasted all through lunch. But, fascinating as it was, it did not take us any further in the clarification of Pockets' message. Where to find a crooked man? I instantly thought of politicans and suggested a scout around Parliament House. Pockets might turn out to be a stringent social commentator. Daniel went off to do this and I found the ingredients and took myself and Horatio up to the roof garden for a drink. I felt that I deserved it.

The roof was hot but the temple of Ceres was cool, for some reason lost in the mists of architectural engineering. I reposed on the bench in front of the statue of the goddess. Horatio prowled off into the undergrowth. The garden was heat-stressed but admirably green, due to Trudi's water recycling. The gin and tonic tasted fine. But I was concerned. Never someone who likes to be involved in strong emotions—I hate mobs and their propensity for absorbing you, which is why I do not go to football matches or concerts—I was nevertheless enmeshed in

Kiss the Bride, which was seething with passions. Ms. Atkins, Ethan, Emily, Tash, Harrison with his wholehearted narcissism. The girls, as well, desperate to succeed. A plot to get rid of Ms. Atkins, too. And it was all surface. Bodies. Faces. I had not the merest notion what anyone might actually be feeling. They were all actors and they were acting. Except Tommy, who seemed much as she was when we were at school together. What were the writers plotting?

I decided that none of this was any of my business. Pockets' magical mystery trail around the city was likely to be much more amusing. I dozed, musing on the crooked man.

I was woken by Kylie and Goss, who had arrived unnoticed and were sitting in the wisteria bower, sipping Diet Coke, nibbling something out of a cardboard box, and giggling.

'Corinna!' exclaimed Goss. 'Come and have some of this sour cherry cake, it's, like, fabulous.'

'I know, I stole some of the apricot cake,' I replied, disinclined to move. 'That Bernie is a very good pastry cook.'

'Come and sit here,' insisted Goss, so I dragged myself to my feet and obliged. They were clean of makeup and I asked what had happened to the day's shooting.

'Ethan cracked the shits with Ms. Atkins,' Goss told me in a high state of excitement. 'He walked out just after lunch. So Tash sent us home.'

'I wonder if he's going to turn up at the party tonight?' put in Kylie, popping another chunk of sour cherry cake into her rosebud mouth.

'Party?' I asked.

'You've been invited,' said Goss. 'Tash asked for you special.'

'Especially,' I corrected.

'That, too. Didn't you get the invitation?'

'Tommy did give me a note,' I confessed. 'I didn't read it.'

Both of them gave me that peculiarly young-person look which can be summed up as 'What's the weather like on your planet?'

'So you'll come,' insinuated Kylie.

'Perhaps.' I did not know if I wanted to spend more time with actors. 'I'll have to see what Daniel is doing. We've got a treasure hunt.'

I told them about Pockets and his paper clues. They were interested but had no insights to offer.

'Weird,' opined Goss. 'Corinna, was it nice to replace Jason?'

'I didn't,' I said, taken aback. 'Bernie was supplied by Tommy because I am cooking for her. Bernie wants to be a pastry cook and she's working for Tommy, not me. I could never replace Jason.'

'Oh, shit,' said Kylie, after a pause and some more cake.

'What?' I demanded.

'We've been getting texts from Jason,' said Goss, as Kylie had apparently been rendered mute by all that cake. 'He was asking how you were going. And…'

'You told him I had replaced him?' I demanded. Bloody texting. I knew it was evil.

'Er…' said Goss. 'Sort of.'

'Sort of?'

'Don't be wild, Corinna, we just said that a girl was working in your bakery.'

'You idiots,' I said angrily. 'Don't you think at all? Jason's a recovering heroin addict! He always said he got off the gear because of Earthly Delights! If he thinks I don't want him anymore he might do anything!'

Then I stopped yelling, not because they were frightened but because they were excited. Their lips moistened, their eyes sparkled. I was flooded with disgust.

'Text him back,' I demanded. 'Do it now.'

'Can't,' said Kylie. 'He doesn't have a phone. He said he was on a borrowed one.'

'I'll send an email.' I got up and, without another word, collected the esky and Horatio and stalked off to the lift. What had those two thoughtless—and that was throwing roses at their mental processes—young women done to Jason? And to me?

I did not seem to be able to avoid emotion, I thought, as I slammed the apartment door and fired up the computer. Horatio withdrew to the safety of my bed as I hit keys with unnecessary force. Curse Kylie and Goss! I wondered if our resident witch Meroe could supply me with a good solid malediction for them.

Dear Jason, I began. *Kylie has just told me what she told you. Don't believe it. I have not, repeat NOT, replaced you. I was doing a favour for a friend. Hope to see you soon*, I concluded. I was sure that this would not work. Adolescent feelings are so sensitive and no one cherishes a hurt like a sixteen-year-old boy. He cuddles it close and relishes it. Damn. Damn. Damn. I really liked Jason.

Just as I was wondering what I could do to get rid of this anger, Jon and Kepler arrived to take me up on an ill-advised promise to check their accounts. They are so sweet together that I could not turn them from my door. And accounts are my field. I provided directions to the tea- and coffee-making facilities and sat down with their books.

And found something to be righteously wrathful about. One of their suppliers had misinterpreted 'double-entry bookkeeping' as 'charge a charity twice, they'll never notice.' I noticed. I accepted a cup of tea from the delightful six-foot Jon and the sugar from the equally delightful Kepler, Asian and the same height as me, and declared, 'This person is cheating you.'

Jon has been an international charity worker for a long time. He looked sad, but not surprised. Kepler, who does frightfully complex IT for various companies, was horrified that someone would rob those who live to do good works. I explained, pointing out the entries and invoices. Twice for the same goods.

'Oh, dear,' said Jon. 'Well, we shall have to find another supplier, shan't we?'

'Call the cops,' I urged. My blood was still hot.

'Oh, yes, that too. I shall talk to that nice Sergeant Nguyen in the Fraud Squad. Just because we're a charity must not mean we are a soft touch. Once that sort of thing gets said it is work, work, work, as Westley says in my favourite film.'

The Princess Bride. I might have guessed.

'Do you want me to write you a report?' I asked.

'If you would be so good,' said Jon, sitting down and cradling his teacup. 'You seem a little distracted, Corinna dear.'

I told him, while typing out a summary of depredations, what Kylie and Goss had done. Jon looked grave.

'That is not good,' he commented. 'Can you contact Jason?'

'Only by email. I've sent one. For what good it will do. I might have lost him,' I said, and surprised myself by bursting into tears.

'Oh, no, you won't have lost him.' Jon hugged me. 'Jason's like the poor. Always with us. And I should know…'

Kepler nodded. I finished the report. They left with thanks. I read the note which Tommy had passed to me. It appointed a Spanish restaurant in Calico Alley as the venue for a 'friendly gathering.' Lorca. I had always meant to go there. At least it was within easy staggering distance.

It had not been a good day. And I had to go to a party tonight! Bugger everything, I thought, and lay down on my bed for a nap. Horatio attended me.

Chapter Eight

Daniel woke me, inadvertently, by rattling the kettle as he filled it. He made tea as I escorted Horatio to the kitchen and sat down heavily. I was on a chair, he was on the table. We were both, if not entirely disgruntled, not gruntled to any noticeable extent.

'I've got a police report on Pockets,' he told me. 'Could help us guess where he might stash his documents. Tea?'

'Yes, please.'

'What's the matter?'

I told him. TV people, mysteries, someone cheating Jon's most worthy organisation. Most of all, Jason. Daniel filled the cups with the beverage. I sipped. It was Earl Grey—so civilised.

'I think Jason will be all right,' he said consideringly. 'He's grown up a lot since he came here. And he knows that the girls are airheads.'

'Even so,' I said.

'We shall have to wait and see,' he told me. 'Let's look at this report and find out about Pockets. Might be good to take your mind off your troubles.'

'That would be nice,' I agreed.

The police report was pithy. Most police reports are. It said that Pockets was a fifty-three-year-old alcoholic ex-businessman with serious mental problems. His real name, before he became deranged, was Robert Banks. He had been on the street for four years, which was a long time to survive, although perhaps the Lemurians protected him. Parents dead, one estranged sister in

Queensland, married and divorced, no children. No prosecutions, several arrests for drunk and disorderly (held for four hours and released), several hospital admissions for alcoholic dementia. Prognosis: dire. Poor Pockets. And I thought I had problems. Nothing like viewing a report like this to restore one's perspective.

'Nothing really helpful,' said Daniel.

'He used to be an accountant,' I told him. 'Previous employment: associate at Mason and Co. Isn't Lena's employer called Mason?'

'Yes, he is,' said Daniel. 'But it's a common name. In any case, it's unlikely Pockets remembers anyone from his previous life, before he met the Lemurians.'

'True,' I said. 'Though memory is tricky. I've known people absolutely demented able to recall in pinprick detail learning to sew when they were five.'

'True again,' he said equably. 'What's all this about a party?'

'How did you know about that?'

'Met the girls in the atrium. They said that you were going.'

'They say a lot of things,' I snarled. 'I'm still thinking about it. I might have to work with them, but I don't know if I want to socialise with them.'

'Well, well,' said Daniel pacifically. 'How about a little walk? *Voulez-vous promener avec moi*, Madamoiselle?'

'*Bonne idée*,' I conceded.

I like walking with Daniel. I fit exactly under his arm. We promenaded down to Flinders Street and then threaded our way through the crowd outside the fast-food places and the bookshop, crossing the road to the old city square. It has a massive hotel on one side, a rather ineffectual fountain (dry) and a plinth on which stands those favourites of Australian legend makers, the Lost Explorers. Burke and, as it happens, Wills, at the last stage of thirst and starvation. They looked just like men who had discovered that the relief party which should have been waiting for them had got bored and gone home. No one has bothered to put up a statue of their rescuer, who made it all the way to Adelaide without losing a horse, much less a man.

Alfred Howitt has been forgotten except by mountaineers. I don't know why we do this. Celebrate the disasters and forget about the triumphs. It's irritating. I looked at the bronze. It was a very good depiction. Burke, or possible Wills, sagged crookedly down in his mate's embrace. The other man—Wills, perhaps—stared blankly out into despair.

'Crooked,' I said to Daniel. 'He's a crooked man!'

To the amusement of onlookers, we started combing the base of the monument. I just caught a slip of parchment as it escaped and tried to flutter off to join all the rest of the rubbish blowing around the streets.

'Aha!' I declared. 'And what do we have now?'

'*Ride a cock horse...*' read Daniel. 'Is Pockets being indelicate?'

'No, I think it meant a male horse in less mealy-mouthed times. "Ride a cock horse to Banbury Cross, to see a fine lady upon a fine horse. Rings on her fingers and bells on her toes, and she shall have music wherever she goes." More or less.'

'Interesting but not helpful,' said Daniel. 'Let's go home and look it up. Also,' he squeezed me closer to his side, 'I think a little nap would calm the nerves.'

◇◇◇

I could not agree more. Having been extensively snuggled, I woke late in the afternoon assuaged, warm, glowing and at peace. Until I started thinking again. Always a bummer, thinking. But I did have a sneaking feeling that I had seen a fine lady upon a fine horse. The idea itched at the edge of my memory and refused to swim into focus, so I ditched it for the present. Daniel was talking on his mobile and sounding soothing, as though he was speaking to a distressed person.

'It will be all right,' he said. 'I'm on the trail. You just have to be patient for a little longer. Yes, I know how hard it is. Of course I know what it's like waiting for a bomb to explode. I'm an Israeli. Don't fret, Lena, I'm on the case.'

He switched off the phone. 'That girl is in a bad way,' he told me. 'I'm concerned about her. But all I can do for her is to solve her problem and find those papers!'

'I suppose—not that I am suggesting this for a moment, you understand—but I suppose you couldn't just grab Pockets and shake it out of him?'

'Torture is rejected by all civilised nations because it is inherently evil and—' he raised a finger '—it doesn't work. The tortured will tell you anything to stop the pain. Beria said, "Let me have a man for four days and I will have him confessing he's the King of England." True, but useless. Such confessions might not have anything to do with the truth.'

'Witchcraft prosecutions,' I agreed glumly.

'Show trials,' he capped. 'Tempting though it is, I can't mistreat Pockets. Life has mistreated him enough.'

'Sorry, it was just an impulse,' I said. 'An unworthy impulse. I'm just cross because I can't recall where the fine lady on a fine horse is.'

'Let's get dressed,' he said. 'Then we can walk along to Lorca and if it turns out to be a frost we can come home. It's really not far. And I'll be interested to see these people you are working with.'

'Ethan invited you especially,' I said, showing him the invitation with a scrawled note from Ethan in the corner.

'Then we should at least buy him a drink,' said Daniel.

I dressed in my going-out-in-summer gear: dark trousers, a decorated kurta with gorgeous blue braiding, and sandals. Then we descended to the atrium, where we met Therese, who had also been invited. She was wearing her trademark natural linen shift, heavily embroidered. Her hands were lavishly decorated with bandaids.

'Beading?' I asked. She laughed.

'Good heavens no, dear, I didn't prick myself that much when I was five. No, I was trying to assemble a flat-pack materials box. I was just about to ring down and ask you to lend me Jason when I remembered that he's gone.'

'Not forever,' I said sharply. 'He's coming back.'

'Is he?' she asked. 'I thought that the girls said...'

'They didn't know what they were talking about,' I assured her.

'That's all right, then,' she said sunnily. I followed her down the steps, hoping that it was indeed all right.

◇◇◇

Lorca is one of the little eateries that practically comprise Calico Alley. I had a great admiration for the Spaniard after whom it was named and I hoped that the food would match his greatness; also, I hoped it would lift my mood. I don't like myself when I'm grumpy.

The first people we saw outside the restaurant door were inauspicious. Three corporate types in the corporate equivalent of a tracksuit (grey marle with a logo on the breast). They were sipping fruit drinks and talking animatedly about a half-marathon. Not my kind of people. And what were they doing here? However, the gush of scent—garlicky, winy, loaded with spices—was encouraging. We passed the corporate persons, two male and one female. I recognised one of them. Claire, the wafer-thin friend of poor Lena. She was bouncing gently in her Nikes and laughing up into the face of a large gentleman who would have been more comfortable in a suit. Claire was fitting in just fine, if these were her employers. The other gentleman was thin as a whip, with that underlying muscularity one sees in long-distance runners. His hair was cut brutally short, perhaps to reduce drag.

'Ten K's every day,' he was declaring. 'Rain or shine. Only way to stay fit.'

That Juvenal with his *mens sana in corpore sano* had a lot to answer for. Though he would have liked Lorca and, after I got inside past the aggressively healthy, I did, too. The menu was written on the wall. All over the walls, in fact. Someone thrust a plate of *patatas bravas* at me and shoved a glass of sangria into my hand. Now that was more like it. I munched a brave potato. They are rendered bold, I suppose, by the spicy tomato sauce. I looked around.

The TV crew was there. Ethan loomed over the crowd, talking earnestly to Tash. Ms. Atkins was scolding Emily. Kylie and Goss were listening to the put-down, mouths agape. Sasha the producer was listening to the writers Kendall and Gordon as they gulped sangria and grazed on anything edible within easy reach. Spanish guitar music was playing. Yes, the Romans could have moved into Lorca without any problems, except trying to educate the locals on the value of the ablative absolute. The place was packed, with barely elbow room to reach for the plates of food scattered around liberally.

Daniel seized a plate of salt and pepper squid, which could only be more un-kosher if it was pork cooked in milk with bacon sprinkles. Therese partook also. I sipped the sangria. It was strong, spicy, and the maker had used good red wine instead of the usual dregs.

'Scrummy,' pronounced Kylie, materialising at my side. 'Isn't this fun? Everyone's here.'

'Oh, good,' I replied. I was still angry with them.

'Have some squid,' said Daniel, swiftly interposing the platter between us.

'Erk,' commented Goss, and they drifted away, which was fine with me. I drifted also, toward Ethan, who had a magnetic attraction for all women. Before I got to him, however, I washed up against the corporate types again. A shove from someone pushed me so that I was nose-to-patrician-nose with the whippet.

'Corinna.' I offered my unoccupied hand. 'I'm the baker.'

'Tony.' He barely touched my fingers. Aha. A fat-phobic. He thought size 20 might be catching. 'I'm with Mason's. We do your accounts.'

'Not mine, theirs. I'm just a professional employeee. Like you. Are you going jogging after this?'

'I run every night,' he said proudly. The light of pure fanaticism gleamed in his dark brown eyes. 'Low-fat, low-sugar diet with plenty of carbs.'

I had no idea what he was talking about. But he was an accountant. So was I. We should have something in common.

'We have a corporate fitness plan,' he went on. 'Gym in the building. Employees have time to work out. Pays off in the long run,' he added, revealing that he was indeed an accountant. 'Less sick leave. We invest in our employees' fitness.'

'And how does that apply to those built like me?' I asked waspishly. How would Lena feel in that environment? Like a couple of tonnes of elephant shit, if I was any judge. Tony looked uncomfortable.

'We try to be inclusive,' he muttered. 'But some people refuse to enter into the spirit.' He took another mouthful of his—alcohol-free, I would bet—sangria. 'Isn't this a nice place?'

'Yes.' I gave up. At least he hadn't offered me any dieting tips. Of course, if he had, I would have been required to take condign action. A Ms. Atkins snub, perhaps, or forcible feeding of empanadas. They were very good little pastry things, I noticed as I bit into one and Tony winced. I hoped that Bernie was taking notes. I looked for her. She was, indeed, taking notes. She was in close conversation with a handsome woman in an apron. Our hostess, I assumed. Good. Where was Daniel?

A server filled my sangria glass again. Peach chunks, yum. I dote on the way the fruit in sangria absorbs the brandy. I circulated a bit, moving closer to the tower of Ethan, and I found Daniel. He was talking to the other corporate trackie.

'So you don't like Lena?' he asked bluntly.

The suit blinked. Plain speaking was not a notable part of accountancy. This one was older than Tony and fatter. A lot of good dinners had gone into constructing that waistline. I grabbed a plate of things on skewers and eavesdropped shamelessly. The older man groped for the food without noticing what his hand was doing. It's a form of sleep-eating and not pretty to watch. It reminds me of guards I had bribed in other parts of the world. The money just appears in their hands. Then it disappears, as the chicken was now doing.

'Perhaps she isn't suited to our corporate model,' he told Daniel through a mouthful. 'She would be ideal for a small suburban firm. If at all. I'm afraid we're going to have to let her go.'

'Don't have a size-twenty tracksuit, eh?' asked Daniel.

'Er, no. Look, this is our brochure. I'm sure you'll find it impressive.'

He shoved it into Daniel's hand and moved away.

'So that was Mr. Mason, Lena's boss?' I asked. 'Have some of these kebab things.'

'Poor Lena,' said Daniel. 'He was very uncomfortable, did you notice?'

'I noticed. Did you tell him that you were working for Lena?'

'I never tell people like them anything that I don't have to tell them. Come on, let's find Ethan.'

We located Ethan in the midst of a competing crowd. Everyone wanted his attention. I wondered what this would do to a young man's ego, and decided that he would have to be a saint not to be monstrously puffed-up. He was awash in a sea of pretty girls. But he sighted Daniel and put aside the damsels.

'Come outside,' he said. 'Can't hear myself think in here.'

And with the force of a battleship, he ploughed his way toward the door, leaving pouting in his wake. Daniel grabbed an enormous platter of tapas and preceded him into the street. There he scored a little table and there was room for me, too.

However, before I could attain my goal, Ms. Atkins summoned me and I went. She grabbed my arm—that arm was going to be bruised before this series was finished—and pulled me close to her. She was all bones: elbow and wrist and collarbones. She made me uncomfortable as she leant in close to whisper.

'Is that hunk your boyfriend?' she asked.

I admitted that that hunk was indeed Daniel, my beloved. Then Ms. Atkins astonished me by saying quite politely, 'Ask him to come and speak to me.' To stagger me she added, 'Please,' a word which I would have sworn was not in her vocabulary.

She released me as I nodded and let me move away from her. What could the Superbitch want with my Daniel? But she had said please. Good manners should be rewarded.

I found Ethan and Daniel sitting on little chairs in the street, scoffing handfuls of olives and talking about camera angles—or so I gathered. I gave my beloved the message. He quirked an eyebrow.

'Careful,' warned Ethan. 'She could swallow you without chewing.'

'I believe you,' replied Daniel, and plunged back into the throng. I could not hear, of course, and he was turned away so I could not read his lips. So I turned my attention to Ethan. He slouched in his chair, easy, grinning, posting pilchards between his lips. He was a very attractive sight. A cross between a Roman emperor and the Ghost of Christmas Past.

'Daniel your bloke?' he asked. I nodded and snitched one of his little fish. 'He always did have good taste,' said Ethan. 'So, what do you think of the TV industry?'

'Noisy,' I said truthfully. 'Emotional.'

'Tense, isn't it? Because we are all trying to make something out of pixels and words. Out of dust and ashes.'

'*Pulvis et nihil*,' I quoted, something which Professor Dion often says.

Ethan, to my surprise, nodded and amended the quote.

'*Ex pulvere*,' he said, '*et nihil laboramus*. And it's a mighty labour and does tend to fray the temper. The trouble is, showbiz would be fine without the actors and the actors would be fine without showbiz. But without actors you have stop-animation, and as much as I admire Wallace and Gromit you can't call it Art, and without TV who would remember the actors when they were offstage?'

'I suppose that's so,' I said.

'So we're stuck with them and they're stuck with us and neither of us is happy. What do you reckon Ms. Superbitch wants with your Daniel?'

'I don't know. She'll have to give him back, mind. Then we shall know. Have you worked with her before?'

'No, and I'll never work with her again if I'm exceptionally lucky. She's everything they warned me she would be. Yes, she's a piece of work all right. Perfect in her way, like a perfect cobra or a perfect black widow spider.'

'Harsh,' I commented.

He leant forward and took my hand. His grasp was warm and calloused, like a builder's hand.

'But true and fair. You've seen how she persecutes poor Emily?'

'I have.' And poor Emily would be rapturous if she could see the gentleness and concern in those brown eyes. Just then Emily looked over and did see us, and gave me a glare of pure malice. Ouch. I released my hand.

'However, she'll get hers,' said Ethan complacently, sitting back in his chair and gathering a few more empanadas. 'God is not mocked.'

This was complicated. In my experience God is frequently mocked, especially when the Melbourne Comedy Festival is on. And which God did Ethan mean? Surely not himself? Did photographers have their own saint?

Fortunately Daniel returned before I had to think of a reply.

'Walk with me?' he asked, extending an elbow. I rose and slid my arm through his.

'See ya, Eth,' said Daniel and we walked down Calico Alley into the arcade. I could have gone back and said farewell to Bernie, but I didn't. Daniel was worried about something and needed my counsel.

'I'm worried,' he told me.

'So I guessed,' I responded.

'Did you guess what Ms. Atkins wanted with me?'

'Not a clue.'

'She wants me to find out who has been playing tricks on her,' said Daniel. 'Chili in her food. Missing shoes. Harassment. And she wants me to find her child.'

'What?' I stopped dead in front of a display of fountain pens.

'She wants me to find her missing baby. Twenty-odd years ago she gave away a baby. She was just starting to be successful as an actor and model and she couldn't keep it. The babe, I mean.'

'Why do you say "it"?' I asked.

'She never saw the child, doesn't know if it's male or female. Her sister took it away and later told her that it had been adopted. Before she could tell Ms. Atkins more, the sister died of a stroke.'

'And she wants to find it now because...?'

'One does not ask the clients for their motivations.'

'Soap opera,' I wailed. 'I knew I shouldn't have got involved with soap operas! This sort of thing is always happening in soaps! Next it will turn out that someone has amnesia or hysterical paralysis or a plane will crash into Harbour Studios!'

'Calm, Corinna, calm,' he suggested. 'I'll start with adoption records. The birth must have been registered. Then we shall continue from there. How I am going to find out who has been playing tricks on her, I don't know. Perhaps I can get Ethan to give me a job as a gofer.' He grinned.

'I don't like it,' I told him. Then the thought which had swum irritatingly just below the surface of my mind rose like a salmon, and leapt. 'Come on. I've just recalled the fine lady on her fine horse.'

We strolled through the city. Melbourne on a warm night is peaceful and charming, except in front of the nightclubs. Children ate ice cream. Students walked, snail-backed with books in knapsacks, deep in discussion. Probably more about boys or girls than Derrida, but engrossing nonetheless. I led Daniel up Swanston Street toward the library. We skirted a woman with two little doggies, each startlingly like Traddles, and ascended the slope in front of that massive pile, scattered as usual with recumbent students who were putting off study until after they had recuperated from their twelve-hour shift in the fast-food industry.

'I don't know about Banbury Cross,' I told Daniel as we reached the forecourt of that great temple of books. 'And I haven't examined the genitalia of this particular horse, but he is fine, isn't he?'

There rode Joan the Maiden, armoured cap-à-pie, lance in hand. Another magnificent bronze. And in the pedestal, another slip of parchment with filthy fingerprints.

'Gotcha,' said Daniel. 'Thank you, Corinna!'

'What does it say?' I asked, trying to read under his shoulder. Daniel unfurled the paper.

'*Rain, rain,*' he read.

'*Rain, rain, go away, come again some other day,*' I sang. 'I can't recall the rest. All I can remember is a parody from a TV show called *HR Pufnstuf* which ends "little witchy wants to zoom, she can't take off on a wet broom" and I'm sure that's not the original.'

'Hardly the true Mother Goose philosophy,' he agreed.

We strolled home again. My grumpy mood, however, despite the revelation of Ms. Atkins' lost child and the other irritants, seemed to have evaporated. So I suggested that we drop back in to the Lorca party on the way and see if there were any munchies left.

We found Ethan outside, beset with girls, drinking Spanish beer and grinning. Daniel joined him. I noticed that the girl whom he had displaced from her chair just sat down on Daniel's knee. Oh, well, she had to sit somewhere. Inside, it was hot and dimly lit. I found a display of prawns which looked lonely and decided to keep them company. Bernie had had the same idea. We swapped crustaceans.

'Having a good time?' I asked.

'I've been nailed for an hour by Mr. Health and Strength,' she said, dolefully. 'He disapproves of cakes and told me so. For an hour,' she repeated. 'Luckily I got some tapas.'

'Come outside,' I offered. 'This way.'

I led her out of the babble and motioned to Daniel to offer her a chair. He stood up, holding his girl in his arms, and Bernie flopped down. I put the prawns in front of her.

'This is my good and deserving colleague Bernie,' I told Ethan. 'Have a prawn. She makes most of those cakes you wolf down during delays.'

'Nice to meet you!' Ethan took Bernie's work-reddened hand and smiled into her abashed face. 'You're a good cook!'

'Pastry chef,' I corrected.

He accepted the correction. 'Of course. Nice to meet you, Chef. How did you make that yummy cake with the cherries in?'

'Do you cook?' asked Bernie in a reverent tone.

'When I can,' said Ethan. 'No good at cakes, though.'

Bernie beamed at him. The other maidens shot her poisonous glances to which she seemed oblivious.

'Your work here is done,' whispered Daniel into my ear, depositing his girl on her feet, very gently.

'Come back inside,' I urged. 'I want you to talk to Tommy.'

'Why?' he asked.

'Because if anyone knows what Granddad Chapman used to call the ins and outs of a duck's bottom, it's Tommy. She adores theatre gossip,' I told him, and back we went into the Spanish fug.

Where we found Tommy, sitting heavily in a chair and drinking what was definitely her fifth glass of sangria. This might prove to be unwise. Sangria is sneaky. It tastes like fruit juice and packs a punch very similar to being hit over the ear with a heavy fist by someone preparing to steal your handbag. The lady in the apron was slumped onto a similar chair but was drinking water.

'Daniel, you remember Tommy. Tommy, you recall Daniel,' I introduced them. 'Daniel is fascinated with TV people,' I lied.

'Really?' Tommy squinted up at my beloved. 'Have a seat, take the weight off. Are you a chef too?'

'Not me,' Daniel replied. 'I like a job where you get to sit down.'

This amused both ladies. Tommy laughed but persisted.

'What do you do, then?'

'I'm a private detective,' he told her. 'Lost children, missing husbands, that sort of thing.'

'Oh, no,' said Tommy. 'Don't tell me that Molly has hired you to find that missing baby.'

Chapter Nine

After that statement we all poured ourselves some more sangria. Daniel recovered first.

'So other people have tried to find the child?' he asked.

'Oh, yes, and no one has a clue. In fact...' she lowered her voice and leant closer, 'some people think that it never existed at all. We can't ask her sister because she's dead. Poor Molly. She gets maudlin when she's taken a few too many drinks and starts blubbing about her missing child.'

'This puts a new complexion on the case,' commented Daniel.

'Oh, take the money and see what you can do,' Tommy advised. 'She might be sincere.'

'Possibly,' I put in. She had said please, after all.

'Worth a look,' decided Daniel. 'And what about the tricks someone has been playing on her?'

Tommy laughed and took a deep gulp of the spicy wine. 'They have been funny,' she said. 'The star on her dressing-room door was painted beige, to match the door. The chili oil in her scrambled eggs—everyone assumed that was Ethan, and Tash ripped strips off him. The day Ms. Atkins arrived and found every left shoe missing. I don't know. Could have been anyone. But I can't see how they managed the latest one.'

'Which was?'

'To meddle with the electronic scales. That's why she went on a fast. Might have just been a weight fluctuation. Mostly fluid, of course. But she went into a snit and didn't eat and that's why she fainted. I can't imagine how you are going to find out who did it. Good luck with that,' she said airily.

'Where did they find the missing shoes?' asked Daniel.

'Packed neatly into a carton next to the rubbish,' replied Tommy. 'Ah! Here she comes at last!'

And into the throng came a thin blonde. I recognised Julie, even though I had last seen her in a box-pleated tunic. Same hairstyle. Same vaguely disconnected expression. She caught sight of Tommy and squeaked. A brief flurry and spirited use of elbows and she was embracing her girlfriend. Then she noticed me.

'Corinna!' she exclaimed. Julie had always conducted conversations by exclamation. 'And who's this?'

'Daniel,' he introduced himself. 'I'm Corinna's partner.'

Julie gave me a swift look which was an exclamation in itself. I admit that I preened a little. Yes, he was gorgeous. Yes, he was mine. Get used to it.

'How's it all going?' asked Julie, waving at the crowd.

'Good,' said Tommy affectionately. 'And I'm not doing the cooking for a change. Time to go?'

'Past time,' confirmed Julie. 'See you, Corinna. *Daniel*.' The emphasis was marked. Which left Daniel and me a little bemused.

'Well,' he said, getting up, 'I've got things to do. Walk you home?'

I thanked the lady in the apron for her remarkable food and followed him through the TV people onto the relatively quiet street. As I walked away, I looked back and saw Ethan take Bernie's hand and kiss it. Well, well.

After that there was not a lot to do but put myself to bed.

◇◇◇

The next day dawned bright and hot. There was a faint haze in the air, which spoke of coming rain. Lately we had been getting downpours which would not disgrace the tropics. Not a good day for bread, but I baked it anyway. Bernie was floating through her work with a delighted and astonished air. I wondered what had happened with her and Ethan, and hoped that she was not about to get her heart broken; but it was early morning, so I said nothing. I have never had a sensitive conversation early in the morning which has not gone horribly wrong.

We made the breads to accompany salads and cheese—walnut, seven seed, black bread, olive bread. They smelt so gorgeous that I hoped there would be leftovers. Just as the thought crossed my mind, a shadow fell across the open door. Bernie looked up and squeaked. I did not, because the looming person was my old friend Rui. He looks dangerous—he used to play for the All Blacks, and Mother Nature has designed Maoris in two sizes, huge and enormous—but he is a sweetie's sweetie. He volunteers for the Soup Run, an enterprise that feeds the lost and strayed, when he is not acting as a bouncer in some of the city's most violent venues. Even there he does not hit people, just hugs them until they calm down. Which they do, quite fast. The Soup Run was contrived under the wimple of Sister Mary, the sort of nun who, in the Middle Ages, used to cause bishops to hide under their lecterns in case she commandeered their mitres to sell and feed the poor. He swept me into a hug from which I emerged rumpled but reassured. Large women are not often held as gently as a day-old chick.

'Corinna! You open again? Got any bread?' he asked.

'Not open as such, just doing a little cooking for a friend. Sorry. But here's a loaf of my special seed bread just for you.'

He demolished the whole loaf in two bites, said, 'Sweet,' and was about to wander away when I laid a hand on his forearm. I might as well have tried to detain a lorry but he stopped out of politeness.

'How have things been going?' I asked.

'Good,' he told me. 'Daniel's been out every night, looking for Pockets' documents. Poor old Pockets! And Spazzo's in the bin. Pockets is a bit lost without Spazzo. But he's been trotting round the city lately. Seems to be on a mission. Well, most of them have missions. We do what we can, and God knows their poor minds,' said Rui, channelling Sister Mary.

'Have you got any idea where he hides his documents?' I asked. Rui shrugged, an interesting movement which reminded me of tectonic plates colliding.

'No notion,' he said. 'Could be anywhere. He gets about, the old Pockets does. Bye,' he said, and went.

'I didn't know humans grew that big,' breathed Bernie.

'He must have eaten his carrots,' I agreed. We finished up the baking. The Mouse Police resumed their nap on the old flour sacks which are their preferred bed. The carrier's whistle—'Hotel California'—sounded outside. We loaded up and were about to leave when Daniel hove into view. He drooped. I had never seen him droop. I embraced him.

'What is the matter?' I asked, concerned. He leant his head, briefly, on my shoulder, then I felt him nerve himself to stand up straight again.

'My client is in hospital,' he said evenly.

'That's bad. What happened?' I asked.

'She tried to kill herself,' he said. 'Luckily she wasn't very good at that, either. Poor Lena. Not that she didn't warn everyone. Posted her suicide note on Facebook. Poor girl! I've got to sit down.'

'Shall I come, too?' I asked. 'Bernie, can you get the stuff packed? Tell Tommy I've been detained by an emergency. Come on, Daniel, up we go.'

I hustled him inside and up the bakery steps toward my apartment. Behind me I heard Bernie ordering Hotel California to lend a hand with the bread. Tommy would just have to cope without me for today.

Daniel was protesting that he didn't need any help but I ignored him. I stuffed him into the bathroom and, as I assembled comfort food, heard the shower going. Good. Washing did not cure anything, but it did make you feel better able to cope. What would assist in the way of comestibles?

I had the very thing. By the time he emerged, damp and sweet-smelling, I had chicken soup on the table. Just as his mother would have made it: luscious, delicately spiced and strong. I watched as he drank it, first reluctantly, then greedily. Greedily was good. I zapped another batch in the microwave. Chicken soup is a cultural artifact. Also, it tastes good, which is more than you can say about a lot of cultural artifacts. Cathedrals, say.

Daniel began to talk. At last. His voice was scratchy and reluctant.

'I got the phone call just as I was coming back from another night trying to track Pockets. I swear he is as elusive as a whiff of ozone. I lost him several times. He just wanders, you see, even he doesn't know where he is going, so I can't guess and get ahead of him. Tiring. Still no idea where his depository is. Then Lena's mother called me. She had no idea that Lena was in trouble. She was very angry.'

'With you? It's hardly your fault...' I ventured.

'Justice does not whisper to an angry and affronted mother. Lena took a whole lot of pills. It'll be a couple of days before they know if her liver is affected. She hadn't said a word to her parents about how unhappy and bullied she was.'

'Why not?'

'It's the same response as I've seen in women who have been raped. It's the rape of the soul, not the body, bullying. The bullied are ashamed. The idea is that if someone manages to bully you, then you must be an unworthy person, at fault because you can be bullied. I know—not logical.'

I thought about this for a while as Daniel sopped up the last of his chicken soup with some of my sourdough.

'Like beaten wives,' I offered.

'Exactly. Oh, if I could get her bosses to myself I'd...'

'Tell me,' I said, sitting down and folding my hands.

'I'd remember some of my Israeli army training,' he told me. 'In unarmed combat. I was quite good at it,' he added. 'There are some holds which are exquisitely painful.'

'It would do them good,' I said.

'Probably, but then they would just squeal the time-honoured bullies' justification: "It was just a joke, can't she take a joke?" And then—' He stopped.

I prompted, 'And then?'

'I would have to kill them, and that is just so illegal. That was wonderful soup. I feel much better. Shouldn't you be getting on with your job?'

'Not for the present. Tommy will manage and I could do with a day off. I'm supposed to be on holiday, remember?'

'You show very little sign of it,' he observed. 'Well, I'd better be going.'

'Where?'

'The hospital. I need to see my client. And with any luck I won't encounter her mother.'

'I'll come, too,' I offered. 'I can distract the raging parents.'

'Corinna,' he said. Then he put up a hand and stroked my cheek, very gently. 'You don't need to, you know.'

'But I am going to,' I said, kissing him.

◇◇◇

I hate hospitals. Worthy places, of course, needed and valued. It's the smell. They smell so clean, so unhuman, with that atmosphere of antiseptic hand cleaner. No smell, in fact, of bread. And the decor is depressing, institution green and cream…

This hospital was made up of an old building married to a new building. You can tell by the floors, which vary slightly according to their composition; old concrete or new concrete. I was trying not to read the signs on the walls when we came into the six-bed ward and saw Lena.

Despair had not treated her well. In complexion she was grey, with a tinge of green. She was connected up to a drip on a stand by the back of one hand, and her eyes were closed.

Sitting beside her was a thin woman in a pink summer suit; impeccably accessorised, well-jewelled, with a Portsea bob and a pair of expensive shoes. Gucci handbag. Oh, dear.

She rose when she saw us and scowled. I took her by the arm.

'A word,' I said. 'I am Corinna Chapman, and I need to talk to you about your daughter.'

'Why?' she snarled.

'Because I have been in her position and I might be able to explain.'

'All right,' she said tightly. 'It's a mystery to me! Why didn't she leave, if they were bullying her? Why didn't she stand up to them? She's always been soft, like her father. I always tried to make her stand on her own two feet. He always just hugged her and told her it would be all right.'

'And her father…' I left the sentence to trail off. She took it as a question.

'Gone,' she snapped. Excellent dentistry. Must have cost a fortune. 'He fell in lust with his assistant and took off. Two years ago. Men! But I wasn't going to let him have the pleasure of seeing me crack.'

'No, of course not,' I murmured, drawing her further away. Daniel had sat down next to Lena and taken her hand. She had opened her eyes and was crying. I could see the light reflected off the trails of tears on her face. So young. I turned my attention to her mother.

'So she never told you anything about work?'

'Just the usual. I have my own business—he didn't get that in the settlement!—and I work long hours. I saw her occasionally. She spent most of her time in her room. She's never been good at making friends. Not even girls from school, and that school cost us a fortune. And of course she's—' she lowered her voice as though about to impart some deep depravity '—fat. I tried. I took her to specialists and sent her to fat camp. Her father always used to feed her chocolates and cream cakes. Junk food. She still eats it when I'm not around to control her.'

I was beginning to dislike this woman. No wonder Lena had been easy to bully. Judgmental, controlling, emotionally distant mother. Missing father. Though I could understand why he had run away. I would have run, too. They tell me Patagonia is nice at this time of year.

'She didn't say a word?' I probed. She didn't even wince.

'Not one word. But she's always been weak. Not like me.'

'No,' I agreed. 'Not like you. Well, I must be going.' I edged away.

Just as I thought I had escaped the mother, in came Tony, the athlete from the night before at Lorca's. He was wearing a suit but he was bouncing in his expensive handmade Italian loafers as though they were Reeboks. I greeted him and he looked at me out of the corners of his eyes, as though a full-size Corinna might be too much for his delicate sensibilities.

'Camilla, is it?' he mumbled. 'What are you…?'

'Just visiting,' I said. 'You?'

'Came to see how our young colleague is,' he said uneasily. 'Of course. We are a caring profession.'

At first I just didn't know what to say to that, then I couldn't say what I wanted to say, so I stood silent and hoped that he should find something organic swimming in his mung beans. Cockroaches, say. Doing breaststroke. He wouldn't get fat-aversion shock from Mrs. Lena, so I unashamedly handed him over to her.

'Your daughter's employer,' I introduced him. 'I'm sure you have a lot to say to each other.'

I left as the lady began on a rant which mentioned 'anti-discrimination law' and 'workplace bullying' in a very satisfactory manner and went over to Lena and Daniel.

'I won't stop looking until I find them,' I heard Daniel say. He patted the girl's hand. On impulse, I leant over and kissed her wet cheek.

'You can live through this,' I told her. 'I know. Been there, done that.'

'You have?' she whispered.

'I have,' I told her. She closed her eyes and almost smiled.

Daniel and I left the Royal Melbourne and started to walk home. It was so good to be out of the hospital and into the street that relief kick-started my mind. I remembered the rest of 'Rain, rain.'

'Let's pick up a taxi,' I urged. 'I've got an idea.'

'Good, because I am all out of ideas,' said Daniel. 'That was kind of you.'

'It was nothing,' I told him. The taxi started in the direction of the art gallery to a merry litany from the driver on how dreadful it was to follow his profession. I listened respectfully because he was right. Taxi-driving is dangerous in the same way as being a prostitute is dangerous. No choice of clients and out on the street late at night. We wished him well in his media studies course and disembarked.

'Well?' asked Daniel. 'Why are we here? Short course on European classical portraits? Actually, that might be rather interesting.'

'Not today. Look at the main window.'

Water,' he said. 'It's a water wall. Always flowing; water on glass. Generations of children have got soaked checking out that it is real wet water. And it is.'

'Rain, rain, go away,' I sang, 'come again some other day. Rain, rain, go to Spain, never show your face again...'

And there was the parchment, swept into a neat pile by a uniformed labourer. He was a little taken aback when we dived on and scattered his pile of old leaves and litter.

'I got lots more,' he offered affably. 'If that floats your boat.'

'Just this one,' Daniel told him. 'Thanks anyway.'

We bought gelati from the van and unfolded the note.

'Oh, no,' groaned my beloved. 'More riddles!'

'*You will find me on Pook's Hill,*' I read. 'Pockets has abandoned nursery rhymes and advanced to Kipling. Puck of Pook's Hill. Wonderful book. Have you read it?'

'Of course. Along with *Just So Stories, Rewards and Fairies, Kim* and *Stalky and Co.*—a rather unnerving collection, by the way. Do you have a copy?'

'Naturally. Come on home, and we shall have a light lunch, a rest, and Kipling. What could be better?'

'I keep thinking about that poor girl,' confessed Daniel. 'Her despair. How she must have felt to do such a dreadful thing.'

'I know you do,' I said and stroked his cheek.

'When you told her you had been there and done that, did you mean...?'

'Not suicide, no, not as such. But I thought about it,' I told him. 'I thought about it a lot. I was a lowly apprentice baker, and the boss was a darling, but his son—I still have nightmares about George. Though rarely,' I assured him. It is easier to impart biographical details when eating lemon gelato, I found. I had never spoken to Daniel about this. Or anyone, really. I took a sustaining lick and went on. 'George hated me because Papa liked me. He's taken over that bakery now, I hear. That's what he always wanted. He tormented me. He was powerful. Like Lena, I had an ambition. I wanted to be a baker more than anything. He would sabotage my recipes, put salt in my yeast cultures, fill my shoes with flour. He never went past me without a pinch or a tweak or a grab at a breast. There was nothing I could do about him. Papa would have believed me but George would have got me. He had powerful friends, he said; I should expect my grandparents to be tortured and killed if I crossed him. He might have done it, too, it might have been true...I have never felt so powerless.'

'So how did you survive?' asked Daniel, slinging an arm around my shoulders and hugging me.

'I had a profession already. I had other places to be. I was older, already at university. Lena is young, has no family support, and only one thing she wants to be. She's trapped.'

'Not anymore,' said Daniel.

'Yes, I don't think that mother is going to let Mason's off with a reprimand. A cheering thought,' I said.

I ate the rest of the gelato. I felt oddly light. We collected a bento box—tori teriyaki, food of the gods, and sashimi for Daniel—and walked home to eat it and read *Puck of Pook's Hill*. An enchanting prospect.

It was, too. Apart from the inevitable feline contingent who just knew that sashimi was designed by Basht to provide an essential food supplement for cats. Daniel did manage to get three-quarters of the delightful fish for himself. The cats got one piece each. Horatio ate his delicately, seeming to pause to murmur 'From the Antarctic shoals, very acceptable,' while the Mouse Police scoffed theirs with gusto and then polished their whiskers in case there might be a scrap left. To massed purring we completed our lunch and got down the book.

Puck of Pook's Hill was first published in 1906 and was written for the author's children. I had visited Bateman's, his house, and reading *Puck* now, I could easily envisage the places. This added to our delight. I found that Daniel had been to Bateman's too.

From the very moment that the children observed a 'small, brown, broad-shouldered, pointy-eared person with a snub nose, slanting blue eyes and a grin that ran right across his freckled face', the story caught and held the attention. We read through the book in the course of the afternoon, pausing only for tea and scones (we felt Dan and Una would have appreciated this) and occasional breaks for stretching. I wondered how Daniel— citizen of Israel—would react to Kipling's Kadmiel, but he was not affronted. 'Those were the bad old days,' he told me. 'With Kipling, you can always say that he wrote as he found. Like John Buchan. But Kipling was wrong about gorillas,' he added. 'He must have been reading Du Chaillu. It's a lot easier to write travel books if you don't actually have to travel.'

'Just ask Sir John Mandeville,' I agreed.

It was a lovely day. But it took us no closer to deciphering the clue which Pockets had left. Where was there a depiction of Puck in Melbourne? I could not think of a statue which might even approximate it.

Just as we were thinking about dinner, the doorbell sounded. Meroe looked surprised to see me.

'Oh, Corinna, I didn't think you'd be home,' she said. Today's wrap was bright red, always an ominous sign. 'I would like you to deliver these to the girls, if you don't mind.' She thrust a wrapped package into my hands. 'Apparently their part requires them to smoke, and I don't want them started on cigarettes. These are herbal and they smell very sweet.'

I invited her in. She flopped down beside Horatio and ran her hands distractedly through her long, coarse black hair.

'Tea?' asked Daniel.

She nodded. He picked up one of her hands in passing and commented, 'You've been in combat?'

Her knuckles were skinned and bleeding.

'Just a little contretemps outside my shop,' she answered. 'Some boys were tormenting a poor old homeless man. I had to be quite firm with them. Fortunately the point police officer saw it all. He came along just as they were trying to be quite menacing, and swept them all up. He seemed amused.'

Daniel provided tea and I provided Betadine and Meroe allowed our attentions.

'But, Meroe, weren't you scared?' I asked.

'No,' she said. 'When you've been bullied as much as I have you cannot stand by and watch someone else being bullied; the Goddess would not expect it. And although I am firmly committed to pacifism, there are times when a right hook can solve many problems.'

'True, true,' agreed Daniel, also much amused. 'Sometimes you have to make the offenders sorry; they gain merit by repenting their actions.'

'I bet they've gained merit, then,' I said.

Meroe is thin and not young, but she's strong. And righteous rage can add strength to anyone. Spiritually aware Meroe in the zone could probably bench press a Volkswagen. Those little thugs would now know the meaning of pain, all right. I repressed an urge to cheer.

'Who bullied you, Meroe?' I asked. She sipped at her Earl Grey.

'Everyone,' she said flatly. 'I was a gypsy. Daniel knows what I mean, don't you, Daniel?'

'Oh yes,' he nodded. 'Watch every shadow, examine every word before it comes out of your mouth. In case it gives offence. In case the bully is heavily armed.'

'Whereas at school I worked out a method,' I said.

'Really?'

'Yes, once they forced me to do their maths homework, I had them by the short and curlies. So I employed one bully to protect me from the other bullies.'

'Ingenious. That's why Kadmiel's people lent money to the king,' said Daniel.

'It worked all right at school. Didn't save me from George, though.'

'It all depends on the nature of the bully,' Meroe advised.

'That's true,' agreed Daniel. 'I had a friend who was in Ravensbrück, darling woman, and when a Nazi hit her, she asked "Why did you hit me?" And then he hit her again, snarling, "Because you asked me why." Under those circumstances there is nothing to be done but try to trust in God.'

This was becoming a little bleak for a summer afternoon. Meroe must have thought so, too, because she saw the copy of the book and said, '*Puck*? Why are you reading folklore, Corinna?'

'It's a book of stories for children which seems to relate to our treasure hunt.' I explained about Pockets and his documents.

'He has other names,' said Meroe. 'Robin Goodfellow, for example. I always thought that Ariel was a Puck figure. I shall think about it,' she added. 'Thanks for the tea.'

We farewelled Meroe and went to bed. I was shaken and in need of comfort and so was Daniel. We proved, in our flesh, that the world still contained delight. And hope.

Chapter Ten

Food and sex—such reliable pleasures. By the time we had risen, cooked pasta for dinner and discussed a couple of glasses of chateau collapseau, we were relaxed and able to think and then, of course, we thought of it. Puck. Of course. Not Kipling's Puck but Shakespeare's Puck. 'I'll put a girdle round about the earth.' Not a statue but a mosaic. It was the work of a few moments to hustle into clothes and zoom down the elevator en route for Collins Street.

The peons were going home as we shoved against a tide of people, all connected to iPods or talking on mobile phones, all as unresponsive as that boy in *Woke Up Dead*. Above the street rose Ariel the Spirit from *The Tempest*, or was he Mercury? And the slogan, 'I'll put a girdle round about the earth.' Very impressive. Daniel found the parchment in the ironwork of a street tree. This time I was stumped.

'*Old Mother Hubbard*,' I read. I recited the rest to Daniel on the way home.

'"Old Mother Hubbard, she went to her cupboard to fetch her poor doggie a bone. When she got there, the cupboard was bare, and so the poor doggie got none."'

'Sounds political,' said Daniel. 'Any ideas?'

'No so much as a skerrick of an idea,' I confessed.

'Sufficient unto the day,' he said, 'is the brilliance thereof. What would I do without you?'

'With any luck,' I told him, 'you won't ever have to find that out.'

Then he created a traffic hazard by stopping and kissing me, in the middle of the street. The passers-by were not impressed and we were advised to find a room.

So we did. Luckily, it wasn't far away.

We passed the evening pleasantly and Daniel went out into the hot darkness to follow Pockets. I put self and cat to bed and slept like a baby. Or perhaps a kitten. When kittens nap, they nap completely.

◇◇◇

Morning announced itself in the usual way and I rose and did all the usual things. Bernie arrived and we began to bake bread and cakes; muffins and cupcakes of all kinds and stripes, which had to be done quickly because they had to be cool before Bernie could ice them. I shamelessly handed over the decoration. I have never had much patience with icing. I wasn't any good at art class, either. And sugar is a difficult medium. When it doesn't glaze, it crumbles.

Still, it tastes nice. I watched Bernie as she whipped fine sugar into egg whites. She was cool and efficient and her very clean hands moved with assurance. Yet she was so young! I was still dropping things at that age. She caught my glance.

'Something wrong?' she asked diffidently.

'No, you are doing it right,' I replied. 'What have you in mind for the cupcakes?'

'I made a lot of roses,' she replied. I had wondered what those white cardboard trays contained. 'They're easy, really. I can show you if you like.'

'Thanks for the offer, but I don't get on with icing. Pity Jason isn't here, he'd love to make flowers for his muffins.'

'Your apprentice?'

'Yes, he's magic with muffins. But he's on holiday. And, I hope, having a good time. He says he has a part-time job as a short-order cook.'

'I've done that,' said Bernie grimly. 'It's not cooking as we know it.'

'So I've gathered. Tell me, how did yesterday go?'

'All right, except for the bust-up.'

'Which was?'

'It wasn't Ethan's fault,' she told me, placing sugar roses onto the shiny glaze with exquisite delicacy.

'I'm sure it wasn't,' I assured her. 'What happened?'

'Wasabi in her lip gloss,' whispered Bernie.

I couldn't help it. I started to laugh. I loathe wasabi. 'But why would anyone think of blaming Ethan?'

'He had a tube of it. He likes hot tastes.' Bernie blushed a pretty rose. 'He brought it along for when we had fish. Then the fish chef went crook when he realised that Ethan was going to put wasabi on his *truite amandine*. So it was a noisy day.' She placed an icing bud exactly on the centre of a cupcake. 'Tommy nearly sacked everyone. I was so scared.'

'I can imagine,' I agreed. Bernie must be spending most of her life on tenterhooks. Employers demand experience, but refuse to risk providing it. Nasty. I realised that I had an authority on what it was like to be young and vulnerable. I started to tell Bernie about Lena. She listened carefully.

'Cruel,' she commented. 'The trouble with bullies is that they pick on the person that no one likes much already. The unattractive ones. The strange ones. They already know that they're out of it. They've already convinced themselves that they're losers.'

'You've seen this?'

'Oh, yes,' she said. 'When I worked in the fast-food world. Not a nice world. I'm glad to be out of it. Corinna, will you give me a reference?'

'A reference?' I had never been asked for such a thing before.

'Yes,' said Bernie, pinkening again. 'To say that I'm all right at cakes. I need references to get a job. And everyone knows you make the best bread in town.'

'Of course,' I said, and seeing her so small and neat and diminished by having to ask, I put an arm around her shoulders and hugged her.

And that moment, of course, was the one that Jason chose to make his re-entry into my world.

He came to the alley door and brushed inside, dropping a backpack on the floor, said, 'Hi, Corinna,' and then stopped dead.

'Jason!' I said, feeling like the classic 'nymph surprised while bathing.' 'How are you? Come in!'

'They told me you'd replaced me,' he said through a hard, thinned mouth. If looks could ignite Bernie would have been a combustion by-product in an eye-blink. 'I didn't believe them. But it's true,' he wailed.

'No, it's not true. This is Bernie, she belongs to Tommy's kitchen. Don't be silly!' I said. In vain. He picked up his pack and stalked out the door. I heard the door of Insula open as he went into the atrium. Thence, I suppose, up to his flat to sulk. Bernie was mortified, almost in tears.

'Oh, Corinna, I'm so sorry,' she wailed in her turn.

I comforted her as best I could.

'Not your fault,' I told her. 'Jason is behaving like a child. Never mind. Let's pack up those cakes carefully. Here comes good old Moon River.'

He was whistling 'Camptown Races' today, as though that made anything better. Doo-dah, doo-dah.

◇◇◇

The kitchen was tense. After yesterday's alarms I suppose that was inevitable. But when I took some scrambled eggs out to the set the cast and crew were all tense as well. Ethan was barricaded away from the rest behind a lot of technological junk. He was, however, eating, which is always a cheering sign. His followers, the crew, sound men, lighting people and so on were with him. On the other side were the actors, pecking at breakfast and sipping at their coffee suspiciously, as though it might be doped with some colourless, odourless South American poison unknown to science. Everyone was glaring at everyone else. It was going to be a long day.

However, there is always food. Tommy inspected Bernie's cakes, thanked me, and was directed to thank Bernie.

'I'm no good at decoration,' I said. 'Bernie did it all. She even brought the sugar roses with her.'

'Well done, Bernie,' said Tommy. Bernie beamed. Well, at least someone was happy.

The fish chef was still furious about the wasabi. The salad makers were sullen. The middle persons were nervous and the underlings apprehensive. I advised Bernie to stick entirely to comments on food and try not to set anyone off. A policy I intended to pursue myself. One thing about working with food is that if you get through the day without any disasters, or no more than the usual number of disasters, then tomorrow really is another (culinary) day.

Besides, I had Jason to think about. The moment when the blood drained out of his tanned face stayed with me. Damn! Now what would he do? Dive back into the world he had previously haunted? The other inhabitants of Insula would not allow a drug addict to continue to live in his grace-and-favour apartment. He would be back on the streets, fed only by the Soup Run, prey to all the monsters who lurked in the shadows. My Jason, who had been doing so well!

Equally, I was extremely annoyed with him, and yearned to clip him over the ear for being silly. I was uncomfortable with all this emotion and not likely to be patient with any more foolishness, so I inwardly groaned when Tash came into the kitchen and leant on my pastry board.

'You heard what happened?' she asked, looking like a milkmaid who has just been kicked by her favourite Jersey.

'I heard.' Several people had told me apart from Bernie. Tash crossed her arms under her considerable bosom.

'Ethan says your partner's a detective,' she began.

'That's true,' I acknowledged. I was cutting bread and I had a large knife, sharpened to a streak, and I was not afraid to use it. Tash watched me a little nervously, as one should always watch people with long, sharp knives.

'Do you think he might be able to find out who's doing this?' she asked diffidently. 'I mean, everyone thinks it's Ethan, but

I really can't see how he could have got into Ms. Atkins' dressing room. She keeps it locked now and she's got the only key. It must have been someone who came in while she was there and I can't see Ethan dropping in to wish her well, can you?'

'No,' I said. Ethan might wish Ms. Atkins many things, but well was not one of them. 'You'll have to find Daniel some sort of job,' I suggested.

'We can do that,' she told me. 'Lots of hangers-on in TV. Will you ask him?'

'Yes,' I said. 'But he's got several matters on at the moment. Why don't you call the cops?'

Tash gave me a scornful look. 'Now you're being funny,' she said. 'Do me a favour! I'm trying to hold together two disparate elements and out of it might come a good series which will make us all rich. Bad publicity and we are right down the gurgler with a lot of other successful Australian series. The crew are solid with Ethan. The actors are with Ms. Atkins—however reluctantly. They've polarised. You can see the problem.'

I could see it, so I nodded. She took a cupcake as a pretext for her visit and stalked away. Still, the cupcake would taste good, as pretexts go. I had just been reading a book about D-day. There were similarities.

Thanking the Goddess that I was not attacking a defended beach under cover of daylight, I continued to make fruit scones, which were required for lunch. When they were in the oven I went looking for the girls, with Meroe's package of inoffensive weeds in hand.

I found them nibbling bacon, lettuce and tomato sandwiches. I delivered the herbal cigarettes in silence. They were the cause of Jason losing his faith in Earthly Delights. And me. I was still angry with them. However, since I was now an investigator, I need to talk to them.

'You heard what happened yesterday?' I asked.

'Like, Corinna, how could we not?' asked Goss. 'She came rushing out of her dressing room screaming. It was terrible.'

'Any idea who did it?' I asked.

'Well…' Kylie hastily filled her mouth with bacon so as to muffle her answer. She pointed her chin in the direction of the film crew.

'Ethan?' I asked, and they both nodded.

'Why would he sabotage his own job?' I asked.

They both goggled at me.

'Come on, think,' I urged. 'If this continues Tash will lose backers and have to call the whole thing off. That would be bad for Ethan, too.'

'He likes practical jokes,' said Kylie. 'And…'

'He doesn't like Ms. Atkins,' concluded Goss.

'On set,' announced Tash, and they squeaked and fled.

Well, that was helpful. I looked at the plate that Goss had thrust into my hand. Bacon, lettuce and tomato. Yum.

I ate it. I had just finished when Tommy grabbed me and hissed, 'Come into the kitchen!' I complied ungracefully. Anyone who seriously annoyed me today was cruisin' for a bruisin'. That included Tommy, who had got me into this. She must have divined something from my expression because she let me go and spoke softly.

'What are we going to do?' she asked.

'What do you mean "we," white man?' I capped the old joke. She didn't laugh. 'This isn't my problem. It isn't even yours, in fact.'

'Yes, it is. They're using our condiments.'

'That was your wasabi? How on earth do you know?'

'From the taste,' Tommy said. I could not imagine gradations of savour in that searing stuff but apparently it was so. 'We mix it with sake. The stuff in the tube isn't mixed with sake. So we can tell that this wasabi was ours.'

'Where's it kept?'

'In the condiment cupboard. Open shelves. Anyone could have taken some.'

'Then we shall have to wait for another incident,' I said.

'Maybe there won't be another incident,' she said, more in hope than in confidence.

'Maybe. But why not thin down the suspect list by closing the kitchen to everyone except the staff?'

'I'll think about it,' she said, and went away to soothe the fish chef, who was declaring that he could walk into a job at Vue de Monde and was thinking of applying.

Nothing more to do except bake. I set out the ingredients for my chocolate cake as Bernie began to bake savoury muffins for the variety of cold soups to be offered. Gazpacho, *potage bonne femme*, avocado and cold beef consomme. The perfect accompaniment would be the zucchini and parmesan muffins which Bernie was mixing. She did make a very good muffin.

'I'm so sorry about Jason, Corinna,' she said to me. 'But if he stays away, would you consider…'

I was about to say something sharp to this neat opportunist, but changed my mind. She was very young.

'I thought you didn't want to be a baker,' I finally announced. 'Only someone who really, really wants to be a baker can work with me.'

'And only then if their name is Jason?' she asked. There was an edge to her voice.

'Probably,' I conceded. 'I never wanted an apprentice, anyway. Jason happened.' I set the electric mixer going. That abolished any further attempts at persuasion.

It was an anxious kitchen and that produces accidents. Flour was spilled, fingers were cut, pots were dropped. Each incident magnified the tension. By the time that breakfast had been cleared away and all my cakes were cooked and cooling, waiting for Bernie's attentions, I was glad to slip into the studio, find a chair, and watch the actors. They were nervous too, but that is standard for actors.

They were shooting a scene where a bride in full wedding gear rushes into the office of *Kiss the Bride*, protesting hysterically about her dress, immediately followed by a dressmaker protesting hysterically about the client. This probably happens often enough in the real world. If you only have one chance to portray yourself as beautiful, the hysteria quotient must skyrocket.

Everything that could possibly go wrong with the rehearsal did. If the lighting was right, the sound was wrong. If the positioning was correct, the camera angles were faulty. And the flyaway veil of the putative bride kept getting caught in things: scenery, doors, Kylie's spiky hair. They played the scene over and over sixteen times before Tash called a halt.

'Get a coffee and grab a break,' she told them wearily. 'I have to think about this.'

She retired to her corner with the laptop and the cast spread out toward the kitchen, where morning tea was being provided. Those cakes looked superb. The crew went into a huddle with Ethan. I heard the sound man talking about 'fuzz.' That was apparently a bad thing, though I associated it with blankets. Kylie and Goss, having collected a big slice of cake each, appeared at my side.

'Corinna! Did you make this yummy stuff?' asked Goss.

'Yes, it's a Greek recipe made with semolina. Do you like it?'

'Mmm,' said Kylie. 'It's so…orangey.'

'It's soaked in orange syrup,' I told her. 'What's wrong with everyone this morning?'

'You noticed, huh? We're scared. We really need this job. And someone is trying to kill off the series.'

'Those tricks? Are they that serious?' I asked.

'Deadly serious,' Goss told me. 'Harrison says that the website was hacked and the profiles changed. And there was the lip gloss yesterday and the chili oil and all the other things. The shoes. I'm scared,' she confessed, leaning on my arm. Kylie leant on my other arm.

'Tash has asked Daniel to investigate,' I told them. The thin little faces lit up.

'Wicked!' exclaimed Kylie. 'Well, that's made me feel better.'

It had, too. Both of them had relaxed. I must remember to tell Daniel how much confidence he engendered.

I was watching the girls nibble semolina cake when Harrison slid into the seat beside Kylie and smiled his angelic smile. He also had a plate, though he had chosen one of Bernie's chocolate cupcakes. A good choice. I told him so.

'Have to watch my weight,' he said. 'But occasionally a little of what you fancy does you good.'

Since he was as lissom as a Greek statue, I didn't think that he had a problem. I still could not believe how beautiful he was. Kylie and Goss were drinking in his profile, and I saw Goss's hand twitch, as though she longed to run her fingers through his Byronic hair.

'Well, well, not happy girls and boys today,' he commented. 'How are you, Corinna? At least you aren't involved in all this...' He waved a long-fingered hand at the clumps of people drinking tea and gossiping in low, stressed voices.

I bit back a retort that my apprentice, Jason, had created an emotional firestorm in my bakery to the detriment of everyone. Harrison could not help it.

'The kitchen's pretty jumpy, too,' I said. 'Things are tough all over.'

'True, true,' he sighed, like an angel mourning the frailty of humanity.

'But I've heard that we're going to be investigated,' he breathed. Both Kylie and Goss gave me indignant looks. It wasn't us, they conveyed. We didn't say a word. How could you think that of us?

And I didn't, because they had been authentically surprised when I announced Daniel's advent. Harrison was getting his information elsewhere, probably from overhearing Tash. He lowered his voice further so that we had to bend down to hear him.

'Apparently he's a very toothsome item,' he said. 'I've got some friends in the business. Never fails, they say.'

I was delighted that Daniel had such a good reputation. This investigation might comfort him for failing to nail Pockets' depository.

'Good,' I said.

'But the thing is, no one must know,' said Harrison. 'If the mags get hold of this then the backers will hear and the money will get up and walk away. So not a word,' he admonished. Kylie and Goss nodded emphatically. I added my nod, and the three of them departed toward the stage as Tash emerged from her conference and called, 'On set!'

I took up the crumb-laden plates and moved toward the kitchen, just as the hysterical bride rushed into the office and declaimed her piece again.

'It's tight in all the wrong places! It makes me look like Kath out of *Kath and Kim*! I hate it!'

This time, when the veil caught in the scenery, Ethan kept filming. The sound man gave him a thumbs-up. The lighting man grinned. The designer started a counterpoint with the bride. 'She's put on weight! She changed her specifications! She won't listen to advice! She's got no taste! I mean, bright white with that complexion? Should have been ivory, maybe with a hint of rose!' Kylie pouted, Goss looked serious, the girl dressed as Tank Girl tapped on her computer console, Harrison sauntered through the set in his bicycle shorts looking ravishing.

And it all went swimmingly. By the time Ms. Atkins emerged from her office to snub all and sundry, dominating the set as always, the scene had been completed and was perfect. The mood of the set changed. Everyone was smiling. Tash was mopping her brow. She said 'Cut!' and there was an outburst of applause.

'Ethan?' she asked.

Ethan collected opinions. Everyone was agreed. This scene, which would occupy perhaps three minutes and had taken all day yesterday and half of today to film, was fine with everyone.

'Okay,' Ethan pronounced.

It was as though they had been offered a reprieve from death. Intoxicated with joy, they rushed the refreshments.

I went back through the kitchen door into a world with which I was familiar. The ones beyond it were very, very strange. Stranger than the ones encountered by falling down a rabbit-hole or walking through a magic mirror.

Tommy was standing in the middle of the floor, clipboard in hand, ticking off people and ingredients and tasks.

'Bernie, icing sugar?'

'Need more,' said Bernie. Tommy wrote that down.

'Pete?'

'More cream,' said Pete. 'Puy lentils, lemons, olive oil—extra virgin, if you please—sea salt.'

'Got them,' said Tommy. 'Who's doing salads?'

'You want to get on to that organic greengrocer,' said Lance the Lettuce Guy, ordinarily a laconic individual. 'Tomatoes were overripe, only fit for sauce. Too much grit in the leeks. Pulpy oranges. Green melons.'

'Check,' said Tommy.

I realised that I had better get to my station, read tomorrow's menu and check my own stores. I hurried across and consulted the list. Tommy carried on.

'Fish?' she asked. The fish chef was still angry.

'The fillets today were a disgrace,' he snarled. 'Had to debone them myself. And messy. I wasted a lot getting them fit to serve. It would be easier to get me an assistant and buy whole fish.'

'I'll think about it,' Tommy promised. I knew what that meant and so did the fish chef. He scowled and put in a spiteful order for Maldon salt. Very expensive and I can't tell the difference between it and ordinary sea salt. But my tastebuds are not very discriminating.

The list asked me for various breads—I was using my own flour, so I didn't need to order it from Tommy—and cakes. By the time the interrogation arrived at baking I had checked the stores and had nothing to request.

The meeting went on and I diverted my mind from Jason by thinking about Pockets' clue. 'Old Mother Hubbard.' I had a feeling that this was one of the nursery rhymes which actually had an author. The rhyme had a nineteenth-century feel to it. In the good old days one had all one's foodstuffs locked up in various cupboards. The lady of the house wore the keys on a chain around her waist, which would have had the valuable side effect of warning the maids that she was coming. All they had to do was listen for the jingle. In those pre-refrigeration days I suppose one could keep a bone in a cupboard. I recalled the meat safes of colonial days and shuddered. How anyone had thrived then I could not imagine.

Tommy concluded her work and put her clipboard under her arm. I surveyed the pastry corner and saw that all the cakes were immaculately iced, filled and decorated.

'Good job, Bernie,' I said. When Tommy came into view I told her, 'Have a look at this display! Wouldn't disgrace a Parisian pastry chef's window. Aren't they pretty?'

'Yes, nice work, Corinna,' she said.

'It was Bernie,' I said. Bernie glowed.

'Nice,' said Tommy. 'Petits fours tomorrow; better get started on them early.'

Tommy moved on. Bernie reached up to the cookbook shelf for the standard work on petits fours, and I untied my apron.

'That was high praise, coming from Tommy,' I told Bernie.

'I know,' she replied.

I took my leave. I always felt a great sense of relief on opening the street door and getting out of Harbour Studios. Maybe I should have taken that holiday when it was offered. The sun hit me and I fumbled for my sunglasses.

Daniel was there. He had a satchel and a smile.

'Corinna! I was just coming to see Ms. Atkins,' he said.

'Oh Lord,' I groaned. 'Back inside, then.'

'Is this a bad time?'

'I don't think that TV studios have a good time,' I replied. 'Tash wants you to find out who is playing all these tricks. Someone hacked into the website last night and recaptioned all the pictures. It's getting beyond a joke. This is sabotage.'

'And a cast of hundreds for suspects,' said Daniel. 'I was coming to see Ms. Atkins about this baby.'

'So there really was a baby?'

'Indeed there was. Born August the eighth, 1988. A boy named Zephaniah.'

'Well, that's one thing about him that will have changed,' I commented as I opened the doors again.

'What?' asked Daniel.

'His name,' I said confidently.

But I was not confident as I led the way through the kitchen. This was too large a group of people for anyone to analyse. As Dylan would have said, too much confusion.

Chapter Eleven

Ethan caught sight of Daniel and beckoned him over to the refreshments table. Daniel did that male thing which excludes speech. He jerked his chin in the direction of Tash and kept walking. I assume that it meant 'hello, mate, nice to see you, but can't talk just now.' It's a sort of shorthand. Women have to use words. I suppose it's evolutionary. One cannot pause for social niceties while tracking the megafauna across the Pleistocene plains. I followed. I was interested.

Tash was talking to the writers, Gordon and Kendall (today's dreads were dyed orange). She sighted me and made some excuse.

The writers moved a little distance away, ears flapping, and Tash took Daniel's hands. I introduced him. Then I joined the writers. I, too, wanted to hear what was said.

Tash gave Daniel a fast, accurate run-down of everything that had happened. It included some things which I had not known—dry mustard in the face powder, for example—and all the incidents of which I was already aware. Then she said, 'It's a very volatile situation. I don't want to call in the police. They wouldn't take it seriously—no one's been hurt—and the backers would have to hear about it then. I need to find this joker and shut him or her down. Can you do it?'

'Well, gang, it looks like we've got another mystery on our hands,' said Daniel, quoting *Scooby-Doo*, a series that he watches whenever he can. 'I can try,' he said to Tash, who had recognised the reference and grinned. 'No point in trying to put me in undercover. What say I just wander around and talk to everyone? Knowing that I am here might suppress the joker, even if I can't locate him. Or her. Or them. None of these tricks needed great physical strength to carry out. Could be anyone.'

'I am not asking for guarantees,' said Tash. Her milkmaid complexion had paled, and she looked like someone had just reported mastitis in her herd. 'You're my only hope,' she told Daniel. And, as Princess Leia had found before her, this is an appeal which never fails. Daniel shook hands on the deal.

'Wow,' breathed Kendall. 'He's gorgeous! Is he in the business?'

'No,' I said firmly.

'Pity,' he said. 'I can see him as a lone avenger, can't you, Gord? A solitary hunter? Vampires, maybe?'

'Vampires are a bit, you know, old,' said Gordon. Her expression conveyed outmoded, old-fashioned, positively archaic. 'Modern police drama? Or he'd make a great PI.'

'He *is* a PI.' I told her. 'Shush, I want to hear…'

'Oh, so do we,' said Kendall. 'This'll make a wonderful script.'

Writers. Worse, almost, than actors. What was Daniel about to do now, and could I help? I wondered, because there was a burning pain in my middle which was called Jason and I wanted to divert my mind. I raised an eyebrow to him; he nodded in the direction of the kitchen, and then went toward Ethan and his collective. I sighed. I had nothing further to do in the food department, but perhaps I could help someone, and do a little light snooping.

I paused in the middle of the floor to locate the area of greatest angst. Bernie was creating icing. Tommy was typing into her laptop. The salad makers were chopping furiously. Fish appeared to be sulking while Meat was turning out a terrine and did not need to be interrupted. I stood beside Tommy and said, 'Daniel's been employed to find out who is playing tricks,' and she jumped a foot at the sound of my voice and nearly dropped the laptop.

'Corinna? That's good. That's very good.'

'What are you doing and can I help?' I asked.

'I'm designing a wedding feast for the writers,' she said. 'They need to do an episode with a caterer and they want some expert advice.'

'And you are certainly an expert,' I said. 'You must have done a lot of weddings.'

'Some,' she conceded. 'Mostly big society ones—you know: "The bride wore a fifteen-thousand-dollar gown designed by Dior." I can't imagine paying that much for a dress, can you?'

'No,' I seconded. 'If I had fifteen thousand dollars there's a lot of other things I would buy. I could really do with a new mixer and a few renovations to Earthly Delights. And there are always books. You?'

'Need a new oven,' she grunted. 'But Jules loves clothes. Not to that extent, however. She's more Scally and Trombone than Chanel. Boutique, you know. Would you serve a prawn roulade with spinach?'

'Certainly. A salad of baby spinach, or a bed of wilted spinach dressed with lemon and oil. And herbs. Or perhaps throw in a few bean shoots and dress it with lime juice, soy, Vietnamese mint and sesame seeds, Asian style.'

'Nice,' she said, and typed busily. 'I usually offer a main of duck breast, alternatively sea perch, and the vegetarian option would be eggplant with tomato and pine nut stuffing. The Greeks call them "little shoes." They're really tasty. Poor veggies have trouble getting enough to eat. Or there's the salad of Puy lentils. That's very nice, too. And ice creams, sorbets and pannacotta for dessert. You have to cater for all appetites at a wedding, and there are always children. And I refuse,' she drew herself up, balancing the laptop perilously on her knee, 'to serve chips, frites, or anything similar. Let the parents take them to the junk food maker of their choice on the way home if they must.'

'As you say,' I said, sidling away. Fanaticism comes in many forms.

Luckily, Lance the Lettuce chose that moment to call for volunteers to chop carrots, and I was able to find myself a job.

Root vegetables are not fun to slice, because they are irregular in shape (someone, somewhere, is probably working on a GM square carrot). I equipped myself with my nice knife and joined the choppers at their long table.

'Corinna,' I introduced myself. The large man in an overall stained with the blood of a thousand vegetables thrust a bag of carrots in my direction and grunted, 'Slices half a centimetre thick, peel them carefully.'

'Don't be annoyed,' whispered Kate, next to me. 'He's had a bad day. Sub-standard veg all round, from depressed lettuce to wormy apples. Here's your peeler.'

I started on the carrots. Kate was in the mood to chat.

'They say that Tash has brought in a detective,' she said. 'To find the joker.'

'That's right,' I affirmed.

'I hope he finds him quick. The atmosphere is getting on my nerves.' She dropped a handful of peel into the compost bin.

'Mine too,' I said. 'And I'm just a contractor. It must be worse if you're crew.'

'Oh, it is. We've mostly been with Tommy since she started out. She's a good thing. Good wages, good conditions, interesting work—always different. It was a bit of a coup that she got this contract. But you've noticed that this bastard uses our things for his jokes. Our wasabi, our mustard, chili oil—condiments. We have them all in this kitchen.'

'I noticed,' I said, peeling carefully. Lance did not strike me as a chef who would be lenient with error. If he said half a centimetre he would mean half a centimetre, and might even measure it. 'But anyone could walk in here. Who do you think it might be?'

'Could be anyone,' she shrugged, which did not impede her chopping at all. 'Actors are all mad. I never met such people.'

'So you think that someone is out to get Tommy?' I asked. I had not thought of this before.

Kate shrugged again. 'She's made a few enemies,' she admitted. 'Some of her rivals don't appreciate her being a lesbian. You can annoy some people just by existing.'

'And that's true,' I agreed. We chopped on in silence. I thought about it. Tommy was a strong personality and did not endure fools with any tolerance. She had always been like that. Her catering venture, Maîtresse, had been very successful in a fairly short time. She must have trodden on a few toes while rising to such eminence that she routinely catered celebrity weddings. Actually, knowing Tommy, she had probably stomped on a few faces on the way up the catering ladder. Would losing this contract have such a bad effect on the company?

Of course it would, I thought as I reached for another carrot. No one would risk their wedding to a company that had a trickster. I had not previously appreciated how very important weddings were to some people.

Carrots completed, I looked around for another task. I could not lounge around in a kitchen. If you're not working, someone will be offended. And find you a really ghastly job, like scrubbing roasting dishes. Luckily Lance came to my rescue with a lot of tomatoes to skin and deseed. I prepared my bowls for boiling water and ice water.

'You're right about the produce,' I noted, prodding a tomato. 'Pulpy and overripe.'

'I told her,' he said through his teeth. 'That greengrocer may be organic but organic shouldn't mean shitty merchandise. Those potatoes were half their weight in worms and soil.'

'I'm sure she'll fix it.' I tried to be soothing.

'That's our Tommy,' he assented. 'They'll know they've been in a fight, all right. But for the present we have to do the best we can with what we've got. For a baker, you slice quite a good carrot,' he added.

'Have you been with Tommy long?'

'Since she was working out of her own kitchen. Now we've got our own premises and we're state of the art,' he told me. 'And I like Tommy. Knows what she wants. High standards. Good luck with those tomatoes,' he said, and went back to stand over the peon who was slicing onions and weeping freely. I remembered being told that weeping was good for the eyes.

This worker was going to be able to see for miles and miles, once she dried her face.

Kate was chatting to the lettuce slicer about the nightlife of Melbourne, in which I had little interest, so I shut up and blanched tomatoes. They were talking about various nightclubs in the city.

'Of course there's always Locomotion,' said the slicer. I had only heard that word in a song by Kylie Minogue, unless someone was talking about steampunk science fiction. I had never gone clubbing. I had never seen the enjoyment in being enclosed in a suffocating mob and deafened. I am, as Goss had once remarked, quite amazingly out of it.

'New one,' said Kate. 'Cupboard. In Collins Street, so you're out of the King Street crush and the bogans don't know about it. It's small and underground. Bit Gothy in theme.'

'What did you say?' I asked excitedly, almost squeezing the life out of a tomato. It squished and slipped its skin obligingly.

'Cupboard,' said Kate, surprised. 'New club. In Collins Street. I've got the card somewhere.' She felt in her pocket and produced one. 'Couple of friends of mine started it. Come along?'

'I might,' I said. Kate considered me for a moment.

'Show the card to the door bitch,' she told me. 'And she'll probably let you in.'

I had not thought of that. One has to pass an inspection before one can be admitted to a club. I had no intention of exposing myself to possible insult. 'Old Mother Hubbard, she went to her cupboard, to fetch her poor doggie a bone,' I said. Kate and Lance looked at me.

'Yeah, right,' said Lettuce Guy. 'What did you think of *Avatar*?' he asked Kate.

Since I did have an opinion on the lack of plot in that movie, we chatted on amicably until all the vegetables were prepared. Then I was at a loose end. Bernie had the baking well in hand and did not need—and would not welcome—my help. Daniel was still wandering round the set, talking to various people. Jason—oh, my Jason…the idiot!—was presumably still sulking in his apartment. I had nothing more to do at Harbour

Studios so I took off my apron and went to tell my partner that I had another clue.

Daniel was talking to the sound people. They were complaining about the difficulties of their profession.

'If it's an outside broadcast, there will be planes flying over, there will be cars, and that will be the moment that the neighbour decides to start up his chainsaw,' said Ali. 'If it's in a studio there will be machine noises, dropped shoes and inconvenient comments. Or coughs, sneezes, farts, belches—humans are very noisy creatures.'

'The life of a sound man is hard,' sympathised Daniel.

'And did I mention electronic interference?' continued Ali, warming to his topic. 'Every person has a mobile phone and a beeper and a pager…'

'Daniel, I'm off, unless you need me,' I inserted into the rave.

Daniel smiled at me and nodded and I slipped away as Ali went on, 'And no matter how many times you tell them to turn the buggers off, there is always someone who forgot or who was waiting for an important phone call…'

I completed my earlier journey and managed to get out into the street without being intercepted. Collins Street, here I come. It was only two in the afternoon, so Cupboard would not be open and I would not have to pass an Exam By Door Bitch.

◇◇◇

I had the greatest difficulty in finding Cupboard. I walked up and down that stretch between Swanson and Bourke several times before I realised I was on the wrong side of the road. Finally I located it between one shop and another; a little barred door which presumably led down a stair to a den of some sort. It was not far from the building with Puck emblazoned above it. There was the parchment, stuck under the door. I pulled it out. Pockets' idiosyncratic handwriting was instantly recognisable.

Three wise men of Gotham, it read. I knew this one and recited it as I headed for home, which presently meant a shower and a gin and tonic, rather stressing the gin, which I felt that I had earnt.

'Three wise men of Gotham, went to sea in a bowl. If the bowl had been stronger, this story would have been longer.' Gotham? Why did I associate that with Batman rather than a rhyme?

Home, hot and tired, I had my shower, put on my loose gown, patted my cat and provided a few treats, fired up the computer and researched Gotham, then took self, cat and esky to the roof garden.

I was clean and comfortable and felt quite good until I saw that the temple of Ceres contained Jason, crumpled into a corner. He looked rough and angry. I sailed in, put Horatio down, and said, 'Hello, Jason,' in as equable a voice as I could manage. 'I'm working on a mystery for Daniel. Want to help?'

'Corinna,' he said. He looked piteously up into my face as I sat down next to him. He had been crying for some time. His eyes were red-rimmed.

'Jason,' I replied.

'How could you?' he choked, and was gone.

Damn again. How was I going to explain to someone who would not stay to be explained to? I might send him an email, I thought. I knew he had a second-hand laptop which the Lone Gunmen had given him as outmoded by several weeks. And we had wireless broadband for the whole building. I doubted that I could express myself well enough in writing to comfort him. But I would try as soon as I finished this drink.

Crossly, I poured myself a stiff gin and sat down to contemplate the wise men of Gotham.

There were a lot of stories about them. Apparently, King John had been about to set up a hunting lodge in their area, which would have been ruinous; huntsmen riding over crops, common land enclosed, winter fodder and wood from the forest cut off. So they behaved like lunatics in front of the King's spies, and he decided that trying to fence in the cuckoo might be catching, and took his hunting lodge elsewhere. Gotham was crazy like the fox. They definitely would have been able to distinguish a hawk from a handsaw, whatever quarter the wind was in. The stories had that odd feel which I had also encountered when Professor Dion read me his translation of Aristophanes. That slippage of humour. Lines that would have had an Ancient Greek audience rolling in the aisles fall flat to a modern audience (i.e., me). Tragedy may last for two thousand years but humour dates quickly. The slapstick Goodies are funnier now than the ground-breaking Monty Python. In my opinion. Anyway, the tales of the wise men of Gotham may have had a medieval audience in stitches around the sooty hearth after their dinner of salt fish and porridge, but they didn't do a thing for me. Though there was something mystic about their valiant attempts to catch the moon reflected in their pond. Presumably the same pond into which they threw the eel, to drown it. Meroe would know.

Oh, Jason! I sniffed into my drink. Horatio hopped up on the bench beside me and gave my hand a lick. I never know if he is trying to be kind or acquiring a taste for human flesh. His tongue was warm and rough. I stroked him. At least someone didn't misjudge me...

Into my temple came two people, loaded down with a picnic basket, and I got up hurriedly.

'No, no, Corinna, do stay,' said Mrs. Dawson graciously. 'Dion and I felt like getting out of our apartments and I suggested a picnic.'

'A good notion,' said the Professor. 'You know, I believe that I am getting old.'

We looked at him. His head had grown through his hair at an early age. He was rosy and sparkling and had certainly not aged in the time that I had known him.

'Really, Dion,' said Mrs. Dawson, pouring him a glass of punch. 'Why do you think that?'

'I thought I saw Jason in the hall,' he said, accepting the glass. 'I spoke to him but he did not reply. I must have been seeing things.'

'You're not getting old,' I said affectionately. 'You'll never grow old! That was indeed Jason, and he is in an almighty snit.'

'Oh, dear. Have some punch. My mother's recipe. Why he is in this state?' asked Mrs. Dawson.

They were both old and wise. I could do with some advice.

'The girls told him that I had replaced him. He is mightily offended and hurt.'

'Oh, those girls, they cause such mischief. It isn't their fault, Corinna, they just don't think. It's this instant communication. Allows no time for considering whether that statement is a wise thing to say. And he was doing so well, too.'

I suppressed a sob and gulped some punch. Champagne and pineapple juice with strawberries and something else—bitters, perhaps? Lime juice? Delicious. Mrs. Dawson was looking censorious and I hoped she might encounter Kylie and Goss before the mood wore off. They deserved a rebuke.

'But Jason has some sense,' commented the Professor. 'I should leave him alone and he'll come home, like Little Bo Peep's sheep.'

'Dragging his tail behind him?' I asked, feeling a little better.

'Just so,' said Professor Dion. He parted a smoked salmon sandwich and gave some of the filling to Horatio, who had been sitting at his side, looking alert and interested, though no well-bred cat would go so far as to beg, like a common mongrel. Horatio accepted the offering and the Professor ate the rest of the sandwich. Horatio dotes on smoked salmon. So does Nox, the Professor's little black cat, which possibly explained why she had not joined us at this picnic.

'So you don't think I should pin him down and forcibly explain to him?' I asked cravenly. I had been thinking that this was the honourable course and dreading it.

'No, Jason knows all about force. It would not have a good effect. In my opinion,' counselled Mrs. Dawson. 'Have a cucumber sandwich, Corinna. How goes the TV studio?'

'Oh, strange,' I said, and explained about the crew, the actors and the tricks. And ate the sandwich. Horatio scored another slice of smoked salmon. I followed up with an exposition of Pockets and the nursery rhymes.

'Well, well,' said the professor. 'You have been having a difficult time! Three Wise Men of Gotham…I haven't thought about them for years. Eh, Mrs. D?'

'Holy fools,' said Mrs. Dawson. 'I sat next to a folklorist at an embassy dinner once—Madras, I think—and heard all about it. Far too much about it, actually, but the alternative was nuclear physics on my other side and I have never had a scientific mind. Yes, I recall that he was fascinated with the concept. The Christian equivalent is St. Francis of Assisi, who actually called himself "God's Fool", bless his heart. Meroe would know more. There is a tarot card called the fool, I believe.'

'Standing on the edge of a precipice, while a little dog tears his trousers. The body trying to communicate with the soul. Jung talked about him,' said the Professor, investigating another sandwich. 'No, my dear chap, you may not have any more salmon. It will spoil your dinner,' he said to Horatio. Horatio accepted this and jumped down. Time for me to depart.

'Thank you so much,' I said to my elderly advisers. 'If Jason should ask you for advice, please tell him that I am happy to have him back if he wants to come.'

'We'll tell him,' they assured me.

I left them sitting side by side on the bench, sharing champagne punch and sandwiches. It might not be so bad, getting old. I collected Horatio and the esky and took my leave. It might have been the punch, but I felt comforted.

Back in the apartment, Horatio went to the couch for his after-walk snooze, and I went to the computer. Holy fools. Would Pockets have known this? Did we have a church of St. Francis in the city? Yes. Lonsdale Street. Aha. That little island of peace opposite all the motorbike shops in Elizabeth Street and the bulk of Melbourne Central shopping centre. It was a long shot, but Daniel had not returned and I was feeling restless. A nice walk with a purpose might be just what I needed.

I left Horatio asleep and let myself out into the street. It was hot and still, that drowsy sort of weather which presages storm. It also presages sweat. I would be dripping by the time I got back. I adjusted my straw hat and hefted my bag. I might drop in at Uncle Solly's New York Deli. I didn't feel like cooking tonight.

I strolled along Elizabeth Street. It was now late afternoon and people were going home, dodging the sun by crowding the shade. I was carrying my own shade with me. My passage was unobstructed.

This part of Elizabeth Street is notable for large motorbikes and larger men with black T shirts and beards that a possum could nest in. Actually I have never examined a bikie's beard for wildlife. He mightn't like it. The air was alive with petrol fumes.

Across the road was the green space surrounding an unassuming little church dedicated to, yes, St. Francis of Assisi, and there was his statue. How this had hidden from the extensive ruination of the city during the sixties I could not imagine. It was a survivor, like Insula. I searched diligently around the base of the statue. No parchment. No papers or litter at all. I wondered where they dumped their sweepings. In a nearby bin, I hoped. I drifted over to said bin and looked inside. Wrappings from fast food, cigarette butts, a pair of sneakers—what sort of story was behind that? They didn't even look worn.

'Looking for something?' It was a *Big Issue* seller. He seemed amused. This was, of course, his corner.

'Yes, a piece of paper,' I told him. I approve of the *Big Issue*. Gives the long-term unemployed a profession and dignity and also, of course, money. To spend on dinner and shelter. This was a youngish man with black curly hair and an affable grin.

'Worth something to you?' he bargained.

'Five dollars. Ten, because I haven't bought a copy of the magazine this month,' I told him. 'Is this where they put the rubbish from St. Francis's?'

'Sure is. What is it? Clue to buried treasure?'

'Sort of.' A reply of which the girls might have been proud.

'Well, I been here since sparrow fart, and the sweeper comes past every hour. Old bloke. Says that people bring things to the church to throw them away just to annoy him. And the derros hang around here. The lawns are nice and flat to lie down on when the grog's got you.'

'Yes,' I said, encouragingly.

'Well, one of them was very careful to put this where someone might see it. I saw it and got it. Twenty, I think you said?'

'Ten,' I insisted. He was waving a piece of parchment. 'Going to split it with Pockets?' I asked, producing the bill.

'Oh, you know 'im? Nah,' he said, taking the money and giving me the paper and a copy of the magazine. 'Can't. After leaving the paper poor old Pockets was picked up by the constabulary for lying down in front of a tram, and they took the poor bugger away. 'Bout six this morning. Sister Mary was here.'

'Soup Run? Of course, she is a Franciscan nun.'

'You know Sister Mary?'

'Yes, I do the bread for the Soup Run.'

'Jeez,' he said. 'I can't take your money!'

'Yes, you can,' I told him. 'It was a fair deal, and if you hadn't picked up the paper, it might have gone forever in the early rubbish collection.'

'All right,' he said, relieved. For a woman devoted to the virtues, Sister Mary engenders tremendous deference. The sort of respect awarded to army, police and Colombian hit men. 'I promise my entire profits will be spent on my dinner. *Big Issue!*' he yelled at passing commuters. 'A cheap way to demonstrate you have a social conscience! Come on! Only the price of a couple of lattes!'

That man would go far. I went home, perspiring. As I walked I unfolded the letter.

Georgie Porgie, it said. I sang it to myself as I slipped into Uncle Solly's New York Deli, a haven of civilisation. Yiddish civilisation. Uncle Solly was there, sitting behind the counter reading a newspaper he always described as the *Hebrew Astonisher*.

'Corinna! Dollink! You look hot!'

'Thank you, I think,' I replied. 'I'm too tired to cook dinner, Solly. What's on your menu today?'

'Sit, sit,' he urged. 'A glass of tea, perhaps? Yes, good, for such a day.' He poured me a glass of lemon-coloured tea from his samovar, which simmered all day on its stand. 'There, that's better,' he said, beaming. 'Catch your breath. I got sausages, you fancy maybe some weisswurst, nice with mustard, maybe some potato salad, maybe Thousand Island dressing for these leaves? Special for you.'

'Yes,' I said weakly. The tea was very hot and refreshing.

'And for dessert I got a special *apfelstrudel*. Just like mother. Your Daniel never tasted the like. All right?'

'Pack it all in this.' I handed over the bag. 'You're a life saver, Uncle Solly.'

He was, too. Since the advent of his deli several of the night-crawlers had tried to rob him. This had always been sorted out amicably, except in the case of the man who had been so unwise as to pull a knife on the respected uncle. The attacker had gone down under an expert assault from Uncle Solly's nephews. They not only took away his knife and broke his arm, they scared him so badly that the word spread that Uncle Solly's was not the place to try a little adventitious robbery. I knew things about Uncle Solly's political connections. He was a powerful man.

Also, he stocked the best weisswurst. He packed my bag with deliciousness and handed it over. And in exchange he asked only money. It didn't seem fair. I waved to the ever-present nephew and slogged my way back to my apartment.

In the atrium of Insula, whence I had paused to relish the coolness, I recited Pockets' latest clue.

'Georgie Porgie, pudding and pie, kissed the girls and made them cry. When the boys came out to play, Georgie Porgie ran away.'

Sounded political. But then, most things did.

Chapter Twelve

Daniel came in as I unpacked my bag and stashed the sausages where no cat could be tempted. Horatio has not yet managed to open the fridge. Like most cats, he is careful of his dignity and will not try anything if he thinks he might not succeed. Or in the process be put in an embarrassing position. I have never forgotten his shame when I had to rescue him from being captured by one paw from the hanging basket of catmint which had been presented to him by Trudi. He had decided to help himself and had been trapped by gravity. He had slunk away and refused to speak to me for days…Like Jason, perhaps.

'Uncle Solly has provided dinner,' I told Daniel. 'Tea?'

'God, yes.' He sank down and rubbed his face with both hands. 'Actors! Crew!'

'You've had an overdose of emotions?' I asked sympathetically.

'If it was sugar and I was diabetic you would have been visiting me in hospital,' he replied. 'But I've spoken to everyone. At length. And once I have recovered my nerve I will tabulate it all. That ought to narrow down the suspect list to the people who had the opportunity to carry out these tricks. Then we will think about motive. Also, I am making progress with the little Zephaniah. Ms. Atkins' child,' he reminded me. 'I have a line on who adopted him. What about you, my angel?'

As I made tea I told him about the holy fools of Gotham, the church of St. Francis and the *Big Issue* seller. I also told him that Pockets was in custody.

'Thank God,' said Daniel piously. 'I can get some sleep tonight. This detective game is wearing on the nerves. That was clever of you, ketschele,' he told me. 'What do you make of Georgie Porgie?'

'Ah,' I said. 'Mr. Google will help me. But for the moment, you will drink your tea, I will put on some music, and we will be peaceful.'

I put on my favourite rendition of Monteverdi's sacred songs and we sat in silence, drinking tea and listening. Sweet, clever, intricate music with a hint of dissonance. Lovely. Outside, as the music finished, lightning flashed and then thunder rolled. That storm was coming along nicely.

'I'm glad you don't have to go out,' I said to Daniel, kissing him. 'It's going to be a nasty night.'

'Perfect for bad deeds.' He grinned at me. 'Let's have some delicatessen,' he suggested. 'I'm starving. Did Uncle Solly give you weisswurst?'

'He did, also a strudel which he says will be better than your mother's.'

'It would have to be,' he said, getting up to put the grill pan on the stove. 'My mother never cooked a strudel in her life.'

'You don't talk about your family,' I said hesitantly.

'They're ordinary,' he replied, unwrapping parcels. 'My mother is a surgeon and my father is a businessman. They live in Tel Aviv. They think I'm an aimless youth and live in hope that I will go back to university and get a good degree, preferably medicine or law, marry a nice Jewish girl and settle down to raise children in Israel. Instead I am shacked up with a shiksa in far-flung Australia, making a living out of other men's evils. We don't get on,' he added unnecessarily. 'Fortunately my elder brother is everything they required in a son, so I got let off the hook a bit.'

I did not want to make a comment which might be considered hurtful, so I shut up and laid out the salads. Uncle Solly does a lovely Thousand Island dressing. I don't know what his secret ingredient is. Not for lack of testing and wheedling. But he won't tell me. I could taste capsicum, tarragon, a hint of chili,

garlic, tomato, chives, paprika—what was it? A smoky flavour…
sort of celery…did anyone smoke celery?

We dined on the delicatessen in amiable silence. Families.
They were a problem.

When the sausages were eaten and the salad bowl empty, I
asked, 'What about Zephaniah, then?'

'He was adopted by a couple called Smith.'

'Oh, that should make life easier,' I said, surprised into irony.
'Not a lot of Smiths around.'

'They seem to have been very religious,' said Daniel. 'They
gave their reference for the adoption as the Church of the Holy
Mother of Perpetual Suffering.'

'I've never heard of that one. Our Lady of Perpetual Succour,
or Help of Christians, yes. But perpetual suffering?'

'I thought it was odd, too. But I don't know much about your
religion. I looked it up but there is no listing for it anywhere.
Not now, of course. I am working on the directories twenty years
old. They were said to live in this church in Eltham.'

'Artists' colony?' I asked. I had watched Eltham change from
apple orchards and wandering watercolourists to close-packed
houses and lots of prams. It is scary how far the city now extends.
You can drive for hours and never leave it.

'I don't know. Surely not even artists would sign up for
endless suffering?'

'They would if it improved their pictures,' I told him. 'Have
some strudel.'

Daniel tasted. 'If my mother had ever made strudel, this
would be better,' he opined. It was indeed wonderful and I
schemed to pinch Uncle Solly's recipe. Once he told me about
the Thousand Island dressing. I must introduce him to Bernie.
This was her kind of cooking.

After dinner Daniel went to his laptop and I went to my
computer to look up Georgie Porgie. All sources referred me to
the amazing career of George Villiers, Duke of Buckingham,
favourite of James of Scotland, who called him 'my sweet wife.'
He was the highest-paid tart in the kingdom, it appeared, got

involved in war (for which he was quite unsuited) and was finally stabbed by a soldier, survivor of his campaign where he had got five thousand out of seven thousand men killed. The murderer was understandably miffed about this. But somehow this did not feel right to me. I was no folklorist but I felt that the George in question must relate to the kings called George, of whom we had had lots. And didn't they call the Hanoverian era 'Pudding Time'? Plus I was sure that I had seen a statue of King George in Melbourne somewhere. Near the shrine?

Thunder crashed. My, that storm was getting its eye in. I logged out before I was forcibly disconnected. Horatio, who dislikes climatic assaults, walked in a dignified manner to my wardrobe and tucked himself inside. That was a sign—Grandma Chapman used to call it 'beast reckoning'—that it was going to be a significant storm. The Mouse Police did not pay attention to thunder. If it wasn't a mouse or rat—or on occasion a spider, pigeon or moth—they didn't even twitch a whisker. They might have noticed a hurricane, but only if it demolished the bakery. I hunted out a few candles, in case the power went out. The night was now as black as pitch and rumbling and flashing like a Steven Spielberg movie. The leafy green things on my porch were suddenly bent over by a lash of wind, and rain came belting down. Daniel looked up from his laptop and said 'Wow!' as the weather slapped the building aside and all the lights went out.

The darkness was enlightened as I lit the candles and Daniel swore fluently in Hebrew. His spreadsheet had gone with the wind.

'Join me on the couch and tell me everything you can remember,' I suggested. 'That will fix it all in your mind. And I'm dying for something to divert me from worrying about Jason.'

'All right, beloved, let's try that,' he said, snuggling down beside me as the rain poured onto the windows as from a large celestial jug. 'You can just hear the reservoirs filling, can't you? And by the way, I am sure that Jason will come round in time. I met him in the atrium and he did actually say "Hey," which is encouraging.'

'I suppose so,' I agreed. 'But you haven't betrayed him. And he thinks I have. Tell me about the TV studio.'

'Well, any one of the crew or the cast could have done the tricks,' he said, settling back and cuddling me to his side. 'And as for motive, Ms. Atkins was the main victim and she really is an unpleasant woman. I spoke to her about little Zephaniah and she said, "My demented sister must have given him that ugly name." And that was all she said. Her principal enemies seem to be Ethan and Emily. The crew might have done it because they wanted to please Ethan. It didn't require much computer knowledge to hack into the website and change the captions. Anyway, these days everyone knows a whizkid geek who can make any system sit up, roll over and beg.'

'We know three of them ourselves,' I remarked.

'Yes, I have asked the Lone Gunmen to see if they can track the vandal. And forestall him if he tries again. The age of the hacker is indicated by the names he gave the actors. Specifically, he described Ms. Atkins as "a big fat ho."'

I giggled. 'She'd really object to the "fat,"' I said.

'And as to the rest, who can say?' said Daniel tactfully. 'Now, the chief suspect is Ethan, because he has the technical knowledge, can't stand Ms. Atkins, and is indignant on behalf of Emily.'

'Yes, but Daniel, he needs to keep this commission. He deferred a deal in the US to work with Tash.'

'True. Emily is very young, has the requisite knowledge and access, is certainly badly treated. She's a young woman from a nice middle-class background. Not too good at school but a smash hit in drama. Just out of NIDA, brimming with ambition.'

'And talent,' I said, and told him about her wickedly accurate imitation of Ms. Atkins. He nodded. In the flickering light, he made a definite image of dark brooding intelligence. The writers had been right. He would make a wonderful vampire. 'But she needs Ms. Atkins to succeed in the profession of her choice. So that means it probably isn't her.'

'Then there's Tommy,' said Daniel. 'This might be an attempt to sabotage her company. What do you know about her?'

'Not a lot,' I admitted. I paused as a crash, similar to a few large lorries colliding, abolished speech. In the silence that followed I heard Horatio give out a faint mew of protest from inside his wardrobe. There was nothing I could do for the poor cat. The storm must be right overhead and appeared to be settling in for a long stay. 'She left school, did a catering course, was apprenticed in one of the top restaurants, then went to London to work in gastropubs. Somewhere along the way she acquired Julie, with whom we were at school, and came out as a lesbian. I had no idea. Came back here, set up Maîtresse, and she has been very successful.'

'Why?' asked Daniel.

'Usual reasons. The food is clever but not so innovative as to be confronting. The ingredients are top-notch. She employs the best chefs and treats them well. All of her staff appear to like working for her, even if they don't precisely like her. Good pay, good conditions.'

'Rivals?'

'There must be some. And sneaking an apprentice or dishwasher into an enemy's kitchen is not unknown. Industrial espionage. The spy is there to find out the secret ingredients and steal the best recipes. Or the mother of bread, in the case of a baker. But I never heard of such a spy actually sabotaging the food. I suppose it could happen.'

'There is a culinary aspect to all the attacks,' said Daniel. 'Mustard, wasabi, chili oil.'

'I thought that they might have been designed to point to Ethan,' I said. 'He loves all those hot things.'

'He says he didn't do it,' Daniel told me. 'He's worried. He does need the contract. He really wants to work with Tash. And if Tash means Ms. Atkins, then he's willing to put up with her. I wonder why she hates him?'

'Could it be that he has failed to succumb to her charms?' I asked.

'It could be that he refused her straight-out proposition.' Daniel hugged me. 'Ethan says that she practically ordered him into her bed and he equally flatly declined to go. He seems to have fallen for Bernie, by the way. His PA, Samantha, is very dark on him at the moment. Ethan's a genius. They are always hard to live with. They think that the rules do not apply to them.'

'Samantha need not worry. I gather that Ethan is not monogamous.'

'No, while he's with someone he's unseduceable—is that a word? He cannot be distracted. But after, as Samantha says, he concentrates his whole attention on a woman and sucks her dry, he gets bored and has to move on. That may be why he's had so many assistants.'

'So Ethan leaves a trail of broken hearts behind him,' I mused. 'Could Samantha have done it, to ruin Ethan?'

'Yes. She's quite able to get close enough to him to pick his pocket of that foul chili oil. He does tend to embrace people, quite absent-mindedly. All they have to be, as Sam remarked, is breathing. And she said she wouldn't trust him with a not-quite-cold corpse if it was good-looking.'

'She sounds quite upset.'

'She's not the only one. Harrison—the one who looks like an angel—is infatuated with the sound man, Ali, who is a straight, married Muslim. Really straight and rather prickly about it. The more abusive he gets the more Harrison follows him around, posing in the best light and giving him melting looks. Ali has been restrained from belting him by his regard for Ethan, whom he says is the only cameraman who appreciates sound. Sound men are always grumpy. It's a hard life.'

Thunder rolled overhead like Thor's chariot going over a very bumpy road. There was a silence after the sound. I heard Horatio complain. Daniel resumed his recital.

'Harrison himself admits that he is infatuated with Ali, whom he is convinced will come around in time. He has always managed to get whoever he wants so hasn't much tolerance for failure. He looks on this production as his next step in a rising career which will get him even more boys of his choice plus

money and fame. He sees himself in five years' time lolling on
the balcony of a five-star hotel, eating caviar with a soup spoon.
Has food issues, too. Devout Buddhist. Thinks that the trickster
is working out some details of Ms. Atkins' karma.'

I regret to say that I laughed. Karmically, Ms. Atkins would
be lucky if she was reincarnated as an earwig.

Daniel went on, 'Gordon and Kendall, the writers, are
offended by the way that Ms. Atkins changes their scripts, even
after they have been debated and endlessly rewritten and given
the seal of approval. The word is that they are a top team, though
their sexuality is murky. No one knows if they are on together or
not. Kendall is supporting a mother with Alzheimer's and Gordon
lives on her own in a tiny flat in St. Kilda. Both are short of
money and surely would not want to ruin the show, from which
they will make a packet if it is syndicated. Kylie and Goss can be
ruled out. They have their big break and so far are doing well.'

'Except that they told Jason I had replaced him,' I growled.

'Except for that,' Daniel agreed, kissing my forehead. 'They
haven't got less airheaded, I admit. I don't think that the soap
opera ethos is a good influence, you know. It's all emotion. No
reason. And actors are so emulous. That girl who dresses in all
the Goth/punk gear, her name is Abby Johnson. She's a serious
young woman, computer illiterate, who just wants to be an
actress and yearns for Shakespeare and Brecht. She's in love with
Ethan as well, but hasn't managed to attract his attention. Yet.'

'Her turn will come,' I predicted.

'Probably. I had the greatest difficulty preventing her from
reciting the whole of the "Make me a willow cabin by your gate"
speech. She has the brain of a peahen but a very good memory.
And she expects this production to smuggle her into theatre.
Not a likely saboteur. In any case, she could not have done the
hacking. She takes five minutes to find the "on" switch.'

'And her character has to spout paragraphs of techno-
babble. Odd.'

'No problem for her. She doesn't need to understand it; she
just has to say it, and she does, flawlessly. Then there's Elton,

who plays Matt, the office boy and PA to Ms. Atkins' superbitch, Courtneigh Yronsyde. I don't quite know what to make
of Elton,' said Daniel. 'On the face of it he is a straight playing
a gay, a calm person playing a neurotic, and a strong-minded
man playing a jittery, overmastered boy. Which makes deciding
on his actual personality difficult.'

'How do you feel about him?' I asked.

'He's hiding something,' said Daniel slowly. 'But everyone
has something to hide.'

'Ms. Atkins?' I asked, settling down cosily for more gossip.

'She's a bit of a mystery,' he said slowly, tightening his grip
on me as the thunder crashed again. I knew that Daniel liked
storms but this one was unexpectedly fierce. I fought down an
urge to join Horatio in his wardrobe.

'In what way?' I asked when I could be heard again.

'Despite the best endeavours of the gossip mags, her family
remains obscure,' he told me. 'This is a little like being under
artillery fire, you know. Without the risk of a sudden and messy
death, of course. Not being shot at always improves your day.
Where was I? Ah, yes. She was born an indeterminate number
of years ago to poor—'

'But honest parents?' I sang the first line of that scourge of
pub singers, 'The Wild Colonial Boy.'

Daniel smiled. 'Not conspicously. Her father was a dealer in
stolen goods—at least, that's what he went to jail for when Ms.
Atkins was a child. Her mother managed badly with three daugh-
ters. One of them was Molly, who joined every drama class and
small production going, perhaps to get out of the house, which
can't have been happy. She worked at various trades to scrape
up the money for more classes. That's when she changed her
accent from lower-working class to middle-American. She got
into modelling. That can be a murky world for the young and
hungry. Somewhere along the way she got pregnant, vanished for
a while, gave birth. I've no idea of the identity of the father of little
Zephaniah. The birth certificate is blank. Her siblings did not do
well. One died of a stroke a long time ago and the other married a

bricklayer and has three children and no interest in acting or her famous sister. There's a suggestion that Molly might have had a brother who was put away in some kind of home. Brain-damaged, I think. As I said, if the gossip mags haven't found out, I'm not going to succeed. They've got more resources than I have. Then Molly married and had a son—another son, I mean—who died tragically. Since then she has had a few high-profile affairs but shows no sign of marrying again.'

'Unsurprisingly,' I said.

'Indeed. Independently wealthy by reason of shrewd investments of the divorce settlement and life insurance policy on her son. But the cosmetic surgery must cost a packet,' added Daniel. 'She doesn't need the money but she does need the break. I had considered that perhaps she was playing these tricks on herself, but I can't see why she would.'

'Neither can I,' I said. 'Who else did you talk to?'

'Marina—she's the editor. Doesn't mingle with the actors, she's post production. There's an editing suite in the studio and she and her minions mostly hang out there. I also talked to the rest of the crew. They are all Ethan's disciples. They would never do anything to hurt his prospects. They mostly despise the show, but that is not their business. Rob, who is continuity, says that they will ride to success on Ethan's coat tails, if he wore coats with tails. So far,' concluded Daniel, 'not a lot to go on.'

'No.' I was beginning to sweat again. The air-conditioning had gone off with the power and Daniel radiated heat. I moved away from him a little. Outside the storm crashed and the wind moaned and inside Horatio cried from his wardrobe.

'The name is curious,' he said.

'What name?'

'Zephaniah. In Hebrew it means something like "hidden by God" or "treasure of God." Isn't there a Book of Zephaniah in the Bible? He was a friend of Jeremiah, as I recall. Have you got a Bible handy?'

'Yes, but it's going to be tricky to read by candlelight.' I fetched it.

Daniel reached into his satchel and retrieved a little book light. It uncurled itself in an eerie fashion and illuminated the old Bible as I leafed through it.

'Yes, here we are, between Habakkuk and Haggai. One of the little prophets. *The word of the Lord received by Zephaniah, son of Cushi.* Hmm.'

He read rapidly. I looked over his shoulder. Zephaniah was one of those severe prophets, who came in wrath. '*There will be a cry from the fish gate and a howling from the second and a great crashing from the hills.*' I was reminded of *Round the Horne*. 'What is your message of hope?' 'We be doomed.' Zephaniah was much concerned with doom. He seemed to particularly have it in for the inhabitants of Moab and Askelon. He added the Ethiopians and Canaan. He had a nice turn of phrase: *And flocks shall lie down in the midst of her, all the beasts of the nations: both the cormorant and the bittern shall lodge in the upper lintels of it: their voice shall sing in the windows: desolation shall be in the thresholds: for he shall uncover the cedar-work.* It finished with a promise to undo all that should afflict Israel, and promised that they should be gathered together again in joy.

'Ah,' said Daniel softly. '*Behold, I shall save her that halteth, and gather her that was driven out: I will get them praise and fame in every land where they have been put to shame.* Pity that it hasn't come true. But we can live without praise and fame, as long as we are allowed to live.'

'Indeed,' I agreed. There was silence for a while. 'That was a very good denounce,' I commented.

'Those prophets, they had passion. Of course, we don't know what they had been ingesting. Apart from despair.'

'Yes, there was a theory that St. John the Divine was eating magic mushrooms when he had all those visions in Revelations.'

'He was probably dining with Ezekiel. Now there was a man with really interesting visions. Dry bones. Burning fiery chariots. Which brings us no closer to finding out why the child was named Zephaniah.'

'No, but it's interesting,' I said. 'Think how he would have enjoyed the present weather!'

Daniel laughed.

Then with rumbling and complaint, the storm moved on. I opened the French window and a gush of cold sweet air flowed in. The lights, however, remained off.

'I think we might as well go to bed,' suggested Daniel.

'You're always saying that…' I said.

'Yes, I am, aren't I?' He smiled at me in the flickering light. I kissed him and blew out the candles.

◇◇◇

Morning announced itself by all the lights coming on at once. It was six a.m. and a clear windy day. I switched off all the lights and did the usual morning things. Daniel, who had had his first night's sleep in ages, was making more coffee as I ventured down to the bakery and found that the Mouse Police had been foraging somewhere wet. They were lying side by side on their flour sacks, licking each other dry, beside a mound of bedraggled prey. Even the rats had found last night's weather impossible to avoid. I disposed of them and fed the cats and put on the mixers.

'Did you lose power last night?' asked Bernie, coming in through the alley door.

'Yes, for hours. It only just came on again. You?'

'Sure did. My dad is furious. I never have managed to teach him to hit "save" often enough. Lost pages of calculations.'

'Poor man,' I said, which was as sympathetic as I got in the morning. 'Bread is on, what have you got to do today?'

'They liked the cupcakes so much that they've asked for them again,' she said, putting down an armload of those flat white boxes. 'I made a lot more sugar roses. It's a good sign, isn't it?' she asked me. 'That they wanted more of them.'

'It's an excellent sign. Good, you can get on with the cupcakes. Use that oven, I don't need it.'

Bernie seemed disposed to chat, which was not my idea of a civilised morning. But nothing to be done about it, so I half-listened as I kneaded and rolled. Kneading is a trance-inducing pastime. It ought to have some sort of mystic philosophical school, or at least a mantra. You can become one with the dough.

'So what did Daniel report about the crew?' asked Bernie artlessly.

'I can't tell you that,' I said shortly. 'Discretion is his watchword.'

'Oops, sorry,' she said, biting her lip. 'What shall we talk about, then?'

'How about some hush?' I suggested. 'Quiet and contemplation.'

Bernie shut up and I went back to kneading. I myself broke the silence after half an hour or so.

'What's the news on the pastry cook's leg?' I asked. Bernie jumped. Like most of Gen Y, she isn't used to silence. I should suggest that she bring her iPod. Jason always had an iPod.

'She's getting better, but she isn't able to stand for long periods yet. Why, don't you like this job?'

'I could do without it,' I told her. She stared at me.

'If you say so, Corinna,' she said, and put on the mixer.

Cupcakes were made and set out to cool. Icing was happening. My bread came out of the oven shiny and smelling delightful. I zoomed upstairs briefly to kiss Daniel and steal one of his English muffins, toasted to a turn, with blood orange marmalade. Yum.

'Are you going back to the studio today?' I asked.

'Oh, yes. Can I catch a lift with you?'

'Certainly, in about an hour. And I warn you, you will not like our driver's musical tastes.'

'As long as he can drive, I don't care,' he said, biting into the other half of his muffin before I could steal it. Horatio, satisfied with his dab of butter, was sitting on the newspaper, having a thorough wash. This meant that Daniel would not read anything which might upset him. A service which Horatio provides without charge. He is a generous cat.

Back to the bakery, where Bernie was to be discovered reading my accounts. While they are public documents available to be read by anyone who wants to pay the search fee, this was cheeky. She jumped again and slammed the day book shut.

'Something I can help you with?' I asked.

'I was curious,' she admitted. 'You're doing well.'

'Thank you. I have no debts to service and very loyal customers. I buy the best raw ingredients, which is expensive, but shows up in the product.'

'I see,' she said.

'Thinking of opening your own business?' I asked.

'I would love to,' she admitted. 'Maybe in LA.'

'You're travelling?' I could not decide whether to be offended or amused so I settled for interested.

'With…'

'Ethan?' I asked. Bernie blushed right up to her immaculate white cap.

'That's where he's going next,' she said. 'To make a film for Spielberg. He's only doing *Kiss* because he adores Tash. He says he'll take me. It's so exciting.'

'Bernie…' I wondered what to say next. This man is not to be relied upon? Don't put your culinary eggs in one basket? Trust not in princes? None of them sounded right. I shrugged. 'Tell me what sort of shop you want,' I said.

The rest of the morning's work was accomplished as Bernie told me all about the small but select patisserie she would establish in Los Angeles; the Middle English recipes she would translate into modern, up-to-the-minute cakes, the number of stars who would patronise her shop, the fame, the fortune. By the time she asked me for my recipe for Bosworth Jumbles the strains of 'Heartbreak Hotel' were already echoing down the alley.

So we loaded up and, with Daniel, set off for Harbour Studios. I wondered if I could properly ask Sister Mary to say prayers for that pastry chef's health and her speedy return to work. I was getting very tired of Harbour Studios and all who sailed in them.

Chapter Thirteen

All was as usual as we carried the cakes into the kitchen. Tommy checked them off on her list. Today was quiches and pies, so I started on my pastry while Daniel drifted around the kitchen, first lending a hand with the salad people. I noted that he had his own knife, a Global by the look of it. Good knives. You can't work in a kitchen unless you have a good knife. Apart from anything else, a blunt knife is much more likely to cut you. Strange but true.

Today the atmosphere was calm. Daniel had that effect on nervous people. Unlike the prophet Zephaniah, who must have been uncomfortable company. Why saddle an innocent child with such a name? Must have been religious reasons. After my recent brush with an extreme form of fundamental Christianity, I found any suggestion of this unsettling. Better I should think about Georgie Porgie and get on with my puddings and pies.

And not consider Bernie and Ethan and the next line, about kissing the girls and making them cry. Why should kissing the girls make them cry? Kicking them would make them cry, but kissing them?

My hands, unregarded, had been mixing and kneading. Soon I had all my packets of pastry wrapped in cling film and in the fridge to cool down. Breakfast was being served so I took a tray and exited into the studio.

Now that I had been informed about the various crew, they were easy to identify. There was Ali, scowling at Harrison. Devoutly straight, being ogled against his will. The makeup artists were working on some of the cast. Ms. Atkins, for example, was muffled under a smock and a towel. I could only identify her by her beautiful feet in her red-heeled shoes. Kylie and Goss were also in chairs, being decorated. There was a hum of conversation. Ethan was eating scrambled eggs and talking about camera angles to his assistant Samantha, who looked sullen. It was unwise of her to fall for Ethan, but he was very attractive. He dominated the crowd by his size and his air of benevolent confidence. He saw me and smiled and my whole day improved. Even though I knew he was a heart-breaking swine.

A very good-looking heart-breaking swine, however. I was surrounded by beautiful people. All of whom needed to be fed, so I went on with feeding them. By the bains-marie I found Emily, who was trying to hold a cup of hot coffee to her mouth. Her hands were shaking. Tears brimmed in her eyes.

I took the cup out of her grasp before she scalded herself. 'Emily, what's wrong?' I asked quietly.

'She's going to fire me,' she whispered. 'What shall I do then?'

'Hold it,' I said. 'She hasn't fired you yet. Don't borrow trouble. And don't despair even if she does. Here, eat some of these eggs. Just a mouthful or two. Come on.' Emily complied. Poor girl. She was used to taking orders. I bullied the rest of the eggs down her contracted throat, then she was strong enough to hold the cup and gulp down her coffee. 'There's always time to despair,' I told her. 'You don't have to do it yet. There, she's calling you. Keep up your heart,' I advised, and Emily sped across the set to Ms. Atkins' side.

'That was nice of you,' someone said into my ear. I jumped and spun, hand ready to box an ear. It was Tash, so I refrained. Milkmaids usually have powerful right arms, exercised by suppressing the rebellious instincts of creatures a lot bigger and heavier than they were.

'It was nothing,' I mumbled.

'She's already lasted longer than any other of Ms. Atkins' assistants,' observed Tash. 'She must have courage. Is that fried bread you have there? I could fancy a piece or two.'

'All yours,' I said, holding out my tray. 'How is the production going?'

'Slowly,' she said. 'We lost power last night and some things have to be rebooted. We're getting on.' Then she was dragged away to answer some urgent post-production questions from a woman dressed in the extreme of Goth chic, who must have been Marina, the editor.

I returned to the kitchen for another load and found myself tasked with refilling the chafing dishes. Tomatoes, mushrooms, little rolls of bacon and kedgeree with smoked cod, which smelt delicious. Various members of the cast surrounded me and thrust spoons into the pots without regard to safety or manners. Everyone was hungry this morning. That was probably a good sign.

Tash clapped and called for rehearsal, Ethan put away his little bottle of chili oil, and I went back to the kitchen to feast on the leftovers and see what else needed to be done. Tommy caught me as I came in.

'Here's your invitation.' She shoved an envelope into my hand. 'Sorry it's such short notice. Do come, Corinna, and bring that gorgeous hunk with you.'

I opened it. Inside was an invitation to the awards dinner of the Caterers' Association. This very night as was. I was about to bin it, then realised that this would be a chance to meet all of Tommy's enemies at once. Provided I didn't partake too freely of their bounty, I ought to be able to interview all of them. I had once overindulged at a Good Food dinner, their hospitality being legendary, but two glasses would see me through tonight. I hoped that Daniel did not have other plans.

I could go and ask him, of course. I wandered out into the studio where the actors were on set and the cameras were pointed, if not rolling. Daniel was sitting on a plastic chair out of the way of the action and I joined him.

'How's it going?' he asked. 'That was a very lavish breakfast.'

'Thank you,' I said, preening a little. 'What are you doing tonight?'

'Following Pockets, if he is out of the hospital.'

'Well…' I put the invitation into his hand. 'Why not accompany me to this bash, which will allow us to meet all of Tommy's competition?'

'Wonderful,' he said. 'That will be an improvement on what I had in prospect.'

Then we hushed, because the rehearsal was beginning.

This plot—God knew which one would make it to the pilot—concerned a bride who was about to change her mind about the whole wedding. It was actually rather subtle, as far as one could tell when getting the story in little bits out of order. The reactions of the staff were interesting. Kylie and Goss, as Chloe and Brittanii, squeaked or delivered devastatingly cynical lines respectively ('I say grab him while you've got him. You can always change your mind later.'). The personal assistant, Elton, playing Matt, camped outrageously. The geek Felicia delivered herself faultlessly of a long technological rave, including a joke pinched from *Red Dwarf*: 'All I have to say is zero, one, one, zero, zero, one, one. And that's my last word on the subject.' Harrison romped athletically through the set in his bicycle shorts, raising the Unresolved Sexual Tension by ten degrees. And Ms. Atkins, as Courtneigh Yronsyde, wheedled, coaxed and finally forced the bride to go ahead with the wedding—even though it was clear that this was not a good idea; her to-be husband was probably a serial killer, and she was sensibly reluctant—in the interests, of course, of Kiss the Bride's profit margin. It was chilling. Ms. Atkins was magnificent.

'She's a bitch, but she's wonderful,' commented Daniel. The lounging crew, to a man and woman, nodded.

'Good script,' I said. Gordon and Kendall looked pleased. They didn't get told that very often, I guessed. The young woman came forward with the clapper, the crew leapt into their places, and I went back to the familiar world to help with whatever was going.

I had crumbles to make today. The choppers had already prepared my fruit so all I needed to do was rub in the butter and flour and stuff the whole thing into the oven. Crumbles are an agreeable compromise between making pastry and serving plain stewed fruit. Hot, with cream, they can be delicious.

I noticed that today's fruit was vastly superior to yesterday's. Tommy must have put a rocket up that greengrocer. Every apple in the basket appeared to have been individually polished. I began to load the gratin dishes with fruit. Bernie was decorating a large work of art with marzipan. Little balls of the stuff were ready to complete her Simnel cake. We discussed medieval recipes as we worked. It seemed a safe subject.

Then it was all done and I needed to get out. The one advantage of being a contractor is that you can go away when the work is done. I could take a walk in King's Domain and see if I could find another parchment. I wondered how poor Lena was getting on. There was no prospect of extracting Daniel before filming was complete, so I bade farewell to my fellow workers and sauntered away into the sunlight.

Hot again, which was regrettable but not surprising. I caught a tram instead of undertaking the long slog up St. Kilda Road and got off near the art gallery. Where was that statue?

I should have packed myself some lunch. I bought a gelato and licked it as I wandered. The grass was dry and crackled underfoot. Only the Australian trees looked happy. This was their kind of weather.

It wasn't mine. The park was dreary in this climate; an English garden transplanted unhappily to the Antipodes and pining for the cool moisture of Kent. I did not find any parchment around the foot or in the interstices of the statue of George, King and Emperor. Damn. All that hot for nothing. I idled near the bin and sighted a leaf of pale yellow in it. Retrieved, it was a clue. I unfolded it.

'*Simple Simon*,' I read aloud, to the hot air. No one was near me to be offended. I sang it to myself as I walked back along St. Kilda Road to the city.

'*Simple Simon met a pieman, going to the fair. Said Simple Simon to the pieman, Let me taste your wares. Said the pieman to Simple Simon, Show me first your money. Said Simple Simon to the pieman, Sir I have not any.*'

Again, Mr. Google must tell me the background. I had a vague idea that piemen were notorious for tossing people double or nothing for their pies. Probably with their very own double-headed lucky penny. I hoped they were good pies, unlike those served to the Ankh-Morpork populace by Cut-Me-Own-Throat Dibbler. But I suspected as much. Pies are deceptive. You can put anything in the filling and the customer only finds out his mistake when he is so unwise as to bite one. I went back to Insula, pleased and hot, for a shower and a drink and a little research. And a rest, if I had to go out tonight. At least the gathering was close. The town hall, no less. I wondered who was catering the event.

Shower, gown, drink, Google. 'Simple Simon' had extra verses, relating to fishing for a whale in his mother's pail and picking figs off a thistle. Which made poor Simon whistle. It was blessedly free from political interpretations, for a change. Just a rhyme to amuse the children. I was not notably amused.

I took the esky, the cat and my current novel up to the roof garden in search of inspiration. Pies? Every café in the city sold pies and some made their own, if you stretched the definition. Was there a pie shop called Simple Simon's? I could not think of one. And Lena's fate still rested in the balance. Damn Pockets. Though the poor man had effectively damned himself. Why did he like to lie down in front of trams? I supposed it was one way to guarantee attention...

The temple was empty, except for the goddess. I set Horatio down and he fell instantly asleep, snared by a patch of sunlight. I poured a drink and sat contemplating the garden. Trudi had done a wonderful job with the waste water. Even the turf was green. It rested the eyes, dried from staring into the hot depths of too many ovens. I closed them. Just for a while. Soon, lounging on the bench, I joined Horatio in dreamland...

When I awoke someone was shaking me by the shoulder. I looked hazily up into an angry face, topped with curly blond hair, bleached by sun and salt water. Jason.

'Just want you to know,' he was saying.

'Know what?' I mumbled.

'I got another job.'

'Good,' I said cautiously. 'What are you doing, which baker?'

'No baker,' he snapped. 'Chicken shop.'

We had often joked about that chicken shop. A franchise, it made fairly tasty chicken dishes for the populace. Like all such establishments it was staffed by students who were probably younger than the produce. The wages were low and the tenure uncertain. But because of this turnover, there was always a job there. The idea that my skilled Jason would be making roadkill chicken was a depressing one.

'Ah, the chicken shop,' I temporised.

'Yair, so I don't need you anymore!' he snarled. Oh, Jason.

'Well, if you change your mind, remember that I need you,' I told him firmly. 'I will always need you.'

'Hah!' he replied.

At this juncture Horatio woke and demanded to know why his peaceful and rightful nap had been disturbed by angry voices. Then he noticed Jason and got to his paws to greet him.

'H'lo, Horatio,' muttered Jason, putting out a hand for Horatio to rub his chin against. 'Lookin' good.'

Horatio purred an agreement. Then Jason remembered his grudge and straightened up.

'Keep in mind,' I told him urgently, 'that this is a misunderstanding. I still want you. I still need you. No one makes muffins like you do, Jason.'

'So you only want me for my muffins?' he demanded.

'Among other things,' I told him, suppressing a giggle. 'Think about it.'

Jason gave me a glare and flung himself out of the roof garden. But I had managed to insert a few ideas into that curly head, and maybe he would reconsider after a few days working in the fug, steam and grease of the chicken shop.

Cheered, I collected Horatio and went back to my apartment for a rest until it was time for the Caterers' Association dinner. Which meant, at least, that I would not be cooking it.

Daniel came in as I was sorting out some clothes to wear. The invitation said 'black tie,' which meant that I would have to glam up several notches from my usual loose kurta, black trousers and wrap. The trouble was that I didn't really have any sparkly clothes. Not since I had given up the world of accounting and donned the baker's overall. I did find a couple of kaftans which had been sent to me from far-flung places by Jon and Kepler, and one of those would do. I was pondering whether to wear the dark-blue floaty one or the bright crimson with—yes—sequins, decided on the red, and turned to kiss Daniel.

I told him about Simple Simon as he showered and dressed in his own gown and accepted a gin and tonic as an introduction to a peaceful interlude before we had to go out and confront the food industry. Daniel in a kaftan is unbelievably gorgeous. He decorated my couch as he sat on it. He sipped and listened.

'Simple Simon,' he said. 'Never heard of it. Him. I got a call from Lena. She's on sick leave for two weeks, which gives us a bit of time. No further bonds have been cashed, so Pockets has clearly put them somewhere safe. I've been working on Pockets, too. Perhaps we can predict where he might stash the stuff.'

'And the joker at Harbour Studios?'

'Nothing further. No tricks since I started. That might be a hopeful sign. You're looking a little shell-shocked, Corinna.'

I told him about the angry encounter with Jason on the roof. He chuckled.

'If he thought he was working hard here, just wait until he does a few shifts at the chicken shop,' he said. 'Now, since the air-conditioning is on again, let's snuggle down and relax. We don't have to cook and we've got an hour or so before we have to get dressed and go and schmooze with the foodies. Let's have a look at that *Doctor Who* episode you wanted to show the Prof. And I could do with a hug,' he confessed. 'My emotions are feeling a bit bruised.'

So were mine. I complied.

◇◇◇

The undercroft of the town hall was adorned with a lot of flowers, wilting in the heat (as was I), and it smelt wonderful. The flowers had been arranged by one of those stem-twisters (bane of Beverley Nichols' life) into unnatural shapes. They looked vaguely alien, as though they might, if not watched carefully, shoot out like triffids and dine on the guests. Daniel was summoned across the room by a large florid cook. I recognised the TV cook, Antonio Domenico. Daniel did not take me with him—he always has a reason for this; possibly he knew how much I detested Tony since he used to come into Pagliacci's when I was an apprentice—so I grabbed a glass of wine from a server and found a cool place near a fan outlet to look at the room.

This was going to be a buffet, and long tables against one wall were already laid with a profusion of edibles. Behind them, servers in eye-catching overalls of blue and white striped cotton were doing things with spoons. I debated grabbing a plate and tucking in—I had my eye on some very attractive prawns—when someone bobbed up and said, 'Corinna! Lovely kaftan!' and I turned to talk to my new friend, who had discriminating taste.

It was in fact an old friend: Irena, who ran a Russian restaurant and—now I thought of it—catered for weddings. She might be a valuable source of information, so I steered her toward the prawns and exchanged the usual amenities as we loaded our plates. She informed me that she had finally cut her ties with her irritating layabout husband, Ivan, who, she said, gave Russian men a bad name just by existing.

'Since he's no longer hanging about in the kitchen annoying the workers, we've been going well. And the young women have stopped quitting. He was monstering them. They never told me. I should have thought more about why they were always quitting without notice. Men! Predators all. How about you, Corinna? Heard you had a partner.'

'Him.' I pointed out Daniel, who was talking to Domenico near the Martian flower arrangements.

'What, Antonio? Surely not!'

'No, the dark one. Daniel.'

'Wow,' she whistled. 'You must have hidden charms, Corinna! He's gorgeous! But handsome is as handsome does.'

'Both is and does,' I assured her. 'I've been working for Tommy of Maîtresse, feeding a TV crew. How about you?'

'Orthodox weddings,' she said. 'Lavish. Sour cream. Borscht like Babushka made. You know. As long as everyone leaves the wedding stuffed to the gills and no more than pleasantly tiddly, it's a great success. "I couldn't eat another bite" is what we want to hear. These prawns are very good.'

'I'm new to the catering industry,' I said to Irena. 'Tell me about the main players.'

'Most of us are niche,' she told me, snapping up another prawn. For someone so small and thin she eats like a truckie. 'Like you, as well. You just do bread. Very fine bread, I might say. I buy your sourdough rye. Perfect for my soups.'

'Thank you,' I said.

'Well, let me see. There are those who run halal feasts for Muslim weddings or kosher banquets for bar mitzvahs; you can tell them by the way they cluster at the kosher end of the buffet over there. Catered by Uncle Solly of the New York Deli—do you know him?'

'Certainly do. He is my honorary uncle.'

'Isn't he a darling?' she agreed. 'Then there is Terry Patel, who caters for those massive five-day festival-type Indian weddings, where you have to feed three thousand guests. I expect that he supplied the Indian treats. There is Renée Dubois, who does elegant French dinner parties for the middle class.'

For the first time I noticed that the banquet was divided into several sections. One was this side, with the striped overalls. A discreet sign informed me that this was *Special Events*. Another was the specialist one, staffed by women in very stylish headscarves and several of Uncle Solly's nephews. The third was attended by young people in deepest green, with ostler's aprons to their ankles. Irena followed my gaze.

'Oh, yes. Well, there was a huge fight about who was going to do the catering for our night of nights. Eventually, we compromised. The two people who had been doing the most yelling got to split the event. This pleased neither of them, of course. Here we have Simply Simon, who really has cornered the huge end of the wedding market. Distinctive overalls, dark green. Run by Simon Gregson. Over there we have Special Events. You jumped. Why? Do you know Tricia Wendemere?'

'No,' I said. 'Just a twitch.'

'Should I introduce you to anyone?' she asked.

'To Simon,' I requested.

Irena gave an 'if you insist' shrug and conducted me through the gossiping throng to a tall man with the kind of figure which spoke of thousands of really good dinners and very little exercise. He must have weighed two hundred kilos, most of it belly. There are fat men and fat men. Some are just so delightful that you want to take them home and cuddle them. Some are mere slobs, and some remind you that Attila the Hun was a man of imposing corpulence. I found myself addressing his straining waistcoat buttons.

'This is Corinna Chapman, a very good baker,' said Irena. 'I really should have a word with Will. Bye-bye,' she said, and kissed me on each cheek. Simon sighted down over his tummy and smiled. He was a big man all over; wide cheekbones, hefty jaw, strong Cro-Magnon brow. Goliath must have looked like Simon of Simply Simon.

'Always good to meet a baker,' he announced. 'Call me Simon. I cater the biggest events,' he said complacently. 'I should have had the contract for the feeding of the five thousand.'

This was evidently a stock witticism so I laughed obligingly. 'Looks like a very good buffet,' I said.

'Come and taste.' He took me by the elbow in a numbing grip. 'Simply Simon aims for food which is acceptable to the most delicate tastebuds—children, for instance—but manages to infuse simple dishes with subtle flavours. We are particularly proud of these...' He snapped his fingers at a verdant server, who rushed forward with a tray of little vol au vents. 'Just a very pure béchamel with asparagus. What do you think?'

I selected and bit. Nice. Not exciting, but nice.

'The asparagus flavour comes through very well,' I told him.

'I think so,' he agreed. 'You might have reason to employ us?'

'I don't think so,' I told him. 'I regret. I am working for Maîtresse at the moment, just while my bakery is closed for the holidays.'

'Maîtresse?' he boomed. 'Oh, dear. I'll give you some advice.' He leant down to my level. 'Make sure you get paid in advance. That woman and her Sapphic slut cannot be trusted. Plus they serve crappy food to up-jumped social climbers,' he added.

'Good heavens,' I commented.

'Now, you are a beautiful woman of excellent figure,' he said, gesturing to a server to fill up my glass. 'Perhaps you would like to visit us? I could give you a lunch the like of which Maîtresse could never offer.'

'I'll have to look at my appointment book,' I excused myself. 'Tell me, Simon, where is your main kitchen?'

'Why, King Street, to be sure,' he told me. 'Until our new premises are finished. Do you like the uniforms? A pacific green, forest green. Nothing to wound the gaze. Unlike dressing your staff in the attire of a butcher. Blue and white stripes, indeed. Oh dear, it's been so nice talking to you, but Antonio is summoning me. *Bon appétit.*' He bulldozed his way through the gathering. I was a little short of breath. I found that Daniel had appeared at my side.

'Why have I suddenly become attractive to men?' I asked him.

'What do men in women require?' he quoted with Blake. 'The lineaments of satisfied desire.' He smiled his dark smile and kissed me. He tasted of asparagus. Simple Simon had got him, too.

'How's the detecting going?' I asked.

'I have been gathering opinions. This is the most gossipy mob I have ever met. If loose lips really sink ships, whole flotillas would have foundered tonight. You?'

'So far I have been told that Julie is a Sapphic slut and Tommy sells crud to social climbers,' I told him. The crowd was pressing us close together but that was fine with me. 'That was Simply Simon, the behemoth over there with Antonio.'

'His name was Goliath of Gath,' murmured Daniel. My own response exactly.

'And Tommy might be cast as David. Have you seen her?'

'Behind the buffet,' he said. 'Talking to Bernie.'

'Have you got enough info yet?' I asked. The evening was beginning to be overwhelming. I have never liked large groups of people.

'Let's just circulate for a little longer,' he suggested. 'Then we can escape before the speeches.'

'Good plan,' I said, and we separated. Daniel went right, I went left. I noticed that the athletic accountants from Mason and Co. were also here. That firm must do the books for all the caterers in town. Mr. Mason was gobbling those attractive prawns and Tony was picking at a vegetable ravioli. Claire was not eating anything. All were drinking imported French water. Sparkling. Gah.

I fetched up in front of the striped buffet again. I reached for another canapé.

'Try the little soufflés,' suggested a woman beside me. 'Are you Corinna Chapman? I buy your bread.'

'I'm Corinna.' I held out an unoccupied hand. We shook.

'Tricia. This is my buffet. Do you like it?'

'Excellent,' I said. 'Really excellent.' Tricia preened.

'We try to make the best for the client's budget,' she said. 'The secret is, best ingredients, careful preparation, pay your cooks well.'

'That's sort of what Simon said,' I remarked. She stiffened. Even blue and white stripes could not make this woman plump and rosy. She was as thin as a fashion model or scarecrow and the pink on those cheeks came from Max Factor.

'Simon? A charlatan, and that's putting it kindly. He's worse than Maîtresse.'

'What's wrong with Maîtresse?'

'Showy food, shameless self-promotion—same as Simply Simon. None of them really care about food. And none of them dare take a risk with it.'

'Such as serving little soufflés at a buffet?' I hazarded.

'Like that.' She nodded emphatically. 'My food is pure alchemy—kitchen chemistry. Eventually the public will realise that the tired old recipes don't cut it anymore.'

'What if they prefer a pie and chips?' I asked daringly. She drew herself up to her full height and snorted.

'Well, if that's their attitude, they don't deserve my food.'

'Quite,' I replied. The soufflé was perfect. I wondered how she had managed to stop it from sinking.

'Besides—' she leaned closer '—I'm told that Tommy is due for a great fall.'

'Like Humpty Dumpty? Why?'

'Rats in the ranks,' she said, and whisked away to coax someone else to try the canapés.

I was full of food, I was overheated and I wanted to get away. Just as I formed the thought, Daniel materialised at my elbow and led me out of the throng. As we finally managed to gain the street, which was relatively quiet, I thought about what Tricia had said. Rats in the ranks? Did Tommy really have a spy in her kitchen?

As they used to sing at the end of *Play School*, it was time to go home. So we went.

Chapter Fourteen

I rose and dressed and did the morning things, still thinking about the conversation I had had with Daniel the night before. Tommy had enemies, all right. Rivals. Fierce ones. I had not known that the food business was so competitive. Only the niche marketers—like Irena—did not strive ferociously to force each other out of the field. Yet you would have thought that there was room for all of them. Still, I suppose there are a finite number of weddings in any given year. I burped. All that emotion and rich food had given me indigestion. Deciding that I would just stick to what I am good at—bread—I went downstairs to admit Bernie and begin the baking.

Bread happened. Cupcakes happened. Bernie's first attempt at Bosworth Jumbles occurred. I was about to warn her that since she was working for Tommy her recipe might be considered Tommy's property, but refrained. Surely that only happened to scientists and inventors. But with this strong sense of competition among the caterers, who knew? They were very good jumbles, anyway. Richard III's martyred cook would have been proud. As I let the Mouse Police out through the alley door I saw someone lurking outside. It was Jason.

'Come in,' I invited. 'Hungry?'

I had never known Jason when he wasn't starving and this lure drew him inside. Bernie and Jason exchanged a long, cool look. I was forcibly reminded of two cats in disputed territory.

At any moment there would be shrieks and claws and flying fur and bitten ears.

'What would you like?' I bustled between them. I make a pretty good shield. Another advantage of being a woman of size. 'Rolls? Bread? Taste one of Bernie's jumbles?'

'Seed roll,' he mumbled and grabbed. We both stood and watched him. He looked tired, I thought, but there were pupils in his eyes and he had not, as far as I could see, gone back on the gear. He was dressed in a clean pair of jeans and a T shirt with a rabbit on the front. 'Yum,' he said, reaching for another.

'This is Bernie,' I introduced her. 'She works for my school-friend Tommy in the catering business. She wants to be a pastry chef,' I added. 'Don't you, Bernie?'

'Pastry is my life,' she said. 'Try a jumble.'

Jason took a jumble as requested and bit and chewed reflectively.

'Pretty good,' he said. 'Maybe a bit too buttery.'

'There is a lot of butter in the recipe,' I told him. 'It's medieval and they had their own cows. Also butter was necessary because they didn't have a lot of raising agents except eggs.'

'You reckon you could cut down the shortening?' he asked, taking another, purely in the interests of research.

'Probably,' said Bernie. 'This is my first try. I'm going to have my own cake shop in Los Angeles. I hope.'

'Sweet,' said Jason, though I don't know if he was talking about the cake shop itself or the dream. 'H'lo, Corinna.'

'Hello, Jason,' I replied. 'Want to sit in on the baking?'

I had said the wrong thing, as I always do in the morning. Jason stiffened, said, 'I got a job already,' and slunk out. The Mouse Police collided with his ankles on their way back inside and he stooped to stroke them before he vanished.

'Boys,' commented Bernie.

'You said it,' I agreed.

'He'll come round,' said Bernie.

'Why do you think that?' I asked, hoping for some crumb of comfort.

'He pinched another cake on his way out,' she told me.

I agreed that this did sound hopeful and we got on with the work.

Daniel joined us for the trip to Harbour Studios. Today's tune was Leonard Cohen's 'Hallelujah.' Whistled badly. The journey seemed longer than it was.

Daniel was intent, today, on being visible, so he went to join the breakfasters while Bernie and I carried in the bread and cakes and started on today's menu. More pastry. I was probably getting more adept with pastry now that I was making so much of it. There had been no complaints, I thought, or Tommy would have told me all about it. In any case, pastry was just the envelope for the filling. All it had to be was friable enough not to break teeth and durable enough to survive handling…

What a world, this food world, I thought as I pounded and kneaded. Who would have thought that it would be so vicious, full of envy, malice and all uncharitableness?

I looked around the kitchen. The salad makers were slicing and chopping like fiends, under the lash of Lance the Lettuce Guy's glare. As I watched one almost screamed at another, 'Will you stop that bloody humming?'

Tension was high again. I caught Bernie's attention and raised an eyebrow. 'Another trick,' she mouthed. 'This one used chili powder. Our chili powder.'

'Ms. Atkins?'

'Yes, and look out, here she comes!' Bernie turned her attention to her icing and I tried to melt into my pastry as the red-suited woman stalked into the kitchen, dragged a chair into the centre of the room, and declared to Emily, 'I'm going to watch them cook my breakfast. Then they can't play any games with the food.'

The maker of scrambled eggs, a small plump girl with dark hair, quailed and dropped a spoon.

'Of course, Ms. Atkins, what would you like?' asked Tommy briskly. Brisk might be the only way to get Ms. Atkins out of the kitchen and back on the set where she belonged.

'A lightly poached egg with hollandaise and spinach,' she declared. Perfect modulation. Her voice carried to every corner of the room. Tommy nodded to Lance and to the egg-scrambler, who already had eggs poaching in their vinegary liquid. I thrust an English muffin into the toaster, and Lance gathered the spinach, inspecting every leaf and nibbling a couple as quality control. The sauce maker began to whisk white sauce with cheese for the hollandaise. All the time, Ms. Atkins sat and stared at us all.

It was unnerving. She had amazing presence. If HM the Q had dropped in for a snack, it might have felt like this did. Nervous. Luckily, I had no contribution to make to the royal meal so I kept making pastry. And pastry had not been implicated in the food-trickster's little japes. Which was a relief. It was shared by Bernie.

'At least there's nothing wrong with the baking,' she whispered to me.

'And there won't be anything wrong with this Eggs Benedict,' I replied in an undertone. 'Lance is interrogating every leaf. Personally.'

'And so far it is telling the truth,' she observed gravely.

Had solemn Bernie just made a joke? I looked around. She was smiling. I returned the smile.

What presence she had, this actress. Enamelled, perfect, from the immaculate hair to the delicate red shoe. She beckoned to me and I hurried over.

Up close, one could see the cracks. The little lines around the eyes and the slackening of the jaw. I wondered how old she really was. In calendar years, not actress years.

'Has your partner found anything yet?' she asked.

'He is making progress,' I told her, striving not to curtsey. 'Shall I fetch him? He's somewhere around.'

She nodded regally. I went in search of Daniel. I found him talking to Ali, the sound man.

'Daniel, you have been summoned to the royal presence,' I said. 'She's in the kitchen and I have to warn you…'

'She's in a mood,' he finished my sentence for me. 'I know. I'm coming. Right away.'

'Good luck with that,' said Ali.

Daniel could soothe the Big Bang. He went to Ms. Atkins, took the scarlet-taloned hand in his, and leant down to talk. He was a reassuring presence. The kitchen calmed as well, now that it was not being glared at. Ms. Atkins' breakfast was assembled and she was escorted out to eat it. Daniel went with her. There was a collective exhalation of relief.

'Well, one thing, it wasn't us,' said Bernie, picking up her icing syringe. 'We have been together all morning.'

'Happened before we got here,' I agreed. 'Before Daniel got here, too. Which might be significant. Well, that's my pastry all rolled out. Pass me some fillings, and let's get this show on the road.'

I made all my pies and quiches. While they were safely stowed in the oven I left Bernie to her own devices and wandered over to talk to the most unregarded people in any kitchen, the washers-up, known dismissively as 'dish pigs.' There were three, clustered around the big machines. I introduced myself.

'You make the pies,' said one, identified as Santo. 'You make grouse pies.'

'Excellent,' agreed the second, who said his name was Rai. Now that I looked at Rai, I was not sure as to his or her gender. Stringy hair, ribby body, loose T shirt and apron. Epicene. The third was a young woman who told me that her name was Laura. They were all university students, hoping to graduate in this kitchen to chopping and dicing before they graduated as accountant, lawyer and business administrator. I asked them how they liked their work.

'It could be worse,' said Rai. 'The leftovers are ours. I'm putting on weight, I'm sure. I've worked in places where you were forbidden to touch a crumb and anyone found chewing was sacked.'

'Me, too,' said Santo. 'Mind you, some places you wouldn't want to risk the food. George Orwell talks about it in *Down and Out in Paris and London*. Gross. Tommy's strict—you should have heard her create when that fork went out with dried egg on it—but she's fair. When one of the machines broke down and we had to wash a whole lunch by hand she gave us a bonus. Also, she sends her green waste to be composted and the untouched leftovers to Feed My Lambs who put on meals for the homeless. All her produce is organic. This is an eco-friendly business.'

'True,' agreed Laura. 'And they do nice vegetarian food. Usually I have to live on mashed potato and wilted salads.'

'Any idea about who's playing tricks with Ms. Atkins?'

'Rotten bitch,' said Rai heatedly. 'Rotten, rotten bitch. She deserves worse.'

'Oh?' I waited to hear more.

'She nearly got me sacked over that eggy fork. You know what egg's like. Sticks like superglue. I only missed it once. Anyone else would have just got another fork. But because God hates me, she got the fork, and she went on as though I'd tried to poison her. Demanded that Tommy fire me right away.'

'Yes, but Tommy didn't fire you,' said Laura patiently. This, evidently, was a conversation which had happened many times before. 'Tommy said it was an oversight and that we'd be more careful in future and she let you stay. Get over it!'

'It wasn't fair,' muttered Rai. I was coming to the conclusion that he might be male, after all.

'Chill,' advised Santo. 'Who's doing it? I dunno. Could be anyone. As you can see, Ms. Atkins has a real talent for making enemies. And before you ask, it wasn't Rai. Rai was with us and has been all morning. But I reckon,' he added slowly, 'that you are looking in the right place. It must be someone in this kitchen. And who knows what he or she will do next? It's all been annoyance level up until now. What if it's drain cleaner or rat poison next time?'

'You spend too much time on Second Life,' scoffed Laura.

'It isn't Second Life,' he said. 'It's detective stories. You don't read enough of them. It's all fantasy with you.'

'Spooky,' said Rai.

'You know,' said Santo, 'I thought that one of us might be Ms. Atkins' lost baby.'

'Does everyone know about this?' I demanded.

'Of course. This is a kitchen. But I can't work out who. Maybe Emily?'

'Find someone else,' I advised. 'The baby was a boy.'

'Oh,' said Santo. 'Another good theory down the tube. There must be some other reason that Emily stays with Ms. Atkins, then.'

'Must be love,' said Laura.

They laughed. I left. It was time to rescue my pastry.

With all my productions safely cooling on the bench, I cleaned up. Bernie was decorating cupcakes. I asked her if she had any suspects.

'No,' she said, distracted by confections. 'Well, no, not really. Can you smash this toffee for me?'

'Finely powdered or just broken into bite-size bits?' I asked.

'Bite-size,' she replied.

I took my trusty rolling pin and pounded. Very satisfying. Toffee breaks like glass. In fact, I believe that film windows were made of sugar at one time. Ideal. You do the stunt and get to eat the pane without the inconvenience of bleeding to death.

Bernie scattered the toffee over her cinnamon and apple muffins. I memorised the idea in order to tell Jason. Then I remembered that Jason was working at the chicken shop and sighed. What a waste!

On with the feast. I had completed my part of it, so I went into the studio to find out how Daniel had fared with Ms. Atkins.

I saw him from a distance in close conference with Ethan. Daniel appeared to be unscarred. No visible claw wounds. Rehearsal was going on, so I sat down to watch. I was becoming addicted to this sort of drama. It was so…dramatic. Cheap emotions and crude writing, but it had power. Like cocaine. Or gin.

Today's plot concerned the organisation of a huge wedding with multifold difficulties: namely the bride's mother, the groom's father, a bunch of relatives and the bride herself, who was having second thoughts about this enormous bash and was trying to opt for a quiet celebration with a few friends and lunch in a restaurant. Ms. Atkins as Courtneigh Yronsyde required that the huge bash go ahead, as she was getting commissions from everyone from the celebrant to the man who put up the tents. The dialogue in this episode was fast; the tension was improving the performance, not damaging it.

'But of course, if you want a *little* wedding,' Ms. Atkins purred, 'we can arrange that…'

I wanted the bride to stand up to her and tell her to go ahead with a little wedding. But the bride crumbled.

'Well, maybe you were right…' she temporised, and was lost.

I went back to the kitchen, determined never, ever, to get married. To anyone. Not even the delicious Daniel, who was standing beside Ethan as the camera was operated. Was Ms. Atkins' baby—now nineteen—on the set? Who could it be?

Harrison did rather obtrude. He was gorgeous, an actor right down to his skin-tight briefs, clearly visible through the lycra bicycle pants, and as self-centred as a gyroscope. A good genetic match for Ms. Atkins. Did we know anything about Harrison? I couldn't engage him in conversation now; he was on set.

I had a thought. Now might be a good time to go down to Simply Simon and check out the waste disposal. It was a nice day for a walk.

Daniel sighted me and hurried to the kitchen door.

'Going somewhere, beautiful lady?' he asked.

'Thought I might wander down to Simply Simon in King Street,' I said, melting.

'Good notion,' he approved. 'I'll accompany you to the car park. My phone has been buzzing like a hyperactive bee.'

In the car park Daniel consulted his phone. He scrolled through the texts. Then I watched the blood drain from his face.

'What?' I demanded.

'Lena. She's disappeared. That was her mother. Oh, Lord.'

'So we have to find Lena as well as the documents?'

'Yes, and the way to do that is to hack into her Facebook page and her blog. Can you go and ask the Lone Gunmen to start work on that? Here's the details. Soon as they can.'

He kissed me and whisked back inside. I thought that I might as well do the King Street search first. The Lone Gunmen would not be awake yet; they did not come out of their hobbit-holes until the day was comprehensively aired.

◇◇◇

King Street is not a charming street. It bears no resemblance to the avenues of Paris. It is lined with industrial and office buildings, built to no aesthetic principle that I have ever discerned. But it was a nice day, for a change, not too hot. I and my sunhat strolled toward Simply Simon, a forest green block in the middle of wasteland.

And outside it was a large, walk-in skip, emblazoned with RECYCLED OFFICE SUPPLIES—HELP YOURSELF. Aha!

The skip was stacked with paper. I sampled the stacks. Documents by the thousand. But which ones were Pockets' documents? Here were government reports, copies of letters, résumés, even what seemed to be a good half of a novel, students' essays, children's drawings. My own accounts for Earthly Delights were there. The whole documentary life of the city was in that skip. Someone might have written a rather good philosophical thesis on it.

I had truffled around in the skip for fully an hour before I remembered that everything Pockets had handled before was smeared with filthy fingerprints, so I began to look for them. It was hot inside this metal prison, and I was beginning to lose patience with my quest when I found a neat pile particularly marked with whorls.

It would be very nice to produce the missing bonds to Daniel, I thought as I ruffled through the dirty pages. Copies of letters from—aha again!—Mason and Co, the firm of accountants for which Lena worked. I sorted to the bottom of the stack.

No bonds. I sorted again to make sure that I had not missed them. But they were not there. Nor was another nursery rhyme clue. Dead end. Damn.

I took a bundle of letters out into the street to read through at my leisure. I still have an accountant's eye. I skimmed the transactions. I noted the dates. I read them again.

Then I stuffed the correspondence into my shoulder bag and walked softly away. Today was not the day to drop in on Simply Simon and ask for the grand tour. I had to think about this.

Meanwhile I had the Lone Gunmen to see and I ought to get myself some lunch. The breeze blew onto my sweaty forehead and cooled me. Something had to…

And where was Lena? Even now she might be holing up in some unsavoury den to complete that suicide which had been interrupted before. Daniel would have to go and interview Pockets again. He had left us no further clues. Which was annoying of him. Still, not much can be expected of one to whom the Lemurians are delivering instructions. I wondered if we could contact the aliens and ask them where the bearer bonds might be. It seemed our best shot at present…

I bought one of Uncle Solly's famous salt-beef-on-rye sandwiches for lunch. Uncle Solly eyed me shrewdly.

'What's the matter, dollink?' he asked. 'That Sabra giving you grief? You send him to me. I set him right.'

'No, not him.' The shop was empty and I needed someone to confide in. Who better than the wise and extremely well-connected Uncle Solly? Uncle Solly heard everything. He might not have been the local representative of Mossad, as popular rumour said. But then again, he might. And this was the financial end of town.

I told him the tale of Lena, Pockets and the bearer bonds.

'Bad,' he said. 'You sit, have glass tea, eh? We talk about this.'

I sat. I had a glass of lemon tea. Uncle Solly could not be hurried. Several customers came in, were served, went out. I lingered over my tea and was about to unwrap my sandwich when he came back.

'I heard of this shemozzle,' he told me. 'Everyone has seen Daniel tracking this poor old mad man across town. All I know is, there is something *schmutzig* about that firm. They do the books for all the foodies. Foodies, pah,' he added. 'They never want to taste my food. Their taste is rotten. All chili like will burn out their bellies in the end. Better they eat honest food and keep the laws.'

'Yes,' I agreed. 'Fashion will make dyspeptics of us all.'

'What you say,' he agreed. 'I ask around, dollink. I let you know. But the word is that firm is in deep. In deep what, I find out. Everyone talks to good old Uncle Solly, what can I do?' He spread his hands, grinned a very dark grin, and let me go.

I carried my bag back to Insula, with a brief detour to the supermarket. I knocked on the door of the Lone Gunmen's shop. It was supposed to be open by now, but they had discovered a fine source of income in abolishing things and finding things on the interwebs, and they only opened now when they felt like some conversation with fellow gamers. Their customer base had accepted this. They got away with their hacking because they had agreed to help the police with any little computer problems they might have. They may have been troglodytes, but they're not stupid.

Gully opened the door, widened his eyes at the presence of a female, and then again at the presence of an armful of Tex-Mex dainties. He opened the door wide.

'Come in,' he said to the junk food. I came with it. I went into their kitchen and unloaded onto the table. I had bags of corn chips, guacamole, Molten Metal salsa, grated cheese, sour cream, a frightful chili dip which dissolved fillings, and a lot of bottles of their favourite drink, Arctic Death, a combination of lemon syrup, soda water, and antifreeze. Or that's what it tasted like to me. I had once brought the Lone Gunmen a lovingly crafted guacamole made by a fervent Mexican cook, who had given it to me as a present. I can't stand chili, so I had regifted it, and watched the Lone Gunmen as they squaffed it. 'Nice,' they told me. 'But not up to Junk Inc's standard.' After that I had surrendered. There was no way to improve their palate, assuming they still had one. Perhaps they really did like the tang of all those artificial colours and flavours. You never know with tastes in food.

'Breakfast!' said Taz gleefully. He began popping bags and loading corn chips onto microwave plates stained red with the blood of a thousand tomatoes.

'Breakfast?' said Rat, wandering in after what had to have been a late night playing the latest game: Bioshock or Heavy Rain. He is called Rat because he retains a little tail of hair at the nape of his neck, like a rat's tail. Fashion has never been a preoccupation for the Lone Gunmen.

'Love that dip,' he said, seizing a handful of corn chips and wresting the lid off the container. 'What's the occasion, Corinna?'

'You've got a new job,' I told them, to the sound of crunching and snacking. 'Daniel wants you to look up this Facebook site and read this blog. It's urgent. The writer has disappeared and she's a suicide risk. So get cracking,' I added. Three heads nodded. Their mouths were too full to reply.

'We'll send it all through to Daniel's phone,' spluttered Gully, always the spokesman. I brushed off a few crumbs and took my leave. Chili for breakfast. How the other half lived…

My place was clean and cool and chili-free. I took a shower and sat myself and cat down at the desk to examine those documents. And eat Uncle Solly's salt beef sandwich. Which was, as always, excellent.

I had a balance sheet and the workings which made up the company accounts. They made fascinating reading. I put on my accountant's hat and examined them closely. What did this company do, what were its assets, its liabilities, its current account? Pockets had marked these sheets with his unmistakable prints. He had handled them. And he had stashed them in the recycling bin. Why? Because he was a fruitcake?

Wait a moment. Pockets had said something about 'corrupt' documents. This had a special meaning in computer science—the code was mixed up. Pockets might have known that. I examined them more closely, adding salt beef crumbs to the biological overload already present. Or did he mean corrupt as in debased? What did those Lemurians want with these papers, anyway?

◇◇◇

Several hours later Daniel arrived. He looked hot and harassed, but had brought a bag of spare goodies, filched from Tommy's kitchen before they were sent off to Feed My Lambs. Horatio rose to his paws to greet Daniel and that hopeful-looking canvas bag. Canvas bags contained cat food. He knew that.

Daniel stroked Horatio, gave him a whole cream bun for his very own, and slumped into a chair next to me. He rubbed his eyes.

'Nothing,' he replied to my look. Horatio licked enthusiastically at the cream, up on the table where he knew he was not supposed to be. I lifted him and his bun and placed them both on the floor. He gave me a severe look, but kept eating. Affront was affront, but a cream bun did not come his way very often.

'I spoke to the Lone Gunmen, they're on the case,' I told my beloved. 'I'll just put on the kettle, you can feast on some leftovers, and I will tell you all about Mason and Co. Also, Uncle Solly is making enquiries. Nothing you can do at present; take a breath, poor darling.'

'You're wonderful,' he said to me. 'Tea, please. I've had my fill of coffee. TV studios run on coffee. Have one of these honey slices. Bernie made them. They're very good. Eight million calories in every slice.'

'And I bet she told Ms. Atkins they were low-fat,' I commented. 'That must be real cream in the bun. Horatio can detect confectioner's cream at fifty paces and wants nothing to do with it.'

'He's a dairy cat,' said Daniel.

I made tea. Daniel ate a sausage roll. He raised an eyebrow at the pile of papers on the table.

'Documents,' I said. 'Put in a recycling skip by Pockets. Not the bonds, sorry, they're not there. But that company is in trouble.'

'Bad trouble?' he asked, biting into another sausage roll.

'Very bad,' I agreed. 'Someone appears to be cooking the books.'

Chapter Fifteen

Daniel laughed. Crumbs showered. It seemed to be my day to be spattered with pastry. I laid my papers before him and pointed out the interesting bits.

'See, here this expense is an expense. On this spreadsheet, it's an asset. And this debt has been hived off to this sub-company so that it does not appear in the profit-and-loss. And I'm pretty sure that those capital expenditures are actually ordinary business expenses.'

'What's the advantage of that?'

'Putting the coffee onto capital? Tax. Don't giggle—that's what Enron was doing. And look what happened to them.'

'Indeed,' he said.

'And another thing…' I put down the papers. 'Why was Lena carrying bearer bonds around town? Hardly anyone uses them anymore. They never ought to come out of the safe.'

'Why?'

'Because they are unregistered and totally negotiable. Like money. Just like money, in fact. In a much more portable form. A bearer bond can be for a million dollars. All in one easily hidden one-page document. Not like carrying a suitcase full of heavy notes.'

'Hmm,' said Daniel, his mouth full of honey slice.

'Admittedly, they are the negotiable instrument of choice for tax evaders and money launderers. They're banned in the

US for that reason. Most financial transactions of any size are done on computer now, anyway. You know, Daniel,' I said, 'reluctant as I am to admit it, there are some crooked accountants. Not many.'

'There are also crooked police, ministers of religion and politicians,' Daniel put in comfortingly. 'There are even crooked rabbis, though I can't think of one at the moment. So you think that Mason and Co. is worthy of a little research?'

'I do,' I said. 'I'll see what's on the public record about them.'

'And I'll check the private sources,' he said. 'I wonder what other interns thought of Mason and Co.? Might be time to find a few. And, of course, find Lena, which means reading that huge email which the Lone Gunmen sent.'

'Can I help?' I asked.

'Certainly,' he told me. 'You would understand a bullied young woman better than I.'

'I wouldn't be too sure about that,' I said. 'But I can try.'

We drank our tea and read through Lena's Facebook entries. It was depressing. Lena had thrown all caution to the winds and exposed her bleeding heart to the cyberspace community, and only a few had been kind. Most replies urged her to stand up for herself and show some backbone and not be so despicably weak. And these were her friends. Two were sympathetic at first. Their names were FaeGirl and GerGer.

Not much longer to go before you finish, encouraged FaeGirl. *Hang in there!*

They're being horrible to you, said GerGer. *Don't give them the satisfaction of seeing you cry.*

But gradually even these people lost empathy. FaeGirl announced that she was unfriending Lena *because of her whining. Suck it up, girlfriend!* she urged in farewell.

And GerGer became positively sinister. *There's a way out if you aren't too weak*, he said.

This was repeated over the entries, recounting the small tyrannies and minor cruelties to which Lena had been continuously subject. Not asking her to sign a get-well card (because the recipient was already sick enough). Not inviting her to after-work drinks (because it was a small bar and they all had to fit in). Not including her in lunch orders (because she needed to go on a diet). Telling her that she was lazy (because she was fat). Leaving cosmetic surgery pamphlets on her desk (because she should consider having all that ugly fat sliced off). Excluding her from the photo of the staff for the annual report (because they were a healthy fit firm). Calling her Fatso, Blimp, Zeppelin, Meatloaf, Bloat, Greedhead. Insults and abuse, nibbling away at her sense of safety. Eroding her self-confidence. *You can escape*, insinuated GerGer. *They'll never be able to get to you once you're safe in heaven.*

'This is torture,' I said to Daniel.

'Torture it is,' he agreed. 'But not illegal. Unfortunately. It would be lovely to get my hands on GerGer,' he added grimly. 'I'll ask the hackers to track him down.'

'And when they do?' I had a lot of faith in the skill of the Lone Gunmen, though none at all in their social abilities.

'We shall have a conversation,' said Daniel.

There was a silence in which Horatio indicated that a scratch under the chin—no, not there, just *there*—would be appreciated. I scratched. He purred. I tried to feel a gentle pity for GerGer and got nowhere. I am not a nice person, really.

Instructive as the entries had been, they gave us no clue as to where Lena might have gone.

'Would she go to FaeGirl?' I asked.

'Not after she had been unfriended,' said Daniel. 'And I haven't heard that she's on the street. Not in the city, at least. We need to ask her mother. How I do not look forward to that interview.' He shuddered slightly.

'I'll come too,' I offered. 'She might not shred you if there's a third party present.'

'I marvel at your confidence,' he said gloomily. 'That woman will see a third party as a valuable extra audience for her grievances.'

'What about her father?' I asked. 'Lena's father. Her mother said that he was always kind to her.'

'A thought,' said Daniel, and rattled keys. He looked up a moment later.

'Her father is on the net,' he said, delighted. 'And he Twitters.'

'What's his profession?' I asked.

'Consultant engineer.' He flourished his fingers. 'Aha, lives in an apartment in Docklands! No wife or children mentioned. We can drop in during the day. We're already at Harbour Studios tomorrow. Good. Very good. Now for some dinner—do you fancy maybe Thai?—and some research.'

I always fancy Thai food. We ate it as we followed the strange and twisting paths of corporate sub-creations that marked Mason and Co., until it got late and Daniel prepared to join the Soup Run, the route of which ought to take him to anywhere Lena might be if she was still in the city. I put self and cat to bed, pleased with a good day's work. Something was definitely rotten in that company. Otherwise why were they hiving off little companies whose sole purpose appeared to be possession of a woundy great debt which ought to belong to the parent company? Gotcha, I thought as I fell asleep.

◇◇◇

I woke with the sense that I had missed something, but I had to go and make bread, so I descended to the bakery, put on the mixers and the coffee pot (those essential bakery tools) and let Bernie in. She looked irritatingly clean and neat and began right away to chat about her private life, in which I had no interest at that hour of the morning.

'Ethan thinks I ought to call my shop the Magnolia Bakery,' she informed me. 'But that's the name from *Sex and the City*. Do you think they'd let me use it?'

'Not a chance,' I told her, seeing as the Magnolia was a real bakery, not a fictitious one. And wondering what sex had to do with the city. 'Anything to do with TV is out of the question. Why not think of another name? It's medieval in theme, isn't it? Why not Ye Olde Cake Shoppe?' I said ironically, pronouncing the extra syllables.

'Brilliant!' exclaimed Bernie.

This is, as the Professor had remarked, a generation without history…

We continued baking. As I let the Mouse Police out to scavenge the alley, Jason came in. He helped himself to a muffin, bit and chewed.

'Not bad,' he said. His cool was a trifle studied, but Bernie was so excited about her new cake shop that she told him all about it and supplied him with a door-stopper of yesterday's rye topped with a slab of cheese big enough to feed a family of mice for a month. Which precluded further comment as I got on with the kneading. He was looking tired, I thought, a bit dishevelled. And he smelt quite strongly of frying oil and chicken. He was working his way through his sandwich with his usual concentration. Jason must have been born hungry. Bernie was concluding her design for her Los Angeles shop as he finally swallowed his last mouthful.

'Need any help?' he asked.

I could have hugged him but I always make mistakes in the morning and I just said, 'Take over the kneading, will you? Bernie needs to do her icing.'

'Okay,' he agreed laconically. He washed his hands with special care and started to beat the dough into submission. This is a very soothing occupation. While doing so, however, he was watching Bernie like a hawk as she beat egg whites for her icing. Jason still wanted to learn. This was heartening. Bernie, also, would probably not mind teaching someone. We worked in silence for a while.

Silence is good. It contains no possibilities for putting foot in mouth. Bernie finished her icing and took out her prepared roses. Jason shoved his tins into the oven and came to look.

'Pretty,' he commented.

'They're easy,' she told him. 'I can show you how to make them?'

'Show me,' he said.

I did the rest of the baking as Bernie showed Jason how to make icing roses (they are easy enough if you have a steady hand

and endless patience, which I do not). Jason made some of his own. They were interesting if a little free-form and he had a heavy hand with the food colouring. Jason's roses were not delicately tinted pastel ones. They were bright red and bright blue.

'I can use them tomorrow,' said Bernie. 'They have to dry. You're pretty good,' she told Jason. 'Come tomorrow and make some more?'

'Thanks,' he said. 'Gotta go get some sleep. All right, Corinna?'

'All right,' I agreed. When he had gone, I just had to hug Bernie. She bore it well.

'I told you he'd come round,' she pointed out. We loaded everything and Daniel, who was half asleep, and to the tune of 'One More Cup of Coffee' we drove to Harbour Studios.

No tricks this morning, so the kitchen was not so tense. The conversation was mostly about a vampire movie, which I had not seen. The lettuce snippers were solidly Team Edward, while the meat cooks—perhaps appropriately—were all for Team Jacob and the werewolf way. I have a writer friend who claims that all literature is a metadrama and this is certainly true with fantasy. Anne Rice introduced vampires like Lestat, truly unhuman and chilling. Then other writers took up the idea and spun it as pleased themselves. Though every such novel I read these days seems to have not only werewolves and vampires, but also fairies. I live in hope of another supernatural creature being discovered. I am getting tired of blood suckers and puppy dogs. And tall, exceptionally beautiful men with long hair…

I beguiled my pastry making with fantasies of what Daniel would look like with hair to his waist. Ooh! I knocked off only as I realised that my hands were becoming too hot. This is bad for pastry. I stuck it all in the fridge and tried to cool myself down as well. I poured a glass of lemon barley water which Tommy supplied for the staff (in homage to Carême, I believe) and drank it. Lovely. Not fizzy. Breakfast was going out and I joined the servers.

As I handed around my tray of toast I wondered if what the dish pigs had said could be true. Might Ms. Atkins' missing baby boy be here? Was someone on this set concealing the dreadful secret that they had been born Zephaniah? There were a lot of people, but the choice was limited by age. Zephaniah must be about twenty. That left out Ethan and a lot of the crew, who tended to the grey-haired. What about the actors?

Now Harrison must be about the right age, and he was an actor right down to his impeccable manicure. On cue—I swear sometimes actors know when you are thinking about them, like cats and children—he sidled up to me and selected a piece of toast. Goddess, he was gorgeous. Dark eyes. Dark hair. Ms. Atkins had blue eyes. But then, I didn't know who the father of this child was. Genetics were not going to be a help. Even if I could remember what recessive meant.

'How's it going?' Harrison asked.

'Looks good from where I'm standing,' I told him. He beamed.

'I thought that entrance was too fast,' he confided. 'I'm only in shot for seconds. I tried a slower saunter but Tash hurried me. I hate,' he said, looking down the length of his classically perfect leg and haunch, 'being hurried.'

'I thought it was very effective,' I assured him.

'Really? Was it hot?' He gave me an electric smile, white teeth, red lips.

'Red hot,' I said. 'Sizzling.' Not even for research would I endure Harrison any longer. Besides, he was hogging the toast. I moved on.

Who else could be the lost Zephaniah? Did anyone show signs of a rigidly Christian upbringing in the Church of Perpetual Suffering? The trouble is that could take people many ways. Look at Aleister Crowley. He was brought up by Plymouth Brethren. And didn't they regret it…

Probably not Ali the sound man. He was so very Muslim. Though he was the right age. Sound men have hard lives: they age early. The world is just so full of noises that are not the right noise. He smiled and declined food.

Just as I approached Ms. Atkins, I heard her shriek at Emily, 'You stupid slut!' She raised that wonderful voice so no one on set could miss a word. 'I said my red shoes! Are these my red shoes? I think not! Look at them! Go on, look!'

She slapped a strong hand on Emily's shoulder and forced the girl to her knees, compelling her to inspect the shoes. They looked red to me. I could not watch this. If Tommy wanted to sack me, she could sack me.

I strode up to Ms. Atkins and grabbed her arm, releasing Emily, who stayed on her knees, crying like a fountain.

'That's enough,' I said firmly.

Ms. Atkins struggled. She might spend two hours a day at the gym, but I spent my life subduing dough and I was stronger than she was. 'You're behaving like a child,' I told her. 'So I'll treat you like a child. Now you are going to your room until you can keep your temper and behave like a grown-up. Get up, Emily, you're not hurt,' I instructed.

The rest was easy. I escorted Ms. Atkins, who had not said another word, back to her dressing room and pushed her inside. She slammed the door on me, which was fine. I gathered up Emily and deposited her in a chair, calling to the kitchen staff for a large brandy. Then I looked around. I had an audience. The cast and crew were standing stock-still and staring at me. There was a long silence. Ethan grinned and made a thumbs-up sign.

'Corinna,' said Tash.

'Can I have your autograph?' asked Harrison.

'You go, girlfriend!' said Kylie and Goss in unison.

Then Ethan began to applaud and the others joined in and I was standing in front of an appreciative audience of actors and crew, blushing.

There was only one thing to do. I bowed, and went back to the kitchen.

There Tommy was waiting for me. I forestalled her.

'If you want me to quit, Tommy, I'm happy to write my resignation as soon as I can find a bit of paper and a pen.'

But she was smiling. 'No, no,' she assured me. 'Stay! I would love to give you a bonus! That has so wanted doing and no one dared to do it. But you can have some of the good brandy if you are feeling at all faint.'

'I think I could manage to feel faint if it is the good brandy,' I replied.

It was. It was Armagnac. I sipped it with a little water. It looked like there was no way that I could get out of Harbour Studios except feet-first. A not-very-nice thought. But I could not loll around here all day. I had pastry to roll out and pies to make.

I had just put the last quiche in the oven and was dusting flour off my sleeves when Emily came into the kitchen. She really was a beautiful girl, even with her hair dishevelled and her blue eyes red.

'Came to thank you, Corinna,' she said softly. 'No one has ever stood up for me before. My Twitter buddies are really impressed.'

'Oh, good,' I said. I was vague about Twitter.

'It's not their fault,' she went on. 'All the people I know are in the business, you see, they can't confront Ms. Atkins. They're sorry for me but there's nothing they can do.'

'And what are *you* going to do?' I asked. 'Have you thought about another line of work where you won't be relentlessly bullied?'

'Oh, no,' she protested. 'This is all I have ever wanted to do. I'm going to be an actor. No matter what. Ms. Atkins or no Ms. Atkins. This is my chance. I've worked all my life for it. Left everything.'

I asked her to sit down and smuggled her one of Bernie's rare not-quite-right cupcakes. I poured her a cup of my own special tea from my own special teapot. She started to talk.

It was a common enough story, I suppose, but delivered with the sort of absolute faith and zeal which sent Joan to the stake. Strict parents who did not approve of her aspirations. Drama class at school. Then the scholarship to NIDA, the cutting of all ties with her family, the loss of every friend she had made. New place to live. New skills to learn. Dance classes which ricked the muscles, memorisation which strained the mind. The girl knew nothing but acting. She seemed not to have seen any films—except ones from which she could learn. Read no books—except theatrical memoirs. She ate, drank, breathed and slept the stage.

'So you see,' she laid a little hot paw on my arm, 'I can't give up, no matter what she does to me.'

'Yes, I see,' I told her. And I did see. 'But I have a suggestion. Stand up to her.'

'I can't ! She'd sack me!'

'No, I don't think so. She hasn't hotfooted it in here to demand that Tommy sack me. Yet. I suspect she's highly strung and overtired and underfed and she just tends to shriek. Try shrieking back. Well, it's an idea,' I said, relenting as Emily's head drooped like a failing flower.

'Corinna,' said another voice. I knew that one without turning around.

'Daniel,' I said, relieved. I really don't like emotion.

'Ms. Atkins has emerged,' he told me. 'She wishes to speak to everyone. Come along. You, too, Emily. She can't eat you.'

Oh well. It had been fun, in a way. I joined the whole crew as we gathered near the food. Ms. Atkins was immaculate, as usual. She raised her head and looked each of us in the eye, one after the other, as she delivered herself of—my God!—an apology.

'I'm so sorry,' she said in her thrilling undertone, perfectly audible even to Ali, who was muttering something about infidels. 'I have behaved appallingly. I am an unadulterated bitch and I apologise to each and every one of you and hope you might forgive me. Especially Emily.' She held out a hand to the girl and Emily faltered toward the star to be hugged gently to the upholstered bosom. 'You have all been working so hard and so well. I am sure that this is going to be a great success. We've got Tash, we've got Ethan and the crew, we've got fine young actors and excellent writers.' The writers grinned, astonished. 'We have to work together,' she said, and I was amazed, because the whole seething mass of resentment was coalescing, in front of my eyes, into a warm pot of something like bouillabaisse. Complex, flavourful and, ultimately, fishy.

But that seemed to be it. Ms. Atkins gave us all a beaming smile, kissed Emily lightly on the cheek, kissed Tash, even kissed Ethan, and they all fled back onto the set in a glow of collective endeavour. Actors.

I went back to the kitchen to tear off my apron and get out of Harbour Studios before I self-combusted. Daniel met me at the door.

'Docklands,' he suggested, and I said, 'Wait.'

I paused at the lunch table and packed a box full of goodies which I had personally cooked. Bernie added some of her baked cheesecake. Then I grabbed the bottle of Armagnac and we left. If Lena's father, Mr. White, wasn't home, then Daniel and I had a picnic. I was in the mood for spoiling the Egyptians. And if there were no Egyptians available, then Tommy would be an adequate substitute. I lifted the box and we stumbled out into the sunlight.

'Phew,' commented Daniel.

'Did you see that? How they all forgave each other like little lambkins?'

'I saw it,' said my beloved. 'I don't altogether believe it, however. Come along. I think it's that building.'

I shelved consideration of the scene I had just observed and followed Daniel through the canyons between the high-rise towers. This was a very expensive apartment building. Not as high as some of the others but well placed to get good views. The glass door was firmly shut and there was a doorman inside. Security.

We pressed the call button. A voice asked our names and purpose. Daniel explained. There was a silence, then a click as the occupant of the flat buzzed us in. A far cry from Insula, I thought, as we were welcomed, bustled inside, ushered into a lift and sent soaring by a uniformed individual with a very professional smile.

We arrived on the seventh floor and were met at the door of the apartment by someone who was clearly channelling Clement Clarke Moore of "'Twas the Night Before Christmas.' There are fat men and fat men, as I have remarked. This one was a cosy armful on the Coltrane model. He was wearing jeans and a yellow T shirt which proclaimed WILL WORK FOR COFFEE. It stretched over his ample tummy. His skin was an agreeable coffee colour, his hair the colour of dark chocolate and he had very white teeth. He smiled. He had dimples. He shook hands with Daniel (my hands were occupied) and led us into his apartment.

'You're friends of my daughter's?' he asked.

'Employees,' said Daniel. 'She hired me to find some missing documents and now we seem to have lost Lena. You're her father?'

'I am,' he said. 'Sit down, do. Coffee? A drink?'

I put my box down on the coffee table. 'A glass of wine would be very acceptable,' I said. I liked Mr. White. His apartment was done in chrome, sage green and cream—oh, you can date decor by the colour choice—but he had put up bright Parisian posters of markets and streetscapes and the whole place smelt of coffee. 'I've brought lunch,' I added. His eyes lit up.

'You're Corinna Chapman, aren't you?' he asked. 'I saw your picture on the Foodie website. You're a baker? I have always wanted to make bread but I just don't have the knack. Fortunately, you do. I particularly adore your seven-seed bread. Bring the box into the kitchen and we shall find some plates.'

I followed him into the kitchen—always my preferred location. It was a proper place, with all the right things. Oven, microwave, dishwasher, fridge, big table, lots of space. I put down the box again and began to unpack.

'I've got sandwiches, quiche, pie, Greek salad and green salad and a baked cheesecake for dessert,' I announced.

'And I've got a rather nice cabernet sauvignon and my friend has just sent me a Calvados which will go very well with the cheesecake, though I observe that you have brought a very fine Armagnac,' he responded. 'Let's eat! I don't usually have company for lunch.'

'Have you seen Lena?' asked Daniel in a strained voice.

'Oh, yes, she's here,' he said, dealing out plates. 'I'll fetch her in a moment. She's been sleeping in. We were up late playing Zenstones. Poor girl, she's had a time. I blame her mother, you know.' He bit into a cucumber sandwich. 'She insisted on Lena being thin. Lena's not going to be thin. All my family were fat and I am not a sylph either. But I'm happy,' he added. 'Very nice sandwiches,' he went on.

'Mr. White,' Daniel began.

'Oh, Roger, please. Lena arrived two days ago, very distressed. She didn't come to me before because her mother said that I didn't want her, now that I've come out. And Lena believed her. I really don't like that woman,' he said.

'She told Lena that because you were gay you didn't want her?' I asked, halfway through a smoked salmon sandwich.

'Just so,' said Roger. 'I tried very hard to be a husband, you see. I mowed lawns, I did the garden, I learnt to cook. I went to nice dinner parties and talked about rolled steel joists. I had a very religious upbringing, you know, homosexuality was sin. I believed it was. I believed a lot of things. I thought I was unhappy because that is man's sinful lot in this wicked world. Then I met a priest who was gay and, I swear, the veil dropped from my eyes. There were sinful men such as I—everywhere! Then I couldn't stay married. I had a fling with a young creature and my wife found out. My world fell to pieces.' He reached for another sandwich; I was glad that I had brought a lot of them. Mr. White looked like Father Christmas who has just been told that far more children were naughty than nice. He chewed thoughtfully for a while. 'But it re-formed and so did I. Now my daughter has come back to me, I've got a dear friend living just down the hall, and I will never, God willing, mow a lawn again. How do you like the wine?'

'Very nice,' I said.

'Robust,' said Daniel.

'I thought so. I went on a little winery tour with my friend and we picked up a few cases of the ones we liked. Yes, Lena can stay here with me. I thought we might buy her some new clothes. Maggie T does a good line for large ladies.'

'But what about her profession?' I asked.

'Ah, yes, well, there we have a problem. She is determined to be an accountant. If Mason and Co. sack her that will become difficult.'

'Did she tell you what they had been doing to her?' I asked.

'No, what?' said Mr. White, selecting a ham and mustard sandwich.

It took me ten minutes to tell her father what Lena had suffered, and he was so horrified that he did not eat another bite. He took several gulps of his wine during my recitation.

'But why?' he asked. 'She's a nice girl. Wouldn't harm a fly!'

'I am beginning to think,' said Daniel slowly, 'that this is not just normal cruelty to the different and other. I think they were trying to get rid of her.'

'Why?' repeated Mr. White.

'Because of something she knows,' said Daniel. 'Can you perhaps wake her? We can offer her some very nice lunch.'

'Of course, of course,' said Roger, and pottered off, distressed. He returned with a ruffled and sleepy Lena, who was amazed to see us.

'Lena,' said Daniel, 'this is important. What do you know about Mason and Co. that would make them want to get rid of you?'

Lena stared at him with her eyes as round as marbles.

'I can't imagine,' she said, and burst into tears.

Chapter Sixteen

Perhaps this had been sprung on the poor girl too suddenly. I bustled around and supplied tissues and a glass of wine, and her father sat Lena down at the table and selected a choice plate of the little sandwiches and pies for her delectation. We let her eat and drink for a while. Indeed I snared another munchie for myself and so did Mr. White. Egg and lettuce, yum.

'Lena, why didn't you tell me what they were doing to you?' asked Mr. White.

'Mum said that you didn't want to know me,' said Lena. 'People have unfriended me for whining. I was just so happy to get you back, Dad! I would have told you,' she said, sniffing.

'I'm very happy to get you back, too,' said Mr. White, also sniffing.

We all had some more wine and a few more little pies. Then I asked, 'Why were you carrying bearer bonds, Lena? That isn't usual.'

'No, I didn't want to, but they said I had to. I was supposed to deliver them to a Collins Street office. Into the hands of Ms. Anita Spellman at Circum and Co. Personally. But then I got into a muddle and my phone wouldn't work and...'

'Yes, yes, tell us more about that,' encouraged Daniel. 'What sort of muddle?'

'They gave me papers to file at the Prothonotary's Office,' said Lena. 'It closes at three o'clock sharp. If your foot's in the way, it gets crushed by the door. You know?'

I nodded. I, too, had broken the land speed record trying to beat the Prothonotary's Office deadline. No wonder I took up baking.

'What was wrong with the papers?'

'Wrong fees. All the assistant would say was that she couldn't file them but I should ring my office and find out what they wanted me to do, so I went outside to do that and found my phone hadn't any power. So I went down the hill to the phone box. When I got through Tony yelled at me that the fees were right and I should get back there and tell the clerk and file the papers and couldn't he send me out to do the simplest little thing. And I went back to the clerk in a bit of a tizz and she said that the fees were definitely wrong and I should go away and try again with the right amounts, and then I realised that I had put the bonds down in the phone box and I ran back but…they were gone.'

'They were picked up by a vagrant called Pockets. You might recall seeing him? Old homeless man in a dustcoat. Mutters about the Lemurians,' said Daniel.

'Yes,' said Lena hopelessly. 'I saw someone like that. And I thought I saw…' She stopped.

'Who did you think you saw?'

'Claire—but it can't have been her. It's just, they had been out for a fun run, twice around the tan running track, that's why Tony was cross, because he had to stay in the office. She'd been wearing the office trackies when I left, and she was wearing her suit when I came back, and it was a nice suit. I noticed it. Navy blue and a white shirt with a big collar. But what would she be doing up that end of town? I must have been mistaken. Claire shops in Mum's boutique, Nothing Over Size Eight. Mum had a lot of those blue suits. Mum lied to me,' said Lena to her father. 'Why would she do that?'

'Lena,' said Mr. White, taking her hand, 'your mother is a very disappointed woman. Her husband turned out to be a poof—a fat poof, at that. And her daughter will never be a size eight. She is very unhappy and when Kimmy is unhappy she tends to spread it around. Let's forgive her and forget about it,' he suggested.

'You need to tell your mother you are safe,' said Daniel.

Lena winced.

'You need not tell her where you are,' I put in. 'Just that you're safe.'

'I can do that, I guess,' she said doubtfully.

'Ring from your mobile,' suggested Daniel. 'In case she has caller identification.'

'Oh, she doesn't know where I am,' said Mr. White. 'At least, she doesn't care. She wanted the house and the car and she got them. I told her I was going to buy a little house in Fitzroy. We communicate only through our respective lawyers. Much better. But even so. Don't want her remembering something more she wanted to accuse me of and turning up on the doorstep to say it.'

Lena winced again. Her father put an arm over her shoulder and gave her a hug. 'Now,' he said cosily, 'how about dessert and some of that cognac?'

So we had cognac and cheesecake, and Daniel and I shortly after took our leave.

'I don't like Lena's chances of losing weight,' said Daniel when we were out in the street again.

'Buckley's and none,' I agreed. 'But she will be much happier with Daddy. Nice man. Do you think she really saw Claire in the street?'

'Possibly. Claire is very identified with Mason and Co. But I suspect that one, at least, of the bonds fell into Pockets' hands. One was cashed, if you recall, and on the same night the whole of the derros' camp was awash with free booze. That does not sound like something Claire would do. And last night I saw poor old Pockets again.'

'Where?'

'On a stretcher on his way to hospital. He had been badly beaten up and all of his pockets were turned inside out. He couldn't tell who had done it or why. But he knew me and he said "dilly dilly" as though it was important. Does it mean anything to you?'

'"Lavender's Blue",' I said.

'Well, I would have said it was more purple than blue.'

'It's a nursery rhyme,' I told him. I sang it. *Lavender's blue, dilly dilly, lavender's green. When I am king, dilly dilly, you shall be queen.*'

'What does "dilly dilly" mean?' asked Daniel.

'I don't know. I suspect it doesn't mean anything,' I confessed. 'Just put in to fill in the end of the line.'

'Right fol der iddle i day, right fol der iddle day,' said Daniel. 'And other meaningless slogans. Is there more of "Lavender's Blue"?'

'Probably,' I said. 'We'll look it up when we get home. How bad is Pockets?'

'I don't know. By the look of it they really worked him over. Why, I can't think. Everyone knows that Pockets has no money. And of course with Spazzo in the bin, he has no protector. But I'm beginning to think...'

'Mason and Co.?'

'Maybe. It seems extreme for an accounting firm. I've asked Sister Mary to keep an eye out. She'll know if anyone unusual is on her patch. Though I grant you that this is stretching the definition of unusual to its limits.'

'Tony in his designer tracksuit would be unusual.'

'I agree,' he said.

'What did you make of Ms. Atkins' apology?' I asked.

'Actors,' said Daniel.

'Yes, but even so! What will happen tomorrow, or the next time that Emily annoys her by being unable to tell the difference between magenta and scarlet?'

'I expect she will smile wryly and murmur that she is very disappointed,' said Daniel, chuckling. 'She can't go back to shrieking again. Not after calling herself a bitch.'

'I wouldn't be so sure,' I muttered. 'I refer my colleague to previous comments on actors. I had a heart-to-heart with Emily.

She's determined to tough Ms. Atkins out, so nothing to be done there. Let's go back to Insula,' I suggested. 'I'm tired.'

'Yes, all this emotion is wearing, isn't it?'

'Have you got more research to do?'

'Yes, I've got the company searches—including Circum and Co., and also the actors. I vaguely suspect that one of the company might be Zephaniah. I found that he left the nice respectable Christian family when he was fifteen and I can't find another record of him. He must have a Medicare number and maybe a tax file number...somewhere.'

'Under one name or another,' I added.

'But probably not Zephaniah. You can stay off the record if you don't get sick or try to establish a credit rating. Otherwise, you are there. He also seems to have taken rather a lot of money with him.'

'Stole the church funds?' I asked.

'No, won the lottery. Really,' said Daniel, as I stopped and stared at him. 'He won more than a hundred thousand dollars. Lied about his age in order to enter.'

'That would mean that he wouldn't need to register for unemployment benefits, or anything else,' I reasoned as we resumed walking. 'That's a lot of money!'

'Yes, I gather he left because the Smiths were expecting him to tithe it to their church. Fifteen and loose in the world with sums beyond the dreams of avarice. Must have been interesting for a boy from a modest home.'

'Challenging, even,' I murmured.

'Indeed. I am looking at Harrison. His background is very sketchy. And he's the right age.'

'I thought of him myself. A complete narcissist. And you would expect a child of Ms. Atkins to be beautiful.'

Daniel smiled. 'They're all beautiful. I need to ask the Lone Gunmen to find that poisonous correspondent of Lena's, GerGer, for me. I am also getting somewhere with the trickster. He made an error when he carried out the lip gloss prank.'

'Which error?'

'He ruled out Bernie,' said Daniel. 'She wasn't there. She was with you.'

'You suspected her?' We had arrived at our own building. The sun was getting into its stride and I longed for a cool drink and some climate control.

'Well, yes, that's what detectives do,' he explained as we went inside. 'The rest of the kitchen staff have been with Tommy for a long time, in some cases from the beginning. They have no reason to want to ruin her. But Bernie is new and desperate for a job. She might not see any harm in carrying out some little commissions for one of Tommy's rivals.'

'But Bernie's a very good pastry chef,' I protested as we gained our own apartment and I slumped down onto the sofa.

'She's ambitious,' said Daniel. 'She has her way to make in the world. In any case, I think that she actually believes Ethan when he says that he's going to take her to LA and help her to establish her cake shoppe.'

'I know, poor girl; he hasn't got a good track record, she must know that,' I said weakly.

'So,' said Daniel, pursuing his thesis, 'if she was doing the tricks, she'd stop once she thought she had a way of escape and a flourishing business in prospect. She's a nice girl and would not like making life miserable for Tommy, who has been kind to her.'

'Do you think Ethan will take her to America?' I asked, which was not on the topic of Zephaniah, but I really was interested. I liked Bernie.

'I have no idea,' said Daniel. 'Possibly she is the love of his life. Such things do happen, eh, ketschele? But I would not be putting any serious money on it, myself.'

'Me neither. Oh well. All right, having eliminated Bernie, who is left?'

'The kitchen staff and Emily,' said Daniel. 'They start early, before the actors arrive. They transport food and ingredients from the home kitchen to the TV set. They have the run of the place from five-thirty till about seven. Provided someone had a key or could jiggle the lock—and that's a pretty paltry lock—they could plant the wasabi-flavoured lip gloss without anyone noticing. You will note that the path to the staff toilets passes Ms. Atkins' room.'

'Very well, but you've just ruled out the staff because they've been with Tommy a long time,' I objected.

'Yes, so I fear that it must be Emily,' he said, sitting down next to me.

'But Emily needs Ms. Atkins,' I objected in my turn. 'And if she's seeking attention, don't you think that this is a bit extreme?'

'Possibly,' said Daniel. 'It's a puzzle. Humans mostly are,' he added. He got up and went to the fridge. 'How about a mineral water with fresh lime juice and a little research? I am myself wondering about Circum and Co. Can you look them up for me?'

'Certainly, to both questions,' I replied.

Horatio was disturbed from his resting place on the keyboard and I fired up the computer. Daniel brought me my mineral water and started work on his own laptop. I was wondering about 'Lavender's Blue.' If that reference to 'when I am king, dilly dilly, you shall be queen' meant that we had to tour all the statues of royal personages in Melbourne, this could be a long search.

I found the song. It was old. No one had an adequate definition of 'dilly dilly' though someone hazarded a guess that it might be a contraction of 'delightful' or 'delicious.' Which did not help at all, as definitions sometimes don't. The early version tempted the girl to stay in a nice warm bed with the singer while other people did all the work, which must have been a seductive idea in the eighteenth century. Otherwise the song yielded no clues and I passed on to company accounts, with which I am much more familiar.

Circum and Co. was not listed on the Corporate Register. I checked twice. The phone book gave a listing for their office in Collins Street, but no company called Circum and Co. had been registered. Odd. I was sure that it had to be horribly illegal to call yourself a company when you weren't. But that was par for the course in this matter. By my count Mason and Co.—which was listed—had committed eighteen offences for which it could be wound up under section 364 of the Companies (Victoria) Code. Or was it section 365? In any case, there was indeed something rotten in this company. Circum and Co. listed their occupation as 'brokers.' A nice portmanteau term that might cover a multitude of disreputable activities.

I paused and rested my fingers and sipped my mineral water. Back to work, Corinna. Circum and Co. had a website. I navigated it. Hmm. They borrowed and lent money on stocks. I had never trusted the futures market, which in my view ought to come under gaming legislation. After all, what was speculation in that market other than a bet that some stock will go down or up in future? The website boasted that it had thousands of Mum and Dad investors, drawn by its 20 percent profits. I snorted. Daniel looked up enquiringly.

'Twenty percent!' I exclaimed. 'This firm is offering a 20 percent return on investment.'

'And that's bad?'

'It's preposterous,' I said. 'The only people who offer that kind of return are crooks or people willing to take huge risks. Look at this website.'

Daniel leant over my shoulder. 'So you wouldn't be putting money into this company?' he asked.

'Not if it was my money. If Mason and Co. has a stake in Circum and Co., then they are on the nose in a major way.'

'Good,' he said, and went back to his own work.

That was enough for me. I exited the computer and went to take a soothing cool shower. I felt that only a strong rose essence would take away the stench of corporate corruption. When I came back Daniel was excited.

'Look,' he said, displaying a website. FIND YOUR ROOTS, it proclaimed. Daniel had called up Zephaniah Smith and got a hit.

'Same as the birth certificate,' I said. '*Mother, Margaret Atkins, aged eighteen*—poor girl. *Father*—aha! *Elijah Hawkes*. His profession is listed as "electrician." A film person?'

'In all probability,' said Daniel. 'So it is just possible that Zephaniah the son and Elijah the father—that sounds biblical—are both on the set at *Kiss the Bride!*'

'Oh, Lord,' I sighed.

We looked at one another. 'Soap operas,' we said in unison.

I had something else niggling me.

'What did you mean, right fol der iddle i day?' I demanded.

Daniel smiled and leant back in his chair. He began to sing in a sweet tenor voice.

'*Young women, they run, like hares on the mountain. Young women, they run, like hares on the mountain, and If I were a young man, I'd soon go a hunting, with a right fol der iddle i day, right fol der iddle day.*'

Daniel could really sing. He had a light, sure voice.

'I bet you learnt that from an old man sitting on the verandah of an English pub,' I said breathlessly.

'Cornish, actually,' he said, and pulled me down to sit on his lap.

'*Young women, they swim, like ducks in the water, young women, they swim, like ducks in the waters, and if I were a young man I'd soon go swim after, with a right fol der iddle i day, right fol der iddle day.*'

He broke off to kiss my neck and a shiver went right through me.

'*Young women, they sing, like birds in the bushes, young women, they sing, like birds in the bushes, and if I were a young man, I'd go beat them bushes, with me right fol der iddle i day, right fol der iddle day...*'

We made it to the bed with seconds to spare. I had never been seduced by song before. It was interesting. After a while, he stopped singing.

We fell asleep and only woke when the sun crossed the window and shot a beam into our faces.

'Busie old foole,' quoted Daniel, brushing at his face as though to push away a cobweb.

'Unruly Sunne,' I agreed, yawning. I could not remember the rest of the Donne poem. Ah, Daniel, what a gift he was. I lay with my head on his chest, tracing the line of hair which ran down his belly with one lazy forefinger. It would be nice to stay in bed all day. But we had things to do and people to locate. Rats!

On the other hand, perhaps Daniel would sing to me again. While working, of course…

It turned out that he had a large repertoire of folk songs and a few very rude ones that I had also learnt at university. We rose and went back to our respective computers to the tune of 'The Sexual Life of the Camel' (which is stranger than anyone thinks). That song had always amused me.

Daniel found an account of the early life of that paragon of boys, Harrison. He also had been adopted, this time by a stage family, who supported his ambitions. His name was actually John Harrison but he had reversed this for screen purposes; Harrison Johns. His website contained pictures of the baby Harrison, naked in a paddling pool and already working on his pecs; the child Harrison, posing winsomely with a puppy; the adolescent Harrison in his Goth phase, channelling Johnny Depp in *Sleepy Hollow*; and the final product, smooth, gorgeous and as self-centred as a geometry compass. His website hinted at a liaison with Kate Ionesco, a famous film star of whom I had never heard. The Harrisons professed themselves to be just bursting with pride at their son's success. They were sure that he would go on to be a major star, as he deserved.

Daniel and I read this puffery while performing a song immortalising the Mayor of Bayswater's charming little daughter. It seemed a suitable accompaniment.

'Well, all right then,' I said. 'It has got to be Harrison.'

Daniel hummed.

'Maybe,' he said. 'But who is the trickster? Harrison doesn't hang around the kitchen. He thinks he might catch obesity from the cooks. Have you ever seen him in there?'

'No, never,' I admitted. 'But the lost child might not be the joker. They might be two entirely separate persons.'

'True, true. Well, I must be up and doing,' he said regretfully. 'Where to?'

'Salino's,' he said. 'Just have to find my shoes. I've set up an interview with several previous interns from Mason and Co. They ought to be finishing work about now-ish. They meet every Wednesday for coffee and kvetching.'

'Can I come too?' I asked.

'Of course,' he said. 'I was going to ask you. You'll know what to ask them.'

'Just let me find some going-out clothes,' I said.

I wasn't too sure about knowing what questions to ask. I had been out of accounting for a long time. Years. Still, the theory remains the same, global financial crisis, boom or bust. Daniel located his shoes under the dresser, where Horatio had abandoned them after a vigorous game of Jump on the Sneaker and Slide. I put on my work garments again. Salino's is an unpretentious coffee shop which has a dedicated clientele who appreciate comfortable chairs, friendly service, waiters who know the names of the regulars and very good coffee. My kind of place.

We walked down through a city which was in the middle of the afternoon rush and found that Salino's was half full, as it always was, day or night. The group at the far table near the kitchen hailed Daniel, and we found chairs and ordered coffee.

The group was composed of three people in suits and one man in jeans. They were all young and had that sleek air of those who know that they are privileged and rightly so, because they are clever and well dressed and deserve to succeed. This is an attribute of the very young and wears off fairly soon, as they are eroded and bruised by encounters with an unfair world. It is not unattractive, however brief.

They introduced themselves as Matthew, Mary, Luke and John.

'Very apostolic,' I commented. They looked at me. Oh, well.

'So you really are investigating Mason and Co.?' asked Matthew.

'Surely,' said Daniel.

'About time,' said Luke.

'They are a disgrace,' said Mary, sipping her free-trade latte.

'Tell me all,' said Daniel.

So they told him all. Mandatory early-morning runs, which bore particularly hard on Luke, who had a damaged knee. Ritual humiliation of those who could not participate in the lunchtime gym sessions.

'I worked in the city and I couldn't even go shopping,' complained Mary. 'But not hopping on a treadmill was impossible. I was so glad when I got out of there.'

'But their business,' I hinted. 'What did you find out about it?'

'Shaky,' said Matthew.

'Shonky,' corrected Mary.

'In what way?'

'Loans secured on wobbly estimates,' said Luke. 'That sort of thing. Futures trading. And at least two sets of books. I thought about complaining about them, but you know what happens to whistleblowers. I just did my time and got out as soon as I could.'

'Which one is the crook?' asked Daniel.

'They're as bad as each other,' said John. 'Tony's all teeth and ears and zeal. Mason's all laidback and smiley and just as greedy as Tony.'

'Horrible pair,' shuddered Mary.

'What I wondered was, why did they take interns? They didn't have to take interns. Did they bring us in just to make us miserable?' asked Luke.

'They brought us in to blame us,' opined Matthew. 'I remember when a bond went astray I was called up and carpeted and they poured shit on me from a great height. I hadn't misplaced the bloody bond. I hadn't even seen the bond. But it was me they blamed. I only got out of that office by promising to be a very good boy in future and signing a statement that I had indeed lost it. It's probably on record somewhere, even now.'

'Unfair,' sympathised Mary. 'They did that to me, too. Said that I must have been premenstrual and advised me to see a doctor. The cheek! I can still see that slimy creep Tony talking about "female problems."'

'No way,' said Luke. 'They must have done it to all of us to cover their defalcations! You too, John?'

John nodded and they all stared at each other.

'You've never mentioned this until now?' asked Daniel.

'No, we don't like to think about our time with good old Mason and Co.,' responded Luke. 'We've got problems of our own—you know, present ones.'

'All right,' said Daniel. 'Tell me all about Mason and Co. From the beginning.'

'They handle the accounts for most of the restaurants and catering companies in Melbourne,' said John. 'This was good, because whenever they had a catered event it was superb. Healthy, you know, but luscious.'

Luke was beginning to put on a little condition and I felt that under the fancy waistcoat a fine corporation was already growing.

'Yes, but after a while you long for a hamburger,' said Mary. 'And I can eat a hamburger without having PMS.'

'And some of those food people are pretty difficult,' said Luke. 'And some of them are downright cheating on their tax. Mason and Co made no enquiries. At all. Also, they are dabbling in high-risk shares and the money they are supposed to have invested in secure stocks might not be all that secure. Not to mention sources of income which no one can explain.'

'All right, they're shonky,' said Daniel. 'Why hasn't anyone done anything about them?'

'Accountants are not like lawyers, who have the Law Institute breathing down their necks all the time. You don't have to join the CA. There's not really anyone to complain to except Companies and Securities, and no one does that unless they're desperate. We weren't desperate. Internships are only for six months and sometimes you get a bad one; so you suck it up and move on.'

'I see,' I said. 'You have your own futures to think about.'

Mary looked at me gratefully. 'You know how hard it is to get a job,' she said. 'We only *thought* there was something nasty going on. We didn't *know*. But if Daniel's going to out them,' she added, 'we can cheer from the sidelines.'

'Bit harsh on whoever is there now,' said Luke.

'We'll get her out before we blow it,' said Daniel. 'If there is anything to blow.'

The table of young people strayed onto other topics and Daniel and I listened, hoping to glean more information. But it was ordinary gossip. Interesting to the people involved but otherwise idle.

We paid for their coffee and left.

'What are we going to do about Lena?' I asked.

'We are going to get some more evidence,' said Daniel. 'And we are going to have a chat with Mr. Mason and Tony.'

'I'll get my running shoes,' I said.

Chapter Seventeen

Meanwhile there was Pocket's clue. Dilly dilly. Lavender's blue. We discussed it all the way home. We came to no conclusion. No statue, location or illustration leapt to mind. Lavender undoubtedly grew somewhere in the city's gardens—it is a nice durable plant and it smells divine—but I could not offhand think where I had seen it. And as to kings and queens, we had lots of both. Royal statues never go out of fashion.

'Well, what do we do now?' I asked helplessly.

'We go see Pockets in hospital,' he replied. 'Or, at least, I do. I know how you feel about hospitals.'

'In that case,' I responded, 'I shall go home and try a little contemplation. Horatio hasn't had his outing today.'

So we parted and I returned to Insula. My 'You have mail' light was blinking. I accessed it. Oh my. The Lone Gunmen had tracked down GerGer, who had advised Lena to commit suicide.

It was her bone-thin friend, Claire.

Disgusted, I collected my esky and my cat and we ascended to the roof garden in our usual state. The temple of Ceres was cool and I set Horatio down to prowl off on his own occasions while I poured a gin and tonic and contemplated, as required.

I got nowhere. I did notice that the garden was looking a bit bruised from the recent storm. Since sitting still wasn't working, I thought I would imitate my cat and prowl, so, glass in hand, I paced along the little paths. We had lavender. Several kinds, as far as I could tell, my botanical knowledge being very limited. And among the lavender, Trudi's blue T shirt was visible as she swore dark Dutch oaths. She looked up and gave me her considered opinion on couch grass. It took some time.

'Certainly,' I said. 'It should never have been invented. I see that Lucifer is assisting.'

Her half-grown ginger kitten looked up when he heard his name. His paws were dabbled with earth. Lucifer loves to get dirty. He is very uncat-like in some ways.

'He is good cat,' said Trudi. 'Gardener cat. Maybe I forgive him for the pigeon. It landed near and he gives a great spring and—paff! Feathers everywhere. Still, they make good compost.'

'Tell me about lavender,' I said.

Trudi sat back on her heels and shed a coil of couch grass into her trug.

'Strong,' she said. 'Smells sweet. Pruned at the end of summer, but not too hard, it will bloom for years. Meroe makes tea from the flowers. What else is there to say?'

'Indeed,' I said. 'Drink?'

Trudi agreed that she could take a break from her epic battle with the weeds, and we went back to the temple of Ceres. Our gardener and all-round useful person takes her gin neat and she had her jar of rollmops to complete the treat. Luckily Lucifer likes rollmops too. We snacked amicably. But I was no nearer a solution for my puzzle. I had just finished my drink when Horatio arrived and engaged in a game of romps with Lucifer. They looked so cute that I could not interrupt them.

Trudi stared out at the garden as she munched her rollmop and swigged her gin. Lucifer grabbed one of Horatio's ears and pretended to worry it, giving tiny little kitten growls. Horatio pretended to punch Lucifer's lights out with his back feet. There was a blur of ginger and tabby and suddenly two cats were at least a metre apart and studiously ignoring each other. Cat? What cat would that be? asked Horatio. Pigeon! said Lucifer, taking off after one.

And on that note, Horatio and I took our leave of a chuckling Trudi. When we got back to the apartment, Daniel was sitting at the kitchen table. He looked grey.

'What?' I asked, letting Horatio down.

'Pockets. He's dying. That beating set off a stroke. And your computer just went bling and look what's on the screen.'

I looked. I had set the computer to search for other mentions of 'dilly dilly.' And this is what it showed me:

> *What shall we have for dinner, Mrs. Bond?*
> *There's beef in the larder and ducks on the pond.*
> *Dilly dilly, dilly dilly, come and be killed*
> *For you must be stuffed and my customers filled.*

'So that's what he meant,' I said.

'The poor old man,' responded Daniel.

I thought of poor harmless old Pockets, who had done nothing except try to destroy himself with any available alcohol and who had been sent to his death by a couple of corporate greedheads for the sake of a few pieces of paper.

'Mason and Co. did this,' I said.

'No evidence,' said Daniel. 'It doesn't take much to steal a life so unregarded. Most of his derro mates would do it for a bottle of Scotch. They aren't talking and no one would believe them if they were.'

'You're right,' I said, and sat down next to him. I didn't know what to do. It didn't seem right to grab Daniel and go back to bed.

'And the Lone Gunmen found GerGer,' I said. 'It's Claire.'

'I thought it might be,' responded Daniel gloomily.

We sat in silence.

Then the doorbell rang. The bell on the actual door, not the one which summons the householder from outside. I didn't want to see anyone and fought the urge to hide under something until they went away. Daniel went to the door and let someone in.

It was Jason. I stared at him and I couldn't even summon up a smile.

'Hey, Corinna,' he said uneasily.

'Hey, Jason.'

'I just come down to ask...' he stopped. 'What's happened? Not Horatio?'

'No, Horatio's fine. But an old man we know has had a stroke,' I told him.

'Oh, well, he's had his innings,' said Jason blithely. So much for Pockets. 'I just come to ask, when you opening Earthly Delights again?'

'End of January,' I told him. 'Why?'

'Want me job back,' he said. 'I been thinking. I talked to the Prof. He said I was an ungrateful young hound and Kyl called me a dickhead. Which sorta means the same thing. I shoulda known those two blondes'd get it wrong. Airheads!'

'Airheads they are,' agreed Daniel.

'I sorta did me block,' explained Jason. I could have hugged him. 'Then Bernie told me that she wasn't goin' to stay. Is this bloke really goin' to take her with him to LA?'

'Who knows?' asked Daniel. 'He hasn't got a great track record in that respect. Possibly.'

'Any road, I wanna come back. Can I?'

Jason gave me a look in which pride and pleading were nicely mingled. Then I did stand up and hug him. He hugged me back, enthusiastically. He still stank of frying oil and chicken. 'Besides, this fried chicken game's got whiskers. I dunno how people eat that shit,' he concluded.

That's Jason. A pragmatist.

'Very well, Midshipman, report to the bridge on the second of February at the usual hour,' I said briskly.

Jason gave a strange two-handed salute, rumpling his curly blond hair.

'Aye, aye, sir, Cap'n!' he said, and grinned.

Then we all had to sit down and have a celebratory drink (beer for Jason and Daniel, fruit juice for me) and somehow, by the time Jason had departed with my copy of *The Forme of Cury*, we both felt better.

'How on earth is anyone who can't really read modern English going to manage medieval English?' asked Daniel.

'He won't have any problem with the spelling,' I told him. 'And he might come up with something for Bernie.'

'What say we go for a walk?' suggested Daniel. 'I want to drop in on Uncle Solly, maybe pick up a little delicatessen. And you want to ask him about Lena.'

'Lena?'

'Yes, we have to get her out of Mason and Co. and find her a new job.'

'So we do,' I agreed.

So we did. The New York Deli was busy and we idled around the shop, picking up some bagels and cream cheese and asking one of the nephews to cut us some smoked salmon. I wondered at the amount and variety of things which could be pickled. Finally Uncle Solly called us over to his corner and offered us lemon tea. Which we accepted.

'Dollink,' he told me, 'that firm? Snookered. Or maybe stonkered. You got anyone in there, you get them out.'

'That was what I wanted to talk to you about,' I said, grabbing at my opportunity. 'Do you know of a nice firm who would like a good accountant intern who has been much bullied because she is plump?'

'Hum,' said Uncle Solly. Momentarily, he looked like an Old Testament prophet confronted by a complex theological problem involving camels. We drank our tea in silence. Then he smiled. The camels were clearly not kosher and all was cleared up. 'Just the place,' he said. 'Wait, I give you address. You call. Take them your girl. Tell them Uncle Solly sent you. And you want the bagels and the lox?'

'We do,' I said, accepting one of his cards with something scribbled on the back. 'Thank you, Uncle!'

'We are put here to help each other,' he said, making a broad gesture. 'Otherwise, why?'

Why indeed. Well, now we had dinner and a solution to Lena's problems. I believed in Uncle Solly. Out in the street, I read the legend on the card.

'Parmenter and Co.,' I said. 'Shall we go and collect Lena and drop in on them now?'

'Getting late,' said Daniel. It was. Another day had galloped past without me really noticing it.

'All right, I'll ring them and set up an appointment. You ring Lena and tell her to write her resignation and get it into an express post envelope right away. Whatever happens, she isn't going back to Mason and Co.'

'Aye, aye, Cap'n,' said Daniel. People were obeying me a lot lately. It was very gratifying.

The pleasant female voice at Parmenter and Co announced that the firm needed an intern and anyone recommended by Uncle Solly was all right with them, at least for an interview. I agreed to bring Lena to them on the morrow. Then I conveyed this to Daniel, who was on his phone, talking to Lena.

'This is all a bit high-handed, though, isn't it?' I asked him as we carried our bagels home.

'Get involved with humanity and you find yourself morally compromised,' he said, unencouragingly.

Still, Jason was back, and we had bagels and lox for supper. Life wasn't all bad. We went home for further research on the father of Ms. Atkins' child. Surely he couldn't be at Harbour Studios as well.

A plane would be crashing into the place any minute now, I could tell…Sharks were about to be jumped.

Daniel was in for a long night scrolling though teh interwebs, so I went down to the bakery to have a look at tomorrow's baking list and decant my mother of bread into various mixers. Jason was back! I could have danced a jig, or possibly a pavane, which is more suited to my size.

All I had to do was solve the mystery of the trickster, and I could brush the dust of Harbour Studios off my stout baking shoes and resume my life, which I liked and I had missed. Technically, it was Daniel's mystery, of course. But we were as one. That solved, with any luck, I would never have to meet an actor again.

That was the trick, as Han Solo had remarked. I thought about it as I sloshed and the mixers rumbled. Not Bernie, I supposed, as she had been with me when the latest offence had been committed. I would have noticed if she had introduced wasabi into my nice clean bakery. Bernie was certainly driven enough to carry out almost any request from someone who would offer her a position as pastry cook. You could taste her desperation to succeed, like chili oil on the shrinking palate. But surely the tricks would have stopped when Ethan offered her a chance to establish her shop in LA? In which she appeared to wholeheartedly believe. No, not Bernie.

I felt better. I liked Bernie and did not want to believe her to be so nasty. The rest of the kitchen had been more or less exonerated on the basis of motive. I could not imagine why any of them would want to ruin Tommy. Admittedly Lance the Lettuce Guy and the fish chef were both temperamental and as touchy as those blue papers on fireworks—you didn't even have to light them before it was wiser to retire immediately—but touchy was not uncommon in kitchens. Of course, if one of the kitchen staff was Ms. Atkins' lost Zephaniah, they could be trying to draw attention to themselves. Some of them were the right age, and Daniel was looking them up as I worked. In default of further information I decided to consider the actors.

What a collection! I set the females on one side. Zephaniah was a boy. Therefore there were only a few possibilities. Harrison had been adopted, but his adoption was well documented and his adoptive family were the stage people Harrisons, not the over-religious Smiths. He had been with them since he was eleven days old. Harrison was not Zephaniah. Ali was also well documented. Devout and pleasantly comfortable religious family who came to Australia from Jordan many years ago. Ali was actually born in Australia. Married young to a nice Jordanian girl and had two children. Ali was not Zephaniah either. In fact the place was replete with people who were not Zephaniah. The writers, Gordon and Kendall, were too old. But what about Elton Karneit, who played the neurotic office boy Matthew? I had paid no attention to him. How old was Elton? I would have to check on Daniel's cast list.

The Mouse Police, emerging from their cave between the dryer and the washing machine, demanded an extra ration of kitty treats to compensate them for their disturbed slumber. They slept all day, reserving their evenings for ratting. I complied. The Mouse Police worked very hard.

It occurred to me, as I went up the stairs again, that there might be one or more tricksters. Operating independently or in concert. Which made the problem impossibly complex.

I shelved it and went to watch the first *Star Wars* film again in the hope that it might clear my mind. It stood up well to the effluxion of time, but my mind was no clearer as I went to bed and slept badly, dreaming in snatches and pieces of lost children in dark tunnels.

Which meant that I rose grumpy and continued grumpy. Daniel was asleep on the couch. He must have gone out again to search for the missing bonds. I did not wake him when I put on the kettle, toasted my leftover bagel and found the cherry jam. Munching and sipping, I inspected the newspaper, then put it aside as too misery-inducing for early morning. The sunlight streamed in through the kitchen window. Another beautiful day, drat it.

Bernie was waiting when I opened the street door and let the Mouse Police out. They had had a good evening, spurred on by extra kitty-dins. Four big rats, seven mice, some a little nibbled. I disposed of them, wishing that I had an owl to feed them to; I hate waste. Didn't I recall a recipe for rats from a Patrick O'Brian book? Squeakers in onion gravy. That was it. I had a feeling that it was not going to feature in my menus any time soon.

Bernie accepted coffee and refused conversation, which was refreshing but a little worrying. Surely her romance could not have gone wrong so soon? It had just started!

But I don't like to talk in the morning anyway. Bernie got on with compounding Middle Eastern cakes and I got on with my kneading. Jason came in as Bernie was laying out her filo pastry under a damp tea towel. She had only met it a few days ago and was now making her own. Bernie deserved to succeed. Jason had never seen filo before and was fascinated. Bernie started to tell Jason all about filo, baklava and similar confections.

It was nice to see her thawing from her frozen calm. Frozen calm is more acceptable than hysteria but neither is nice to be near. I was listening, because Bernie was describing making her own filo and I didn't know anyone who went that far. The process sounded dire, as peasant processes often are. You wouldn't want to undertake making paper unless you had a chunk of time on your hands. Or, come to think of it, cider or pickles. Or anything.

My mind does tend to wander while kneading. I slung the dough into tins and shoved it aside to rise. There were savouries to be made and I looked hopefully at Jason.

'Feel like compounding a few muffins?' I asked.

'What sort?' he asked briskly.

'Cheese,' I said. 'Zucchini and Parmesan, onion and poppy-seed...'

'Sweet,' he said, and went to wash his hands.

Jason was back! I could have danced except that I don't, not at that hour of the morning. But I did start to sing.

Jason and I have found a mutual liking for work songs. So it was to the accompaniment of 'Go Down, Moses' and 'Deep River' that Bernie made her syrups and Jason made his muffins and I supervised my bread. Bernie did not know the songs but, after an astonished pause, began to join in. She had a light, small soprano voice which went well with Jason's tenor and my alto.

The Mouse Police woofled their noses at the scent of lemon and rosewater. Now they would have been an appreciative audience for rat baklava. I could not see it catching on, though. Not even with Bernie's scented icing.

'*Go down, Moses! Way down in Egypt land, tell ol' Pharaoh to let my people go...*'

Bernie was getting into the swing of it, and we sang lustily as the confections emerged: spicy, sweet, salty, tangy withParmesan and ground pepper.

Someone joined in from the street door. It was Mrs. Dawson's thready elderly voice, as true as it had been when she had learnt music as an extra at her finishing school in Switzerland. She was immaculate in a light tracksuit in beige with an apricot silk scarf. We finished the song and grinned at each other.

'Ah, Corinna,' she remarked. 'I know you are not open for business, but would you have a loaf of that rye to spare perhaps?'

'For you,' I said, imitating Uncle Solly, 'the world.'

Mrs. Dawson took a deep sniff of the bakery air.

'One of the best smells in the universe, baking,' she told me. 'Ah, Jason, there you are. So nice to see you back in your rightful place.'

Jason ducked his head and muttered something. Mrs. Dawson examined him with those sparkly old eyes which could effortlessly see through a steel door or the pretensions of any grandchild who was telling fibs about the provenance of her toffee apple. He evidently passed her examination, because she gave me a charming smile and the correct sum for the rye bread, which I had wrapped for her.

'Corinna, a word?' she said, and I went with her into the darkness of Calico Alley.

'Sylvia?' I asked. I still had to concentrate not to call her 'Mrs. Dawson.'

'I understand that you are looking into the affairs of a certain Margaret Atkins,' she said.

I was taken aback. I would not have thought that Mrs. Dawson and Ms. Atkins shared any social circles. Mrs. Dawson was diplomatic and academic; Ms. Atkins was a working-class girl and an actor.

'Yes, she has asked Daniel to find her missing baby.'

'That used to be common,' observed Mrs. Dawson. 'So hard to explain, now, to the new generations. The position of a young girl at the time was dire. Help was not going to be forthcoming. They really had to do as they were told.'

'Yes,' I agreed. I was wondering where the conversation was going. Mrs. Dawson usually got right to the point. And I still had loaves in the oven.

'I used to know Molly,' said Mrs. Dawson. 'A long time ago we were known to each other. And if you are looking for that baby, there is something you should be told. Perhaps you would be kind enough to convey this information to Daniel. In confidence, of course.'

'Certainly,' I assured her. 'What is it?'

And she told me. Thereafter I went back to the bakery and worked the rest of the morning in silence.

Gosh. That was a piece of news and no mistake…

Bernie and Jason completed the preparations and loaded the van, chatting pleasantly about *The Forme of Cury*. Apparently they had discovered a pear honey cake that ought to take LA tastebuds by storm. It did sound delicious, though honey is hard to manage; as Bernie had said, give it half a chance and it burns, and few people go out of their way to taste black cakes. Then Jason went into Insula to go back to bed, having consumed a pile of leftovers and taking a basket of others to feed his never-failing appetite. Jason suffered not only from night starvation but from morning starvation and afternoon starvation as well. Poor boy.

The driver was whistling 'Go Down, Moses' and was very surprised when Bernie and I joined in. Daniel would have to make his own way to Harbour Studios today. I left a note saying where I had gone and arranging to meet him in Docklands to convey Lena to her prospective new employer.

Everyone was in their accustomed places as we lugged the baskets and trays into the kitchen. Lance the Lettuce Guy unbent sufficiently to offer me a taste of his Thousand Island dressing, which was not as good as Uncle Solly's. But a very pleasant dressing. I said so. He smiled.

The air was full of the smell of sizzling bacon, another of the premier scents of the universe. The usual cast was present. The usual things were being done. I settled down at the pastry table to make—as it were—pastry. Bernie was whisking her icing. All was well and went quietly until I went to the table to get a cup of coffee, which I felt that I had deserved.

Then I noticed a newcomer. He was very tall. He was dressed as a Great White Hunter (a type I have always despised), though he had doffed his solar topee, perhaps in deference to the ladies. He was in close conversation with Tash. I drifted across to offer refreshments. Actually, I was snooping.

The Great White Hunter was wearing khakis and a T shirt which was marked WILDLIFE FOR HIRE. Unusual, even for a TV set. I came within the ambit of conversation and held up my tray.

'Breakfast?' I asked. His pale blue eyes examined me and dismissed me in an eye-blink. His offsider, however, grinned.

'Yes, please,' he said. 'Whatever you've got.'

'Tea, coffee, munchies,' I replied. This man was as attractive as an iced gin and tonic on a hot day. He had long black hair, worn in a ponytail, dark eyes which snapped with intelligence, and curiously beautiful long hands. But his air was the most interesting thing about him. He was charismatic. Even among actors he was magnetic. He was small, shorter than me, and thin but wiry. A pleasant contrast to his tall aloof partner.

'Leonidas Cohen,' he introduced himself. 'We're bringing my tiger tomorrow. Have you got any anchovies?'

'Yes, lots,' I said. 'Tiger?'

'Tabitha,' he said, hopping into the breakfast muffins, which contained bacon and tomato. 'These are really good,' he said through a mouthful of crumbs. 'Tabitha. Beautiful girl,' he enthused. 'Most beautiful tiger I have ever had. Must get a cup of coffee, Sean,' he said as an aside to the GWH.

I conducted him to the coffee machine. He was still talking.

'Surely they're not going to risk a tiger in a TV studio,' I offered.

'No risk,' he told me. 'Not much risk, anyway. She's been with me since her mother rejected her when she was born. She thinks I'm her parent. Or at least her brother. Worked with tigers all my life. We used to be circus people until animal rights came along. Now we supply wild animals to films and so on.'

'There's a lot of demand for tigers?' I asked.

'Oh yes,' he said. 'And bears and dogs and cats and even pigs. Very bright creatures, pigs. Brighter than most dogs.'

'Really?' I had not been so interested in a conversation for ages.

'Sure. Sean mostly works with lions and his sister is parrots and birds generally.'

I should have guessed that the GWH was a lion tamer. He looked just like one.

'I have cats,' I said lamely. He patted me with an unoccupied hand.

'Good on you! You'll like Tabitha. Tigers are like cats. They are cats. Just very big, and if they get cross and scratch you, you need surgery.' He grinned and drank his coffee. I considered this. I would never take a cat, as it might be Horatio, into a TV studio. He'd hate it.

'But what about…the noise? The lights? Won't she be scared?'

'I'd never take Tabitha anywhere if I thought she was going to be scared,' he said, suddenly solemn. 'If she thinks I'm her brother, I think she's my sister. But she's been on film sets and in noisy places since she was a kitten. She was born in winter and I carried her around with me in a sling in case she took cold. She slept in my bed until she got too big. No, Tabitha will be fine provided everyone stays calm.'

'What a hope,' I said, gesturing at the crowd of babbling, arguing actors.

'Oh, they'll be all right,' said Leonidas Cohen, giving me a forty-watt grin. 'Amazing what a calming effect a tiger can have. We'll bring her along tomorrow and be in and out in two hours. They just want her to walk through the set, one side to the other, as though she is following a bicycle courier. That young man.' He pointed to Harrison, who was condescending to Emily and drinking herbal tea. 'I'll be concealed on that side.'

'Sounds simple enough, I suppose,' I admitted. 'Why did you ask me if we had any anchovies?'

'The reason I asked is that they are Tabitha's favourite fruit. She adores anchovies.'

'Really? Does she prefer the Spanish or the Portuguese?' I was interested in a tiger's view of this perennial contest.

'Portuguese every time,' he told me. 'Any more of those muffins?'

'I'll get some,' I promised, and did.

'Of course, with cats you find that there are up cats and down cats,' he observed. 'You will have noticed that yourself.'

I had. Some cats elevate to a height as soon as they are startled and some dart under the furniture. I said so. He nodded approvingly.

'Just so,' he said. 'You know your cats! So we use the cat's natural tendency. If we have an up cat, then she does the climbing. If we have a down cat, then she does the crawling through tunnels. Training consists of rewarding the animal as soon as it does what we want it to do, every time.'

'No punishment?' I asked.

'Never!' He choked with indignation, swallowed some coffee and explained, 'If you hit a cat it will just assume that you have gone mad and remove itself from your vicinity. Not only is punishment cruel, it's stupid, and I try not to be stupid. They all have their favourite treats. Not the ones you would think of, either. I have had a tortoise who loved strawberries, a python who doted on chunks of mango—green mango, mind—and a wombat who would walk through walls for parsnips. Not carrots. Or potatoes. Just parsnips, lightly steamed, with butter.'

'There's no accounting for tastes,' I said, interested. 'My cat Horatio loves cheese but I have had cats who liked tomato and basil sauce or broccoli above all things.'

'They're all individuals with individual tastes. What was I talking about before? Oh yes, natural tendencies. Wombats will follow their trainer, like they followed their mum when they were babies. Kangaroos lie still when stressed. You have to know a lot. And you have to let the animal tell you what it wants to do. There are days when Tabitha has in mind a nice bask in the sun and then there's no convincing her that she should get up and amuse the people. We're partners. We both have to earn our living. But you can't expect a tiger to know that.'

'No,' I agreed.

He smiled his sunny smile. 'Better get back to Sean,' he said. 'Before his Great White Hunter act starts to get on that nice director lady's nerves. It does, you know, after a while.'

He went away briskly.

'I never thought we'd get the tiger past the board,' said Gordon to me as I gathered some more muffins.

'So I have been hearing,' I replied.

'It's going to be massive,' said Kendall, eyes glowing. 'The tiger has been hired for a wildlife wedding. The van breaks down and the tiger gets loose. And she follows Harrison into the office.'

'Then what happens?' I asked.

'Everyone freaks until Ms. Atkins reproves the tiger and it lies down at her feet. Courtneigh Yronsyde is more feral than the tiger, you see.'

'I see,' I said.

'Mind you, I still think that the skydiving sequence was a blast. Ethan was all for it but Tash said we couldn't afford the insurance. So we had to rewrite it,' said Kendall.

'But the tiger stayed in,' said Gordon complacently.

Tomorrow looked like being a really interesting day.

As I fed the crew, I made up a list of the actors whom Tabitha should consider selecting for her matutinal menu and then went back to the kitchen. Somehow the prospect of a tiger made the day seem less dreary.

'Tomorrow,' said Tommy. 'Thank God, it's the very last day at Harbour Studios.'

I had to concur.

Chapter Eighteen

But meanwhile there was lunch to prepare. Bernie was working beside me. She seemed to be worried about something. She was biting her lip.

'Corinna, can you read Middle English?' she asked.

'Sort of,' I told her. I had read Chaucer for HSC Literature, after all.

'What's this funny sort of *d* thing?'

'That is a thorn,' I said, relieved that I had remembered something from all that study. 'You pronounce it as a *th*. The rule with Middle English is to sound it out, say it aloud. Spelling was optional in the fourteenth century.'

'I wish it was now,' she muttered. She was reading a recipe for 'Gyngerbrede.' It did not appear to be true bread, I found as I read it. It was more like a French confection called *pain perdu*. It involved boiling a quart of honey, for a start. That must have counted as conspicuous consumption in the old days.

'For your shop?' I asked.

'Yes,' she said distractedly. 'If I can make it work. I must ask Ethan. He didn't come round last night,' she told me.

Oh, dear. I produced one of the Old Sayings.

'He's a very busy man,' I said.

'Of course he is,' she replied.

We got on with the pastry. Emily had arrived with the Super-bitch's order for breakfast. She was still eating those little quiches which Bernie made so well. Bernie abandoned the intricacies of Middle English and started on the quiches.

'There's going to be a tiger tomorrow,' Emily told us.

'So I hear,' I said. 'I've been talking to Leonidas Cohen, the tiger person. The tiger's name is Tabitha,' I added.

'I'm so scared,' confided Emily. She put her little hand on my floury arm.

'Why?' I asked. I was confident that Mr. Cohen and his tiger would be a good team.

'What if anything happens?' asked Emily in a little girl's voice which rasped like a nettle on my patience.

'It's very unlikely,' I responded.

'Well, aren't you scared? It's a wild animal,' said Emily.

'Wild animals are a lot meeker than wild actors,' I told her. 'Bernie, how are those quiches coming along?'

'Just about done,' said Bernie. 'She likes them a little wobbly in the middle. There we are,' she said, deftly dishing up the tiny quiches and adding a handful of Lance the Lettuce Guy's carefully selected spinach salad. Emily gave us a reproachful look and left.

'What was she on about?' asked Bernie.

'Heaven knows. Seems to be trying to start a panic about the tiger for some reason. Who can tell with actors?'

'What do you think this might be?' asked Bernie, shrugging and returning to her recipe. 'I guessed that "lech" must be "like" but what is "y-spyked"?'

'The "y" is an "i",' I said, bending to the oven. 'Sound it out.'

'I-spi-k-ed,' she said. 'Oh, spiked. He means that you put a clove in each diagonal bit. Nice. Thank you, Corinna... Corinna?' she said tentatively.

'Hmm?' I was snipping burnt bits off the edges of one of my quiches. This always happens and can easily be rectified.

'There's something I have to tell you.'

'Spit it out,' I suggested.

'Tommy's offered me a job.'

'Great! Which job?'

'Er, yours,' she said.

'Wonderful,' I said. 'When can you start?'

'You don't mind?' she said, astonished.

'Not in the least,' I told her. 'Never wanted to do this in the first place. What say I finish tomorrow and then you take over?'

'Wonderful,' she whispered.

It was, too. Now even if Ethan did his celebrated eel-wriggle to avoid commitment, Bernie would have a job. And I wouldn't. The thought was delightful. Back to my own bakery, with Jason making muffins, singing merry spirituals in the morning. Wonderful, as Bernie said.

We translated the rest of the gingerbread recipe as we finished the baking. Bernie boiled a pot of honey as required, mixed in the pounded pepper, saffron, ginger and cinnamon with the breadcrumbs, and left it to set in one of the smaller baking dishes, scored into diamonds and spiked with cloves. I didn't know what it would taste like but it smelt very festive.

In the back of my mind I was considering Mrs. Dawson's information. There had been something constrained in the way she had spoken. Did Mrs. Dawson, who seemed so respectable, have a child that had been adopted out at birth as well? The ages did not match. Mrs. Dawson was seventy at the least, and Ms. Atkins was perhaps forty, so they would not have met in a maternity ward.

Harrison swanned into the kitchen to ask if by any chance we should have lamb's lettuce, which his naturopath had recommended. As it happened, Lance the Lettuce Guy had the said herb, and supplied Harrison with a handful. His offer of Thousand Island dressing was rejected. As the young actor turned away I examined him. Gosh, he was beautiful. But was he any relation to the blue-eyed Ms. Atkins after all? It seemed unlikely.

'Corinna,' he said to me, 'have you heard about the tiger?'

I told him that I had.

'It follows me,' he said excitedly. 'Right across the set. I'll be in shot for minutes.'

'So will the tiger,' I reminded him.

'But I'll be the star,' he said artlessly.

'Enjoy your salad,' said Lance the Lettuce Guy sardonically.

The rest of the morning passed uneventfully. That was good. I like uneventful. Daniel had arrived and was flitting about, chatting. No one played any tricks. The crew were arranging the filming of the last segments of the previous episode and rehearsing the advent of the tiger. A hiding place, shielded from the cameras, was prepared for Leonidas Cohen. All he had to do was call Tabitha across the set. All she had to do was to come halfway into the room, pause, then lie down at Ms. Atkins' immaculately shod feet. Then get up and slouch to Leonidas, who would reward her with anchovies. Then, presumably, she would get back in her travelling cage and be transported back to Werribee, to get on with lying in the sun. Her preferred occupation, apparently.

It seemed safe enough.

Meanwhile, it was coming on to lunchtime. I checked the menu for tomorrow. Lance would be making an *anchoiade*— anchovies did seem to be swimming into my life lately. Nothing unusual in the list. I waved to Tommy, farewelled Bernie, packed a picnic for the White family and found Daniel on the phone in the loading dock. I realised that I still hadn't conveyed Mrs. Dawson's message. I decided that it could wait. Daniel looked very worried.

'I just got a call from Spazzo. Pockets' old friend. He wants to see me urgently. Can you handle Lena on your own?'

'Of course,' I told him. 'See you at Insula later.'

Daniel kissed me and left in the direction of the city.

◇◇◇

I was admitted to the pristine apartment block and rode the elevator to the home of Mr. White.

There was another person in Mr. White's apartment. A tall saturnine man with paint stains on his T shirt and his hands. He was introduced as Penhaligon Roberts.

'I've got one of your paintings,' I said, shaking the spattered hand.

'Really? Which one?'

'*Winter*,' I told him. It was a small oil study of a roaring fire in a hearth. In front of the fire was a sleeping black cat, stretched out, paws crossed over its nose. It was a lovely thing. One of the few original artworks that I owned.

'They sold very well,' he admitted. 'And Shadow asked for her model's fee to be paid in fish. Nice to meet you!'

'Lunch,' I said, offering the box.

Mr. White and Lena led us into the kitchen and set about making tea. Lena looked better. I said so.

'I feel much better now I've got out of that horrible place,' she said. 'But I'm scared about this interview.'

'I'll come with you,' I said. 'And anyone that Uncle Solly recommends is worth meeting.'

Lena assented and we sat down to eat Tommy's leftovers. Though they hadn't precisely got a chance to be left over quite yet. I noticed that the artist was wearing a T shirt on which the words FEED MY LAMBS could be discerned under the paint. I asked him about it.

'Such a good idea,' he said, wiping his mouth. Those little tarts were very crumby. 'Piles of food gets wasted in Melbourne every night. And there are always hungry mouths. So we arrange that if a restaurant has leftovers, we can use them. Not scrapings from plates, of course. But when there is a whole pot of beef stew left over, we can use it. And we profit from other people's misfortunes.' He grinned. 'Recently Frantic had a whole wedding feast prepared and then they had to give it to us.'

'Why?' I asked.

'Bride ran away with the best man,' he chuckled.

I didn't seem to be able to get away from weddings.

'Then there was a complete dim sum banquet which had to be chucked out because the person it was designed for died suddenly. The Chinese would consider eating that food very unlucky. But the homeless thought the *bai pan* was fantastic. This is Tommy's food, isn't it?' he asked.

'It is,' I said. 'I'm her pastry cook at present. Do all of the restaurants donate to you?'

'Most. The good ones. No good cook likes their productions to go to waste. Our only holdout is Simply Simon. Simon freezes his leftovers. Runs a very tight kitchen, I'm told. Still, there's always one,' he said, and took another pie.

Roger White was looking at Penhaligon with melting tenderness. It should have been ridiculous in a man of his age and weight, but it wasn't. This must be his dear friend who lived down the hall. Things had, at last, worked out for Roger White. I was pleased.

We finished lunch. Lena refused the slug of the good brandy that her father urged on her to elevate her spirits. I approved. It would not be a good plan to arrive at an interview reeking of cognac, even if it was good cognac.

'Now, Lena dear, don't worry,' he said encouragingly. 'Just smile and talk slowly. You can do it.'

He gave her a hug. We left.

I marched Lena through the city at her preferred pace, which was slower than mine. We did not talk much. When we arrived at the office block which contained Parmenter and Co. she stopped, shook herself, and dragged in a deep breath. Determination was evident in both her chins.

'You don't have to come,' she said.

'Yes, I do,' I replied. 'I have to introduce you.' I wasn't letting her go into this ordeal alone. Also, I wanted a look at Parmenter and Co. I trusted Uncle Solly, but I wanted to see them for myself.

It was a pleasant office, with lots of leafy green things of the sort Trudi was wont to sneak onto balconies when the tenant's resistance was low. The decor was green and cream. Were there no other colours in the world? The receptionist showed us into a large office where two women were sitting behind a conference table.

Parmenter, I presumed, was the older lady with white hair and a twin set. Co, I assumed, was the younger lady with a severe bun and a nose ring. A tad incongruous. I like that.

'You must be Lena?' the older lady asked the younger of us. 'And you would be...?'

'Corinna,' I told her. 'A friend of Uncle Solly's.'

'Ah, that man,' said the younger lady. 'Couldn't you just take him home and cuddle him? I'm Deirdre Parmenter, and this is Rosemary Walker. Sit down, please. Lena, tell me why you want to be an accountant.'

Lena paused for so long that I was afraid she had forgotten how to speak. Then she said, 'Order.'

'Order?' asked Deirdre.

'Numbers,' said Lena. 'They are so neat. So satisfying. Simple. No emotions, no fuss. Just pure order.'

The two ladies looked at each other and Rosemary smiled. That was the point at which, I am convinced, Lena got the job.

'Right,' she said, and asked Lena about her studies, her experience, her background. When she mentioned Mason and Co, the ladies exchanged another look—one so profound that it ought to be called a Look. Horatio was very adept at the Look. It was a cat thing.

'You're better out of there,' said Rosemary. 'Monday start do you? Good. Usual pay, base grade until we find if we suit. Month's trial. All right?'

'Yes,' gasped Lena.

We floated out of Parmenter and Co. Lena was in a hurry to get back to tell her father, so I let her go with good wishes and idled along. One problem solved. Fantastic. Now there was only the lost bonds and—of course—the actors.

I dropped into Reader's Feast for a rummage among the new crime books. Then I wandered back to Insula for my gin and tonic and my rest. Things were working out. For a change.

Drink, rest, all very pleasant. I was about to open my new detective story when my mobile phone rang. I fumbled with it. I do not approve of mobile phones.

'Ah, Corinna,' said Daniel's voice. 'Can you join me at the derros' camp?'

'Certainly,' I agreed. I found my straw hat, took a bag and my backpack, and strolled out into the sun.

Down the steps on the other side of the bridge and through the fine, disinfectant-smelling pines to the river bank. Most of the drunks were out, canvassing the streets for loose change. I met Daniel by the boathouse.

'Here I am,' I said.

'So I see. Love the hat. So useful if we meet a hungry donkey. This way, I think,' he told me, and I followed him along the bank. It was cooler by the water.

Renovations had been taking place. No wonder the council wanted to get rid of those unsightly old men. Since cities are no longer using their fresh water as a convenient way of disposing of toxic waste, river banks have become desirable. This was a nice place to stroll.

Apart from the ever-present danger of being run down by a Lycra-clad bicycle fiend, of course. We avoided two of them, who flashed past without regard to mere pedestrians. Daniel was alert. I took his arm and could feel his excitement through the muscles.

'Agreeable as it is to promenade with you at any time, what are we doing here?' I asked.

'Ah, philosophy,' he teased. I shoved him gently.

'Come on,' I said. 'Tell me! I've got a secret to swap,' I hinted.

'I spoke to Spazzo,' said Daniel, leading the way along the river bank. 'He confessed that he pinched the bonds from Pockets' stash. And he told me where he put them. In here.'

We had stopped beside a decorative bench that the council had scattered along the bank of the Yarra. It was made of some kind of material which looked like porcelain, and had been painted with flowers. It also functioned as a box to contain council property, secured with a padlock.

It took me half a minute to snap back the padlock. At that expensive private girls' school which had blighted my youth, they always told me I would learn skills which would stand me in good stead in my adult life. Well, they were right. That

was where I had learnt to pick locks. The box creaked open
and Daniel dived on a stack of papers. Mostly newspapers, but
inside one were a number of sheets of carefully engraved paper.
I examined them.

'They are the bonds,' I told my beloved. 'Oh, well done, Daniel!'

'I couldn't have done it alone, metuka,' he said, kissing me.
'Right, now let's lock that box again and I have a few phone calls
to make. And will you come with me to see Pockets?'

I assented. I leafed through the bonds as Daniel made his
phone calls. They were very pretty. Also very valuable. Their
face value was more than a million dollars. I was suddenly
scared. How could I carry this much worth through a city
with pickpockets? I stuffed them down the front of my shirt,
next to my skin. That was uncomfortable so I put them in
my shoulder bag and clutched it to my chest. That would do.

I looked at the bench. The bench was decorative. I identified
the flowers painted on it, and experienced an authentic cold chill.
This bench had herbs. Rosemary, basil, roses and…

'Look at the bench,' I whispered to Daniel. He looked.

'What about it?' he asked.

'That's lavender,' I said. 'Lavender's blue, dilly dilly, lavender's green. But you said that Spazzo pinched the bonds from
Pockets. Pockets can't have known where they were. Why did
he give you that clue?'

'Perhaps the Lemurians told him,' said Daniel.

◇◇◇

After that we were silent until we stood in intensive care, looking
at the shell of a man, all festooned with wires and tubes.

'Pockets?' asked Daniel.

There was no answer. We stayed for a while, feeling helpless.
Then Pockets opened his eyes. They were a pale watery blue in
his grey face and seemed to be fixed on the far distance.

'We found the bonds,' said Daniel. 'The men who did this
to you will be sorry.'

'The Mother Ship,' murmured Pockets. 'The Mother Ship
has signalled. They are coming for me.' And he fell silent.

Presently all the alarms began to beep and we were ushered into the waiting room. A harassed nurse came out of the cubicle.

'No point in waiting,' she said. 'He won't wake again, most likely. Poor old man,' she added.

We echoed her as we went out into the sunshine again. Poor old man.

'And now,' said Daniel, 'for Mason and Co.'

◇◇◇

Mason and Co had a newish office, impressionist prints on the walls and a decor of green and—what else?—cream. That Martha Stewart has a lot to answer for. The receptionist did not want to call Mr. Mason and tell him that we were there, but Daniel, who had made his request for an interview in a very quiet voice, stared at her until she fidgeted, looked away, and hit the intercom. My beloved was possessed of righteous rage and that is not something that any receptionist school teaches its pupils to combat. We were directed to the second door. I noticed two other people in the waiting room who also apparently wanted to see Mr. Mason. Two size-20 ladies in suits. They came into the office behind us.

'Mr. Mason,' said Daniel, 'we have something for you. Something that Lena lost.'

'She's resigned,' Mr. Mason told us. His healthy fat appeared to have solidified into something resembling Rocquefort. I had never seen a man look so unwell and be upright. Beside him Tony stood, bouncing slightly in his sneakers. Claire had been looking out the window. Now she saw me and paled, raising a hand to bite at her fingernails.

'I know,' said Daniel. 'She has another position now.'

Daniel gestured to me and I produced the six sheets of engraved paper. I was about to hand them over—Mr. Mason had stretched out a trembling hand for them—when one of the large women who had been waiting intercepted them.

'What do you think, Mara?' asked Daniel.

'Oh, certainly,' she said, riffling through the pile. 'I'll have to do some further tests, but they look like fakes to me.'

'Fakes?' demanded Tony angrily, after pausing a little too long.

'But you knew that,' said Daniel in that same dead-quiet voice. 'You knew that your share issue and loans were secured on worthless paper. Nice engraving, though. A professional job. Did you do it?'

'I don't know what you mean,' said Tony unconvincingly.

'This is Detective Inspector Mara Shields,' said Daniel. 'From the Fraud Squad. And this is Ms. Anna Dietrich. From WorkSafe. She's going to investigate the persecution of your intern Lena. With particular attention to an Internet stalker called GerGer.'

Claire started to gnaw the other hand. Then I actually internalised what Daniel had said.

'Fakes?' I exclaimed. 'They're fakes?'

'Yes,' said Daniel. 'That's why Pockets filed them in his corrupt documents stash. He knew they were fakes, too.'

'But they had to get them back,' I reasoned it out. 'Someone else might have found them, examined them, and then their whole sandcastle would collapse.'

'Precisely,' said Daniel. He turned back to the accountants. 'I can never prove,' he went on, 'that you arranged for poor old Pockets to be beaten so badly that he is presently dying. You deserve to go to jail for life for what you have done.'

'Ridiculous!' puffed Mr. Mason, eyeing his visitors with loathing. 'Get out of my office before I call the police!'

'They're here,' said Mara Shields. 'Have a look at this warrant,' she added. 'I'm going to need all of your records. This is going to take some time. And your trading ceases from this minute.'

Tony broke first. With an athletic spring, he dived for the door. And somehow fell over my foot, which I had inconveniently stretched out to ease a momentary cramp. He came a purler. He hit the floor so hard that a copy of Seurat's *Grande Jatte* fell off the wall, revealing a hidden safe. Mara Shields' eyes lit up.

'Thank you, Corinna,' she said to me.

'My pleasure,' I replied.

And there seemed to be nothing more to say. My last glimpse of Mason and Co was this: Tony still lying on the floor, imitating a rug; Mr. Mason sagging back into his chair; Claire chewing her nails; and Mara Shields opening the safe to disclose a bundle of memory sticks within. And thus Lena and Pockets were as revenged as we could manage in a society which has forfeited blood feuds.

Drained, we stumbled into the street, hailed a taxi, and had ourselves conveyed home to construct some stiff drinks and order takeaway pizza. I needed alcohol, salt, grease and crunchy bits of burnt salami. And I got them. Horatio likes salami, too.

'To Pockets.' Daniel raised his gin and tonic.

'To Pockets. May the Mother Ship convey him safely to Paradise,' I said.

We watched *Doctor Who*—I still cannot decide about the new one—and went to bed early. No more scouring of the streets for Daniel. He needed the sleep, and so did I. We snuggled together with our cat for company and comforted each other for loss and pain and loneliness.

And tomorrow there would be a tiger.

Chapter Nineteen

Six am. Daniel rose and made breakfast. Toasted English muffins, yum. I munched them and inhaled that first cup of coffee which scarcely seems to touch the sides and descended to let Bernie in. She was accompanied by Jason, who was carrying some of her boxes. They were discussing the difficulties of using medieval spices.

'The trouble is, they used so many flavours,' complained Bernie.

'That was how you demonstrated that you were rich,' I told her. 'Come in. Watch out for the Mouse Police. They even used to gild cloves. With real gold. How did the gyngerbrede work out?'

'Have a taste when we get to the studio,' Bernie invited. 'It's got a really strong flavour. Might be too strong.'

'Then cut the spices in half and try again. You might try another flavoured honey, too. What about lavender honey with lavender flowers sprinkled on it instead of cloves?'

Bernie instantly saw what I meant. She and Jason began on the day's baking while discussing it. I got on with the bread. It was a nice peaceful morning. Most unusual.

I was thinking about poor old Pockets' lonely death. Then again, he was sure that the Mother Ship had come for him, and perhaps that made him feel better. His Lemurians would not desert him. And perhaps that is all you can ask of any religious system...

We completed the baking without incident. Jason accepted his basket of goodies and departed for his own flat. His mood of acceptance had stayed. I was pleased. I hoped that the next time something happened he would not react so precipitately. He had doubted me so quickly.

Then again, I am hopeless with emotions and know nothing whatsoever about adolescent boys.

Bernie and Daniel and I loaded the trays and boxes into the van. This morning the driver was whistling an old Lulu song. I had heard it as a child. *'I'm a tiger, I'm a tiger...'* I sang softly. Oh yes. Today would contain a tiger. Which is not something you can say about most days.

The kitchen was keyed-up. Tommy was standing in the middle of the floor, clipboard in hand (that universally respected symbol of authority) making announcements.

'You can go into the studio to look at the tiger,' she said. This was sensible. The staff were going to do that anyway. 'She's due at ten,' said Tommy. 'So I want all the preparations done by then. Get on with it,' she advised, and we scurried to our places.

It was a case of all hands on deck (as Patrick O'Brian would say), and I missed my midshipman as we cut, kneaded, chopped, mixed and whipped. Lance the Lettuce Guy had bought a Thousand Island–dressed salad from Uncle Solly on my recommendation and was still mulling over ingredients. Something made Uncle Solly's dressing better than any other that he had tasted. There must be a secret ingredient.

'It's a sort of celery taste,' he said. 'You know, Corinna? Yet it has an overtone of smokiness. But you can't smoke celery.'

'I never tried,' I admitted. 'I know what you mean. I've asked, but he won't tell me.'

'Perhaps you should beg,' suggested Lance. He was making an *anchoiade* for his salad of boiled eggs and spinach. His off-sider was rinsing spinach leaves with wincing care. The speed of a really efficient kitchen is like one of those massive Victorian steam machines. It huffs and groans a lot but it turns out millions of widgets. Crunch, thump, puff. I stashed my pastry to cool down and turned my hand to grating carrots for Lance. Bernie was making savouries with the speed of sound. Each little toastie was topped with smoked salmon, whipped cream cheese and a sprinking of lumpfish roe. This was sustainable, unlike caviar. Her hands almost blurred over the trays. Breakfast was already out and my carrots were finished, so I grabbed a tray and exited to feed some actors.

I felt better about them, knowing that I was going to leave them soon. And they really were decorative. There they flocked: Kylie and Goss in full makeup, nibbling scrambled eggs; Harrison condescending to feed Emily little bites of toast as she took up Ms. Atkins' hem; Elton, whom I now knew was too young to be Ms. Atkins' Zephaniah, drat it; Ethan, drinking nightblack coffee; Tash, ploughing grimly through a bacon and egg sandwich as though she were due to be executed and wanted to die full. I asked her what was wrong.

'Oh, Corinna, it's you,' she said. 'Animals. Children are bad enough, but animals are the pits. I wish I hadn't agreed to this. But one of the backers adores tigers.'

'I was impressed with the tiger wrangler,' I said. 'Leonidas Cohen.'

'The little man? Yes, I liked him more than his partner. This is costing us a fortune in insurance alone…' She ate another bite of her sandwich. 'And I don't like guns on set.'

'Why do we have guns?'

'Not a real gun, a tranquilliser gun,' she told me. 'Over there, arguing with Ethan about sight lines.'

I saw the Great White Hunter, now bearing a rifle, gesturing at the set. Ethan was shaking his head.

'He needs a clear line of sight so that if the tiger runs amok, he can shoot her with a tranquilliser dart,' said Tash unhappily. 'Ethan says he can't stand where he wants to stand because he'd be in camera range. The tiger's due at ten. Oh, shit,' said Tash, finishing the sandwich. 'I have a bad feeling about this.'

'Have some more food,' I suggested. 'Try one of these tomato and bacon muffins. My apprentice made them.'

'Bernie?' asked Tash. 'She's good. Ethan wants to take her to LA. Or so he says.'

'No, my own apprentice, Jason. Do you really think Ethan will take Bernie to Los Angeles?' I asked.

Tash shrugged. 'He's never promised anything like that to any of his other amours,' she said. 'He might really be smitten. Serves him right for working on a soap,' she said vengefully. 'I swear, the plot line is infectious. Have you heard the rumour that Ms. Atkins' lost child is working on the set?' she asked.

'Yes,' I said. 'And it might be true.'

'Complications,' sighed Tash. 'Just what I need.'

I moved on. At least the muffins would be comforting.

I circled the rest of the cast, refreshing my tray as needed. Everyone was excited about the advent of the tiger.

'Her name is Tabitha,' I told Kylie and Goss. 'She's very tame, apparently.'

'Oh, tigers are sooo cute!' exclaimed Goss.

'And sooo cool!' agreed Kylie.

'There once was a lady from Niger, who smiled as she rode on a tiger,' I said. They had never heard of this, or limericks at all, I suspected.

'Really? Could we ride on her?' asked Goss excitedly.

I went on, hoping to restrain their excitement. If a tiger was indeed a cat, no one would get to ride on her. Not without considerable protest.

'At the end of the ride, the lady was inside and the smile on the face of the tiger,' I warned. They thought about it, brows wrinkling.

'Oh, she wouldn't eat us,' said Kylie.

'Not when we like her so much,' added Goss.

I passed on. Some ignorance is invincible.

Ms. Atkins was breakfasting in her room, as usual. No tricks marred her morning serenity. Thank God. Emily had completed her sewing to her satisfaction. Gordon and Kendall were excited. It must be fun to see your words turned into action. They were haranguing Ali about getting a microphone close enough to the tiger to record a purr. He was telling them that he had arranged the sound for many actors but there was nothing on a tiger on which to attach a throat mike, unless the tiger had pierced ears.

'Besides, maybe she won't feel like purring,' said Ali sourly. 'I wouldn't, if I was asked to lie down at that infidel woman's feet. Nice idea, guys, but can't be done.'

Kendall and Gordon knew when they were licked and surrendered gracefully. After all, they had lost out on the skydiving wedding, but they had retained the tiger. They were ahead, at least on points.

Breakfast was concluded. Lunch was well in hand. I had got myself another cup of coffee and was leaning on my bench, listening for my oven timer and sipping the ambrosial brew. I heard a stir in the studio and went to the door to observe.

A large cage, lined with canvas to preserve the modesty of the occupant, was being wheeled into the studio through the big doors. A whisper went through the set. The tiger had arrived. Escorting her was Leonidas Cohen. He saw me and grinned.

'She's in a bit of a mood today,' he confided. 'Nothing a few treats won't amend, though. Everything set up for us?'

'I think so,' I replied. 'Tash is over there, she'll know. Your partner is here. With his gun,' I added, with distaste.

'He does so love his firearms,' said Leonidas, waving at the Great White Hunter, who had won his argument with Ethan and had a good bead on the set. His rifle was raised. I disliked the sight of him. The idea of someone shooting any creature was horrible. Even if it was with a tranquillising dart, rather than a bullet. I was so glad that soon this would be over and I could stop associating with the TV world. Leonidas Cohen, it seemed, felt the same. 'Right, let's get this done,' he said.

I went back to the kitchen to take out my last pies and turn off my oven. When I came back into the studio I joined the rest of the kitchen staff lined up along the kitchen wall.

I had not realised how very big tigers were. Tabitha eased herself disdainfully out of her cage and gave a rousing sniff. Then she sneezed. Apparently she didn't like actors either. Leonidas came to her, attaching a leash to her collar. She lifted her lip in a half-growl. Great. A premenstrual tiger. He allowed her to lick some sort of treat from a thing like a table tennis bat and led her through the silent throng to the other side of the set. There he left her as he walked across to his prepared position and Tash said 'Action!'

Leonidas had been right. A tiger does have a calming effect, even in a TV studio. She was so large and so heavily fanged and so beautiful. Her stripes were perfectly aligned. Her ears were delicately fringed. Harrison made his entrance and the tiger slouched after him, belly to the ground, as though she was hunting. Harrison turned, registered her presence, and froze. Kylie and Goss, as required, screamed. Abby the geek girl fainted across her keyboard. Then Molly Atkins emerged from her room, made an imperious gesture, and the tiger lay down at her feet.

'Perfect,' said Ethan.

Which meant, in film parlance, 'Do it again!' So they did.

Harrison entered, the girls screamed, Abby fainted, Ms. Atkins reproved the tiger. Each time, Tabitha walked off the set to Leonidas, received her reward, and was led back to her entrance again. She was behaving beautifully. I was delighted. We might get away without any incident at all. That must be the end of it. They had done seven takes.

'One more,' said Ethan.

Leonidas protested. 'That's enough, surely,' he said. 'She's getting bored.'

'Just one more,' insisted Ethan. Nothing is more implacable than a camera person who thinks that the next take will be unimaginably perfect. Leonidas shrugged.

'This will be the last one,' he said. 'Come along, Tabby, soon be out of here.'

The tiger gave him another half-growl, but allowed him to lead her back to the same tedious place she had been minutes before. Her tail was switching. This really ought to be the last take. If Tabitha had been my cat, I would have been putting down the comb before she scratched me.

'All right, this is the last,' agreed Ethan.

The kitchen staff gathered up personal belongings and we prepared to return to our labours. I was just thinking about maybe another cup of coffee when it all went wrong.

Tabitha followed Harrison onto the set, paused, lay down as required. Then Molly Atkins, perhaps remembering old photos of tiger hunts, planted a spike-heeled red shoe on the recumbent tiger's neck.

Tabitha had been tried. She had been required to undertake the same boring routine all morning. She had complied, for the sake of the rewards and because she liked Leonidas. But no one had ever explained to her that she had to bear a sharp heel in her neck, and she did not mean to endure it patiently. She stood up abruptly, tipping Molly Atkins off balance into the desk behind her. Molly lay still. Harrison and Emily flung themselves on her, screaming. I thought I heard a voice shriek, 'Mother!'

Tabitha was annoyed. She did not like loud voices. I saw the Great White Hunter's finger tighten on the trigger. So did Kylie and Goss, who with one accord leapt to the tiger's defence, screaming, 'Nooo!' They hung about her, arms around her neck, competely spoiling the GWH's aim, and at that moment Tabitha banged into the set and caused the protective screen to fall on Leonidas Cohen.

The tiger was puzzled. Where was her treat? But she could smell something very agreeable. She raised her head and sniffed.

Then she shrugged off the girls, quite politely, and nosed into the audience.

No one has ever measured the degree of panic produced by an unexpected tiger on the staff of your average kitchen. Tabitha was surrounded by people and chairs and suddenly I knew what she was after. Lance the Lettuce Guy was standing on a chair, screaming, and Tabitha was pushing at his apron with her nose. At any moment she would raise one of those dreadful clawed paws and…
Disaster loomed like an iceberg in the path of a very big ship.

I fled into the kitchen, grabbed the jar of anchovies, spilt it into a mixing bowl and called, 'Tabby! Come along, Tabby!' into the screaming mob. I had no chance of being heard but I saw the tiger's head come up. At last, she seemed to be saying. Someone who gives out the rewards for being a good tiger. Because I'm worth it.

People fell over her as she slid through the throng. There were crashes. Lance the Lettuce Guy had been making anchovy dressing, that's why she had selected him. Tabitha doted on anchovies. But my mixing bowl contained a whole jar of anchovies and Tabitha meant to have them.

I led her into the kitchen and shut the door, closing out the chaos without. Tabitha pursued her anchovies and I set down the metal bowl so that she could eat them in comfort.

I had never been so close to a tiger. She could have killed me with one casual slap of those massive soup-dish-sized paws. She slurped up the anchovies and then looked hopefully for more.

'I don't know if we have any more,' I told her, just as I would to my cat Horatio. 'Let me look.'

I crossed to the store cupboard. Tabitha drifted along behind me, making not a sound except the click of her claws on the lino. Outside, I hoped that someone was extracting Leonidas Cohen from under that pile of masonry and speeding him to my assistance. But for the moment there was just me and the tiger.

I found another jar of anchovies and replenished the bowl. Tabitha licked at them delicately this time, then sat back on her haunches to give her whiskers a polish. I had now run out of anchovies. Bugger. But she had just eaten a lot of salty fish, how about a drink of water?

I filled the mixing bowl. Tabitha watched me with golden-eyed benevolence. Someone who understands a tiger's requirements, she seemed to be saying. She lapped.

Then she rolled her huge length over and indicated that a scratch under the chin would complete her repast.

I knelt down and scratched as requested. What else could I do? Up close, she smelt of straw and fish. Her fur was amazingly soft. She was an astounding beast.

'Tiger, tiger, burning bright,' I said to her. 'In the forests of the night. What immortal hand or eye dare frame thy fearful symmetry?'

It was fearful. Every stripe was in exactly the right place. She was a superb artistic creation. Blake knew what he was talking about, as poets usually do.

Then I heard the sound which Gordon and Kendall had wanted to record.

Tabitha was purring. I was sitting on a kitchen floor with a purring tiger. I froze momentarily, and Tabitha opened an eye, wondering why I had stopped. So I started again. She was very cat-like. Her whiskers laid back against her muzzle in just the same way as a domestic cat's. But her teeth were like daggers in her tawny jaw, and I judged that it was about time someone came to rescue me before Tabitha got bored again.

Just at that moment, the door edged open and Leonidas crept inside. Tabitha gave him a sniff of greeting, got up, aimed a lick at the side of my face, and allowed him to attach her purely symbolic leash. That was an interesting interlude, she conveyed, but I'm ready to go home now.

He led her out toward her travelling cage. I decided that I might just stay on the floor for the present. It was quite a comfortable floor. Outside there was dead silence. I could imagine Leonidas leading Tabitha to her cage, escorting her inside, shutting the door, summoning labour to wheel the cage out of the studio into the car park, and close the big doors. And as soon as that happened...

The noise broke out again. Doubled and redoubled. The whole of the kitchen staff, led by Tommy and Daniel, erupted through the door. They collided in the doorway and struggled to get in. I suddenly felt very tired.

'Corinna! That was so brave! Are you hurt? Bernie, find the brandy! No, the good brandy! I got a new bottle!'

Daniel took my hands and pulled me up into his arms.

'Come, sit up in this chair. Are you faint?' he asked.

'No,' I said, realising that I spoke the truth. 'I'm fine, really.'

Lance was still complaining. 'It's karma,' he said. 'She picked me out of all of us to attack.'

'She didn't attack you,' I explained, trying to be heard over the babble. 'It's just that you smelt of her favourite snack. It was the *anchoiade*. She loves anchovies. And I'm afraid I've used them all,' I added.

I didn't feel faint, but I would never turn down a glass of the good brandy. I sipped and began to feel very pleased with myself. I had done the GWH out of his shot. Tabitha was fine. And well fed. And safely out of Harbour Studios. A good morning's work.

'Corinna,' said Daniel, 'that was very brave. I swear, my heart was in my mouth. Are you sure you're all right?'

'Not a scratch,' I said. 'Here, have some brandy. You look like you could do with some, more than me. I'm fine. Truly. What's happening on set?'

'Oh, you should come and see it,' he said affectionately. 'If you feel strong enough.'

'Of course,' I said.

Even so, he kept hold of my arm. I had given Daniel a shock. Further shocks awaited us.

◇◇◇

On set, Molly Atkins was sitting in a chair, with Harrison and Emily on either side. All were weeping freely.

'But how?' she sobbed. 'How did you know?'

'Easily,' I said. Someone needed to get the explanations over with so we could get on with serving lunch. 'Why don't we all sit down and have a nice cup of something?'

Tommy, who had never been slow on the uptake, summoned her staff and soon people with trays were moving among the actors. They distributed tea, coffee, chocolate and fruit juice, with a selection of Bernie's toastie treats and muffins left over from breakfast. Soon everyone was snacking, nibbling and sipping, which was great because it meant that they were no longer exclaiming, screaming or expostulating. Tash, who was reproving Kylie and Goss for protecting the tiger, took a cup of hot chocolate and let them go. She gestured to me to take over. Everyone sat down and soon only Daniel and I were standing.

'My colleague,' I said, emboldened by Armagnac, 'undertook to find Ms. Atkins' missing child. In case anyone was wondering, there was indeed a child. He was christened Zephaniah, poor kid, and adopted by a very religious family called Smith.'

'And expired at an early age of acute nomenclature,' observed Ethan. There was a laugh. Tash gave him a glare which would have smelted platinum. He subsided.

'When he was fifteen he won the lottery. Left the Smiths. Vanished out of history. At least under that name.'

'There are several people who might be Zephaniah on this set.' Daniel took up the tale. 'Harrison was adopted. But his adoption and subsequent career do not match what we know of Zephaniah. The other thing I was asked to research was, who was playing food-based practical jokes? Was it someone trying to ruin Tommy? Was it someone trying to injure or offend Ms. Atkins? Neither of those motives appeared to match the people available.'

'Then it started to make sense,' I said. 'Due to information received.' I was not going to expose Mrs. Dawson to this lot. 'We found out that Zephaniah was not the only child of Ms. Atkins. We were told, in fact, that she had borne twins. Both had been adopted out. Both might be playing tricks to seek her attention. Possibly also to revenge themselves on a mother who had deserted them. Was that the reason, Harrison?'

General sensation. All eyes turned to the beautiful boy. He did not blush or lower his gaze. He was used to the admiring public gaze.

'It wasn't me,' he said. 'I knew she was my biological mother. But I had a lovely adoptive mother. I couldn't have been happier, more supported in my talents. I didn't want to become a star—as I shall—because of her patronage. I was going to do it on my own. But when I saw the tiger attack her...'

He leant on Ms. Atkins' shoulder. She patted his curly head.

'My son,' she said in her compelling throaty voice. 'Oh, my son.'

There was a silence. Then Ethan asked, 'Well, who was playing the tricks?'

'You played one,' I said. 'I saw you squeeze your pocket. You made an electronic doodad to make Ms. Atkins' scales register higher so that when she weighed herself she seemed to have put on kilos. Did you play any of the others?'

'No,' said Ethan. 'Really,' he protested. 'I thought they were trying to frame me! They were all hot spices, and you know how I love hot tastes.'

'Exactly. Who would want to injure Ms. Atkins and frame Ethan and ruin Tommy? Someone who had been bullied unmercifully by Ms. Atkins, and rejected by Ethan, who had replaced her with someone from the kitchen. You weren't trying to ruin Tommy, were you, Emily? Just Bernie.'

'I thought she'd be sacked,' muttered Emily. 'Then Ethan'd come back to me.'

'No chance,' Ethan told her, taking Bernie's hand.

'Emily!' exclaimed Tash.

'There's more,' I said, holding up a hand. 'Let me tell you a story.' Out of the corner of my eye I could see Gordon and Kendall taking notes. Curse them. Everything is grist to a writer's mill. 'A young boy who knows he is born in the wrong body. He is told that all sex and probably gender is sin. But it is too painful to stay in a body which is totally wrong for him. Then he gets a sign from God. He wins the lottery. He has enough money for gender reassignment surgery. In some distant land, where no questions would be asked and no one would know. Thailand, perhaps.'

'Malaysia,' someone muttered.

'Zephaniah is soon dead,' I said. 'And home to Australia comes…Emily.'

'It's true,' said Emily. 'I played the tricks. I did change sex. I am Ms. Atkins' child. Now let me go…'

She made as if to stride to the door, but Harrison and Ms. Atkins caught her in their arms. She resisted for a moment, then subsided into their embrace, weeping freely.

'And that is all,' said Daniel, taking my hand.

'And I got it,' said Ethan with great satisfaction. I realised that he had been filming throughout. The whole thing. The tiger, the accident with Ms. Atkins, the wholehearted confessions. I just stared at him. He grinned.

'All in the can,' he told me.

I couldn't help it. I began to laugh and couldn't stop.

'But tell me,' said Harrison to Emily. 'Did you know about me?'

'Of course not,' she told him. 'How could I know? I haven't seen you since I was born.'

'Sister,' said Harrison, rolling the word around his tongue.

'Brother,' said Emily, through her tears.

'Daughter,' said Ms. Atkins, getting into the act. 'Son.'

Soap operas.

Tash cleared her throat. 'Well, that's all been interesting,' she told the assembly. 'Now back to work. We've got the last scene to finish. Tonight we party, but today we work. Ethan, you ready?'

Ethan was clutching Bernie's hand.

'I never knew,' he said dazedly. 'I never knew she was a trannie. I never thought…I never noticed…'

'It's all right,' Bernie assured him. 'We all have things to regret. I once tried to make a fish-flavoured chocolate mousse. Don't stress on it.'

'Ethan?' Tash's patience, which had been much tried, was audibly wearing thin.

'Right,' said Ethan, kissing Bernie and putting her firmly aside. 'I shall summon my minions. All right, minions?'

The crew resumed their places. Makeup artists flocked in to repair faces. Ali grumbled about the sound quality. Abby complained that collapsing onto the keyboard had ricked her back. Emily dried her tears. Ms. Atkins stood up and shook herself. Kylie and Goss, who had indulged themselves with hot chocolate, smoothed their costumes and pushed back their hair. In an incredibly short time the TV crew were filming the last bits of *Kiss the Bride*.

Daniel and I withdrew to the kitchen to help with the preparations for the conclusion-of-filming party. All that emotion, despair, terror, joy; it was instantly put away. How could anyone do that? I was still feeling shaky.

But there were cocktails to mix and sorbets to freeze. The set broke for lunch, which we duly served. Bernie's gyngerbrede was very moreish. Then the actors returned to their profession, and Daniel and I were out of a job.

I have never been so delighted to be unemployed.

'So you don't mind about Bernie taking your job?' asked Tommy. 'I told her I wouldn't take her on if you objected.'

'Oh, I don't object,' I said. 'But what will you do if Bernie goes to LA with Ethan?'

'She'll be here for months,' said Tommy. 'By then Alicia's leg will be recovered. And Ethan hasn't won any endurance awards for his affairs. Either way I'll get some very good cakes. And she'll get some useful experience. Things are hard in the catering trade at present. Everyone who's seen *Masterchef* thinks they're God's gift to cuisine. You've really got to shine to get noticed. So you'll come to the party tonight?' she asked, handing over an envelope which rustled. 'Don't forget to take your knives and so on, will you, when you leave?'

'I won't forget,' I told her. 'It's been…fun,' I added.

'Sure has,' said Tommy. She shook my hand.

I collected my apron, my knives and my cap. I stuffed them all into my bag. I kissed Bernie goodbye and agreed that her Green Lady cocktail was very acceptable for a hot day. Daniel accepted his payment from Tash and waved to the crew, who were involved in a ferocious discussion about using a green screen.

Then we left the studios and walked into blessed sunshine.

'That,' said Daniel, 'was weird.'

'Tell me about it,' I agreed. 'I'm a bit at a loss. I've finished my job. I've been given an honourable dismissal from Maîtresse.'

'I've finished my job too,' said Daniel. 'We've revenged Lena and Pockets, found the bonds, found the trickster. That sex-change came as a bit of a shock. How did you work it out?'

'It just came to me,' I said. 'There was a bit in the paper about gender reassignment clinics in Thailand. I don't know that anyone would operate on a fifteen-year-old in Australia. Not without parental consent. And I couldn't see those parents consenting. But Zephaniah had the money. It must have seemed like a gift from the deity.'

'It might have been,' said Daniel. 'I have always thought that God had a funny sense of humour.'

'But I got the motive quite wrong,' I told him. 'I was looking for a familial one—but Emily just wanted to get rid of Bernie. And to be revenged on her mother, too.'

'This will be a salutary lesson for Ethan, too,' said Daniel.

'Yes, I expect it will. And Bernie's position seems relatively secure,' I said.

'And the tiger was not injured or even more than passingly affronted,' said Daniel.

'And the girls are probably forgiven by now,' I mused. 'Things move fast in the TV world.'

'But that does leave us at a loose end,' said Daniel. 'Would you like to see a film? Visit a museum? Art gallery?'

'No, I'm knackered,' I realised.

'Then let's go home and take Horatio for his walkies and lounge about and do nothing, until we go to this party tonight,' he suggested.

That sounded like a very good idea. When I checked my email I found one from my friend Lucy, offering me a couple of weeks at her house in Apollo Bay. Sun. Sea. Good food. I would have to ask Daniel how he felt about a holiday. I was coming round to the idea that they might be a good thing, after all.

Chapter Twenty

It looked like a promising party. I now felt differently about the actors. I had not wanted to feed them. I had been blackmailed into being Tommy's pastry chef. But I was now out of a job, free, clear and unemployed. Daniel had been enthusiastic about Apollo Bay and Jason had agreed to feed the kitties in exchange for unlimited access to my cable TV. I felt light and sociable. Everyone who had been involved in the production was invited. There was a party from Insula; Meroe, invited by the girls, Therese Webb, Kylie and Goss, Jason (probably invited by Bernie) and Mrs. Dawson, who accompanied the Professor, who was invited by Kendall, who had attended his Latin classes at the university before embarking on a literary career. The world is full of people who went to Professor Dion's Latin classes. There seemed to be more actors and crew than I had seen before. These, I realised, were the behind-the-scenes people: editors, computer people, technicians. All of whom were hopping into the cocktails with an avidity born of relief. Filming was over. *Kiss the Bride* was, as Ethan had said, in the can. Its future fate could be left on the knees of the Gods of Film.

Bernie carried a tray of drinks toward us.

'White Lady, Green Lady, Sex on the Beach,' she said.

'In my experience, sex on the beach is productive of sand in the underpinnings,' I told her. 'I'll have a Green Lady.'

'And I'll have a White Lady,' said Daniel, smiling at me. 'How's it going, Bernie?'

'Good,' she said. I did not know if she was referring to the party or her own career. 'Everyone seems to like the drinks. What a day! Is every day going to be like this?'

'Once you get off this TV set,' I told her, 'your career will be of unexampled dullness. Why? What's been happening?'

'That triangle—' Bernie jerked her chin at a clump of people on the set '—has been carrying on since you left. Dull…' She thought about it briefly. Then she nodded her neat little head. 'I could get to like dull. Thank you, Corinna.'

She passed on through the crowd, dispensing drinks. Daniel and I clinked glasses and sipped. Icy and profound. Gin, lemon juice, white of egg, something green. I could feel it doing me harm. Lovely.

Mrs. Dawson had accepted a cocktail, but Professor Dion had somehow prevailed on a server to fetch him a glass of red wine. Kylie and Goss bobbed up beside us.

'Corinna!' said Goss. 'The tiger man's here and looking for you.'

'Leonidas Cohen?' I asked. 'Where?'

'Here,' said Leonidas Cohen, surfacing. 'They asked me to the party, but not Tabitha.'

'How is she?'

'She drank a lot of water when she got home,' he said. 'How many anchovies did you give her?'

'As many as we had,' I told him. 'Two jars. Well, one and a half.'

'Oh, that's all right then,' he said, relaxing. 'She's quite a big tiger, she can stand that much salt.'

'Yes, she is big, isn't she?' I recalled.

'I'm so glad you were there,' he said, taking my hand.

'My pleasure. Has there been any legal trouble about it?'

'No,' he said decisively, snapping his white teeth. There was something intensely cat-like about Leonidas Cohen. 'Everyone heard me tell that fool photographer that Tabitha was getting bored. She didn't do anything wrong. When she couldn't get her treat from me, she went looking for the scent of anchovies. When that idiot cook panicked, you took over, very intelligently, and had the sense to isolate her from the mob. Then it was just a matter of me getting out from under the collapsed set and putting her back in her cage. Tabitha was completely vindicated,' he said, and took a deep draught of his cocktail.

I got the impression that Leonidas didn't like people much. But I was glad that Tabitha was well. She was the most beautiful cat I had ever seen. Leonidas passed on to talk to some animal-loving editors.

Daniel and I drifted toward the centre of the room. A mathematician friend of mine once told me that you can map the movement of people at parties. The drift looks random, but it isn't. There is always a focus, sometimes two foci, around which the party revolves in slow circles. The focus of this party was the triangle of Harrison, Emily and Molly Atkins. They were holding court in the middle of the space, sitting on plastic chairs and accepting homage.

Daniel and I, accompanied by the Insula group, drifted that way accordingly.

'My, they are handsome,' said Mrs. Dawson. She had taken a second drink, which was unusual for her. She was also right. They were beautiful. Now that I looked at Harrison and Emily, I could not believe that I had not noticed their resemblance before. Both slim, dark, lovely. The hormones and the surgery had given Emily rounder, more female contours, but the bone structure was their mother's. What anthropologists call gracile. Graceful. Sweet flesh lay gently on fine bones.

'They certainly are,' said the Professor, adjusting his glasses.

'Now if only we had been able to find Elijah Hawkes,' sighed Daniel, 'the plot would be all wound up.'

'Elijah Hawkes?' said Mrs. Dawson sharply. 'You didn't mention that. You were looking for him?'

'The father of those delectable twins,' explained Daniel. 'He was an electrician, and we did wonder if he might be working on the show. This is a soap opera, you know. We have already had the revelation of the concealed twins. It would be nice to have the missing father, as well.'

'In accordance with the unities,' agreed the Professor.

Mrs. Dawson seemed to be about to speak but Tash called out, 'On set!' and we all fell silent. Tash was radiant. She looked like a milkmaid whose freshly shampooed, garlanded cows had just won the blue ribbon at the show.

'We have finished filming,' she announced. 'Apart from post, *Kiss the Bride* is in the can. Ethan will be showing a bloopers reel tonight which I hope that you will all enjoy. But we have a few awards to present first. To Ali, sound man of sound men.'

She called him up and gave him a perspex plate on a stand. In deference to religious sensibilities, it just had the word *Ear* engraved on it. Ali scowled. Sound men do not talk much. But he bowed to the assembly and was cheered back to his place.

'To Ethan,' said Tash. She gave him a trophy in the form of a perspex eye. He leant down from his careless height and hugged her so hard that she squeaked. There were tears in his eyes. Bernie jumped up and down in her place, fortunately putting down her tray first.

'To Marina, our editor and post-production person, whose hard work is still to come,' said Tash. Marina, who was among the animal lovers, came forward and accepted a perspex trophy with a thumb drive embedded in it. Then the rest of the cast were called, each to receive the actor's trophy, a bridal headdress encased in plastic. Professor Dion remarked that they resembled laurel wreaths and were doubtless well deserved.

'More like a wooden foil,' I muttered, and he chuckled. He himself had told me that retiring gladiators received a wooden sword as a prize.

Kylie and Goss received their awards with becoming modesty. They had behaved very well, I thought. Rising at five, makeup and hair, staying on their diet, never complaining, not a slip until their defence of Tabitha, which did them credit, at least with me. This production ought to do their CVs some good.

Tash would have to give them a high mark for skill, intelligence and good behaviour. They came through the throng to show us their prizes. I admired them.

'I did wonder if I really wanted to be an actor sometimes,' Kylie admitted. 'Especially early in the day. I don't know how you do it, Corinna, getting up at four every morning to do your thing.'

'I'm going to sleep in till noon for a month,' declared Goss.

'But it was such fun,' said Kylie. 'Wasn't it?' She sounded wistful.

'I suppose so,' I said. I didn't want to dampen the celebrations by telling this pair that serious steampunk machinery would be needed to drag Corinna anywhere near a TV production in the future. Me for the nice quiet early morning; just me, Jason, the Mouse Police and the yeast. Kylie and Goss hugged me, one from each side. They were still wearing their stage makeup and smelt sweetly of Max Factor and gin. Then they dived for the hors d'oeuvres. They were no longer on a diet, bless them.

I collected one of Bernie's toasties. It was cream cheese topped with chives. Yum. Mrs. Dawson put a hand on my arm. 'Corinna,' she began.

'Have a savoury,' I offered, holding out the plate. 'Sylvia, maybe you would like a chair instead,' I added. She was as pale as milk. Professor Dion, who had stratospheric social talents, summoned a minion and sat her down.

'Whatever is the matter, Sylvia?' he asked.

'It's nothing,' she said, with a return of her hostess manners. 'It is rather hot in here. I shall just sit still for a moment and I will be fine. Can you bring Daniel over? I would like a word with him. And you, Corinna.'

'Done and done,' I said. I waved to Daniel, and he detached himself from Tash's audience and came to my side.

'Mrs. Dawson,' he said. We grabbed a couple of chairs and sat down, close enough to hear her over the party babble.

'You mentioned Elijah Hawkes,' she said slowly.

'I was tasked with finding Ms. Atkins' lost baby,' said Daniel. 'We finally located Zephaniah. But there was another child, and that was Harrison, and his birth certificate had a father's name on it. And it was Elijah Hawkes. Why do you ask? Did you know him?'

'I was married to him for forty years,' she said.

We sat stunned for some moments.

'I did talk about the unities,' said Professor Dion apologetically.

'My husband, if he was female, would have been called a complete tart,' said Mrs. Dawson. 'Dearly as I loved him, some girl only had to flash her bosom in his direction—sometimes not even in his direction—and off he would go. A standing cock has no conscience,' she told me. 'He was so charming and so kind and so funny that I got used to it. He always came back to me,' she added. 'He was the only man I had ever met who could always make me laugh.'

'My dear,' said Professor Dion, and took her hand.

'Mostly he confined his attentions to intelligent, well-prepared young women who knew what they were doing,' she continued. 'But when he met Molly Atkins, he fell in lust head over heels, and she with him. And Molly Atkins was not a well-prepared young woman. She conceived. And she would not consider an abortion.'

'Sylvia,' said Professor Dion, with deep sympathy. She tightened her grasp on his hand.

'The affair was over by then, of course; they never lasted. Molly came ramping up to the house to confront him. He wasn't there to confront. He never was,' she said with a flash of bitterness. 'So she had to make do with raging at me. But there wasn't a lot I could do. I couldn't make "Elijah Hawkes"— how that man loved his secret life—go back to her. She could have ruined his career, but she isn't vengeful, really. I offered her an allowance, and I took her to hospital myself when the time came. She was delivered by C-section—she never saw the children, she didn't even know there were two. And she didn't care. Then she decided that she wouldn't keep the child after all. It would constrain her future as a model and an actress. Which they would have, of course. I offered to take them but she would not give them to me. I had not thought of them for years until the girls got this job. Then I heard a name I had not heard for such a long time.'

'Goddess have mercy,' said Meroe. She fumbled in her bag and came up with a pinch of greenish dust. This she flung over Mrs. Dawson, muttering some sort of spell. Sylvia, who would retain her social skills through a hurricane and fire storm, nodded a thank you.

'I echo my learned colleague,' I said. 'What do you mean to do now, Sylvia?'

'You know, Corinna, for the first time in a long time, I really don't know.'

'I do,' I said. 'Come along.'

'Do you know what you are doing?' asked Daniel in my ear.

'Hope so,' I replied. Now what relationship would work? Sylvia was technically a stepmother, but stepmother wasn't going to cut it. I needed a relationship which would have instant cred-ibility and also not be threatening to this fragile new mother-and-children triangle...Aha!

I escorted Mrs. Dawson through the people until we stood in front of the triangle. All three of them looked up at us.

'Harrison, Emily,' I said, 'this is your grandmother Sylvia.'

'It's you,' said Molly Atkins, reverting instantly to Superbitch.

'It is I,' replied Mrs. Dawson. 'Hello, Molly.'

The twins examined her. Slim, elegant, dressed in a milk chocolate linen shift, emblazoned on one shoulder by a huge gold Minoan brooch. Draped in a cotton wrap patterned with fire-drakes, borrowed from Meroe. Immaculate, stylish, unashamedly old in the same way as a priceless antique shouts its antiquity. They approved.

They sprang up and embraced her, one on each side. Young face, old face, young face. They were a picture. By someone like Caravaggio.

After that Molly Atkins had to accept the fait accompli. I like my faits to be accompli rapidly. I hate waiting.

'What happened to Elijah?' asked Molly.

'He died a few years ago,' said Mrs. Dawson.

'I hated him for a long time,' said Molly.

'Oh, so did I,' said Mrs. Dawson. 'For daring to die and leave me alone.'

'Let's have another drink,' suggested Molly. I summoned Bernie urgently and she came forward bearing cocktails. I had another one too. That had been a huge risk. Then I left Mrs. Dawson with her new grandchildren and let Daniel find me a chair by the kitchen wall. Lance the Lettuce Guy was there, full of excitement.

'I've got it, Corinna!' he exclaimed.

'What have you got, Lance?' I asked wearily.

'The secret ingredient to Uncle Solly's Thousand Island dressing.'

'Wonderful,' I said. There was a long pause. I went on, 'And are you going to tell me what it is?'

He looked around to see if anyone was listening. No one was. Next to us was a spirited debate on the virtues of long as opposed to short Jacobean stitch, between the wardrobe ladies, Therese Webb and, of all people, Tash, who apparently sewed in her spare time. Lance the Lettuce Guy leant close and whispered in my ear, 'Lovage.'

'Never heard of it,' I told him.

'You try it,' he said, perfectly sure of himself. 'I munched my way through all the European herbs trying to duplicate the taste. I am sure that it is…' he dropped his voice, 'lovage.'

'Well, I hope you and the…' I dropped my voice in turn, 'lovage will be very happy together.'

'Oh, we will,' he said delightedly.

'Fairytale endings all round,' commented Daniel.

'It's a judgment,' I said. 'A judgment on me for getting involved in soap operas. Yea, a judgment.'

'Shall we go?'

'Not yet,' I told him. 'Surely that has to conclude the revelations. Of course, at any moment a plane may crash into the studio. Or possibly someone may reveal that they have been someone else all along, they just lost their memory.'

'Or were possessed by the devil,' said Daniel gravely.

'Or were dreaming,' I added.

'Corinna?' It was Bernie, looking guilty. I knew what she was going to say and tried to forestall it.

'I won't tell a soul,' I promised.

'You knew?'

'I saw you talking to Simply Simon at the banquet,' I told her. 'I know you were spying for him. But you didn't tell him anything important.'

'He offered me a job,' whispered Bernie.

'But now you have one,' I stated.

She brightened. 'I do, don't I?' she said.

She kissed me and swam off through the crowd.

'And that,' I told Daniel, 'is the last revelation.'

'Positively the last?' he teased.

'Absolutely,' I said firmly. I swigged my drink. It was very good. Maybe green chartreuse? That was the only thing I was intending to investigate any time soon.

Thereafter, it was a nice party. Jason was claimed by two young things who professed themselves agog to know all about being a baker. And gave him a lot of information about being an actor. The bloopers tape was playing on an endless loop. On it Molly Atkins planted her foot on Tabitha's neck and was knocked backwards by the tiger's abrupt objection. Harrison and Emily flung themselves on her, the girls embraced the big cat, and I led her away from her assault on Lance the Lettuce Guy's apron. I had never seen myself on film. I was huge. Compared to the rest of the cast, the only person who would outweigh me was Tabitha.

But that was all right. I did not want to be an actor. I wanted to be a baker, and I was. So that was all right. All shall go well, nought shall go ill, Jack shall have his Jill again, and all go well, as the nursery rhyme said.

Several hours later we made our farewells. We had to go home to pack for our holiday. Ethan was discussing her medieval cake shop with Bernie. Ali, with fruit punch, was talking about the value of silence with the Professor (with more red wine). The kitchen staff were swapping recipes. Tash was talking about bobbin lace-making with Therese, who had offered to give lessons. Molly, Sylvia, Harrison and Emily were still entwined in familial affection. Everyone was happy and no one was quarrelling. Time to go.

I actually had my hand on the door when Leonidas Cohen shoved through the crowd and called my name. I paused.

He thrust a huge bouquet into my arms.

'From Tabitha,' he said.

We stood outside in the cool night air. I examined my blossoms.

Daniel began to laugh. 'Tiger lilies!' he said.

I kissed him.

Recipes

Medieval cookery is simple enough (not counting making comfits, which is a bugger), but you need a good modern redaction of the original. Any Society for Creative Anachronism website has them. You will find some dishes strange. The amount of spice, for instance, is greater than modern usage. That's how you demonstrated that you were rich, in the old days. No tomatoes, peppers, potatoes, avocados, eggplants, etc., as America has not been discovered yet, except by all those highly civilised people who have been living there for millennia. On the other hand, the bread is wonderful. When you have a cold Sunday afternoon, bung on the oven and start kneading.

Note that cooks writing books in medieval times accepted that they were writing for experts, so they do tend to say things like 'cook until it is cooked' and 'mix until it is as you like it.' Ingredients are never measured. They say 'take sufficient flour.' Medieval beginners started off as children in a castle kitchen, twirling the roasting jacks. Anything is an improvement in conditions from twirling the roasting jacks…

Use your leftover bread to make:

GYNGERBREDE

1 jar honey
several handfuls of coarse breadcrumbs
pinch of saffron
1 teaspoon cinnamon or 1 cinnamon stick
2 teaspoons powdered ginger or chunk of ginger root
1 teaspoon powdered cloves
lots of whole cloves, to decorate
red colouring, if you like

Bring the honey to the boil, then take it off the heat. Skim any scum off the top. Pound the spices together into mush (or use powdered spices), then mix the spices and the food colouring into the honey. Drop in handfuls of breadcrumbs, stirring well. You will have a mixture which is not quite crumbly, like the base for a cheesecake. If you overdo the breadcrumbs, add more honey. Press the mixture into a greased baking dish, slice it into diamonds, and put a whole clove into the centre of each diamond. Leave it to set. Delicious, very strongly flavoured. Sort of like baklava. You can vary this by making, for example, a lavender-flavoured gyngerbrede with lavender honey and dried lavender flowers on top. Or a rose one with petals. It was meant to provide a sugar hit for a cold night. Needed due to the bouncy, enthusiastic exercise known as medieval dancing.

SAINT BRIGID'S BREAD OR
BARA BRITH OR BARM BRACK

This is a rich celebration bread, using expensive dried fruits and spices. The 'barm' refers to an ancient word for yeast. For all you linguists.

6 cups strong bread flour
1 teaspoon mixed spice
¼ cup caster sugar, or 1 tablespoon honey
1 teaspoon salt
1 package dried yeast

300 ml lukewarm milk
150 ml lukewarm water
4 tablespoons softened butter
2⅓ cups chopped dried fruit—raisins, figs, currants, dried
    apricots, candied peel...

Mix the flour, spice, one tablespoon of the sugar (or all of the honey), salt and yeast. Pour in the water and milk mixed together. Combine well, adding the rest of the sugar. Make a sticky, soft dough. Plump it into a clean bowl to rise for about an hour. Then drop it onto a floured surface and knead it into a flattened oblong. Spread the butter on it, add the fruits, roll it up and start kneading again until it is all more or less incorporated. It looks like a speckled sedimentary rock but tastes much better. Let it rise again for half an hour. Oil a round cake tin of about 23 cm. Pat the dough into it and leave it to rise again for another half an hour. That dried fruit is heavy. The yeast needs to get its little pseudopodia going in order to raise it. Then glaze the top with milk and bake in a moderate oven for at least 45 minutes. If the top starts to scorch, cover it with foil. It's cooked when you tap the bottom and it sounds hollow. Most of my ancestors only got to eat this to celebrate a wedding or a birth. Enjoy.

PEA AND HAM SOUP

1 ham hock, ask the butcher to split and break it for you
    (those lads get a massive kick out of being asked to
    break bones; it is a little worrying), or several slices of
    bacon, crisped in the microwave
1 stick celery
1 carrot
1 onion
3 leeks
2 cups green split peas, soaked overnight. Any soaking cuts
    down the cooking time, but if you forgot or the dog
    drank the water, use them out of the packet and just
    cook the soup for longer.

I make this soup in two stages. One, I boil the ham hock in about two litres of water for several hours, until the flesh falls off the bones. Then I remove the bones and cut up the ham. I cool the stock overnight and skim it in the morning. If you are making vegetarian soup, of course, omit this step. Don't throw away the water—add the vegetables and the ham and the peas and simmer it all for about three hours. If you are using bacon, just put all the ingredients into the pot, add water, and cook gently for the three hours until the peas are melted. Leave it to cool, then blend it, and sprinkle the bacon on top. Do not be alarmed if, when you come to reheat it, this soup has gone solid. That's a good sign. *Pease porridge hot, pease porridge cold, pease porridge in the pot, nine days old*—as we used to sing while skipping. This reheats very well in a microwave, stirring after each minute. Serve it with rye bread, if you have a good baker.

For more of Corinna's recipes, please visit the Earthly Delights website, www.earthlydelights.net.au

To receive a free catalog of Poisoned Pen Press titles, please contact us in one of the following ways:

Phone: 1-800-421-3976
Facsimile: 1-480-949-1707
Email: info@poisonedpenpress.com
Website: www.poisonedpenpress.com

Poisoned Pen Press
6962 E. First Ave. Ste 103
Scottsdale, AZ 85251